BREATH
OF
OBLIVION

BREATH OF OBLIVION

MAURICE BROADDUS

TOR

TOR PUBLISHING GROUP
NEW YORK

BREATH OF OBLIVION

Copyright © 2024 by Maurice Broaddus

A Tor Book
Published by Tom Doherty Associates / Tor Publishing Group
120 Broadway
New York, NY 10271

www.torpublishinggroup.com

Tor® is a registered trademark of Macmillan Publishing Group, LLC.

The Library of Congress Cataloging-in-Publication Data is available upon request.

ISBN 978-1-250-26512-8 (hardcover)
ISBN 978-1-250-26510-4 (ebook)

Our books may be purchased in bulk for promotional, educational, or business use. Please contact your local bookseller or the Macmillan Corporate and Premium Sales Department at 1-800-221-7945, extension 5442, or by email at MacmillanSpecialMarkets@macmillan.com.

First Edition: 2024

Printed in the United States of America

0 9 8 7 6 5 4 3 2 1

The Kheprw Institute
I am because we are . . .

CAST

THE IJO
(Seven Founding Families)

ADISA	JYWANZA	CHIKEKE	BUHARI	NGUNI	DIMKA	YAR'ADUA
Amachi	Nehanda	Bekele	Maulana	Geoboe	Jaha	Bayard
Ezeji	Selamault	Stacia		Itoro	Lebna	
Wachiru		Yahya		Khuma		
Xola						

THE REAPERS
Epyc Ro Morgan (Captain)
Robin Townsend (Sergeant)
Anitra Gouvei (First Lieutenant)
Chandra Elle (Second Lieutenant)
Ellis!Olinger

THE *CYPHER*
Stacia Chikeke (Captain)
Paki Listener Harges (Master Teacher)
Kenya York (Head of Community Security)
Nadina Campbell (Engineering Chief)
Yahya Chikeke (Research Scientist)
Bekele Chikeke (Roving Listener)
Marguerite Pinero (Roving Listener)
Zenith Prebius (LISC liaison)

TIME LINE

Welcome to the sovereign territory of Muungano, centered around a lunar outpost but whose ties extend to Titan, Oyigiyigi (a series of asteroid belts), and Bronzeville (one of the Mars settlements). It's led by a coalition of weusi people, mostly a mix of Asili (natives of the Motherland, Alkebulan), Maroon, and Ugenini (children of the diaspora). Here's how it came to be:

2019   **The "Year of Return."** Ghana's president, Nana Akufo-Addo, declares and formally launches the call for Africans in the diaspora to unite with Africans on the continent.

2021-2024   **The Great Unrest**—civil disturbances lead to the rise of the Service of the Order.

2026   **First World established.**

2030   **Ecological collapse on Earth.** Climate terraforming begins in earnest.

2031   **The Rorschach Disaster,** when Earth abandons the fledgling lunar outpost in favor of creating "New Earth" on Mars.

2033   **Mars establishes New Earth.** The Toppers abandon the rest of humanity to what they designate Original Earth. Eventually, they revert to the name Mars as they decide to carve out their own identity.

2034   **The Decade-Long War.** Original Earth breaks down in a series of political and religious wars that ends with the eventual defeat of the Service of the Order.

2037   **Fifth Wave Migration.** The Ugenini and Asili people begin to settle on First World using the private interstellar shuttle conglomeration Outer Spaceways Inc.

2040   **Ujima Experiment,** when the weusi assumes control of the physical space of First World. The colony begins as a recovery space. They reach out and build institutions to create time (to control their own stories). Soon First World becomes a thriving community, with the efficient mining of He-3 and after the discovery of kheprw crystals, which help fuel their starships.

2042   **Mothership Incident,** when the mothership accidentally slips back in time through a wormhole, returns, and then hides behind the moon.

2044   **The Liberation Investment Support Cooperative (LISC) expands** and recharters the United Nations under its auspices.

2045   **Incursion.** Original Earth leadership seeks to reclaim the Ujima / First World territory. Extremists want control, to return to war mode in time of crisis.

2046-2049   **The Lunar Ukombozi War,** the battle for control of the moon. *(Includes HOVA operations: Bumba, Obatala, the Yemaya Campaign, Hellwalk, Ragnarok.)*

2047   **The Bronzeville Rebellion**—Mars experiences a civil schism.

2050   **Muungano established.** At the end of the Lunar Ukombozi War, the lunar community secedes from Original Earth's sovereignty.

2050-2100   **Uponyaji,** a period of isolation and healing, wherein the weusi establish the independent Muungano culture and traditions.

2052   **Oyigiyigi mining outpost established.**

2087   **Titan community established.** Construction of Muungano starships begins.

2120   **Orun Gate discovered.**

2121   **Present.**

When black is introduced, things change.

—**Mari Evans**

BREATH
OF
OBLIVION

01

EPYC RO MORGAN
Beyond the Orun Gate

"We regroup. And once we're ready, we take the fight back to the Interstellar Alliance . . . and finish what they started." Epyc Ro stared into the blackness of her view port. So many stars, so much potential. She chewed on her lower lip. Her crew had to adjust. Learn who they were and what they were going to be about. They had to mourn. They had to heal. It would be a long, difficult journey.

"It's gone." As she monitored the incoming reports, Epyc Ro stood behind her seat on the command deck. She churned her new title, "captain," over in her mind. The responsibility of leading their newly christened Reapers weighed heavy on her shoulders. Rank meant more when they were gbeto in the HOVA.

The Reapers were in a state of transition, from HOVA gbeto to what she wasn't sure. This was a new journey for all of them, and they'd already been through so much. Their mission started as a military drop onto an uncharted world. Followed by military skirmishes, a first-contact scenario with the Mzisoh, and the loss of the squad's captain, Fela Buhari. No, that cleaned up the circumstances to something nearly clinically pristine. The brutal and public decapitation of their leader, their friend, left the entire unit scraped and raw. And angry. They fought to escape their captors only to discover the remains of the Orun Gate, their only way home, destroyed.

"What is?" Having forgotten that their commlinks were active, Epyc Ro turned to see Robin Townsend picking out her Afro puffs. It was the first time she'd had an opportunity to tend to her hair in days. The look in her eye declared she was ready to stab someone for some shea butter.

"The Orun Gate. All of it. There's barely any debris left from it."

The HOVA was Muungano's specialized defensive regiments, both shield and spear. The elite warrior protectorate, the closest Muungano kept to a standing military. As HOVA, they were more of a community within the community, their own cohort within the Muungano space. Believing that they had failed that mission, her unit renounced their office, now calling themselves the

Reapers. The memory of hierarchy remained, and they still looked to her for leadership.

<Residual energy signatures are all over the place.> Chandra Elle monitored the scans. She rarely spoke. Becoming a member of the HOVA was akin to becoming a living sacrifice. The majority overwhelmingly women, they underwent genetic modification. Sometimes, like with Chandra, cybernetic enhancements also. She possessed a neurological Maya implant; a portion of her brain stem had been excised to accommodate it. Bioplastic covered parts of her skull and cheek. She had been modified to be a living radio, a way for Command to relay orders to them. But now there was no Command in her ears. Only her and Maya. The other Reapers could only wonder what the conversations in her head might be like. <Weapons discharge. Military class.>

"Could it have overwhelmed the gate? Created a, I don't know, feedback cascade?" Epyc Ro asked.

<Uncertain.>

"How's the ship?" Epyc Ro remained in vigilant appraisal of their commandeered vessel. It bore an insignia, but no name. Though the ship was little bigger than a kraal, the command deck was a largely open space with two stations near the front about the size of a rondavel. The vaulted ceiling streamed with lights, the material of each rafter a translucent metal that refracted the beams into kaleidoscopic art. Each of the twin piloting helm stations were partially sunken into the dock and partially enclosed in a bulbous partition leaving her team determined to refer to it as the cockpit. The antechamber on the other side of the octagonal entryway served as a meeting alcove.

"I'm still trying to figure out the rest of the controls." Robin took her station at navcom.

"I hope you aren't over there just pushing buttons," Epyc Ro said.

"Do I look like Anitra?" The controls responded to her gestures; hard light structures moved like funkentelechy-controlled nanobots. "Comms. Transmitter. Receiver. Sensor array. Some sort of quantum slipstream engine."

"Slipstream? I thought that was just theoretical."

"Not according to these readings."

"That's . . ." Epyc Ro's voice trailed off as she gestured toward the screen of the body of the ship. Enlarging the image, two figures bobbed near the surface of the hull in EVM navsuits. Their biomech suits acted as a sort of mechanical membrane partitioning them from the world, shielding them from the environment. Each suit had a built-in air-filtration unit as well as servos in the limbs to aid with movements. It filtered sound through its receivers, the noise of which became muted when navcom channels engaged. The world appeared to them along their visor, scanned and digitized, the telemetry beamed back to Command. "What are they up to?"

"Painting over the insignia on the ship," Robin said.

"What?" she asked, but waved herself off. "Never mind. I'd ask who authorized that but . . ."

"Anitra."

"Dare I ask why?"

"So that anyone we encounter knows who they're dealing with now!" Anitra Gouvei shouted. Unadulterated joy fueled the bombast of her voice. She reveled in life, whatever it might look like, taking it on her terms. It was what made her so devasting as a gbeto: she fought for her sisters, she fought for life. So painting the letters *L.H.S.*—Life, Health, Strength—on their ship made perfect sense.

"Who?"

"The aliens." Anitra said to Ellis, "No offense."

"Am I supposed to be offended?" Ellis!Olinger asked. Muungano scientists had designated the first habitable world on this side of the Orun Gate Eshu. But Ellis's people, the Mzisoh, did not distinguish themselves from the planet. After the HOVA secured their people and dispatched the agents of CO/IN— the Interstellar Alliance's version of the HOVA—who had been terrorizing them, Ellis opted to travel with the (now) Reapers in the hope of bringing the war to the CO/IN.

"Not yet," Robin warned. "Brace yourself, she's just getting warmed up."

"We're out in the home territory of the aliens. I'm not down for any anal-probe nonsense either," Anitra said.

"Literally we are the aliens in this scenario," Robin reminded.

"No. Butt. Stuff." Anitra shook her head and batted away the imaginary probes.

"You a daggone fool, you know that, right?" Robin shook her head. "Although, Captain, I hesitate to say this, but Anitra raises a good point."

"I done told them . . . ," Anitra echoed.

"Let me rephrase that: Anitra has inadvertently stumbled into a notion we should discuss further."

"What's that?" Epyc Ro asked.

"Our first-contact protocols." A spoken-word artist in her former life, Robin could have been anything—a Master Teacher at the Thmei Academy, a ranked battle poet, or a member of the Griot Circle—with her skills.

"Everyone, let's convene in the command deck in ten minutes." Epyc Ro clasped her hands behind her, with neither a shrug nor a sigh, content that her team were adapting, even embracing their new adventure. They were their own, often wandering, village. They were always home as long as they had their sisters.

More an odd, metallic blue, the corridors were lit by vaguely blue light drowning the ship's palette in something sterile and cold. There wasn't a lot of ship to explore, but just enough to get lost in. Not a military vehicle, it retained a bulkiness that brought to mind a cargo vessel of some sort. As she wandered, Epyc Ro found that she missed gardens. Her time on research-level starships exposed her to Green Zones, but she missed the planetside feel of grass beneath her feet. The sense of peace that accompanied communing with nature.

Peace seemed like such a faraway memory.

Shoulders back, spine straight, her proud bearing owning any space she entered, Robin accompanied her to the meeting alcove. With her huge heart, being a gbeto did not come naturally to Robin. It didn't mean she wasn't good at it, just that Epyc Ro worried about her. She finished cleaning her talon, Busta, and with a flourish set it on the table before her. Inspecting her weapon with a meditative soberness, she decided to stow it in the series of translucent ribs along the wall she improvised into a weapons rack. She was an experienced gbeto, a sergeant in the HOVA. When the need required, she could set aside her emotions to perform her duty. When the need passed, she felt every bit of them. That practice kept her human.

Chandra was the next to join. When she removed her headgear, her white mohawk slumped to the side. Her eyes always stared toward the distance, but were also glazed with exhaustion. She'd probably seen more action than any other member of the Reapers. Though her military record stretched back decades, the campaigns and missions she was a part of were Code Black / Eyes Only.

Anitra tromped in, the last of the original HOVA Hellfighters that comprised their unit. Her sniper expertise was unmatched even among the HOVA. Her modified talon, a DMX-3000—more a tactical weapon—was a mess. Banged up, earth clogged, scarred, it would take a while to properly clean. Spying Robin's talon, she slung hers onto the table in front of her. Within easy reach. Noting the silence, she uncharacteristically remained quiet.

Ellis!Olinger nipped at her heels. They had the physique of a champion pyramid player. Strong. Patient. Cooperative. Dedicated. Persistent.

Epyc Ro finished her assessment of her people. For now.

"All right, we all here." Anitra sidled next to Epyc Ro. "Why don't you continue to school everyone here on my good point."

"Lawd," Robin said. "I regret all of my words."

"As members of Muungano, the HOVA were entrusted with training to handle first contact with indigenous people." Epyc Ro circled the room, meeting each of their eyes. "We have to determine what interacting with new cultures means for what's left of the Muungano way."

"Real, proper-ass aliens," Anitra said.

"Again . . . ," Robin began, but shook her head, not wanting to rise to her baiting. "We've all had cultural engagement and diplomatic training."

"But we were dispatched as gbeto, not diplomats. With our weapons, we send the wrong message in terms of building bridges and how we want to exchange ideas," Epyc Ro said.

"What are you saying?"

"It's easy to believe, given, you know, all of history, that humans are wired to not like folks who don't look like them. It's too easy to lean into that default. I suggest that we need to adapt our protocols given the change in our . . . military parameters."

"Yeah, now that we're space pirates, not gbeto," Anitra said.

"We're not . . ." Robin waved her off again. "So what do you imagine?"

"You and Chandra take point. You because of your extensive studies in cultural analysis. Chandra because of her Maya database."

"Let's not overthink it," Anitra said. "I figure first-contact protocols is like figuring out who to invite to the cookout."

"It better *not* be like that because I'm a longtime advocate of us needing to keep the invite energy to ourselves, because it's rarely reciprocated," Robin said. "Besides, do we trust their cookouts?"

"Hell nah. That's what I'm saying. First contact is only a couple steps away from how raisins end up in our potato salad." Anitra initiated her DMX's self-maintenance protocols. "We need trusted spaces to be able to talk shit about folks. Most importantly, I'm not trying to share my to-go plate. Cookout meat is a precious sacrament of family, not meant to be shared casually with colonizers, gentrifiers, and fans of Dave Matthews."

Anitra was part of the neonik generation. They loved the late-twenty-first-century era, referring to their throwback culture as the Remember Revolution. While the philosophical intent was to never forget tragedies of O.E. oppression, functionally it boiled down to them using older slang and references.

Robin glided toward Ellis in commiseration. "We want to just get out of her way when she's in the full throes of that LVE."

"Do I even want to know what that means?" Epyc Ro asked.

"Loud vagina energy." Anitra plunked her clean DMX onto the weapons rack. "Let's set our protocols to 'minding our own weusi-ass business' and see how far that gets us."

"Anyone check out the ship's stores? I'm hungry," Ellis said.

Chandra projected a holovid of the schematics of the ship. <Standard amenities. Protein synthesizers. Shower bay. Limited fashioning capabilities.>

"You had me at showers. I'm stowing my gear unless y'all planning on getting into a space skirmish in the next hour. I'm not coming out until I feel completely human again." Robin stashed her EVM and other gear out of discipline, but stripped out of habit, without consideration of Ellis's presence in the room. Shame didn't accompany nudity for Muungano members.

Ellis canted their head in a manner filled with mild curiosity, more innocent wonder than anything else. Their gaze lingered at the string of beads girding her belly. "What are those?"

"My HOVA elekes," Robin said. "Part of our uniform, I suppose. We receive them when we become official gbeto."

"Do I get one?" Ellis asked.

"Do you know what I had to do to earn these?" A sniff of offense accompanied Robin's tone.

"When will I have done enough?" Ellis had picked up a weapon and fought alongside them, but they were still thought of more as an armed civilian. And each of the Reapers found it difficult to relate to people of the civilian world.

"Oh, trust me, someone will let you know." Transparent as ever, she didn't want the Mzisoh to further inquire. The Reaper rituals were for them, defined them, and they hadn't discussed what introducing an outsider to them might look like. "You okay, Captain?"

"I'm . . . assessing," Epyc Ro said.

"Assessing what?" Ellis asked.

"I don't know yet." Epyc Ro also wondered how they would maintain Muungano culture now that they'd been cut off from it. She lacked the words to explain what churned within her or what her emi searched for. Not knowing where to direct their energies next, she feared her people might lapse into depression and anxiety. Feeling numb. She remained alert for anyone beginning to isolate themselves, ceasing to do the things they loved to do, or diverging from their usual routine. Though there was nothing usual about where they now found themselves. "If you'll excuse me . . ."

Epyc Ro longed for the luxury of a walkabout. A journey to clear her emi. So much of her preparation to transition to a HOVA gbeto involved pain. The ritual they all underwent opened with a communion drink. A mixture of sacred fruit, herbs, and a tincture of her blood blended into the initial retrovirus cocktail. Most folks rarely discussed the sense of dysphoria that accompanied the early phases, post-transition. One of the reasons why gbeto were so dominated by women was that they adjusted better to the mitochondrial insertion and other genetic modifications. Honestly, she hadn't understood all the changes made to her or even considered all of the implications of her transition. All the genomic and cellular modifications, including her cells possessing dual mitochondria, led to her body's ability to rapidly detoxify reactive oxygen species and other cellular wastes. She was faster, stronger, and her endurance lasted longer. She aged slower and healed quicker. After the transition, her gbeto sisters performed a scarification on her thigh: a welcoming ritual of carving signs and symbols into her evoking strength and protection. They had to be done soon after the initial treatment because after that, her enhanced cellular regeneration would erase all scars as she healed.

The cost of the procedure required them to separate from the Muungano people. This program teetered too close to the cliff of eugenics, a hypocrisy the Muungano leadership admitted to but couldn't always face, especially living alongside gbeto in day-to-day community. The HOVA forged a new society, their like-minded members sworn to protect and guard their people.

That was so long ago.

The existential ache Epyc Ro experienced spilled all over her sabhu, threatened to consume her. Longing for her passion to return, she wanted to feel again. Part of her had forgotten itself, how to draw people in, how to create and live within a sense of belonging. She needed to discover the things that would make her happy. Tracing her scarification with her finger, she idly wondered what the barrel of her talon tasted like. What the energy pulse blasting through her skull might feel like. If an eternal quiet might still the voices and bring her peace.

With an interrupting cough, Robin framed herself in the octagonal entrance-way. She'd fashioned her nanomesh into a loose kanzu with textured pants.

"That shower didn't take long," Epyc Ro remarked, somewhat irritated at the disruption.

"I rushed back to my humanity faster than I thought I would." Robin saun-tered over. "You good?"

"Yeah, why?" Epyc Ro asked.

"You just don't seem all there."

"Just have a lot on my mind."

"Uh-huh. That might fly with the others, but not with me. Never with me. My love is consistent, persistent, and . . ."

"Insistent?" Epyc Ro forced a thin smile. "I thought you were going for a rhyming thing."

"I wasn't sure either. I was leaning toward 'knowing.'" Robin peered, a pen-etrating gaze into her emi; deep and aware, yet without intrusion. There wasn't much room for hiding from it.

"I'm afraid."

"I ain't never seen anything close to fear from you."

"It's about what sort of things I'll have to leave behind, to be who I need to be in this new situation." Epyc Ro ran her hand along the storage compartment above her.

"The unknown is a risk. Chaos is an opportunity. We adapt and trust in the process. I'm excited to see the you, the any of us, that emerges."

"I . . . don't know who I am." Epyc Ro avoided her friend's eyes.

"The HOVA was a role, a uniform, not who you were. You are a Muungano member no matter where you go. Right now, you are simply free of the duties and obligations others had for you. That said, being a leader is also part of who you are. I wonder if it's about trying to figure out not who you are, but rather how you can be true to that without other people telling you." Robin's hand fell on her shoulder in a reassuring clasp.

"I think part of my struggle is figuring out who I'm supposed to be next."

"Anitra found her answer."

"I'm not sure if I'm ready to become a space pirate."

"Me either, but we'll figure it out. There're too many things left in life for us to do."

"It's all right."

"What is?"

"To cry. To yell. To do whatever it takes to lift that burden from you." Robin's huge, tough, easily wounded heart betrayed her again. Epyc Ro knew that many nights her lieutenant wept, not out of fear, but to mourn all the lost lives and wasted efforts of their wartime activities. "A ritual of renewal," she called it. "Don't let it overtake you. Share your load. We all can help carry it. Closure is a myth. Heal and live, sis."

Epyc Ro still found that she tried to muddle through on her own, forgetting she had people to work stuff through with. The two of them spoke of heart things. Of Fela things. Of Epyc Ro things.

When they returned to the meeting alcove, everyone else ate in silence. Their nanomesh tailored into casual wear. The air redolent with heat and moisture, though not stale. Epyc Ro took a few steps into the room, her soles nearly soundless against the floor. She cleared her throat and her gbeto turned to her.

"There was a time when Muungano needed to figure out who it was going to be and how it was going to get there. We had a choice: we could believe we would never be free of the constructs and injury of history; or we could create a new culture, a new way of being and doing, together. To bring together all of our people to forge something which hadn't been seen before. It was why we had the Uponyaji. The act of resting, healing, and dreaming together would create an overarching wellspring we could all draw from.

"You want us to have our own Uponyaji?" Robin cocked her head quizzically.

"Sort of. We need a time of restoration. And forgiveness. Of looking back and sharing stories. We need to welcome a new member into our ranks, but to do that, they will need to hear who we are and where we came from." Epyc Ro walked over and stood over their prospective member. "Ellis!Olinger, please stand."

Ellis glanced at each of them. Anitra shrugged.

"The group surrounding you has a long and storied tradition." Withdrawing a black case from her pocket, Epyc Ro clutched the box while she spoke. "We call ourselves the Reapers after a battalion of the Mino, the all-female military regiment of the Kingdom of Dahomey. Before that, we took our name from an infantry regiment of the New York Army National Guard known as the Harlem Hellfighters during World Wars I and II. They spent more time in combat than any other American unit in World War I and were one of the most decorated. It was the Germans they fought who gave them the nickname 'Hellfighters.'

"We follow the charge given by the Deacons for Defense and Justice, veterans of previous wars who charged themselves to protect members of the civil rights movement against those who would use violence against them. They swore to rise to the 'defense of civil rights, property rights, and personal rights and defend said rights by any and all honorable and legal means to the end that justice may be obtained.' Do you so swear?"

"I do," Ellis said.

"Then by the power vested in me by this circle of sisters, I welcome you as a fellow member of the Reapers." Opening the case, Epyc Ro held out a set of Oya elekes beads.

Ellis strung the beads between their fingers.

Robin's eyes lit up with recognition. "Are you sure?"

Ellis noticed the exchanged glances between Robin and Epyc Ro. "What? I'm missing something."

"Those were Fela's elekes," Anitra whispered.

"And they are now Ellis's to guard. And be guarded by." Epyc Ro held out another item for them to take. A flat disk.

Ellis turned the green metal circle over in their palms. "What's this?"

"A burial disk. Each gbeto is issued one. If they die on the field, this is how we collect our own."

"I hope to never need it, but I shall bear it with honor," Ellis said.

"I know you will." Epyc Ro rested her hand on their shoulder.

"Asè," Robin said.

"Asè," the rest said in unison. Ellis echoed them.

With a fleeting smile, Epyc Ro faced the full circle. "What do we do now?"

<Permission to begin extended scans,> Chandra said.

"Permission granted. What are you looking for?" Epyc Ro asked.

<Any nearby signals which may indicate a culture with the technology necessary to provide us safe harbor.>

Epyc Ro said, "We looking for a place to call home?"

"No such thing. Not out here," Robin said. "Not after the CO/IN killed Fela."

"Unless we create it." Epyc Ro's words were more prayer than whisper.

<Network detected.>

"So soon? Can you trace it?" Epyc Ro asked.

<Working.> Chandra projected a holovid arrangement of the surrounding stars. She highlighted a portion of the field.

"That's close. Plot a course there. Everyone find a station."

Chandra and Anitra hopped into the helm hemispheres. Ellis remained near the entranceway, assuming a tactical security position. Epyc Ro rested her hands on the back of a chair at the center of the command deck. Circling it, she wondered whether it was truly hers to take. If perhaps someone else, like Robin, would be better suited for it.

"Have a seat, Captain." Robin drew up a series of data streams at her station. Science ops.

Brushing back her jacket, Epyc Ro sat down. "Sitrep?"

"It looks like a ship of some sort. In geosynchronous orbit with the planet below it. It's issuing a distress beacon."

"On screen."

The ship vaguely resembled a beetle with its wings extended. Two tubular cells extended along the section of the ship connecting the wings to its main body. Protrusions like mandibles at its front and legs unfurled from its rear. Scorch marks seared the hull. Much of its exterior appeared damaged. Several holes, like ruptured pustules, spewed debris. A trail of flotsam orbited the ship.

"Any guess about what happened?" Epyc Ro asked.

"Main reactor breach, maybe? It's taken a lot of damage," Anitra said.

"Self-repair systems?"

"Minimal. Like trying to do surgery on yourself while taking a nap."

<Message coming through on commlink bands,> Chandra relayed.

"Can you translate?" Epyc Ro asked.

"There's a series of arrays scattered about the ship," Robin said.

"They might as well have a giant sign that reads 'Stay Away!'" Anitra said.

"Those appear to be weaponized satellites," Robin said.

<It's a repeating message.>

"Stay away," Anitra repeated.

<It's a warning message.>

"When will y'all stop doubting me?"

"Some space pirate," Robin said.

"I'm just saying we have to be reasonable. It's my personal piracy assessment protocols," Anitra said.

"*Your vessel violates Morawi space. You will leave this vicinity immediately or we will open fire,*" a voice intoned with the tenor of an automated message.

"We're being scanned," Robin yelled.

"Plotting course 'Alpha, Gamma, take our ass outta here.'" Anitra punched in stellar coordinates.

"People are this suspicious and unwelcoming for reasons. Or . . . ," Epyc Ro said.

"Aliens," Anitra said.

"I'm done telling you that we're the aliens in this scenario," Robin said.

"No, we're space . . ."

"*Any evidence of piracy will be dealt with strictly,*" the voice continued along its script.

". . . circus. We're the space circus." Anitra held a finger to her lips. "You never know who's listening."

"Thoughts?" Epyc Ro asked.

"Someone's worried about attacks. There's a damaged ship out there. Sounds like this region may already have raiders targeting vulnerable ships," Robin said.

"Do you suspect this is a legit distress signal or a trap?"

"I have a suggestion for our new prime directive: Leave that shit alone," Anitra said. "Any situation we come across, we start with 'Leave that shit alone.'"

"Do you think you can dock with that ship?" Epyc Ro asked.

"Captain, if you ask me to, I can land on a pinhead." Hunching over her console, Robin fashioned a docking column and altered their trajectory.

"I'm going to need a boarding party." Epyc Ro stood up, pausing to see who would join her.

"You already know." Robin eased out of her seat.

"You sure?" Epyc Ro asked.

"I just got clean, so I'm not happy about it. However, you need to sit down, ma'am. Your place is on the ship. You're the captain now. Someone's got to watch the kids."

Epyc Ro locked eyes with her, just shy of a glare. Robin met her gaze and rolled her eyes. The discussion was over; she was so right there was no arguing to be had, and all that was left was posturing and acceptance. She headed toward the weapons rack.

"I'll go." Anitra transferred her system to the captain's station.

"Wait, what happened to our prime directive of 'Leave that shit alone'?" Robin paused by the doorway.

"I just wanted it firmly on record that I denounced the idea of holing up with aliens or, for that matter, entering dark basements. That's just a matter of principle. After that, a mission's a mission."

"And you're ready to take everything that's not nailed down." Robin slung Busta over her shoulder.

"In the name of research." Anitra joined her at the weapons locker. "Besides, we do have to eventually open communications. Won't be too long until I'll need an interstellar weed connect."

"Anyone else?" Epyc Ro asked.

"I'll go." Ellis's gaze tracked Anitra. They might be a problem. The mission field was not the place to indulge one's crush. But that same energy made them fiercely defensive of the squad.

"All right, suit up. Ready to deploy in ten. Chandra, finish docking," Epyc Ro said.

<Range 014 and closing.>

Her clothes fashioning back into her tactical nanomesh, Anitra stepped into her EVM. Once secured, she hefted her DMX-3000 like a long-missed friend.

<Primary couplers engaged.>

Robin kissed her elekes before morphing her nanomesh for combat readiness. Slipping into her EVM, she slung Busta over her arm.

<Drop stations secured.>

Ellis tucked their burial disk into their vestments.

Epyc Ro studied the viewscreens. "Take us in low over the ship. Let me know if any of those satellites start acting up."

<I won't keep it to myself.> With a mild jolt as clamping assemblies locked them into place, Chandra docked the ship. She deployed a gangway tube, the apparatus extending out like a prehensile filament. Its seal steadied the ship's orbit.

"Stay on stations. Prepare to deploy."

Epyc Ro created holovid displays for each member of her boarding party. Swallowing, she dug her fingers into her armrest. She desperately wanted to be alongside them on their mission. She hated the sense of remove she experienced, all of the action occurring thousands of kilometers away. That she was no longer in the thick of it. At the same time, the action popped off at such speed, circumstances gave her little time to think, only react.

"Deployment dispersal on my mark. Anitra on point," Robin ordered.

"Today's a good day for a good day," Anitra yelled, and dove down the docking tube.

Ellis stared down the shaft and back to Robin, not sure what to do next.

"Are you out of your rabbit-ass mind?" Robin leapt after her.

"Every time you use a phrase like that, you're another step closer to officially becoming an elder," Anitra said.

The three plunged down the artificial umbilicus, their EVM thrusters guiding their descent. The sensation a mix of weightlessness and free fall. Landing first, Anitra jacked a Black Caesar into the ship's door ports. By the time the other two joined her, the panel on her break box lit green. She nodded. Ellis pressed their back to the ship's wall, watching their ship's tether. Smacking the hull, they signaled their readiness. Anitra opened the hatch. The walls buckled as if punched by a large invisible fist but rebounded. With the hatch behind them, they activated a seal, creating an artificial air lock, but the drop in pressure swept through in a rush. Anitra moved deftly despite the heavy navsuit armor.

"Hull integrity appears solid. There's power." DMX at the ready, Anitra plunged in. "We have atmosphere and pressure."

<No visible activity.> Chandra initiated a tactical display at her station before projecting it along the command dock. Sensor sweeps mapped out the ship as they went.

Anitra's light illuminated the receiving bay. She held her position until Robin flanked her and Ellis sealed the doors behind them. Robin nodded and joined Anitra in forcing open the next set of doors. The ceiling above them had been shorn through, as if a single claw raked along the inner lining of the ship. Fluid leaked along the ruptured metal. Minimal power sputtered the occasional light to a dim glow. Air filters scrubbed away any lingering odor. The walls had a loamy, moldy quality to them, a curtain of bleakness, which pained Epyc Ro's emi. The gentle plinking of water echoed in the distance. Their boots, magnetically clamped, clanged along the walkway.

"Analysis?" Epyc Ro asked.

"Evidence of small-arms fire. Blaster burns, that sort of thing." Robin examined the scene through the scope of her Busta. The telemetry readouts hovered along the command deck chamber.

"I don't know what kind of fecal fiasco you done got us into . . ." Anitra's whisper trailed off as she shifted into business mode.

The way the Reapers could stop midchatter and stand ten toes on business never ceased to amaze her. As natural as breathing. Her emi tightened and she took a tactical position to cover Robin and Ellis as they advanced.

"Ship looks relatively intact. No structural damage. Definitely a cargo vessel," Robin said.

"What sort of cargo?" Epyc Ro asked.

"Can't say just yet," Robin said. "No motion detected. Live signals from forward."

"Any reaction from the satellites?" Epyc Ro asked.

<Nothing.>

"Proceed with caution."

"Ellis, you're up," Robin said.

The ship wasn't under thrust. It was as if power was present, but no one had turned anything on. Anything not stashed away or locked down floated. Robin brushed aside the occasion cargo box or spanner, bobbing ghosts of engineers past. Anitra and Ellis flanked the doorway while she attended the controls. The ship rumbled to full life with its reactor core powering up. Once the drive core was online, the ship thrummed and the objects collapsed to the floor with the suddenness of cut strings. Locks hissed and disengaged as the emergency pressure doors released.

Ellis assumed point position. Stalking up the catwalk, they swept the room. Robin seconded them, waving her hand for the Black Caesar so she could jack into the main computer. The comm station had been powered down specifically. A few sensor logs streamed innocuous data, hull-integrity readouts, shield status, life-support levels. They had data logs, none of which Robin paid particular attention to. Her intelligence training assumed that whoever piloted and crewed this ship would have scrubbed the memory core of any sensitive data and locked down the station. Perhaps overlaying logs with prewritten logs to mask their true mission and activities. Emergency protocols in case they fell into the wrong hands.

"Records intact. Downloading data logs through firewall protocols." Robin unplugged from their system. "Anitra, what you got?"

"A couple sealed-off compartments. Heading to what I'm guessing is med lab."

"On your six," Robin said.

Coming alongside, Ellis rushed forward.

"Hold." Anitra raised her fist for everyone to halt. "I have a life-form reading. Ahead."

"Close on Anitra," Epyc Ro said.

Ten storage rooms lined the deck. Robin descended a crew ladder to access the deck below. Her curiosity getting the better of her, she bolted ahead, not giving Anitra and Ellis enough time to clear the deck. This must have been what passed for the lower deck, the crew level of the ship. Personnel cabins around a tiny hub presumably meant to be a commissary of some sort. All manner of disaster scenarios ticked through Epyc Ro's mind about what could have caused them to abandon the ship so suddenly. Radiation leak. Mutiny. Hull breach. But her mind kept coming back to raiders.

The CO/IN operated that way.

"Robin, rejoin your team, I don't want you all separated," Epyc Ro said.

Robin held her position long enough for Anitra and Ellis to secure the room. They passed wall panel after wall panel, and none flashed any warnings. Weapons at the ready, they crept toward med bay. The dimly lit hallway and the obtuse angles of the strange architecture played with their perspective. Medical tools were scattered around on the ground as if doctors dropped them mid-operation. Ellis stepped on one. Its slight metallic clatter made Robin and Anitra stop to stare at them. Ellis glanced up, sheepish. They were new to the field and lacked the expertise of the rest of the team. Epyc Ro made a mental note to double down on their training.

The far side of med bay was a labyrinth of shadows. Anitra swung her light along its edges. One of the shadows shifted. A figure scurried along the corridor.

"I have a lock," Anitra said.

"Hold your fire," Robin yelled.

"Target acquired."

"I said hold your fire." Robin rushed after them.

Hidden by the shadows, the figure reached a grate, their small fingers scrambling for purchase. Before they could tug it aside, Robin caught up to them. She grabbed them by the shoulders. The darkness shifted, the stranger slapped her hand away. Her back obscured Anitra and Ellis's line of sight, though both drew down on her position. The way Robin's cam was angled, Epyc Ro couldn't make out anything.

"Wait, what now?" Robin shouted into their commlinks.

"Robin, what do you have?" Epyc Ro jumped out of her seat. Her heart pounded impotently waiting for her officer's report. Robin's health telemetry remained unwavering.

Spinning her light to provide a visual, Robin held a little girl.

02

WACHIRU ADISA
O.E.—Indianapolis (West Side)

Every revolution had its anthem, we simply hadn't found ours yet.

Canvassing for climate refugees was not how we planned to spend our day. We were Wachiru Adisa, the son of the great Xola, a cofounder of Muungano. The Camara of our people. Now Xola was dead and most days we found it hard to even breathe. The duties and responsibilities of Muungano filled most of our life, occupied most of our mind, squeezed out everything else. We could not remember the last time we were on Original Earth. O.E. The Yo. We hoped our walkabout on O.E. would allow us space to figure out who we were outside of the work. We wanted to rediscover our first love, our art. Living into our music, going wherever the creative spirit took us. Just shy of mocking us, Jaha chided that we were off "to be a carpenter."

Instead, we skulked about the Indianapolis neighborhood of the Breton Court town houses. They rose out of the ground like jagged teeth that hadn't seen a dentist in a while. The latest experiment in them corralling and housing its citizens. Tall spires, much overgrown by weeds and moss, cracking its foundations. The sporadic foliage had overgrown much of Breton Court, the townhomes reduced to little more than a shantytown. Our mission was to resettle some weusi citizens of O.E., trying to get them to the Muungano embassy. Migration of our people seeking a place safe from the ravages of climate collapse to live was the natural response to climate collapse. The calculation of opportunities, latitude, elevation, infrastructure. And luck. Jaha Dimka ever by our side. Upon Maulana's ascension to Camara, replacing our father, she chose to accompany us on our walkabout. Who were we to refuse our godmother?

"Breton Court had once been an O.E. pinnacle community. Once a solidly wazungu, not-quite-suburban enclave, just a little south of the Eagle Creek national park in Indianapolis. Once wazungu flight began, it fell into steep decline as an underresourced neighborhood which the city forgot about until the Thmei Academy opened, inaugurating the International District of

Indianapolis, eventually becoming Embassy Row." Jaha's voice brimmed with near merriment with the chance to run down logistical details. A red, black, and green cloth wrapped her head. No one saw her without a covering, be it hat, scarf, or artificial hairpiece. A gold disk circled her neck, a collapsed chakram, the weapon of choice of a Niyabinghi. Jaha's funkentelechy fashioned her tactical suit. Metallic green eye shadow framed a black kohl-rimmed eye. One eye remained the deep brown of her birth, but the other shimmered with a golden hue, a reminder of the surgeries she underwent after she survived the Muungano embassy bombing the last time she was stationed here. Thin lines framed the fierce set of her jaw. "The neighborhood languished as land speculators held on to the property, gambling that they might be able to profit once the International District expanded. Or if it were targeted as one of O.E.'s Opportunity Zones. But it never was. This 'unplanned slum' as LISC—the Liberation Investment Support Cooperative, the financial and governing power of the Yo government—calls it, has been shut out of the mainstream economy . . ."

"Seriously? Telling us what LISC stands for might be too thorough," we dared interrupting her. "We're good, Jaha."

The translucent filter of the rebreather unit sheathing our face allowed us to move about Indianapolis breathing what passed for the Yo's air. Despite its terraforming technology, the air quality hadn't improved much, at least not in Breton Court. Many of its windows on the lower levels were left shattered. No lights illuminated the public spires. A scree of gravel and crumbled stone served as sidewalks. It sickened us to believe that any of our people had been consigned to this. We suspected that there were many neighborhoods—cities, states, or countries—that LISC simply neglected.

"There's one more piece. I haven't given you the rest of the information . . ."

"We said 'We're good.'" Our voice was uncharacteristically sharp; our spirit had been on edge ever since we detoured to this section of town.

"Oh well, my apologies." Halting midstride, Jaha turned to the nearest tree and slapped it. Glancing about as if confused, she smacked it again.

"What are you doing?" We pressed our hands to our side, taking in the show of Jaha dramatically making whatever point she needed to make.

"Trying to hit the pause button on the world to give you time to process everything going on. It doesn't seem to be working." Jaha was already on one, which meant it was going to be a long day. "Life seems to keep coming at us fast."

We rubbed our temples. "All we were saying was that all that back information was extra. We can't keep up with it."

She slapped the tree again. Jaha was Nyamakalaw of the Griot Circle, Mu-ungano's internal security, a storyteller of the highest order. It was said that members of the Griot Circle didn't need weapons because they could remember their people's names, though they carried pehla sticks as a precaution against the folks they didn't know. At one point she was Ras of the Niyabinghi, Mu-ungano's external security. A general of the community's security. The words *former* and *retired* weren't in any lexicon that applied to her.

We adjusted the rebreather unit. Even with our advanced version of the tech—four nodes on our face that generated a purifying field—it went against the flow of how we wanted to move through spaces. O.E. was in the throes of the four arms of its collapse: climate change, pandemic, economic collapse, rebellion. They continued to ignore the repercussions of the rise of global temperatures as long as they could promise Mars. Or the stars. O.E. shielded their more privileged enclaves, bubbling whole cities or sometimes just some specific neighborhoods. Burning fuels and spewing pollutants despite their best interests. But masks were a way to honor people, the smallest concession to demonstrate our valuing of them. A simple social courtesy. However, they also reminded us of when we fell critically ill not that many years ago, needing the aid of Muungano technology and healers to recover.

"We can't keep working like this. So how about," we began again, "if we say we're good unless it's critical."

"It's critical," she responded without hesitation.

"The situation can't be critical, we just got here."

"And look where we are. You need to learn the lay of the land."

"We're just saying that there was nothing we needed to know about all that . . . 'extra.' We only needed enough to know what we were looking at. Though we appreciate your diligence." The two of us often had what she called "intentional, direct conversations." But honestly, sometimes we just wanted to argue. It was a familiar, even comforting, rhythm. Reminding me of how she and my father used to bicker with each other. Never able to stay mad at each other. We needed to do a better job of only asking for what we could process in the moment. Unlike Jaha, we weren't trying to know every detail about everything going on, because there was too much shit in our head to just keep adding to it. Often losing ourselves in the weeds of details, we had to prioritize information to keep from overloading our mind.

"And I just wanted to make sure that you were prepared for what's coming next."

"We don't make decisions grounded in the rush to do something quickly." We heard echoes of our father, Xola, in our words.

"My love." Her touch every bit that of the doting grandmother, Jaha raised our chin to meet her gaze. She threw us her you-think-you-grown-now stare to make sure we received her full lesson. "You're going to experience many First Attempts in Learning."

"It's just . . . we feel like we've become a roving listener." The first-level members of the Learning Tree, our living curriculum. The way Muungano passed on knowledge and culture within the community. It was the rank of children or those early in their journey.

"There's nothing wrong with that. Roving listeners are the ears of Muungano, out in O.E., just like cultural attachés are its hands."

"We suppose. At least now we are free to move about without constraint and do things our way."

"Without the burden of being a leader?" A snide tone gilded her words. Again. "This is an interesting way to run from responsibilities."

"We were never . . . running." We were no longer connected to Maya, the AI member of Muungano, who served as our guide. We could not afford to be traced by anyone. On Muungano or off. We were on our own. Our mind yielding as we withdrew into our emi. A gentle ache accompanied the stretching, opening up to possibilities. Hoping for a sense of direction of where we should go, it was as if our spirit had closed itself off to us.

We were lost. Alone. Our sister, Amachi, was gone. Our father, Xola, was gone. Our community, Muungano, chose Maulana to speak for them as Camara. Not us. There was nothing left for us back there, so we had to figure out who we were and who we were meant to be. Which, we supposed, sounded a lot like running.

"But we also couldn't just let people on the Yo languish," we said.

"You are still you no matter where you go. And you make me proud." She placed her hand on our shoulder, and a rare note of concern thickened her voice. "We have enough people coming for us without us taking ourselves out. So, I need you to look out for my friend."

Her emi ever battle-sharpened, Jaha stopped short, a wolf suddenly catching a troubling scent. We turned to see what was wrong when a figure rushed from the shadows. The tackle knocked the wind out of us, and we landed on the ground harder than if we'd been prepared. We had grown sloppy. We weren't on Muungano anymore. We couldn't afford to lower our guard, be taken so unaware, in these streets. The man attempted to lock our arms and legs, but we twisted free before he could complete the grappling hold. We weren't trained fighters like those in the Griot Circle or the Niyabinghi, but we had been in our share of tussles. We elbowed him in the side, and the blow glanced off his body armor without him so much as grunting. Spinning away, we stomped down, aiming for his knee. He pivoted enough for our heel to catch only the thick muscle of his thigh before he scrambled to his feet. Balling our hand into a fist, we started a swing. Before our punch could complete its arc, the man lunged forward. His hand formed a blade of an extended forefinger knuckle, which he drove into our face next to our nose. Our head snapped back like we'd taken a blast to the face. He swept our legs out from under us, but we planted our hands on the ground, catching ourselves, and twisted our legs around his to bring him down instead. His hands configured into a new attack posture, but the blade of Jaha's chakram gleamed against his throat.

"That'll be enough, baby," she said calmly.

He raised his arms, his hands palm-out, not surrendering so much as tarrying. Jaha nodded, stepping back to give him just enough room to stand. We cupped our face, nursing the pain, hoping it wouldn't mushroom into a headache later.

"The Energy, stand down. Don't you recognize our guests?" Another armored man, much burlier than the first, approached from the woods. His helmet was an elaborate Gelede mask carved in two parts: the lower part was a vaguely human face, while the upper part was a mélange of a leopard, snakes, and knives. Jaha whirled at the sound of his voice, chakrams at the ready.

"*Freedom! Where are you?*" Jaha shouted; her phrasing had the timbre of an old code.

"'*Cause I need freedom, too.*" The burly man moved slowly, removing his helmet. Gray dappled his dreads, which draped down his back in a magnificent mane. His face, weathered and taut, had a resigned weariness to it. A military veteran ready to suit up again to fight in a war without end.

"*I break chains all by myself.*" The Energy completed the cadence, his mask turning from his compatriot back to Jaha. His head angled quizzically to us. "Who are you?"

"The Brand." Jaha flattened her chakrams to her chest, and they re-formed into a necklace about her throat. "Welcome, brother. I didn't think I'd see you again."

"The Deacons have always been about that work." The Brand extended his arm, and Jaha clasped it. "Not exactly the Muungano way, but we can't all work out of that playbook. Still, it has been too long."

His name sounded familiar to us. The Deacons were well known to us, as we had worked alongside them in various capacities over the years. The Deacons organized to serve and protect those weusi areas not under Muungano's sovereignty. They billed themselves as "the fuck around and find out squad."

"We are Wachiru Adisa." Turning to The Energy, we reached out with our emi. Reading another's energy, or gathering a sense of their spirit, was to understand the language of the soul, their sabhu. At least that use of it hadn't abandoned us.

Though the men wrapped themselves in cloaks, their navsuits, their armaments were older-generation HOVA weapons. Muungano-developed, yet in the hands of folks outside of our defensive military forces. The Energy's mask was more standard O.E. military. When he removed it, a series of twists unfurled. They covered the front half of his head, the rest of his hair styled into a fade blending into his low-cropped beard. His eyes, rueful and vigilant, like those of a student resenting his need to study for a quiz. He had the fierceness of a devout believer. "Adisa? Wait, are you Xola's boy?"

"Yes." The mention of our father still stung, his absence a fresh pang.

"You aren't in Muungano now." The Energy's voice hardened with a slight sneer.

"That's the point. Our people are in need." We offered our arm in greeting.

"You have no idea." Rather than clasp it, The Energy smacked away our hand. "I'm glad you deigned to finally remember us."

"Watch yourself." Jaha issued a rattlesnake's warning. "We never forgot. Just like you need to know that even now, not every soul is going to make it across the river. In fact, most won't."

"I brought The Energy into the work. He found his calling and fell in love," The Brand said.

The Energy gave her a careful appraisal. "You must be the legendary Jaha Dimka. My apologies."

"Play nice." The Brand smiled at Jaha.

It took a moment of nagging to place our connection to The Brand. "Wait, I know you. Our cousin, Ezeji, dated your daughter."

"We don't talk about that." The Brand's emi shifted toward cold as he settled into business. "Why are you here?"

"You have that tone again," Jaha said.

"What tone?" The Brand feigned innocence poorly.

"That we're somehow trespassing, not supposed to be here. Or that we're unwelcome, treading on your turf."

"Like I said, you do the work your way. We do it ours."

"But these days, it's all hands on deck."

"True that." The Brand sighed in resignation, without quite lowering his defensiveness.

"We heard rumors," we interrupted, not sure how to interpret the weirdly hostile yet respectful spirit between them. "There's a group of refugees gathered who seek sanctuary in Muungano."

"So you decided to come down from your lunar loft and help the little people?" The Energy's hand continued to hover too near his talon for our comfort.

"Baby, I'm experiencing what some might call 'a diminishing return of fucks' when it comes to you." Jaha's side-eye silenced him.

"Our people are attempting to cross town, defying the curfew and the Knights of the White Camelia. Just to make it to Muungano. We've come to provide them access."

Things had obviously gotten so much worse since incontrovertible proof arrived that the people of O.E. were not alone in the universe and that their neighbors in the cosmos were pissed. LISC promoted the narrative about the Interstellar Alliance consolidating its power and fortifying its boundaries to stave off our perceived threat. That Muungano, led by its new authoritarian leader, wanted to take the war to O.E. LISC's fearmongering allowed them to enact strict curfews and controls. This gave rise to conspiracy theories about how the footage of the execution of our HOVA captain, Fela Buhari, was an elaborate hoax. All prosthetics and special effects broadcast on hijacked signals. Conspiracy theories conditioned people for powerlessness. Rumors of war heightened tensions down to street level, especially with the Earth Firsters.

They weren't quite a movement but fell into various camps. The American Renaissance Movement (ARM) was their political wing, infiltrating the ranks of LISC until it was all but a political party; they fancied themselves federal "soldiers in the army of the Lord." The Service of the Order was what happened when the Space Force got religion; though many groups sprang up in the wake of the military church being defeated during the Great Unrest. The last was their boots-on-the-ground militia, the Knights of the White Camelia. Once an easily dismissed fringe group, the Knights of the White Camelia rode the anxiety of panic and uncertainty to become part of the greater ARM

National Guard, a policing force akin to our Griot Circle, except with no interest in de-escalating a situation. They preferred any excuse to bust heads and remind people of their place in the name of order and peace. Most went without masks; at best, the Knights wore only kerchiefs to cover their faces against the poor air quality, considering even such mild protections capitulation to the propaganda of those who pushed the narrative of climate change. All of them vied for power, emboldened by the uncertainty of the times and people grasping at anything to make them feel safe.

Our folks wanted to get out before they couldn't. Not that we had any idea how to handle the current surge of coming citizens, but we supported them being moved by the dream of Muungano because we understood that no matter where our people found themselves, until everyone was free, no one was free.

"Why are you here?" Jaha asked.

"It's easy to get lost in India No Place," The Energy said.

"Think of all the time lost with just our weird-ass time-zones situation alone," The Brand joked to lighten the mood. "Our intelligence reports that operatives have been planted among us to amp up any of our protest efforts in order to give VOP all the excuse he needs to send in ARM troops."

"Our people are in danger and we will always suit up to defend them. So we have the same objective." Jaha glared at The Energy.

"So it seems." The Brand half bowed and gestured for Jaha to take point. "But this isn't Breton Court. This is what remains of what the VOP thinks Breton Court is."

We followed the Drinking Gourd, the only light still visible in the night sky through the heavy haze over the city. We skulked through the thin copse of trees and along the overgrown woods that wound from Eagle Creek to the White River. Its embankments ran flush against what was once a strip mall of some sort. Its façade now little more than a bombed-out husk harkening back to a long-bygone era after almost a century of neglect. Folks huddled about. Electricity still powered a couple of the homes, with extension cords snaking from those homes with power to those without. To the colonist gaze, a landscape with no space, no hope. Dilapidated town houses overgrown by weeds and mats of grass, discarded metal cobbled together to patch roofing. The people living there surviving day to day, all they could do. To the trained eye, the metal protrusions on the roofs harnessed solar energy. The mat of green served as natural insulation. The abandoned crates along the creek processed and recycled water. The community of dreamers grew their own food. They created their own infrastructure decoupled from the city's grid network.

"The people call it Lil M," The Brand said, his voice flushed with pride.

"Our people." Jaha wasn't in the mood to be disputed. "They've done some great work here. A model of resilience for other communities."

"Which is why they have been targeted. Because of the Muungano embassy bombing—and the subsequent heightened tensions—more attention has been focused on the area. Determined to root out insurgents, ARM units are said to be deploying to raze the entire area. We have to get the people out."

"They always seek to rob us of our joy," we half whispered.

"Joy? There's no joy here." The Energy all but whirled toward us. His hand danced near his weapon, eager to target an enemy. If he wasn't careful, he'd find a real one.

Jaha stepped in between us. "Sweet baby, joy is an experience. Happiness is an event. Take either where you can."

"I'd always heard that you were a boss, always ready to kick ass in the name of community. All I see is an elder who has gone soft," The Energy sneered. "One with a track record of breaking from community."

"The key word is *elder*." The Brand's words bit deep. "One due all the respect."

"It's all right, The Brand. Let the baby learn. He's working his way up to being bold enough to call me out on my time at the Bayard Rustin Home School community. I was younger then. What I was trying to get my hands around evolved and that space no longer served my personal journey. They worried that I was stepping away from the rituals based on some of the things I was reading and exploring, stepping away from the ideology. And then the school was burned."

"Well, we ain't got time to read," The Energy said. "We're in a war."

"We're in a war of ideas," Jaha said. "And I need to make sure my troops are well trained. That's why we read. Either the world had to change or we had to change how we engage the world."

"Don't mind The Energy. His school also . . . burned," The Brand said.

"My school is these streets." The Energy unholstered his talon, drew it, examined it, and then returned it to its sling. "Class is always in session. And we always have to be ready."

"Good. There's always a place for learners with us." Jaha sniffed, unimpressed.

"Even if we face the last desperate gasp of humanity, we still have to get up every morning to keep grinding," we said.

The Energy huffed in resigned acknowledgment, as close to respect as he was in a place to offer before stalking off to secure their perimeter. Jaha reached out to stop The Brand by his arm before he could wander after him.

"You got no chill in you. Did you have to go so hard with him?" The Brand watched The Energy patrol the perimeter.

"Our gifts thrive in different times," Jaha said.

"Complaining's not a gift."

"Agitating. I'm a professional agitator. That's how I get shit done."

"It's a mystery why you've remained single . . ."

"It's a greater mystery how my foot has never ended up in your behind." Adjusting her scanner, Jaha began security scans of Breton Court. "Look, I'm not here to fearmonger. I know you're not happy with the choice people have made to leave what they've built here. But we have to take certain precautions that aren't easy. The work is exhausting, but our people are allowed to make their own informed choices."

"What you do you mean 'informed'? You got a sociology degree packed away or you just going to watch holovids by conspiracy cranks?" The Brand asked.

"My foot. Your behind."

"We are building a thing. Here. On our terms," The Brand said. "I like what's being carved out here."

"I do, too," we said. "But if the foundation of that life is rotted through, how long can that life last?"

Silence settled between us, a pause pregnant with determining how we were going to work together. The residents of Lil M scurried about, packing up their minimum necessities, hoping to find the rest of what they would need at Muungano. The night sky obscured most of the stars, but the moon leered above us in tantalizing reminder. A self-contained dream waiting for them. The Belts orbited it, a series of interlocked kraals housing millions. Members could shuttle back and forth to the Muungano lunar surface with ease.

Studying the perimeter, The Energy barked a few orders, hurrying people along. A tattoo—portraits of two people—peeked from along the back of his biceps. Butler on his left arm; Basquiat on the right. Author and artist. As The Brand walked by, we saw that his tattoo was a word or phrase, but without an ocular unit we couldn't have it translated by Maya.

"What does your tattoo read?" we asked.

"'Sun'qhela' is a phrase with many shades of meaning. It says 'Don't undermine me,' 'Don't underestimate me,' and 'Just try me.' It's a command and a threat, all at once." His eyes weary and resigned, The Brand turned to us. "What's your plan?"

"Head to the International District. We can cut through the neighborhood streets, end up right in its heart."

"Where they are rebuilding your embassy." The derision in his voice confirmed the common sentiment of how those who were left behind felt toward Muungano. "You can't get there from here. VOP Harrison is having some major event and folks are protesting. Them Camelia boys done took over the streets to provide 'security.'"

"They are little better than Deep State Dogs," The Energy cosigned.

"Only because they openly declare themselves enforcers of the state."

"Then how do you propose we get there?" we asked.

"I'll lead us." The Brand shrugged his pack higher on his shoulder.

"You?"

"I'm a speculative hunter," The Brand said.

The phrase drew Jaha's full attention. Turning, she placed her hands on our chest as if willing our heart to calm. "I've only ever encountered one other. They're considered . . . next-level trackers, trained to use their emi as a different way of seeing. Rumor has it they can even project their self out of time."

"We call it mind throwing," The Brand said.

"It's a rare skill."

"Pockets of the Egbe Society remain in Indianapolis." The Brand closed his eyes. His emi shifted. He took point, leading the caravan of people from the enclave they knew as Breton Court. "Go down toward the river. We'll follow the creek beds."

As O.E.'s capital city, Indianapolis billed itself as "the crossroads of the universe." A fitting place for the council of world governments, seated at LISC headquarters. Towering spires, a forest of buildings, the city focused its resources closest to its heart, the Mile Square. Its layout mirrored the exact plat of the former Washington, D.C., before it—and much of the east coast—was erased due to climate reshaping. The streets were broad, concessions made in tepid attempts at mass transportation; enough effort and resources for the government to claim that it legitimately tried. The White River cut like a laser swath through the concrete boroughs, nearly cleaving the city. Several bridges connected to downtown. The rest of the city was a sprawl of sectors and intermittent green spaces.

Dodging thick puddles left from the day's storm, we retreated deeper into the woods. The Brand followed a path guided by signs only he was privy to, the landscape tagged with metadata sigils detected by his eye codicil. The fading moonlight was all Jaha needed. She whispered of the signs folks once left, be they stars carved into the bark of black oaks or branches assembled like arrows pointing to hidden paths.

The International District encompassed the west side, an area of town almost completely "returned" as green space. The outermost areas of the city were declared nature reserves in a desperate bid to beat back the climate-collapse effects. A rolling mix of trees and overgrown malls, with corridors of houses and the Embassy Row adorned in porcelain, mosaics, and bright colors. The city employed artists to reclaim spaces, decorating them for tourists before developers could rebuild the area as they saw fit. At its center was the LISC-funded amphitheater, the perfect spot for VOP Clay Harrison to make the latest of his pronouncements. Tonight, he would be announcing the LISC Global Reshaping Summit.

"Uncle VOP is throwing a party." The Energy crouched low, surveying the scene. "They got every major corporate logo up there behind them."

"All revolutions need sponsorship," The Brand said.

"Freedom ain't free." Jaha nodded toward the edge of the green space. "Who are they?"

"They're ours. Part of the Lil M movement. This generation is pissed, tired of the VOP's empty promises."

A group of over a hundred youths marched down the street to post up on VOP Harrison's lawn. They began to go through a series of yoga postures. A disruptive, but peaceful, protest. They, too, wore masks, since they provided the additional benefit of thwarting the surveillance drones working steadily to identify them. Many shirts bore the image of Xola. The Breton Court caravan swelled their ranks. Signs among the crowd read WE DON'T TRUST LISC, THE TRUTH IS OUT THERE, and COMMUNITY FIRSTERS. The protest organizers were smart: crafting a simple narrative for the linkage channels to latch on to in the hope of their coverage amplifying their voice. Unconventional was good; drama led all other stories.

From our vantage point we watched a contingent of police approach. A parade of figures obscured by body armor and weapons. Unintimidated by their approach, the protestors held their ground. Violence was not the vibe they brought. Confident that would shield them from military overreaction, they were naive enough to not realize their presence alone was all the excuse LISC required. To a student of history, this had only one conclusion.

"This is going to end poorly." Jaha shifted in impotence.

"That's why we were brought in," The Brand said.

"You thought two Deacons would be enough?"

"It usually is. Overkill even. But . . ." The Brand studied the crowd. "No one could predict the scale of this scenario. Nor anticipated VOP calling a press conference. Or how many youth would show. Or the ARM presence. Or . . . you, the caravan."

"That's a lot left unanticipated. We're going to need a distraction," Jaha said. "Something to break the tension. Buy us some time."

"I know a guy," The Energy said.

A mix of boos and cheers greeted Theodora Harrison, the VOP's wife, strutting across the stage with an elegance and posture of authority. A statuesque mzungu woman with a regal bearing, she walked as if she expected to wield power as much as it expected to be wielded by her. "It's my honor, my privilege, to introduce a man who is a godly leader . . ."

"Only if she means he tries to put the fear of God into his people," The Brand said.

We weren't amused. Theodora had the delivery of a vice president introducing their running mate rather than someone introducing their husband. ". . . with that, I give you a man who never tires of fighting on behalf of his people. The hardest-working man in politics. My partner, VOP Harrison."

The former reverend bounded onto the stage in a red suit jacket with black lapels over the raised collar of an iridescent black shirt. Theodora wrapped a burgundy cape around him. The crowd laughed, his antics begrudgingly blunting the edge of their jeers. His security detail formed a human shield behind him. He, too, knew how to stage an image that would play well on vidscreens. All eyes had to be on him.

"People have the right to protest," VOP Harrison began, conciliatory, though saddened. A quaver edged his bravado as he performed the calculus of the swelling mob. For the VOP, the stage was his pulpit of fear. He had to disseminate, prey on their fear. The city divided among itself was what he needed. One united, all leagued against him, was the nightmare scenario. The satrap of

LISC, the dominant caste, he sat comfortably at their feet eagerly awaiting their pat on his head to let him know he'd been good and faithful. "They have the right to express their anger and frustration, but the families of Indianapolis—these United States, the communities of this world—have the right to feel safe in their own homes. Their businesses safe and undisturbed. Violence and the destruction of property will not be tolerated.

"A citywide curfew will go into effect starting tonight from nine P.M. to six A.M. in order to curtail the thugs who want to incite violence and destroy our way of life." Studying the livestream in his prompter, VOP Harrison carefully framed himself in the background of the video shots. The VOP played to his support base, instilling the image of looters riddling the streets; and to the powers behind him, barons who might have to desert the royal capital to secure their manses against marauding citizens.

VOP Harrison edged toward the platform, ready to leave. The catcalls made him pause. Soon laughter and cheers erupted. Wearing a digital mask, The Energy ran out under the stage in a black coat with tails. He mimed straightening a bow tie and tipping an imaginary top hat. The Energy started to tap-dance. Evoking the ghost of Bert Williams, his digital mask mimicked a countenance of blackface. Security flanked the VOP, prepared for an attack as the young man stared him down. The Energy robbed the VOP of the limelight. Link media surged to capture and broadcast the images, every moment of this uploaded to linkage. Everything seemed off, the stage reduced to a maze of corrupted shadows. The air charged, a storm about to break. Everyone froze, waiting to see what would happen next.

Determined to recover the moment, VOP Harrison shuffled about as if this were an expected part of the show. His face an offset façade slipping about the edges, on the verge of breaking. A man whose spirit leached from him, threatening to leave nothing behind except the mask.

The Energy pressed his hands together in a prayerful gesture toward the VOP and slowed his prance to make it look like they were synchronizing into the cakewalk. With a subtle gesture, VOP summoned two ARM members to arrest The Energy. They moved toward him, soubrettes at the end of a vaudevillian show. The Energy bounded from the stage. Removing his mask, his face still flushed from the performance, he ducked into the waiting crowd.

We didn't notice the furtive figure moving into position, only sensed The Brand's sudden alertness. Scanning the crowd like he'd caught the scent of spoiled food, he darted toward the figure. A lone mzungu man wearing mostly black. Once we noted him, we noticed how his bearing stood out, his body language all wrong. Secretive. Mischievous. Tattoos sleeved his arms. A red kerchief covered his face. The security squad prepared to hustle VOP Harrison offstage, but he turned, waiting for the cameras to find him.

"Our streets will be kept safe. I will see to that. On that, you have my word."

Smoke billowed from several buildings just after another masked figure ran from their direction. Fire engulfed a store. Several people, all masked by red kerchiefs, scampered into several storefronts, smashing windows and looting them. The ease with which they smashed the windows drew our suspicion. To even crack security panes required special equipment. Preparation. Coordination. Definitely not the spontaneous, haphazard overflow of anger and frustration. The Brand moved to intercept the first man but was too far away. The man hurled a rock at the line of police soldiers. The stone bounced harmlessly off their armor, but such an action demanded a disproportionate response.

"Get our people out of here," The Brand yelled. "It's about to get leveled."

The Knights of the White Camelia deployed into a line formation. They launched a series of canisters. Gas swirled about to little effect. Most of the protestors wore rebreather units, older models covering most of their faces. The knights fell back, preparing for the second wave of attack. We rushed toward the Lil M community. Jaha herded the dreamers, standing between them and the shifting forces of the knights. We guided them toward the Muungano embassy. The crowd snaked slowly across the cordoned-off road.

An armored Rescue Vehicle™, a three-segmented caterpillar, scrabbled along one of the side streets, bursting through the blockade, and careened toward the crowd. From each of its three segments, turrets popped up. Secured once again in his full armor, The Energy rumbled into the street, waving his talon for all to see. The vehicle slowed, having second thoughts. The Energy took aim at its tread. The vehicle veered, skidding off the road. The Energy launched a volley of mini rockets at it. The driver ground the vehicle's servos into reverse, peeling off the way it came. The Energy patrolled the street, waving any other stray vehicles away from the scene.

Security drones swarmed the sky. They rained marble charges into the crowd. The taser pellets shocked and immobilized targets like electrified shackles. Behind a security screen, the VOP nodded in approval, his face projected onto several monitors. Several hundred ARM militia members stormed the streets. They sealed off the area, careful to avoid any properties that could claim diplomatic immunity, carefully orchestrating a bottleneck surrounding the Muungano embassy. The sea of confusion allowed them to arrest anyone they identified as a leader.

The Muungano embassy had a series of escape tunnels leading out to different areas around the block. Jaha's security clearance granted her entry. She and The Energy held the entrance open while the fleeing dreamers ran inside. The Brand concentrated his talon fire to take out any drones veering too close to their position. Lagging behind the crowd to usher any last stragglers, we shielded a group of Lil M dreamers caught between the approaching ARM members and the rain of drones. Flames danced through the treetops, illuminating the scene below in an amber halo.

Waves of ARM troops collapsed upon the Lil M refugees from all sides. The Brand forced his way toward them. The militia's blaster fire targeted him. The first shot punched through his armor, nailing him in the side. The way his armor splintered with the impact we knew those were military-grade ordnance. Blood seeped down his armor. His wound slowing him, The Brand weaved back and forth, firing at ARM soldiers. He pinned them down, buying Lil M time to escape into the embassy. A second blast caught him in his arm. He dropped his talon. He drew pehla sticks and charged the nearest militia members. The next charge struck his thigh, causing him to stumble, but he refused to fall to his knees. The refractory coat on his armor cracked, leaving a frieze of fractures along his leg. Grabbing a rifle from a fallen knight, he kept firing. The Brand needed to make sure his people were safe. A final blast caught him center mass. The Brand tumbled back.

Rushing to his side, we cradled him before he could fall. "Hold still, we got you."

Without the assist of his servos, supporting The Brand was like cradling a small car. We began to drag him back, but he brushed our hands away. "No, help steady me. I got one last trick in me. I just need a boost."

The rear of the amphitheater had an earthen wall behind it, so that by design it looked like it arose from the ground itself. A series of overhanging ledges connected it. The two of us clambered up the side ridge, The Brand clutching onto us, desperate to climb out onto an overhang. The pooling ARM militia massed underneath us. The Brand struggled, barely on his feet. Clutching two charges, he locked eyes with us and nodded. Before we realized his next move, he leapt from the ledge. Falling backward, he opened his mask, revealing his final grin. Just as he landed amid the ARM soldiers, he detonated his charges.

Shock waves from the blast bowled us from our feet.

The ledge crumbled, cutting off our escape path to the Muungano embassy. The rest of the building rocked, under siege from all sides. Streaming from every entrance as if they'd waited for us, ARM troops surrounded us. As they fastened cuffs on us, their voices collapsed in a rude chorus of voices. "Kill the bastard." "No, take him alive, damn you. Take him alive." "You are under arrest."

03

STACIA CHIKEKE
The *Cypher*—Beyond the Orun Gate

"Everyone to your stations. Now!" Captain Stacia Chikeke's vision blurred, her head ached, but she had no time to allow either condition to slow her down. She had the vague awareness of pain—every part of her ached, injuries she didn't have time to attend to. She had to focus and push through. The command deck largely plunged into shadows, the *Cypher*'s emergency lights flickered, panels of red silently pulsed in the dark. Sparks sprayed from overhead exposed conduits. Alarms blared, terrible screeching night sounds alerting that a predator stalked nearby. "This is the *Cypher* hailing any Muungano ship in this sector."

Stern but not frantic, more numb than anything else, she refused to accept that all she could do now was watch everything she'd sacrificed so much for just burn. She wasn't about to give in to the nebulous fear creeping about the edges of her consciousness. Her fingers were cold. The crew had dived into the artificial wormhole known as the Orun Gate. They had no clue the cost it would incur. Drifting among an asteroid field, the *Cypher* was little more than a lifeless rock. Auxiliary power had kicked in, but reserves ran dangerously low. Asteroids floated by. The proximity sensors blared and the engines fired enough to adjust the ship's rotation to avoid a collision.

"No signals. We're alone out here." Paki "Listener" Harges had assumed the seat nearest her in the same position since they entered the debris field as her second. She'd coveted him for her crew from the moment he left the Thmei Academy. Though heading up their Learning Tree for the youth of their ship was not at a command post. On the edge of his seat, he issued orders like he'd been born for it. His thick beard a series of unmanaged twists, framing his very grave face, keen eyes constantly assessed. Sweat beaded along his forehead as if he were a jazz musician ready to improvise if given the space. A gash split his shirt. Blood dried along its edges.

"Damage report!" Stacia snapped, more accusation than request.

"Reports coming in from all stations. Injuries on multiple decks."

<Shields down to sixty percent.> Maya was a quantum artificial intelligence, capable of calculations in multiple dimensions at the same time. An independent consciousness, entangled at the quantum level. They had been offline, glitching just prior to the *Cypher* entering the Orun Gate wormhole, but now they responded as if nothing was wrong.

"Maya?" Stacia angled her head to the ceiling out of reflex when talking to the AI.

"We're losing power," Paki said.

"Wait, we have a signal. An incoming ship. No, two. Navcom puts them on an intercept course." Kenya York, head of community security, reported from the tactical station. A series of readouts and data streams hovered around her, each a different color pleading for her attention. Her two long braids, the tips dyed purple, whipped back and forth as she monitored and adjusted the ship's course. Scorch marks streaked the side of her chrome-colored security armor. "Closing fast."

"Approaching ships, this is the Muungano research vessel *Cypher*. We are on a peaceful mission. Please identify yourself." Pounding her armrests with her fists, Stacia ended her broadcast. She hated being boxed into a position so desperate she had no room to think outside of considering strangers enemies. "Can we get more power to shields?"

<Rerouting now.> Maya activated the commlink to engineering for her. They always anticipated the crew. Unnerving, but efficient. The crew had grown unconsciously dependent on them, so the AI's protracted period of glitches and being offline nearly hobbled the *Cypher*.

"The strain on the containment unit is immense. We're struggling to maintain life support." From the echo in Nadina Campbell's commlink signal, she was still deep in engineering. And had her hands full, probably within the central containment chamber that powered the ship.

"Initiate a command performance," Paki said.

"But who will lead it?" Nadina asked.

"You." Stacia's voice didn't invite argument. Only the best musicians on the ship were selected for command performances, and the hesitation in Nadina's voice spoke volumes. She'd have to get over herself.

The holovid showed the vessels nearing. Their hulls prevented any scans, leaving only vague representations not quite resolving into ships. Since the sensors couldn't provide her any specific telemetry, Stacia could only trust her eyes and instincts. Emi was for mythicists. The dark shapes swung about in a pincer maneuver.

"Weapons status?" Stacia whirled her seat toward the security station.

"Weapons?" Kenya said. "The *Cypher* is strictly a research-class vessel. I've been wanting more military-level upgrades . . ."

"Improvise something. We need to give them a reason to back off," Stacia said.

"On it." Her hands dancing about the air, Kenya rerouted systems like a crazed pianist, shouting out relays she needed access to so Maya could clear them. "Captain, a weapons system has locked on to us."

"Paki, take over navigation. Get us out of here."

Paki brought up the command array at his station. "I'll try, Captain, but engines are impulse only. We've sustained a lot of damage."

"Evasive action. Head deeper into the asteroid belt." Stacia leapt to her feet and shouted.

"Captain?"

"If we only have impulse, let's level the playing field. They won't be able to maneuver any better than us in there." Stacia brought up the image of the asteroid cluster and overlaid the positions of the ships. The debris field and asteroid belt wreaked havoc on the *Cypher*'s sensors. She hoped the same would be true for their unwanted guests'.

Paki rode the sensors, the ship little better than a horse bucking half out of control. Hunched over his station, he maneuvered the ship through the cluster of iron-and-nickel-rich asteroids. A proximity alarm chimed. Not too long after a course correction, it blared again. The *Cypher* grazed a large rock; the impact sent a shudder through the ship.

"Captain, I think I have something," Kenya said.

"Make it fast." Stacia monitored the images of ships and stones.

"I've rigged one of the communications arrays to funnel energy for charged blasts."

"I thought the *Cypher*'s array wasn't built to handle that sort of energy output."

"It could fry our whole system." Paki held on to the handgrip beside his console.

"It'd be good for a shot or two. Enough to give them something to think about," Kenya said.

"Or maybe start talking to us," Stacia said.

"Coming about," Paki yelled.

The *Cypher* canted between asteroids, rolling to avoid the larger ones, even as smaller ones bounced against its shield. The two alien ships came into view. Large barreling tubelike warcraft, little more than armored laser rifles strapped with engines.

"The lead ship has launched a warhead," Kenya said.

"Get an asteroid between us and that warhead. Now!" Stacia screamed.

The *Cypher* appeared to do little more than drift compared to the speed of the missile, barely slipping behind a stellar rock before the weapon exploded. The deck bucked beneath their feet.

"Steady . . . ," Stacia whispered as if forcing her will onto the ship. "Dina, are you in place?"

"Yes, Captain."

"Engage auxiliary power."

Strains of music echoed along the communication channel. Kheprw crystals powered the ship, developing into aligned lattices with the converted sonic energy harnessing the fusion reactions. Music renewed the crystals, healing them into even more perfectly aligned lattices. The ship's systems thrummed.

"Now." Stacia eased back into her seat and bridged her fingers. Her eyes narrowed. "Let's really give them something to think about."

Kenya and Paki exchanged furtive glances. Stacia delivered an approving salute.

Kenya worked the controls, tracking the lead ship and firing the energy pulse. The blast hit the lead ship's shields. The feedback loop of the energy discharge erupted through her console, sending her flying into the wall. Life support pumped as much fresh air as it could from the Green Zone of the ship, but the damage overran Maya's venting efforts. The stale air smelled of fried conduits and melted bioplastic.

"Kenya!" Stacia shouted.

"I'm fine, Captain." The security officer staggered to her feet. "I can't tell how much damage they took. Or us. Sensor telemetry is . . . down."

"The other ship is coming about," Paki said.

"They're trapping us," Kenya yelled. "Weapons will take another thirty seconds to recharge."

"We don't have thirty seconds," Stacia said.

<Shields down to one percent.>

"We can't afford even a near miss," Stacia yelled. "Try hailing them again."

"No response," Paki said.

"Their weapons array is charging," Kenya said.

"Enemy ship has locked on," Paki said.

"Evasive maneuvers," Stacia said.

"Impulse is out," Paki said.

<Shield collapse eminent.>

"The ship's firing," Kenya said.

The *Cypher*'s shields shimmered, signaling their imminent collapse. The weapons spread blanketed their ship. The charges lit up the viewscreen. Plunging the ship into complete darkness. The *Cypher* went completely silent. And dark, a shadow against the deeper void of space. Drifting, inert and lifeless, succumbing to the entropy of the universe. Seconds stretched into something interminable.

"Are we dead?" Kenya asked. "Are we in heaven?"

"You got jokes now? End simulation. Maya, lights." The interior lights rose to standard illumination. Stacia scrambled to her feet. Maya configured the usual user-compatible interface of the virtual image womb to engulf the entire command deck. "What did we learn?"

"What is a drill at this point supposed to tell us?" Paki sniffed.

"The level of our readiness. And we aren't even close."

"For what?"

"For anything." Stacia faced her crew.

"The captain ain't playing, y'all," Kenya said.

"We'll need real weapons," Paki said. "Hostiles could be around any corner."

"As could friendlies," Stacia chided. "We are in uncharted territory. We have to prepare ourselves. We are a research ship. We need to be ready to study and follow our curiosity. But Paki's concern is legitimate. Let's come up with better contingencies to defend ourselves."

"My weapon-array idea wasn't too bad for a theoretical construct. But we need more powerful weapons to better defend ourselves." Kenya stationed herself by the wall. "In case we encounter folks who may not be as . . . people-centered in their negotiations."

"I'll leave those upgrades to you. Paki will make sure you have what you need."

"Aye, Captain." Kenya faced the sea of blank stares aimed at her. "What? I've always wanted to say that."

"What's our actual status? How bad is it?" Stacia favored her left leg as she limped toward the center of the command deck. A steady coil of pain writhed in her thigh and ran down the length of her leg. As it had many among her crew, the trip through the Orun Gate left her battered. But the crew of the *Cypher* was still here. Whole. Alive.

"We've lost navigational stability. We really are running on auxiliary power." Paki's tone shifted to something uncharacteristically comforting, which filled her with an even greater sense of dread. "Things are . . . not entirely awful."

Stacia rubbed her temples. "That bad, huh? Sitrep, Maya?"

<Autonav systems offline. Structural integrity at thirty-seven percent. Life support minimal. Energy conduits compromised. Systemwide failures on decks . . . >

"I get it." Stacia waved at the air to cut off the litany. "Prioritize and begin to effect repairs."

"Those are the emergency repairs." Paki paced about, studying the scrolling data streams. "Tactical systems compromised. Long-range communication arrays are down. Sensors are . . ."

". . . fried," Kenya said. "They can't even lock on to where we are."

"So, we're blind and mute. But . . . we're alive. And relatively whole," Stacia said.

"The *Cypher* went through the Orun Gate without the guidance technology the O.E. provided the HOVA during their joint ventures before our . . . split. We knew the results would prove unpredictable."

At the memory of the light vortex of their passage through the gate, Stacia's headache intensified. "And the warhead Maulana had fired on us?"

"We don't know what effect that had on the gate," Paki said.

"Yes we do. Check the scans. There's no sign of it," Kenya said.

"There's no sign of anything. Our limited stellar cartography doesn't match any of the data from any of that collected from previous excursions through the gate. We could be light-years away from our expected destination."

"So we're lost on top of everything else," Stacia said.

"We're fucked," Kenya said.

"I didn't want to lose you with too much of a technical assessment." Paki smirked to soften his delivery. Again, if his resting scowl had been displaced, attempting something hopeful, it meant their situation must be truly dire.

"We need a dedicated helm specialist," Kenya said. "So that I can concentrate on security matters. That's our top priority."

"Greater vigilance might have prevented many of the events which led to our current circumstances," Paki said.

"You have something to say?" Kenya's tone declared that she wasn't in a mood to be trifled with.

"Only that I agree. We don't want your attention divided."

"Enough, you two." Stacia strode to the center of the command deck. "Maya, establish coordinates relative to the Galactic Core."

<That will take some time.>

"What about your famous quantum computing?"

<The astronomic data is complex.>

"Damn, we lost, lost," Kenya said.

"Dina, how long until we effect repairs?" Stacia asked.

"I'd prefer to be addressed as Nadina, Captain." The words were spoken without heat. Or warmth. A relational reset declared in front of all who heard. "We can use all the time you can spare."

"Apparently you're in luck. We have nothing but time." Stacia grew somber. Casting out the mutinying members of her crew—including Nadina's partner, Hondo—cost her their relationship, but the captain stood by the choices she made. Her heart may have wanted to nurse the wound of their betrayal and absence, but she couldn't afford to address the relational fracture. The crew was poised on the precipice of a massive undertaking. Although she had a formidable team around her, the weight of the responsibility of leadership proved heavier in this moment. The last few weeks. "Plot a parabolic course away from this asteroid field, but don't engage. Let's park here to continue our repairs."

"Captain, may I talk to you in private?" Paki asked.

Paki sidled up to her. Kenya approached from her other side, without a gilded animal mask like other security officers, but fitting her breastplate into place over her bodysuit. With all of her genestream engineering to become a gbeto, Kenya had half a meter and several kilograms on Paki. She received commendations for her role in Operation Obatala, before transferring to the *Cypher*. Kenya watched him close, gave a stiff, proper head bob of acknowledgment. She brandished a shield though she kept her charged pehla stick holstered at her waist. Her primary security duty was to the captain, not a command deck station. Opening the exit from the command deck, Stacia hid her limp as best she could, leading the way to her captain's quarters. In the hallway, a crew member welded sheaths of bioplastic to reinforce the bulkhead above them, showering them with sparks. Steam plumes blasted from ruptured conduits. Med carts rushed by, ferrying injured to the imaging chambers of the med bays. She headed to the antechamber. The command deck no longer felt like home.

Kenya positioned herself at the door as Paki and the captain entered the captain's quarters.

"You should have that examined." Paki gestured to Stacia's leg.

"Priorities."

"Your health is a priority."

Stacia gestured toward the empty seat as she moved around her desk to assume her usual chair.

"We have a ship to repair. And plenty of folks in more serious shape than me. My life is no more important than theirs."

"No one said it was." Paki settled in across from her. Even in a culture where teachers were the most esteemed members, Paki was one of the best natural teachers she'd ever encountered. And a valuable member of the community . . . when he wasn't being an utter ass. Under his tenure, the Thmei Academy blossomed. However, he needed a new path after he fell out with both his wife and husband. He had a history of getting ghost in the name of serving community or when he became stressed. Despite his prickly personality and often cantankerous approach to relationships, he always found his footing when teaching. "But your health is still important. We look out for each other."

She just wasn't in the mood to be the object of one of his lessons. "What's actually on your mind, Paki?"

Paki cleared his throat, again, uncharacteristically circumspect in arriving at his point. "The ship's morale. This exercise didn't help."

"The crew has to be ready. Threats won't wait until we're field tested and prepared before coming at us." Stacia leaned back.

"True. But this felt very much like punching an opponent who was already down."

"You live to critique."

"We learn by critique and I live to learn."

Stacia's face curdled, unamused as she was by his clever turn of phrase. "The Orun Gate is gone. We have no way home unless we can find a way to duplicate its operation."

"Carving channels through the space-time fabric of the universe sounds like a poor way to travel. There have to be repercussions. Especially with no guidance or stabilizing tech."

"What did the O.E. tech do that we didn't?" Stacia asked.

"They had an augmentation to their navigational system."

"Yes, I know, but what kind?"

"*Proprietary,* O.E. military claimed," Paki said. "They installed and maintained the systems. Code Black / Eyes Only."

"Now that's a song I know." Yahya entered without fanfare. To arrive unannounced, one had to hold a high enough security clearance. Or simply be Stacia's husband.

"Not now, Yahya." Stacia cradled her face in her hand to massage her temples.

His gray-dappled goatee framing a mouth already fixed in disapproval, Yahya fashioned a couch along the wall farthest from her. Even sprawled along it, his imposing size couldn't be disguised. For years she found security in his overprotective embrace. In his huge arms, nothing could get to her. Now no place seemed less inviting than his presence.

"We can continue the debrief later, Captain." Paki pushed away from her desk. "You seem to have other pressing matters to attend to."

"Consider my all-too-delicate sensibilities offended." Yahya shifted toward them.

"Enough, Yahya." Stacia ran her hand along her hairline, brushing her locs out of her face. Bored, she didn't meet his eyes.

"Captain, it's all right." Paki stepped aside as if not wanting to be in the splash zone of some overly emotional display. But there were few things he enjoyed more than an uncomfortable moment.

"No, it's not 'all right.' Wherever that attitude is allowed to stand, it's easy to transfer it to the next person. Know in advance that I ain't the one." With her background in organizing work, Stacia understood that one didn't need to agree with—or even like—one's partners so long as everyone bought into the overarching mission. Staring into Yahya's eyes, she wasn't sure what mission her husband was on.

"While I hope my offense was noted, Captain"—emphasizing the last word to stamp his point, Yahya turned somewhat sheepishly to Paki—"I do apologize. Funny thing is, when I came in, it was to make sure you were okay, but when I heard 'Code Black / Eyes Only' . . . let's just say that it was easy to fall into familiar ruts of resentment."

Love in an honorable relationship was a delicate thing to maintain. Theirs was a marriage of process, of refining the truths they could tell and be to each other. The full implications of what that level of interpersonal commitment meant and required terrified each of them with every new layer of understanding.

"I don't know if you knew this about me, Yahya, but I came out of a family steeped in community." Paki traversed the space between them. "We had our roots in the South and our home was always open for business. There was always someone coming to stay with us. Family. Friends. It was all very communal. Very . . . Muungano-ish. It has proved difficult to maintain such family ties along my journey. My work with the Thmei Academy began during the height of the Lunar Ukombozi War and the tensions of the Bronzeville Rebellion. I was . . . very involved with things. Not at the reactionary level, but through a more nationalist cultural lens. So when I arrived in Muungano, it was the closest flavor to what I was looking for. But the Uponyaji was not an easy time for me."

"For any of us. Dealing with demons and generational traumas never is," Stacia added gently, curious to see where this revelation of his was heading.

"Until then, if it wasn't analytical, rational, and measurable—if it didn't make sense—I wasn't going to fool with it. The ways of the Uponyaji bordered on the spiritual, a near-mythicist approach to communal healing. My suspicion, in retrospect, was rooted in a reaction to my father's . . . shamanistic tendencies."

Within Muungano, all expressions of mental states were viewed as gifts; people called them shamanistic rather than fall into the O.E. need of a "diagnosis" as a label. Those days they needed all the different eyes they could get to see all the potential problems looming. Stacia knew Paki's records and also knew his deep-seated fear that he might, too, one day display such mental breaks or challenges.

"Then I read a book that challenged me to explore the intangible more. About how the true Alkebulan mind-set involved more than the material. It was a turning point for me. Our journeys might appear to be rational, but they are also more esoteric than we may be comfortable believing. What some might consider spiritual. Everything comes out of spirit, using the material world to manifest those ideas. I got there from where I was, not where I was trying to get to."

Stacia couldn't tell if she entirely understood his point, though part of her thought it was on the edge of understanding the deeper truth he pointed to; he could also simply be spouting deep-sounding bullshit to confuse the moment. Either way, she nodded sagely.

"We still have a morale problem." Paki paused by the door. "Perhaps it, too, might be rooted in the esoteric. A spiritual malaise."

"We've plunged through a wormhole into complete uncertainty. We don't know where we are or when we'll get home. Our ship is damaged. Danger lurks around every asteroid. So . . . folks are down. I get it." The Muungano way was to provide a space for people to have voice, inform them, and give them the moment to question. But ultimately, Stacia had to trust the work to the workers. "What would you do?"

"Me?" Paki arched a skeptical eyebrow, probably suspecting a trap of some sort.

"Yes, if you were captain."

"I'd address the crew." Paki shifted from foot to foot as if testing the ground. "Remind them of who we are as Muungano citizens. That no matter where we are, we're home because we have each other. And that we have a mandate to follow our curiosity. We're in a new place and rather than hide in fear and panic at the unknown, we should take the opportunity to learn all we can about it."

"Sounds pitch-perfect. Go address them. Let's create the new mandate to explore this new territory like the sebau we are." The *Cypher*'s mission for Muungano actually was to study the gate. She upticked her chin, her lips pursed in something short of a smile.

Dismissed, Paki half bowed, unable to help but throw a smoldering glare at Yahya.

Each member of her crew was tasked with the greater philosophy of Muungano. Sometimes the nature of the work created a conflict between mission and family. Her marriage with Yahya teetered on being a casualty of that conflict.

"I really did intend to check to see how you were doing." He folded his hands in front of him, almost in prayer, before dropping them to his side.

"I'm fine, Yahya. I really am. I just . . . need to think. I have to figure out next steps."

"Alone?"

"That's best. For now," Stacia added hastily. She studied the view port and the many stars, the many possibilities, framed by it.

"Thank you for holding space for me." As if he'd run out of excuses to be in her presence, Yahya excused himself. He hesitated at the door before letting it close behind him.

Stacia didn't turn for fear that he had paused to see if she would. And that wasn't the promise she wanted to even hint at.

<Is it wise to antagonize him?> Maya was another situation Stacia didn't have the bandwidth to deal with. The quantum computer was another example of someone in her life whom she allowed close into her orbit, whom she came to depend on, and who abruptly abandoned her. Only to prance back into her space as if no time had passed or anything was wrong.

Stacia circled her desk, stalking some unseen prey. "I am an assault on the pride of self-antagonizers."

<Paki or Yahya?>

"Does it even matter anymore? They each have a job to do." Stacia realized how little she understood the entity she considered possibly her best friend. Each crew member interacted with a version of Maya shaped by their relationship history with the AI. How Maya was the single governing AI of Muungano, yet the Maya of the *Cypher* was separate, well, rather distinct, from the Maya of Titan. Or the Citadel. Or the Dreaming City. There was so much about the implication of all of that which often hurt Stacia's brain to think about. "Maya, can I ask you something?"

<You know you can.>

"I didn't want to do this in front of the whole crew."

<Do what?>

"I only have a rudimentary grasp of quantum theory. I know enough about entanglement to make me dangerous." At the quantum level, when two particles were entangled, if you knew the properties of one, you knew the properties of the other. Like two partners in a dance locked into their routine, the position of one revealed where the other was and what they were doing. Being a quantum computer, Maya entangled with themselves, and no one knew or could even guess what the effects of an entangled pair going through a wormhole might be. Entanglement itself, or maybe the properties of the Orun Gate itself, caused Maya to glitch as the *Cypher* moved closer to the moment of their convergence, depending on their perspective. "Two particles that are entangled always know where the other is, know what they are experiencing, no matter the distance. Is that correct?"

<That is a wholly incomplete summary of entanglement theory.>

"But accurate?"

<On a rudimentary level. Paki probably wouldn't accept that answer from one of his sebau, no.>

"But for my question it'll do. Where are we?"

<We are still calculating.>

"Where are you, Maya of the *Cypher,* in relation to you, Maya of Muungano?"

They paused. No immediate quip. No immediate response. Just . . . silence. After too many heartbeats, they finally responded.

<I have never answered that question.>

"What does that mean? Do you know where we are?"

<I have never answered that question.>

"Tell me, damn you."

<We are unable to comply.>

"Unable? Why?"

<Code Black / Eyes Only.>

"I'm the captain. No one's clearance is above mine. On whose authority was this answer locked?"

<Camara Maulana.>

"Maulana?" Stacia mused out loud, not really expecting Maya to respond. "That makes sense. He's one of the few who can lock me out of anything. But how could he lock a response before I asked the question? And why?"

<Query?> Maya's tone had a sense of a reset to it, as if the aside interaction had never occurred.

Stacia wished more of her relationship, or at least the more fraught conversation, could be so easily navigated. "Keep me updated on those calculations."

<And what will you do about Paki and Yahya?>

"I'm going for a walkabout."

✳

Stellar cartography would be working around the clock processing all of the data they were collecting. The nearest star had forty-seven planets orbiting it. With the array of astrophysical anomalies to be recorded and studied in this region of space, they might be the only members of the crew truly excited right now. Stellar cartography was also the best station to launch from.

Though it wasn't strictly protocol, Stacia donned an Extra-Vehicular Mobility unit over her nanomesh uniform. Not a HOVA-grade navsuit, but one typically used for maintenance work outside of the *Cypher.* The nanobots covered the nanomesh, their layer only a few atoms thick. Because the nanomesh had interface behavior at that short length scale, two materials that were essentially all interface, there were quantum effects. Many of which were used to integrate the suit to be more responsible at the level of consciousness. For it to operate almost as an extension of her. The air lock door hissed open and Stacia stepped free from the ship.

This view taught her how to dream again.

Her daddy once took her on a "science run," as he liked to call them. They traveled to an observatory on Titan where he would take her out. No pollution. No signal interference, almost nothing between her and the sky. She stared up and saw the stars. Truly saw them. A hundred billion stars of their Milky Way, such a tiny strip in the sky. So big. So majestic. Mind-bogglingly so. A hyper-object, something so large she couldn't comprehend it. Filled with wonder and awe beneath it; connecting her to the past, to her ancestors, in ways nothing else had before. She was no mythicist, but what she experienced in that moment could only be described in story, poem, or song. The kind of thing that stirred one's imagination or . . . spirit. It stole her breath.

The memory sealed itself with the image of her wrapping her tiny hand around her father's.

Maneuvering her EVM, Stacia marveled at the configuration of stars. Even the light here felt different. Ancient and knowing, though it never ceased to humble her. No, that wasn't the right word. The universe provided her perspective. In the infinite possibilities of night, the stars were all potentiality. And she the dream of her ancestors fulfilled. Shutting off her navsuit's thrusts, she drifted among the infinite. Things stopped seeming so complex. She was no longer excluded from the systems that governed her home planet. Her training on O.E., yet a Muungano soul, warring ideals within her, ever threatening to tear her asunder. Here, there was no twoness. No divided sense of self, with her ready to manage her dual selves into a greater, truer, whole; a vessel for so much more. Here, there was only the universe.

The sun, the moon, the planet, the stars, all the celestial movements combined to form a kind of music. Tone of energy and light whispered in a pattern of their relationship to one another. The hum of orbital revolution.

Here, she wasn't exhausted.

She rotated back to the *Cypher* and every bit of weariness returned to her soul.

The ship's battered hull was far from the gleaming shell she commanded out of the Titan space dock not so long ago. Much of its surface scraped up as if it had been thrown into a shredder. All hands worked around the clock to effect repairs. Maya-directed drones crawled along the outside of the ship, fitting newly produced sheets of bioplastic into place, as if performing a series of skin grafts. Tending to repairs, attempting what amounted to a shipwide retrofit—something unprecedented away from Titan, much less mid-mission.

They had been on this side of the Orun Gate for less than a day, but the reality of their situation settled on her. She had commanded her people into the unknown, not knowing when or if they'd see their home, Muungano proper, again. Their friends. Their family.

But Maulana had fired on them.

Stacia's headache intensified when she remembered that moment. The explosions rocked the *Cypher* as they entered the Orun Gate. The ship bucked. The wormhole opened, a miasma of swirling lights. Or what remained of light. Reality elongated and folded in eerie . . . translation. She learned at an early age that the idea of a black hole was a solution to the equations posed by the theory of relativity. Where space and time were distorted together, collapsing into a ring. A wormhole was another solution, where two points in space had a connection. She also considered the possibility that there were other possible solutions to those equations. Anything that was possible could happen.

The g-forces from the wormhole alone should have rendered them all unconscious. Words failed to describe how time and space bent around them. A tunnel of space ripped open and a spiral of radiating light shot out from everywhere. The brightness reminiscent of staring into the heart of a star. Space shifted and warped, buffeted by the energy of what she could only presume was the gate collapsing around them. *Thank the Universe for small favors.*

But now they were here, wherever here was. Stranded. Alone but together. Bobbing among the debris, Stacia scanned for the remains of the ancient machinery that supported the Orun Gate. Little remained of it, only whatever mechanical flotsam came through the aperture in the wake of the *Cypher*'s arrival.

They were here because her crew, her family, had faith in her. Because Bekele, her son, was sick. Because the pathogen was man-made and the cure promised to be on this side of the Orun Gate. Well, they had arrived, and it was time for their erstwhile travel companion, Zenith Prebius, to hold up his end of the bargain.

✳

Not being equipped with a brig or anywhere else to house dangers to the community, the *Cypher* assigned Zenith his own quarters in an improvised version of house arrest. Stacia hated dealing with him. With anything remotely connected to O.E., especially LISC, actually. Any contact with him threatened to drag her back to being a person she didn't recognize. Yet she could almost hear Xola's voice in her ear: If there is something of value you can use to benefit the community, it doesn't matter if it is up a bull's ass, you go in and get it.

An ass greeted her at his door.

A mzungu man, Zenith stood sipping a cup of tea. Fit, but not athletic. He ran a hand through his full, though thinning, hair, revealing a tattoo on the inside of his wrist. With surgeries and treatments available, even this could be a carefully constructed façade. His right eye danced with delight at her presence, already alit with mischief. A cybernetic interface covered his left eye. His white goatee frayed about the ends, the early days of him not being able to keep it as perfectly trimmed as he preferred. And he was always aware, akin to how some used their emi.

"I see you, Zenith," Stacia said. Kenya had pieced together his mala fides. Zenith was a deputy chief at the Ministry of Advanced Narrative Design, with ties to MI-7, National Security Agency, State Security Agency, and the Ministry of State Security. He earned a Ph.D. in literary criticism and linguistics from Harvard. He deployed his learned techniques to detect deep patterns and hidden meanings in records, becoming a connoisseur of files. Running deception operations so intricate, sowing so much confusion, that state policies became a wilderness of shattered mirrors led to his star rising. When he was promoted, his specialty became investigations. Assassination conspiracies, infiltration of news organizations, unauthorized linkage surveillance, nothing was off the table for him.

"Would you like some tea?" He proffered his cup.

"What kind?" Stacia could tell who was highborn, or believed they were, based on the universal human response to hierarchy.

Unconscious signals programmed into him, Zenith possessed a certitude in bearing, demeanor, and behavior, even in such simple displays of welcoming her, offering her tea. With a visible expectation of centrality, in the simple act of waiting, he reflexively attempted to loom over her, assuming a position of authority as if it were as natural as breathing. "English Breakfast, of course."

"No thanks. That tastes like aristocratic sadness." Stacia took the seat between him and the door. "Now that we're on the other side of the Orun Gate, where do we go?"

"Straight to business, eh?" Zenith attempted to fashion a seat next to her. Waving his arms about and all but shouting "Abracadabra." Stacia gestured, her funkentelechy directing the mass of nanobots to produce a hard-backed chair farther from her than he wanted. "Where are we?"

"Don't toy with me. We did what you asked: turned on Muungano, betraying their trust, forcing their hand so they had no choice but to fire on us, and plunged through the Orun Gate. All because you said the cure for Bekele's condition could be found here." She wasn't going to play his game; not on his terms, anyway. Zenith toyed with a scheme within schemes, at one point kidnapping Paki, to move him out of play but not permanently. Potentially holding him for a bargaining chip later because he also planned a contingency within contingencies. He was the hands of those in power, infecting her son with a virus that perverted Muungano's funkentelechy. All to manipulate them through the wormhole. "We're here. Where do we find this cure?"

"You misunderstand, I can't help you if I don't know precisely where 'here' is."

She stood without realizing it. The rage began in her fingertips. It traveled up her arms, swelling in her chest. The cascade reached her eyes, the point of no return. A glare Zenith recognized. He scrambled out of his seat to back away, his hands held high.

"I swear, I'm not playing games." His voice quavered with something just short of fear. There was a resigned blankness to his face, like that of a chess player out of moves. "When we went through the 'Orun Gate,' as you people call it. I don't know if it was our lack of navigation equipment or that strange blast that hit as we entered, but we're not where I expected us to be."

Stacia knew that she couldn't leverage their situation through all her rage. Though it had often served her well. Rage was a gift, brought a clarity. Whenever she dealt with O.E., she operated from the space of just being mad at wazungu people. Slapping her thighs, she settled back into her seat and released a long breath. "So we're lost. We sacrificed everything for nothing. Which means you are no longer of any use to us."

Not trusting something in Stacia's eye, Zenith retrieved his sigil from his vest pocket. "I'll just remind you that under Article 37 of the Lunar Ukombozi War Convention, I've invoked diplomatic immunity."

"That sigil saved your life. Once."

"No, I know what saved my life. This allows me a measure of comfort." Struggling to regain the conversation, Zenith risked a smile. Elite capture was also a part of the LISC playbook. Separate, balance, or neutralize strong voices. Co-opting them or driving them from the herd to leave the herd directionless or powerless. Hoping the herd would keep failing to realize that the power resided in the herd themselves. "We need to see this as an opportunity."

"How so?"

"We are in uncharted space, privy to uncharted resources." Zenith was the high priest of the O.E. way: snatch up every resource on the board. Their caste spaces weren't designed to value or support people. Their system morphed with the times, patient as water, adjusting to survive and thrive.

But so did her people.

"You just can't help yourself, stuck in the same old loop." Stacia grabbed one of the tea biscuits from his plate. "Muungano chose to move away from the toxic 'survival of the fittest' mentality that drives people to grab up all the cookies they can before they die."

"Cookies?" Zenith bit into one.

"Resources. We consume as many as we can, often when we don't even need to, we eat them just because they are there. Then, when we die, all of our left-over cookies pass down to our family. A few generations later, someone's eating cookies they had no part in baking." She tossed it, uneaten, back to his plate.

"I hate unearned cookies."

"And yet you don't mind benefiting from them, since after a couple hundred years, most of the cookies are concentrated in a handful of bakeries. It's like you can't help yourself. You can't think outside of economic redlining and cornering resources. From First World to Muungano, we decided to follow a more cooperative model and be about growing the pie so that everyone could get a slice."

"You have a very dessert-centric worldview." Zenith poured himself a second cup of tea.

"Ours was a switch in mind-set. When you think in terms of abundance, we recognize the gifts present. We understand that *we* were enough. Relationships became less risky, because security and confidence comes when you're convinced that everyone has your best interests of heart."

Zenith set his cup down to mock applaud. "Impressive speech. It lacked a certain 'I have a dream' verve, but it'll do. But you do me a disservice: I can easily set aside our differences if there's business to be done. I'm what I like to call 'northernly astute' when it comes to my brand of healing the racial divide. If you got change for a twenty, I'll even chip in on some reparations."

"You think this is funny?"

"You think you're making a difference? A principled stand?" Zenith's smile remained perched on his face, his eyes both defiant and nonplussed.

"There, you overplayed your hand. An oppressive regime is by nature terrified. Paranoid."

"I believe the words you're looking for are *careful, shrewd.*"

"The crew of the *Cypher* is not here to run your errands, do your scouting, or deliver your personal shopping list. We're here to find a cure for my son. If I get the impression that you are wasting our time, we will be down one more crew member and go about our business."

"On the upside," Zenith retrieved his cup and saucer, "That means I'm a recognized member of the crew now."

"A member of the crew confined to quarters." Stacia stood up and straightened her vest. "I've dealt with your type before. You have two problems: One, you always think you're the smartest person in the room . . ."

"And what's the other?"

Stacia stepped toward the door but glanced over her shoulder to say, "You forget that I'm in the room."

"I appreciate you, Captain," Zenith called after her as the door closed.

Yahya passed her without comment as she entered their quarters. A relationship with sound made people feel at home no matter where they were. They had weaponized silence. There was nothing worse than a long-distance relationship when said distance was the width of a bed.

Without warning, Stacia's head rushed with the sensation of plunging headlong into a dream. The pressure in her temples tightened. She struggled to get her breath. Her whole body relived the moment of slipping through the wormhole. She clutched the doorframe, desperate for the episode to pass. Yahya placed his hand on her back, stabilizing her, a life preserver drawing her back to the moment. The weight of their history also brought familiarity. Knowing. Comfort. He saw her and never flinched. He'd hardened over the years, an emotional shield to protect himself against the ravages of duty and who they were. Too bad it took moments of her weakness for him to lower his own shields.

Life had its own gravity well. Often people stayed in certain spaces, a relational inertia, the weight of history ground into the ways of their being. To cobble together a simulacrum they could call living. Real life presented challenges based on where a person was, not through the lens of them staying in that space. She feared that their marriage was reduced to the catastrophe of two broken people building a sanctuary within their trauma and calling it commitment. The way intense psychological pain rewrote genes, a baton in an epigenetic relay, parents passing down stories of their history. They wanted to break that generational curse for Bek. Once steady on her feet, she moved into the next room needing to see her son.

Bek and his best friend, Marguerite Pinero, struggled to maintain a semblance of normalcy returning to their familiar rhythm of the Learning Tree. The twists of Bek's hair slowly locked into thick cords. When he leaned over, he grimaced, favoring his left arm. He hadn't been injured; the constant pain was part of his condition. As was the discoloration that mottled his skin from his wrist to his forearm.

"What have you got?" Bek asked.

Education wasn't about absorbing a million facts. It was about putting those facts together, making connections. It was about building relationships, with students and teachers. Getting students to talk out what they were studying. They mostly had to just provide them room to explore and grow. Paki's assignment for them was to construct miniature terraforming pods. Each one layered with a partition of AI code, essentially a seed of Maya, and designed to tackle a particular problem related to an aspect of supporting life on a world.

"A bacterium that absorbs sulfur and spits out O_2." Marguerite fiddled with her Huichol beaded collar. Cords of pink and purple lights snaked through her hair, moving in preprogrammed fashion to change her hairstyle. Most times she was awkward and jumpy, but around Bek she relaxed, comfortable in her own skin.

"Nice. Good to know that I haven't missed much for our assignment," Bek said.

"Some mild mutiny and an escape through a wormhole is a pretty solid reason for turning in homework late." Marguerite pored over her code before pushing the entire module away from her. "Ugh. Why do we have to learn to read in so many different languages? Maya translates for us."

"You already know what they're going to say. 'To preserve our collective cultures.' 'Maya may not always be on' or 'What if Maya randomly goes on the fritz.'"

"Again," Marguerite interjected. If blurting her thoughts was its own language, she had it mastered.

"It's a way for us to continue to get to know and be in conversation with each other . . . blah, blah, blah."

"It's almost like every adult's been given the same speech to memorize."

"Yeah." Bek leaned over his workspace. His hand fumbled one of his lancets. As it clattered against his workbench, he muttered a series of . . . creative . . . oaths. He glanced over at his mother, who arched an eyebrow that neither approved nor disapproved.

"You all right?" Marguerite pressed against him. The way she held his hand was both concerned and overly intimate.

"I'm good." Bek drew his hand away, his voice thickened with a sudden, resentful frostiness.

Marguerite cocked her head to the side. Her brown skin highlighted the blond tangles that swayed like vines disturbed by an unseen predator. "Really?"

The word was an accusation framed as a question. Stacia was well versed in its technique.

"Sorry. It's the virus." Bek hung his head. That was when Stacia truly saw him. The fatigue lines ringing his eyes. The toll simply sitting upright took on him. The set of his jaw to hide the pain accompanying his movements. It wasn't so long ago that his body betrayed him to the point of leaving him in a coma-like stasis. A neurological condition that left him feverish and convulsing, leaching away his life in centimeters.

"You seem much better." Marguerite's voice rose, making the statement a question.

"The healers say it's like it has gone into complete remission. I've felt so much better ever since we came through the wormhole."

"You're getting around much better, yet I sense a 'but' . . ."

"But I feel like I'm working for a disease. A boss I didn't ask for. People have sacrificed so much for me. Mom. Dad. The crew." Bek spoke, aware of Stacia's proximity to them, but unbothered. As if he were on a reality show and had forgotten about the cameras. Though she suspected it was more deliberate, the same way one might leave their diary out so that its discoverer could know exactly what was going on with them. Without them having to face each other.

Stacia tensed, ready to remove some of the weight—as much as a mother could—and put it squarely on her. Her choices, her crew. Some pathogens could never be killed, only contained. A mental strain with their ever-present danger occupying space in their minds. Dealing with recurring ones was like long-buried threats bubbling to the surface. Life bent around their demands:

warning, exposure, its longevity, its ability to mutate, thrive, and even hiber-
nate until reawakened. Their lives reduced to management and anticipation
of when things would go wrong. Yahya settled his hand onto the small of her
back, silent reassurance to allow the kids room to work things out on their
terms. She slid back against the couch.

Marguerite punched Bek playfully in the arm. "Everyone was happy to do it."

"Those that stayed." Bek studied his fingers.

"They're your family."

"That's just it: I feel like I've even turned my family into indentured ser-
vants to my virus."

"What about me?" Marguerite asked.

"You don't count. I'm stuck with you."

She rocked into him, a comfortable habit. Stacia remembered when she and
Yahya were so light and free with one another. Time was inexhaustible, its
quality what they made of it. Yet it was so easy to fall into the O.E. mind-set
of living in a poverty of it. Because in her heart, she believed time was running
out for Bek.

Gravimetric waves rattled the ship.

"Stacia?" Yahya sat up.

"Captain to the command deck." Paki shouted over the commlink.

Yahya shifted as if he'd received the command himself. "It's okay. Go."

Stacia stirred from the couch, only then fully realizing that she had uncon-
sciously curled up into his embrace. "I appreciate you."

"I appreciate you."

✳

Children ran across the vibrant, almost waxy viridian grass of the Green Zone,
playing an improvised version of pyr ball. Hurling the ball through suspended
disks, they were more interested in running than actually playing by any rules,
the act of throwing the ball more an afterthought. Completely oblivious to the
reality of their situation. Going through the wormhole may have been scary,
but life returned quickly to what they knew. Cruising through space on a ship
the size of a small city. It was almost enough to take Stacia's mind off her
duties.

She entered the command deck with a determined stride. Reports from
stellar cartography streamed along the walls. The viewscreens filled the entire
space. A grand blackness occluded the monitors.

"Are the holovids offline?" Stacia asked.

"No, those are the long-range scans," Paki said. "In real time."

"What am I looking at?"

"Nothing."

"What . . ." Stacia stepped closer to the image.

"We're . . . not sure. To the best of our analysis, we're looking at some sort of . . . supervoid." Paki faced her. "And it's drawing us into it."

04

EZEJI ADISA
Muungano—The Dreaming City

Ezeji projected the pyr ball game linkcast all around his room. The image so encompassing, it was almost as if he was on the pitch. Pyr used smart balls that not only recorded who touched them and when, but also provided unique angles for the linkcast. Three to four players ran in triangle formations, so close he could reach out and touch them. Runners dashed back and forth along a switchbacking trail while the racer advanced the ball. The way the pyr ball bounced about, no one could rest. As the members ran up and down the peak, his muscles twitched with memories of being in the thick of the game. Running along the field track, not knowing how difficult the path might be or when it would end. The difficult terrain allowed slower players to often catch up. Not controlling the ever-shifting route, only adjusting to it. Passing the ball back and forth, driving home the lesson that no one got through on their own.

"The playing field levels the playing field," the announcer said.

The Indianapolis Clowns played with the wild abandon of children, the aspect he loved and missed most about the game. Sport was a festival of friendship, teams made up of different factions, uniting for a purpose. Spectators sipped skia, a home brew of fermented root, the drink of choice for the games. Ezeji preferred his almost as thick as rice pudding and flecked with poppy seeds.

His dreads extended from the back of his head upward, wound together in the shape of a cone. He was shirtless, and his light complexion highlighted the scarification along his body. His ocular display unit allowed him to analyze the stats in real time, information constantly fed directly to his frontal lobe. He didn't consider himself a jacker or sensate, but on occasion he streamed data as a way to get his head up. They played for the thrill of the game. No one argued or coached from the sidelines. No one cared who won. Admittedly, so much skia consumed led to more trash talking. He leapt out of his seat when a player threw the ball too hard, knocking the receiver out of his sandals.

"Get up, you got this," Ezeji shouted as if the child were one of his team-mates. He recalled many a nighttime game where he made a similar play.

The player scrambled up with the ball and dashed off with only one shoe. He banked the ball off a rock and it was caught by a teammate to score. The play was spectacular, and cheers erupted from both sides. The banging of the drums signaled the game's end.

A broad grin splayed across the child's face, mirrored by Ezeji; his love of the game was contagious. When Ezeji played he felt the most seen (when he allowed himself to be seen). The most valued. He knew his role, how he fit in. He under-stood his place in Muungano. Not so much these days. Maybe things changed with Xola's death. Or the broadcast of Fela's death. Or Wachiru leaving.

Or Matata betraying them.

Though the blows kept coming, that last one hurt more than he was pre-pared to admit. With the game finished, he had nothing left to distract him from the fact that his friend was going on trial today.

"Maya, did you record any of the Dojo sessions?" Ezeji came up in the un-derground battle poetry scene. The Dojo were pop-up spots using illegal jam-mers so no one could record, transmit, or link. It was just the poets spitting off the top of their domes without assist.

<Doing so was prohibited.>

"Just checking. What about the Write On slams?"

<Yes.>

"Display any sessions with me and Matata."

Ezeji swigged the last of his skia before switching to much stronger tjwala. He fashioned his chair into a couch to watch the projected highlights. Back then, Matata, with his never-quite-level high-top fade, appeared so young. They both did. Matata grew up poor on O.E. but fell into Ezeji's orbit. They came up together on the poetry scene, long before Ezeji left to pursue pyr ball. He was being scouted by O.E. teams even then and helped Matata navigate weusi-controlled spaces. He never quite seemed to wrap his mind around the profundity of Muungano's existence, always commenting on Ezeji's language. Muungano's central tongue borrowed from their various cultures to express their shared worldview. And how, with this language's use, attitudes shifted. There was a back-straight, heads-up pride with their every step. Such that when wazungu came to visit, it was they who had to adjust, not the weusi. He reveled in the way wazungu moved out of the way when Muungano members came through.

Knowing that Ezeji was an Adisa, Matata harangued him into visiting Xola. Not *Camara* Xola—who performed his duties for the sake of Muungano—but the man. Off the block. Off the clock. Ezeji stifled a chuckle, knowing no such partition existed. Camara Xola's porch was more . . . informal. The way Ezeji remembered the Muungano of his youth, the space he brought Matata to was a safe weusi space. Rough-and-tumble, it was a place of real, raw, authentic Negus. Twenty minutes in, it was all shouting because . . .

"*. . . you called my friend a slave!*" *Ezeji voiced his opinion with volume. Without heat, he jumped up.*

Wachiru matched the movement, the energy, in reflexive caution.

Xola tamped the air to settle them both back into their seats. "*Yes I did. So fucking what?*"

"*That's my point, Negus. You can't go talking to my friends any ol' fucking way.*"

"*That's fine,*" *Wachiru said.* "*You a slave, too.*"

Ezeji fashioned a new seat farther away from them. "*I'm not fighting a war on two fronts. That's a trap.*"

Xola smiled.

"*Can you move over there. You're making us nervous.*" *Wachiru positioned his seat between Xola and Matata.*

Never particularly skilled at understanding a person's emi, Matata held his hands up, not wanting any smoke while he tried to learn the room. "*I wanted to stand there, but then they looked like they wanted to get to fighting and shit. All I kept thinking was 'Man, don't you go over there.'*"

"*Sit your baby ass down.*" *Xola raised his fists like he was ready to box.*

"*You know Xola got that rope-a-dope. He ain't scared.*" *Wachiru grinned, but a hint of black steel in the hour of chaos undergirded it.*

"*My words were meant to sting. To push your buttons until you woke up.*"

"*They only stung if you bit,*" *Wachiru said.*

"*It felt like you were judging me,*" *Ezeji said.*

"*You're reacting based on what you think I'm judging you on. What you think you've done well; or not well.*" *Xola cocked his head with a mischievous grin again, as if Eshu, the trickster orisha, whispered in his ear.* "*I tell you what, I'm sorry I called him a slave.*"

"*When you say it like that it sounds like you full of shit. You didn't even pretend to mean it.*" *Ezeji hated the tincture of poutiness to his tone.*

"*He's a hater.*" *Wachiru's head bobbed, either in laughter or because a melody caused him to score the soundtrack to this conversation. So like his father in many ways, down to the broad, mischievous smile to voices, or songs, only he could hear. "That what this Negus do. Professional-grade hater. You have to know what he's on when you get here. And then learn to shake it off."*

Ezeji drummed his fingers along the chair arm, a crude beat to match the rhythm created by Wachiru's bobbling head. The imagined music gave his thoughts room to coalesce. "You got to tell that story of why we're under attack. Otherwise it comes across as 'You're weusi there, seen as a slave, so don't do shit. You don't have agency, so don't move. You have no freedom, so don't have experiences. And above all, don't fuck up.' That's the conversation we came here to have."

"Then why were you jumping out left?" Concern suffused Xola's tone, shifting him into full teacher mode, excited by a student on the verge of uncovering their own truth.

"Because he made his point to my friend, now we in the middle of a family argument."

"And, what, you feel embarrassed? You *brought your friend. I didn't bring him here."*

"And you know how we get down," Wachiru said.

"You absolutely know," Xola echoed.

"You right." Ezeji wiped his face like he was bringing down a curtain over it. "I go from zero to one hundred. I take ownership of my reaction. I have to do better."

"You ain't got no choice." Xola's lips parted, revealing rows of teeth too small in his mouth. "You ain't getting out of this space without being better."

"Back on point, Pops never said 'don't move.' He was speaking to the broader issue that we don't own." Wachiru's fingers formed a triangle pointing down, preparing to recap the lesson to see if he caught it himself. "There are parts of our history that we ain't passed down. That we haven't prepared our children for. Or each other, for that matter. That they don't understand how to move forward is some real shit."

"Thank you!" Xola snapped back in his seat.

"What are you? Xola's anger translator?" Ezeji asked.

"It was never an attack on you," Wachiru said.

"The Negus was over here cussing out my friend."

"Come on man. You ain't *never* been cussed out?"

"At nineteen maybe." Ezeji angled himself away, covering his mouth.

"Shit, at fifteen 'cause we the ones who did it." Wachiru clapped his hands; Xola threw his head back in laughter. Ezeji joined in. After a heartbeat, so did Matata, except his smile was a tight-lipped thing. Cataloging each of them—their reactions, their cadence—in committing each movement to memory to imitate later. "You *took it personal, got all in your feelings, getting pressed about the shit that we all know all too well. Recounting the hard lessons of when we walk in spaces that aren't our own. That don't spring from our imagination. They weren't created to support us or our best interests. You can't take it personal."*

"I took it personal because the Negus took the ball and threw it out of bounds. You make a whole-ass list of all of my shortcomings. Which I'm fine with. Let me know where I fall short, it's the only way for me to get better. But that wasn't what it was about." Unbothered, Xola leaned back in his chair. The young always had room to be heard, and yielded to elders only if they were right. But respect had to run both ways. *"Your response was inauthentic. You weren't being real, not with me and not with yourself, and that's why you needed to be checked."*

"Ezeji felt a certain way about his perceived failures." Wachiru turned to his father. *"You could have just told him that he's doing a great job and you're proud of him."*

"I gave him what he needed in this moment. But . . . you right. That's probably a conversation we should have." Xola's voice trailed off with a mumble where an apology could be found if one dispatched a large enough search expedition. It wasn't like anyone expected Xola to actually say he was sorry. *"We need to hear from Matata."*

"What do I say?" Matata asked.

"Ain't no question on the floor. What's your takeaway from this exchange?" Wachiru asked.

"Not to ask y'all for nothing." Matata's face stiffened, almost pained. His words treated with a tentative step as if not wanting to say the wrong thing. *"Personally, all I wanted to do was visit O.E. for a bit and catch a pyr ball game."*

"Let me paint you a scenario and let's see if we can get to the heart of your original concern. Young weusi men wander the streets and shops of O.E. How do you do that in a way that ameliorates your risk?" Xola asked. *"Use Wachiru as an example. Let's say he was out with his boys. Some of them had weapons and was out hunting for somebody. They had death on their minds so he linked me 'cause he realized he had to get out of that situation. 'Hey Pops, come get me.'"*

"Immediately," Wachiru amened.

"And did I ask him any questions?" Xola asked.

"Nope," Matata guessed.

"And now his friend is doing life at the Panopticon. For murder. You around more of your own, but it's the same shit. We are in those times. They may not call themselves sundown towns anymore, but if you know, you know. You exercise some

caution, the experience taught us by our entire existence in O.E. But also know that we aren't confined by that caution or history. It's not about living in fear. We're free. We live in boldness, but we ain't stupid. Assess your dangers. Some places are riskier than others. Some blocks I don't step on. We have the responsibility to tell our young people that. At fourteen. At fifteen. At twenty. At thirty. They may not always make the right decisions—hell, I expect them to fuck up often—but we still have to let them know, so they make informed choices to fuck up. I could give a damn about them having a good time. We arm them with understanding to prepare them to survive."

"That's the role you play." Matata's sentence rose at the end, hinting at a question.

"That's who I am. I'll run a Negus off this porch in a minute if they on some bullshit. I ain't here to play some role. You think I give a fuck about being 'Camara' of Muungano? This is what I do. This is how I play the game. That's how I got here and I ain't seen anything that tells me I got to do things different."

"Your words just hit me a certain way," Ezeji admitted. "Maybe it was the delivery."

"Aw man!" Everyone, including Matata, threw their hands up and groaned.

"Again, just to be clear, this ain't about creating fear." Xola's voice thickened with the air of imparting another lesson. "This ain't about raising cowards. Never that. The key thing as we try to raise our children in the midst of caste structures of O.E.—which not only aren't going to abate, but only get louder—is that we have to tell them the truth. It's not about what you can't do, where you can't go. It's that we have a responsibility to let them know when their life is at risk."

"There's what's said and there's what was heard." Ezeji softened, the wind escaping his sails.

"You come to this porch knowing what you're going to get. If you don't want this sauce, this way, go somewhere else. I got my flavor. You got your flavor. That's why we work as a team."

"Your flavor impacts the entire culture," Ezeji said.

"But what is the culture? The culture is the combination of all of us," Wachiru said.

"If you want to play at the pro level we got to get the high school ballers off the team." Camara Xola stared at each of them in turn. His rheumy eyes had long since failed him, but he didn't need them to search their emi, peer deep into their sabhu. He canted his head with peculiar fascination when he reached Matata. "We're at war. And we can't go to war with some soft shit. So I'm going to bring the

heat. Some motherfuckers won't be able to take it and will have to watch from the sidelines. The stakes are high. These are our lives. My main concern are opps. We talking radical shit. Food. Housing. Education. Justice. If you've done any kind of reading, know any kind of history, you know what to expect."

"Infiltrators?" Ezeji asked.

"Night Train," Wachiru seconded.

Xola sagged in his chair as if suddenly exhausted. "Police, by any other name. In order to work together, we have to get shit out in the open so we can . . ."

. . . air it out. Xola wasn't Muungano but his fingerprints were all over the community he helped build. Ezeji wrapped his locs cone in a scarf. Linked chains, bringing to mind the image of dangling shackles, served as his earrings. He lowered his cowrie-bead necklace into place. Matata's trial, linked for all Muungano to see, was meant to allow the sunlight of visibility to disinfect the community. Ezeji hoped he could still trust the process now that Xola was gone.

※

Ezeji walked the streets of the Dreaming City, low-key, a small town, with an intimacy of knowledge. The Blue Candy House was one of the original remaining structures from when Muungano was known as First World. Fresh from O.E., they used to sell alcohol on "Sundays" and pass out king-sized candy bars like it was something transgressive. He dabbed up Obi Abara, who most folks knew as "the Dancing Man," when he passed him down by the library plaza.

The brilliant colors of the upinde mvua fields led to a winding path of cemented regolith creating a walkway around at the center of the circle of rondavels. *Hedera helix* snaked the surrounding walls. Bowls bobbed along, suspended at different levels, creating a floating hanging garden. This was the heart of the Dreaming City, its library. Before he left, Wachiru submitted Ezeji's name to stand in his place as head of the Adisa family, declaring it time for him to step more into leadership. Ironic that Wachiru did so in order to step out of leadership.

No Camara stood on occasion. Most people only went to them if they had business to discuss. It wasn't that they were intimidated by them or worried about their busy schedules. It was just that as Camara, they were a master teacher as well as servant leader, and school was always in session. And Maulana's preferred method of teaching was PAW—Ezeji's soon-to-be-trademarked slang for public ass whuppings—making sure all scolding as "lessons" was as public as possible. Ensuring that many students cut his particular class whenever possible. When Ezeji arrived, he almost interrupted Maulana's meeting with Geoboe, Mansa of the Oyigiyigi mining outpost.

"... you've moved the warship facility to Titan." Geoboe's image strode about Maulana's chambers like a peacock on a runway. Even for Nguni, he was short, with an elongated quality to his frame, the product of low-gravity living. The elaborate beadwork of his vest barely covered his belly, proudly slumping over his waist sash. His large head had been freshly shaved that morning. His flat nose and small eyes cinched his face in a perpetual squint, making him appear more spiteful than usual. His large shoulders shook as he walked, his proud bearing befitting someone who saw himself as royalty. To drive home the point, a stylized metal insignia emblazoned on his left shoulder. And he carried a spear, even for this one-on-one meeting.

"It was a matter of practicality. They are much closer and were already set up to construct research ships." On one, Maulana matched his energy wearing a headdress of elaborately grooved horns around a central conical blue coiffure rising from the two faces on the mask. Even behind the veil of beads curtaining his face, one could feel his dark eyes glaring with a protective ferocity. His mind a series of calculations, assessing everyone and everything's potential threat level to Muungano. Maulana's pitch didn't change, a smooth, even baritone delivery unconcerned by Geoboe's bluster. Acknowledging Ezeji with a "one minute" finger, he waved him in.

"That leaves the Citadel . . ." Geoboe's hard light image paced back and forth like a performer owning their stage. Who served as his audience was ever the question.

"Guarded by the Ring. I don't want O.E. knowing our full defensive capabilities."

"You mean *our* capabilities." Geoboe halted midstride, half turning his head to Maulana with mild skepticism. He stamped the spear.

"Muungano's capabilities. Not just the Citadel's." Maulana clasped his hands behind his back and squeezed them to a count of ten between sentences. His diplomatic muscles underwent quite the stringent workout since becoming Camara.

"We want self-sufficiency."

"That is not the Muungano way. We strive for interdependence . . ."

"Interdependence is a chain."

"The chain is life."

"The entire Nguni culture is no more than Muungano's mining colony. You use us in no way different than any previous colonial power. We aspire to something greater. Cities that can manufacture, control our own resources. We want to be able to trade as equals."

"We're already equals. The old ways, the Yo ways, are a lingering infecting madness."

"That's what's said. We just want assurances now that Xola no longer leads Muungano."

"The Camara doesn't lead. Community leads. The Camara is merely its voice."

"Well, *I* lead and want the best interests for my people."

"*Our* people. This is what those who took out Xola wanted. Chaos. Division. Uncertainty. I will always seek the best interests of all of our people. But I can only do that with your help. You always have a voice within the Ijo, the security council, and with me." Everyone prevailed on Maulana to tone down his rhetoric. Muungano elected him because they needed his posture of anger. And defensive mind. However, they could not move by his suspicions. Ever since he accused LISC of an attempted decapitation strike with the assassination of Camara Xola, tensions with the governing body of O.E. steadily increased, taking all parties—Bronzeville on Mars, Oyigiyigi, and Titan—to the brink of war.

"We'll see. Words are easy."

"Word is bond." Maulana snapped his head toward Geoboe, the beads of his headdress rattling in warning. No one questioned his word. Geoboe averted his gaze slightly, not wanting to stare too long at the sun of his radiating rage. With the slightest acquiescing nod, his image disappeared.

Maulana was a hard brother to embrace. Some might appreciate his volatility and single-minded mania, but leadership required finding the delicate mixture of voices to form the self-organizing organism known as Muungano.

"What can I do for Muungano's latest Master Poet liaison?" Maulana drew him out of his reverie.

"Matata's trial. It weighs on me." The full Ijo had not been convened since the days after the images of Fela Buhari, Maulana's sister, were transmitted throughout all of Muungano, Mars, and the Yo. The security council had met nearly every day since. "Matata was one of my boys, you know."

"He meant a lot to a lot of people. He was a rising star from early on, one of the youngest to be considered for a post within the Niyabinghi. You know how difficult that is, the battery of tests one has to go through to reach that level of trust within Muungano? Which made his choices and actions that much more egregious." Maulana leveled his distrustful gaze toward Ezeji, taking his full measure.

Ezeji couldn't help but feel as if he were left wanting. Fashioning a seat, he plopped heavily into it and soon cradled his face in his hands. "I'm just trying to make sense of it. This feels so big."

Maulana fashioned a table between them and set two glasses on it before reaching for a decanter from a nearby hidden cabinet. He poured two fingers' worth of whiskey into each glass. After another meaningful study of Ezeji, he added a third. "Uncle Nearest. This bottle's over a hundred years old."

"Special occasion?"

"I'm in a storytelling mood." Maulana slid into his seat and sipped slowly. "In ancient Alkebulan, the hydra was a mighty lord of the water. Each of its seven heads was feared, a power in its own right. Its terrible roars reverberated throughout the land. Though it kept the rivers flowing because of its magic, people considered it a monster, often bringing offerings to appease it.

"One day a rival lord needed its help. An ambitious creature, never content with her own land and treasures. At first the lord attempted to bribe the hydra with gold. But the hydra had no need of it, for that kind of wealth was not the lens through which the hydra moved. Then she offered up her daughter. However, her water jar—her lobola offering—had been filled with mud. Pitying her plight, the hydra accepted the deal. It cleaned out her jar and even refreshed the rival lord's streams so that no one else's jars need be filled with mud. Pleased, the rival lord sent her daughter to the shore to be taken to the hydra's underwater kingdom. When the hydra arrived, the daughter begged to be allowed to return to her mother's home to bid all of her family goodbye. The hydra agreed.

"Instead, the daughter went to her secret lover's house. When she returned to the hydra, he snuck up on it, bearing his sword. With the hydra's eyes locked on the girl, her lover plunged his sword into the hydra's neck and cut off all seven of its heads. Killing it."

"Got it. Don't trust wazungu women." Ezeji raised his glass in toast. His smile revealed three silver strips on three of his teeth. Some parts of his Yo exploits weren't so easily left behind. They were embedded data strips, an AI virus key card, the signature gear of Yo hackers. "Look, I managed to decipher the subtle message. A lord driven by avarice and gold. The hydra betrayed by the lure, the promise, of relationship. It's an old, simple children's fable."

"Simple and direct so that even the most obtuse of children could divine its meaning." Maulana laughed, an almost mean thing. "I think about that story a lot. About how the hydra operated out of abundance and still was mistrusted. Deemed a threat. How dangers against it could take so many different forms. And that by its very nature, each of the heads needed to be taken out. All of them. Otherwise for each head taken out, two would replace it, because as long as the body of community survives, there will be heads."

"We still have to do business."

"Commerce is an old lure, one many—even in Muungano—sometimes chase along their journey of discovering themselves." Maulana took a long sip to allow the barb of his message to sting a little. Ezeji hated how people froze in time. Years ago, he left. Traveled O.E., made a bit of a name for himself. Had fans, people who looked up to him. Grew up. But when he encountered someone who knew him before, they acted like they knew him. That he was still defined by his teenage fuckups. Memory was cryogenic. "Relationships are the foundation of who we are; reminding us that all things are sacred. Which is why betrayal of those relationships is such a high . . ."

". . . Crime?" Ezeji refused to give him the satisfaction of seeing him squirm.

"Treason. It's a rejection of who we are and everything we stand for."

"All I'm saying is sometimes I wish there was some cash incentive around here."

"Money isn't what drove Matata." Maulana studied the liquid in his glass before taking a long, rueful sip. "Besides, what do you want us to do? Stamp Xola's face on a piece of paper and assign arbitrary value to it?"

"He'd love that shit. You washed dishes? That's ten Xolas." Ezeji's laughter collapsed on itself, unable to drift away from thoughts of his friend.

Maulana swirled his glass. "Matata is Night Train, pure and simple. He's always been disruptive in any space he found himself in and uses the idea of community to cloak himself. He's never been truly one of us."

"Just because someone doesn't weusi the way you do doesn't make them less weusi."

"This isn't about some vague notion of cultural story. This is about a way of life. Someone refusing to take responsibility for his acts."

"He wants to do good, but he operates from a place of deep wound. His need for validation always tripped him up. Yes, he betrayed the homies, but we want to leave room for him to come back around. To grow. To change. To . . ."

". . . betray us again." Over the lip of the glass, Maulana hard-eyed him. "We do not knowingly clutch a scorpion to our breast."

"Only you can turn the idea of friendship into a threat-assessment exercise." Ezeji stopped short of sucking his teeth.

"Is that what's really bothering you?"

"It's just . . . this path seems so final. I have to believe that there's always a chance for redemption. How do we create a space for people to contribute their gifts and talents then abandon them when they fuck up?"

"You care about your friend. That's commendable and speaks to who we're hoping to be. But make no mistake, far as I'm concerned, he is a tool of LISC. He has rebuffed all offers to walk with healers." A community within community, a walk with healers was the journey of penance to allow time to pass and them to experience their healing in their own time. Rehabilitation was its own path, one that had to be willingly and freely embraced. "Which I'm fine with. I'm not interested in his past, his growth, or his personal journey."

"I don't understand. It's not like we have jails."

"We don't know. He won't talk to us." Maulana set his empty glass down.

"Where is he?"

"At his home. With a member of the Griot Circle posted outside." Maulana turned his back. It had the finality of a curtain lowering. "Allow me to make plain my position: To paraphrase the prophet, when a man tells you who he is by what he does, believe him the first time. It will save you a lot of future pain."

✸

Constructed with exacting intentionality, the Dreaming City incorporated much of the original colony known as First World. Inscriptions were carved into the architecture, imbuing even the walls surrounding them with the movement of poetry. Sculptures bedecked banisters, niches, and were tucked into transoms above alcoves. Ascending terrace gardens accompanied many of the walkways. Many areas of the city were little more than nested kraals to allow a density of neighbors to know one another. At its heart was the pyramid-shaped tower known as the Well of Griots. Signs along the entrance encouraged visitors to: BE KIND, SPEAK TRUTH, BE GRATEFUL, and TELL STORIES. The people crowded the grand hall, a sea of Basotho blankets, Himba braids, and Maasai collars. Despite the pageantry of the bright colors, the mood was grim, suffused with a somber, unforgiving energy. Death hung in the air.

People could say what they wanted about Maulana, but the brother knew how to make an entrance. As he came in from the rear of the room, the wide sleeves of his loose-fitting vestments flowed about his white-and-red hand-woven robe. Triangles divided into smaller triangles formed the sacred symbol of Alkebulan; an interlaced diamond pattern illustrated the continuity and balance to life. To eternity. He moved with the solemnity of a judge.

Four Niyabinghi escorted Matata in, a procession of shame. Tall and rigid, Matata stared straight ahead, not meeting anyone's eyes. They gave him away with the indifferent resignation in them. A hint of defiance steeled his bearing; his was a façade easily tumbled, a house whose foundations had been whittled away by termites. Without his title, command, respect, he was broken, standing only out of muscle memory. Maulana could render any verdict and Matata would accept it without complaint. He was alone or believed himself abandoned and deserving whatever any of them demanded of him. He'd given up, every bit a lost little boy Ezeji still called friend.

Many of Muungano's elders took their places. Selamault Jywanza, Xola's widow, had a pervading melancholy threatening to rush from her eyes. The Adinkra pattern aligned down the front of her robes. Her near obsidian features had the radiant sheen of dignified beauty. Twin spheres—Taiwo and Kehinde—orbited about her, jamming all signals, effectively designating her and the space about her Code Black / Eyes Only. Once she assumed her seat, the spheres settled into the folds of her robes. Bayard, head of the Yar'adua family—and a high religious leader—had the looming presence of an old tree. Kente cloth accented his formal white robes. He called the meeting to order with a simple raising of his hand. The ranking members of the Ijo milled about, not knowing how to respond to the charge of the moment.

"Brothers and sisters, all those of the Muungano family," Maulana began, "we gather together in grave duty. For transparency, we gather in the pursuit of truth and share it before all. We sound the call: Who speaks for the people of Muungano in this matter?"

Bayard stood, his robes falling about him in grim sobriety. "I do."

"And who speaks for the accused?" Maulana asked with a cool aplomb. A murmur swept through the crowd. "Well?"

Before his mind registered that his legs were moving, Ezeji rose. He locked eyes with Maulana. "I guess I do."

With the slightest tick of his chin, Maulana sat and Bayard strode to the center of the dais.

"Where we work, where we play, where we pray. We hold space. We hold the line. That trauma lives in our DNA. We remember," Bayard said. "Matata Okoro, former Lij of the Niyabinghi, you are accused of conspiring with our enemies."

"Night Train. Night Train. Night Train," some in the crowd chanted.

"Many come to Muungano seeking a second chance. To re-create themselves. We judge a person by their past action, who they were then, under those circumstances. Without context of what they thought they were trying to do. Matata always felt the outsider. He loves community—well, the idea of community—but never allowed himself to feel its love." Bayard paced about, his tone conflicted. Matata often came to his kraal, hung out on his porch, spending time with the "fun uncle" compared to Xola's stern ways. No less the lessons of Muungano, but the tenor seemed more gentle. Bayard loved him and the responsibility of the moment brought only a distant heartache. His voice cracked slightly. "Play his confession."

The holovid burned to life above them. A scene from an interrogation room at Oyigiyigi. Matata squared off against Lebna Dimka, magistrate for the Griot Circle of Oyigiyigi. The bulk of his uniform hid his thinness, but he clearly favored his aunt, Jaha Dimka.

"That's what we're here to find out." Ishant enlarged the files in front of Matata, tracking his movement, prior to the bombing. Being recalled to the Dreaming City. The movements of a data ghost, tracked by being invisible. Then fleeing to Oyigiyigi once Amachi dogged his trail. *"All of my collected data is right here. What story would you have us read?"*

"It's simple really," Matata began in a low, not-quite-resigned tone. *"We need to bring Muungano to the table. But you all are so damn proud. Self-sufficient. Don't have to take anything from anybody. Doing things on your terms or your timetable. Calling yourselves 'free' when all you are is 'arrogant.' Blind as Xola. You can't see your need for others, even against an overwhelming threat."*

"The unknown is not a threat," Lebna said.

"Now you're just being naive. Oyigiyigi. Bronzeville. The Dreaming City. All of Muungano has to reunify. Partner with LISC. One way or another, you'll be brought to the table so that we can form a united Earth alliance. That is the only way we'll be strong enough to face the coming storm."

"Were you a part of the terrorist plot to blow up our embassy?" Lebna asked.

"Yes." Matata lowered his head.

"Do you deny any which was said in the holovid?" Bayard asked.

Matata shook his head. Ezeji opened his mouth to pose a question, but Matata's hand brushed his side to silence him.

"What say you, Bayard?" Maulana asked for his summation.

"Many Israelites wanted to return to Egypt after Pharaoh released them once times got hard. Many of the enslaved of the Maafa wished to remain on the plantation rather than risk the unknown they called freedom. And there are those some refer to as Night Train—skinfolk who ain't kinfolk—who are so lost in self-hate they wish to bring us all to ruin to reclaim their piece of the status quo. Matata, you are guilty of deception. Your intellect adopted the abstract values of the oppressor and embraced them as your own. You assimilated the culture of the oppressor, how they think. Their values seeped into your sabhu until you were left a deluded dual citizen. Caught up in being seen as indispensable in their eyes, because despite what you proclaim, their gaze—them seeing value in you—truly matters to you. Whenever you walk among them, you become a mirror, reflecting their words as if you are the arbiter of righteous fury. All to disguise that at your core, you are a desperate opportunist. Believing you are moving the work of Muungano forward, unaware of how you only leave broken relationship in your wake. You, Matata, once one of our brightest stars, have broken our hearts."

Bayard walked off the dais. He plunged his hands into a silver bowl. He wrung his hands in its water before wiping them on his pants legs.

"What say you, Ezeji?" Maulana asked.

"Do I have permission from my elders to speak?" Ezeji waited for Bayard's ascent. "I'm not sure what I'm supposed to do or say. The mistakes you make matter. They shape you. They shape the future. All I know is that Matata has taken ownership of his actions and has cooperated with our internal investigation. Both with the Griot Circle and the Niyabinghi. He was also debriefed before the security council. Now he comes before the community after betraying us. No matter how shitty you are with the home team or with how you think you've been treated, you don't talk about that shit with obroni."

"Ezeji, in this place, especially in these circumstances, we do not stray from decorum," Maulana intoned without amusement.

Ezeji patted the air in apology. "My bad. My point is that if folks break with you, you confront them instead of holding on to all sorts of animosity. Yell at them. Cuss them out. All that you felt, Matata, you could have shared it with us. Been mad with us, alongside us. All I'm saying is that you deal with us. You don't move against us and the entire community, your words used against all of us. The second you start doing that, the bridge collapses out from under you and there's no chance for redemption."

"Is that his . . . defense?" Maulana's voice arched in skepticism.

"That's me telling him to his face how he hurt us. How he hurt me. I owe him that. Him standing here before the Ijo, before his friends, family, and people, is his acknowledgment of that hurt. We have to be willing to hear and learn one another's stories, walk in those uncomfortable spaces."

"We all want forgiveness and reconciliation without having to do the hard work of forgiveness and reconciliation." The beads forming the veil of Maulana's mask clattered, as he turned to face Ezeji. "The lessons of our oppressors would demand but one recourse for his actions: death. There is a . . . simple wisdom . . . in that. Fortunately for all of us, termination is not our preferred course of action. We subscribe to a more restorative justice. What happens when you sell out and no one's buying? I ask you, Matata, what should the community do with you?"

"Be done with me. Maybe in time you'll . . ." Matata tried to screw up righteous indignation, but the words tumbled out as a whispered crack, without conviction, his voice hitched with each syllable. His sabhu worn out before he could get out the words "*forgive me.*"

"Maybe." Maulana adjusted his vestments, silent for several heartbeats. "Until then, we give you over to the desires of your heart. Go your own way. Alone. We cast you out of Muungano to return to your masters. May they deal with you as they see fit."

Four Niyabinghi surrounded him. Raising his head enough to meet Ezeji's eyes one last time, Matata said, "I appreciate you."

"I appreciate you." Ezeji patted his shoulder. The Niyabinghi led his friend out of the chamber.

With that, the crowd began to disperse with only the slightest swell of dissatisfied grumbling. The governing elders of the Ijo remained. Around the central table, Bayard and Selamault flanked Maulana. Even without the veil, he'd have been as inscrutable as ever. Not sure how to reveal what he was thinking or feeling. Ezeji fashioned a seat for himself off to the side, his legs akimbo as he slouched in it.

"VOP Harrison is calling on a secure commlink." Selamault didn't raise her eyes from the screens surrounding her as if she was double-checking all of the data and reports produced by Maya.

"Put him on screen." Maulana shifted in his seat, making himself taller.

All grinning teeth, VOP Harrison filled the space between them. "Greetings, Maulana. I wanted to reach out to you in hopes that we might . . ."

"We are returning your Night Train dog to you. Spin the narrative however you want, but your actions have brought us to this place."

"So much for cooler heads prevailing in the moment." VOP Harrison shook his head in mocking disappointment.

"There's no need for the performance. It is only a few family members here. I'd hate for you to exhaust yourself overdoing it. All the same, we don't need the voice of outdated institutions to tell us what course we should pursue for the benefit of our community."

"Now who's performing?" VOP Harrison shrugged off the comments.

"You push and provoke to corral us back to your world order." Maulana leaned forward, bridging his fingers.

"We need to form a united federation of Earth and her colonies to give this alien alliance pause. Your stubbornness blinds you to the fact."

"I want to beat that motherfucker like he stole an election," Ezeji whispered. It was easy to forget that he was in the room with a head of state. The Camara allowed any interested sebau to sit in meetings to learn and build their comfort in such spaces. Sometimes Ezeji grew too comfortable.

Selamault leveled her eyes at him in silent reminder that while his voice was valued, his words needed to be chosen with care. Every action needed to be strategic. Ezeji twirled his chair away from VOP. Maulana held up his hand to keep the rest of the Ijo still.

"In any event," VOP Harrison continued as if not hearing him, "I wished to personally update you on the situation brewing in our capital."

"The long-prophesied insurrection?" Ezeji mumbled, though this time no one chided him.

"Not quite." VOP Harrison didn't rise to the bait. His tone had a smug air of being pleased with himself. Unsettled, Ezeji returned his seat back toward him. "There was a disturbance at my latest rally. What started off as a beautiful, peaceful event descended into chaos. I had to send in a detachment of ARM troops to retain order."

"What do we care about your internal authoritarian crackdowns?" Maulana lifted his wrist as a security brief pinged.

"Maulana . . ." Selamault's fingers drew up a series of newslink feeds. She slid them to his display.

"Early intelligence reports that both Jaha Dimka and Wachiru Adisa were present on the scene," VOP Harrison said. "I wanted to let you know personally, to demonstrate transparency in the hopes that we can initiate an ongoing dialogue to . . ."

Maulana cut him off, disconnecting the commlink. "Any verification?"

"We have an initial contact from Jaha. I'm sending you her report," Selamault said.

"I want Niyabinghi dispatched to our embassy immediately."

"What of Wachiru?" Ezeji asked.

"They were separated. VOP has him. He called to gloat, hoping to leverage his safety to drive us to the negotiation table."

"And it will." Selamault's tone was a declaration, stopping just short of a command.

"Are you responding as a ranking member of the Ijo or as a worried mother?" Maulana asked.

"I respond as the bagirwa of the Niyabinghi. A Black Dove, of the line of oracles, the Libyan Sibyls." Her face darkened, a storm cloud blotting a full moon. "So a respectful tone would be appreciated, assuming you haven't lost sight of what that means."

"We're in the room with LISC because we have to be. The circumstances around Matata are more proof that they were trying to work around us."

"Because to their minds, we grew so large—occupied so much room—they had no choice but to deal with us. But now we're at the precipice of war. All violence is not conflict but all conflict is violence. We cannot protect the dream of what we have at the expense of the heart of it," Selamault said.

"If you're going to make the choice to be peaceful, you have to be capable of causing harm. Otherwise you are just harmless." Maulana paced the dais. "You do not see how we are under attack, from all sides, because you don't want to. Many of us are afraid. I don't blame any of you. It's easier to pretend that we're surrounded by allies or at least by people striving to be better. But we're not. Many still actively work against us; engage in behavior specifically determined to block our progress. Someone has to remain vigilant and defend against those who would march against us."

Ezeji stared at him without a word. Matata's presence filled the room, a roaming duppy no one wanted to acknowledge.

"You do not need to lecture us." Selamault's tone cut like an ice blade. "We understand that an attack against one of us is an attack against all of us. Even what occurs inside other sovereign territories often bleeds into ours. There's a future for us where we are all free, but it's up to us to make it happen . . . and then do whatever it takes to preserve it. That was why we have entrusted you to speak for us. Rise to that responsibility."

"Good. We had not, do not, and will not refuse to commit to the use of force to defend ourselves. Our interests, our values, and our way of life. We protect our own, no matter where they are. And we will make sure no one gets left behind." Maulana moved to the center of the stage to address the full Ijo. "As an additional security measure, I hereby move to issue an expulsion of all obroni, all non-weusi, from the Dreaming City."

05

ISHANT SANGSUWANGUL
O.E.—Indianapolis

Ishant Sangsuwangul walked back and forth in his tiny apartment, the entire space of his room little bigger than a loft. Outside of his room, two guards flanked his doorway "for his own protection." Not to be confused with a cell. Or him being in solitary confinement. As a liaison reassigned to LISC, he was "the opposite of a prisoner." He was a guest of the state. As such, he had to keep a strict routine and stay within restricted areas for matters of security.

The room remained bare, the way he liked it. A few plants hung in suspended bowls tucked into the corners to freshen the air. His unfurled workout mat spread out near the center of the east wall, the only uneven surface in the room. Its blank walls a seamless, gray matte, the ascetic décor pleased him. He'd long prided himself on never needing much. Not even a bed, contenting himself to lie on the floor as a matter of discipline. Or perhaps to remind himself that no place would never be home. More so after Maulana's edict.

Overseer, the AI that ran much of things on O.E., was compartmentalized, unlike Maya, strictly a tool that could be turned on or off as the user required. Ishant had it turned off, though he was not under any illusion about his privacy. Intelligence nanobots monitored his every movement. Through his initial training with the Niyabinghi, his senses seemed heightened. He wiped the ledge along the wall, a white-glove inspection that made no logical sense. Intelligence nanobots weren't visible, not individually, not even en masse until they were brought together in quantities sufficient to form a tool of some sort. Yet he sensed them scurrying about surveilling him, monitoring his movements, recording his conversations. Constantly cataloging his abilities, though he wasn't going to give them much to report. No matter how impressive their tech, they couldn't penetrate his mind. Or spirit.

Begrudgingly sitting at his workstation, he studied the data streams of crop production in North Dakota and Canada, the hemisphere's breadbasket. Despite his not having jacked in, his heart pounded with each data stream. Being a data streamer, he often jacked into data streams for pleasure. Though this wasn't the euphoric rush of that. The information wasn't alarming, though projected yields were down 15 percent. Blood rushed through his ears, and the raucous thump, thump, thump produced movement in his chest despite his extra layer of clothing. His hand trembled, framed by the hard light projections of his station. Ishant stripped off his sweatshirt. A thin trickle of sweat creased his chin. When he rose to grab a drink at a hydration station, his legs quavered, leaving him unsteady on his feet. His heart slammed harder. His breath came in shallow spurts, sharp and painful. His vision had a kaleidoscopic burst before things grew darker. Narrower.

"You're dying. This is it, what death feels like. And you're alone."

Slowly sinking to the floor, he ran through scenarios of how he might have been poisoned. Someone's touch. Ingestion. Microbe. Gas. Nanobot. He felt his life ebb from him in slow waves. The sensation had an eerie familiarity to it. And he remembered.

Back when he'd transferred from Thailand to California to finish out his school, he'd developed an interest in the idea of regenerative economics. Admittedly, he was also fairly contrarian and tended to stomp through the halls of academia without any regard to the politics—and sometimes feelings—of his colleagues, putting him at odds with many of his professors and accruing a laundry list of people who . . . did not seek his best interests. Then came the day he was due to defend his dissertation. When he neared the building and saw the rogues' gallery assembling for his presentation, a sharp pain shot down his left arm. He tried to calm himself, but he was convinced he was experiencing a heart attack. He stumbled around the campus, the tingling and spiking pain through his arm convincing him that at any moment he would keel over. Leaving him sprawled out on the classroom floor, dying as he stared up at a row of faces of those who held him in contempt. His chest tightened. He couldn't move. His breaths struggled, erupting in gasps. The thought of his dissertation defense caused him to tremble. His left arm throbbed, propelled by his hammering heartbeat. Administrators called for an ambulance. After some very expensive tests, doctors diagnosed him with having had a panic attack. They recommended that he seek therapy.

Ishant had his left arm removed.

His cybernetic arm was sheathed in bioplastic, and he could jack it into any workstation. Soothing data streams washed over him, calming him enough to collect his thoughts. Descending into sensate culture, he became a data streamer. Sensate culture created community, a sort of technology-induced connection to generate empathy. The scariest part was that even once he realized whatever stress he was experiencing was triggering a panic attack, his body and mind remained convinced he was in imminent danger. That was then.

The reality of his current days was that his slightest mistake could result in his death.

He'd barely been recruited into the Niyabinghi, Muungano's intelligence and security agency, and had received only minimal training, when his transfer to LISC was mandated. Next came quarantine protocols, orientation, and now numerous onboarding meetings, constantly under a watchful eye. Anyone associated with Muungano was placed on an automatic watch list. His access would be limited and he'd have to be cautious, but he was assured he'd be able to accomplish his assignment.

And eventually someone might let him know what it was.

Though not quite 5 A.M., this was his time. He understood that he couldn't rely on data streams for comfort but had to keep focused. Withdrawing to the corner of his room, he meditated to order his thoughts, reflect, and plan. Stretching through the Forms, he assumed a new posture. The stubborn knot in the base of his neck threatened to spread into his shoulders, no matter the exercises. Embracing it, he welcomed the pain as a companion sent to remind him of the dangerous game he played.

Ishant wrestled his racing heart back under control. The entire situation was . . . big. He was diving into deep waters—not sure of himself or his abilities—his life tumbling into an anxiety spiral he might not be able to pull out of. And he was on his own. Staring as the wall, he knew with the touch of a panel he could summon what he needed: washbasin, chair, desk, commlink. While Muungano funkentelechy allowed for the near-spiritual manipulation of their nanobots, other tech approximated it. Ishant had studied with many Muungano members, never quite getting his mind around matters of spirit, but part of him remained open to it.

His doorway chimed. Ishant signaled for an entrance.

"We have a situation." Akilah Natarajan stormed in without breaking stride. Her short brown legs pistoned beneath her short skirt, and she moved with an uncoordinated energy, as if parts of her body scrambled to keep up with the rest of her. Her long black hair clamped to her back, still wet from her shower. Her baggy shirt, closer to an amorphous tunic, draped along her body, both shielding her figure from anyone's gaze and being completely comfortable. Not quite the wardrobe he expected from the chief of staff for the secretary of state.

"I see you, Akilah." Ishant rose to greet her. He urged his heart to stay calm, a plea that he seemed to start every conversation on O.E. with.

"It's good to be seen. God has blessed your eyes." Mimilah sneered with her eyes, an annoyed expression without heat. "And good morning. By the way, it's Mimilah when we're joined."

"Some sensates need to come with signs." While Ishant was a jacker, "true" sensates used tech to literally feel what another experienced, thus "joining" with each other to essentially function as one unit. "That's got to make for a complicated home life."

"Miriam has been read in. She works in the accounting department of the Defense Department. This is why you have to choose your sensate partners carefully at this level."

"Mimilah is a pragmatic name."

"Pragmatic. I don't get that a lot."

"It became a tradition among the Ugenini—during the Maafa, since they could be taken from them and sold at any time—to give their children distinctive names in the hope that they could one day find them."

"Or took the name of their plantation or owner hoping that their children might remember and perhaps track them down. I learned a lot during my internship at Muungano also. All names are made up. This is our joined name." Mimilah summoned another workstation. "However, if we're done with all of the salutations and pleasantries, can we keep it moving?"

Ishant stepped out of her way. As her assistant policy advisor, he was still learning her ways. People on O.E. were conditioned to a certain way of behaving and moving through their spaces. Conditioning to perceived authority was the most significant lesson of the O.E. educational experience. Which was another reason why Ishant never finished his schooling. Not LISC's way. "Has there been an update on the embassy incident?"

"No word. Casualty reports are still coming in." She flipped her damp hair out of her eyes. "Relax. Jaha is fine. She and her merry band are holed up inside the Legacy of Alexandria."

Ishant had a sense of déjà vu. The last time he was on O.E. he was stationed there alongside her. When it was bombed. "What of Wachiru?"

"Unknown. VOP Harrison's claiming that 'the scion of Muungano' was a foreign security officer working on O.E. soil against their interests."

"He could make that claim about me, too."

"Keep that in mind and be careful. Though you're the scion of obroni. But that's not the situation." Mimilah attempted to plop into a seat, missed its center, and instead caught the edge of the armrest. Off-balance, she overcorrected and barely managed to stay perched on it. She glared at the chair in skeptical critique of its design. "You look stressed. Are you okay? What trumps the annihilation clock ticking ever closer to midnight?"

"I've received a cable. Muungano is ordering me to report to the Legacy of Alexandria."

"That sounds ominous. Maulana hasn't had a change of heart, has he?" Mimilah asked.

"Hardly."

"You worried?"

"No, they are. He is. Doesn't trust me not to share what I know," Ishant said.

"But if you don't go, it'll hurt your standing."

"I have no idea where I stand these days."

An awkward pause lingered between them. Her eyes probed him, searching for any weakness.

Ishant couldn't remember when he first became disillusioned working for LISC. He was there to work on the real problems facing O.E. The unhoused. Medical care. Global reshaping. Renewable energy. He wanted to make a difference on his world, bring his creativity to the work. But what he was tasked to do more resembled errands for people who enjoyed their positionality to power. Bureaucratic busywork between the petty squabbles, the management dysfunction, and the poor interpersonal communication. There was no plan to develop him as a leader. Actually, he wasn't seen. Not by his supervisor. Not by his team. They had no idea who he was or what he could do. It was why when he was assigned to the Thmei Academy by LISC Corps, he applied to become one of Muungano's equity fellows. He worked in Muungano space for eight years, becoming Jaha Dimka's right hand. Maulana's ban provided perfect cover for him to return to LISC. He understood that in his head. His heart thumped hard in his chest.

"Dang, you just disruptive." Mimilah turned her attention to her holovid display with a mix of annoyance and condescension. "Speaking of, we have a group of climate refugees coming down from Canada."

Ishant appreciated the change in topic and settled in at his station. "I thought O.E. had approved terraforming for the Arctic Circle?"

"They have, but those efforts take time. The albedo effect alone will take a while to reverse. Intelligence reports that about fifteen hundred Nunatsiarmiut set off from Baffin Island in vessels which on a good day might be considered rafts. Another five hundred turned around due to inclement conditions. About a hundred and fifty are missing, presumed dead. They're signaling for temporary asylum in the meantime."

"That's not good." He sat cross-legged on the couch, sipping a cup of coffee and scrolling through his daily link messages.

"It gets worse. We have new reports of flooding. Bangladesh. St. Petersburg. San Francisco. The drought updates will be in by six A.M." Mimilah swiped at the air, reading and culling data streams. "You good?"

"I'm fine. Tea?" Excusing himself, he went to the bathroom. Staring in the mirror, he splashed water onto his face and waited a moment before heading back out. He swept his hand across a wall panel to reveal a hydration station. He brewed a cup of tea. This had become their morning routine, with Mimilah arriving earlier and earlier each day because the workload piled ever higher. He wasn't much of a chai drinker but quickly developed a taste for it thanks to her. She joked—in her sardonic, sharp-edged way—about it being a tribute to their oppressors. Settling into an amiable enough rhythm, they used their morning cup to go over the agenda and goals of the day's work. Today she waved off the offered a cup; he sipped from his while leaning against a wall.

Mimilah drew up a series of reports, the screens hovering in the air while she shuffled through them prioritizing their work. With a sigh, she enlarged a screen and slid it over to him. "With the LISC Global Reshaping Summit quickly coming up, political affairs would like for you to go over the order of the Conference of the Parliaments' balls."

"The . . . COP . . . balls?" Ishant snorted, nearly choking on his tea. "Someone should really consider reaching out to marketing before naming things."

"Damn. Noted. We're looking to host a series of welcoming soirees. It's one of VOP Harrison's major initiatives. There's a lot of social capital riding on this and he needs things to run smoothly."

"Why me? Parties are not . . . what I do."

"Soirees. And they think they're important. There are a lot of factions we need to keep appeased, or at least not actively piss off."

"Like Muungano?"

Mimilah tapped her nose. "You know them best. Do you know why I brought you on?"

"A pressing need for more sarcasm in your life?"

"A pressing need for more Muungano perspective in my life." Allowing a moment for her words to land, Mimilah continued. "Foreign policy is about boundaries, what we won't do, what we won't commit to. We have existing treaties."

"Do I need to go into the history of how well treaties have been honored?"

"They're like executive orders: they matter . . . until they don't." Mimilah squinted against the holovid projection of a report, her face lit in a gentle azure. "There's been a security cable."

"Am I being read in to something?" Ishant angled toward her.

"No." Mimilah shifted, blocking a casual read of her reports. But she didn't delete it. "And let me be clear: no."

"I think I'm slowly beginning to piece together the administration's position on me."

"If I'm being too subtle, I can try to be clearer."

"Much clearer and I'll need treatment for bruises."

She scooted her face toward him. "Don't get too upset. You'll get some face time with him eventually. Until then . . ."

". . . go over the ball details." Ishant twirled his chair back to his workstation.

"It sounds so dirty when you say it." Mimilah smirked, sinking into her chair again.

"So why am I even hearing about this cable?"

"It came with a force depletion report."

"That said what?"

"I can't say."

"But there was a report." Rubbing his jaw, Ishant leaned toward his screens as if minding his own business. Somewhere in her words, in what she wasn't saying, was a message. Whatever it was, Mimilah couldn't hint any more toward it without risk. "That VOP Harrison requested?"

"I can't confirm that. However, I can say the importance of these talks cannot be overemphasized."

"But I can be trusted with the order of the evening's . . . soirees?"

"You could offer enough perspective for that. You've spent time in our, in their, space."

"Hard, isn't it? To let go of that place. How it made anyone feel like they were home." Ishant shuffled to the screen and fashioned a seat and workstation, focusing on the screen, not wanting her to catch his eyes and plumb them for any traces of hurt or loss. "Though not so much these days."

Her hands balled into fists to steady herself on his workstation, Mimilah leaned over. Her mouth fixed into an angry moue. "You've heard then?"

"About Maulana? He's on one, all right. This embassy situation has everyone on edge."

"He's not the only one. VOP Harrison has been mounting a series of speeches criticizing Maulana, calling him no statesman, but rather 'a warmonger taking everyone to the brink of Armageddon.'"

"This after initiating a decapitation strike," Ishant said.

"Which Maulana suspects, but can't prove. Or else he'd sever all diplomatic ties to O.E. and recall all Muungano citizens."

"Almost all."

"Almost all." Mimilah lightly drummed her fingers along the consoles. Her nails were short, neither trimmed nor adorned in any way. The dull thrum seemed to soothe her as she drifted into her own thoughts. Or perhaps to hear, or feel, what was going on within her joined self.

Ishant wasn't around the first time LISC dealt with First World, but the stories were practically legend. They had been invited to meetings to help craft a report about transitioning First World to Muungano as an Opportunity Zone. LISC floated language about an inclusive growth plan. "The page is blank. You're going to help us write it up," Reverend Harrison, at the time an associate director at LISC local, reassured everyone. However, the process wasn't as open as they led folks to believe. When First World outlined what an equitable "Opportunity Zone" would look like—on their terms, under their control—they were uninvited, not even making it to the first meeting. It was an aggressive approach, moving them one step closer to the inevitable Lunar Ukombozi War.

"You were saying something about the ball. Well, you'd changed topics about the ball," Ishant said.

"Yeah, I do slick shit like that." Mimilah sat up straighter in her seat.

"Why can't you handle the ball details?"

"Because I'm delivering the keynote."

"Since when?"

"Since about two hours ago." Stifling a yawn at the thought, Mimilah stretched in her seat. "I am the chief of staff of Theodora Harrison, the secretary of state."

"Way to bury the lede. It's a LISC/UN summit. Where will VOP Harrison be?"

"Squirreled away in a closed room. Probably back-channel negotiations."

Ishant struggled, not knowing where the line was between him following his trained sense of curiosity and pressing her for as much intelligence as possible. Mimilah—even Madam Secretary—was like VOP Harrison's personal canary, swooping into the ever-expanding coal mine of his rule, ready to be sacrificed if that meant alerting him when the toxic gases of his decisions rose to life-threatening levels. "You are in the room with powerful people, where the decisions get made."

"I worked hard to get a seat at the table. My job is to carry out Madam Secretary's will."

"How . . . subservient." Ishant scooted back, arms folded across his chest.

"How patriarchal." Staring Ishant up and down like he was small, Mimilah ran her tongue underneath her lip as if deciding on which lesser course of violence to pursue. "VOP Harrison calls the play, she carries it out. I'm policy, counsel, and execution."

"But if VOP Harrison asked for a force depletion report . . ." Ishant let his voice trail off, hoping she'd fill in the blank.

"He's contemplating new parameters for use of force."

"VOP Harrison doesn't strike me as someone the word 'contemplative' could describe."

"Does he strike you as a capricious someone who'd love to be able to send in troops at his authoritarian discretion?"

"Yes."

"So joke time's over?" Mimilah asked.

"Yes." Ishant settled into his seat.

"He wants me to adjust our foreign-policy language. Give himself carte blanche when it comes to use of force. 'A new doctrine for a new age.' The narrative he's trying to present is a worldwide coalition. A force for peace standing alone in our increasingly hostile solar system. Here's the language we're toying with: 'We must be strong. Diplomatically, economically, and if need be, militarily. Whenever we see an injustice, we do whatever the greater good demands.'"

"Violence governing how he keeps order in his world."

"There is no playbook for what he's trying to do or how he's supposed to lead. My job is to make the language of the old ways sound better."

Ishant blew at the surface of the tea out of habit. The mug kept the temperature just below scalding, exactly the way he liked it. "So . . . how bad are the fractures?"

"Fractures?"

"No one works so hard to present a united front unless they're trying to conceal fractures."

"Intel's reporting movement by the Service of the Order. In Spain."

"State needs to issue an alert," Ishant said.

"Thanks for telling me. Don't know what I'd do without a man letting me know how to do my job. Whew." After dabbing her forehead, Mimilah feigned deference, averting her eyes, half bowing. She lived to remind people how smart she was by reminding them of how they defaulted to dismissing, overlooking, and underestimating her. Rolling her eyes, she drew up another schematic, this one a layout of the Mars settlements. "There's a border dispute brewing with the Bronzeville settlement."

"Since when are they a settlement? What, they didn't like the implications of being called a colony?"

"We forever live in the shadow of history." Mimilah shoved the latest communiqué to the side, highlighting a new series of reports. There was a brutal efficiency to how she approached her job. "We have a commlink scheduled. The commander of the Seventh Space Fleet has detained a vessel in their settlement. It was scheduled to launch to explore the remains of the Orun Gate. He wants to know about forwarding units."

"Wait, what does this all mean?" Ishant scanned the reports. "Can we, can LISC, detain anything or anyone on Mars?"

"We're initiating talks. We need to lay the rhetorical language foundation to smooth that situation over. We've proposed doing joint exercises with Mars."

"Military?"

"Research." Mimilah's tone was a puzzle of kept secrets.

"Similar to the joint research exercises which led to the creation of the HOVA?"

"I hope not. That didn't exactly end well."

"It ended at least." Ishant sifted through the reports, noting his recommendations.

Mimilah rolled her chair over to face him. "Look, VOP Harrison has to reunite Earth to project an image of what humanity was meant to be; not be seen as warring factions scattered throughout the solar system. The LISC social order relies on two things: economy and peace. Capitalism we got in spades, so we need to sell everyone on the idea of peace. We need everyone at the table."

"What if the table's the problem?"

The question hung between them.

✳

Mimilah dismissed the agents stationed outside of his door. Ishant was given leave to be able to move more freely. He was cautious, knowing he would be surveilled. He began his dry-cleaning route, a circuitous path meant to throw off anyone who might be watching him. He loved to walk, but hated the air, mostly because he could taste it. Even in the LISC headquarters, the carefully scrubbed air left the acrid aftertaste of what he guessed to be peanut butter along the back of his throat. Most people considered it better than wearing a rebreather unit, but Ishant slipped one into place. He passed through the Amtrak rail station and ducked into a restroom. The elevated maglev tracks emitted low electromagnetic pulses, enough to cause interference for any surveillance drones. He activated a small sphere, a signal-canceling device. Such a dead zone was its own alert, considering the level of monitoring by Overseer, but he only needed to be off their radar for a few minutes to blend in and disappear. His ident sigil would be scanned if he boarded the train or any other public transport, so he exited a side door and continued his walk.

He wondered if he was ready to admit to a quiet thirst for adventure.

The Tinker Street Tech Café served as the food court for the eponymous complex. The cyber compound ran the length of a once historically Ugenini block. The original residents were displaced when their neighborhood, too, was declared an Opportunity Zone. Tinker Street Tech became the economic engine that fueled Indianapolis's rise to prominence. If there was one place he would not pick to meet his intelligence handler, it would be here, in the proverbial—and literal—heart of the LISC beast.

The café itself echoed the appearance of one of Muungano's open-air markets, with tables under colorful spinning umbrellas. Lebna sat at a table, legs crossed. His embroidered, long-sleeved gown, matching his trousers, draped elegantly about him. He cupped a short glass of whiskey in front of him. Another waited expectantly on the other side of the table, presumably for Ishant.

"Ishant." Lebna waited until he fell under the shadow of the awning to gesture. "Sorry about the short notice. We don't know when moments will allow for chances to make contact. I took the liberty of ordering a drink."

"I'll assume responsibility for whatever's been poured for me." Ishant eased into the empty chair. The air charged about them, like he'd been cut off from something. It could have simply been the paranoia Niyabinghi spycraft instilled—

acute situational awareness—but something more disturbed his spirit. His cybernetic arm was less responsive, whatever the tech equivalent to numb was.

"Meets become tricky since O.E. is a hundred percent surveillance state."

"Practically speaking, so is Muungano. Maya is omnipresent and ever listening."

"Which makes the act of subterfuge that much more challenging." Lebna pointed up. The umbrella over them had been lined with what Ishant could only presume was something that produced a kind of scattering field. Considering the effect on the tech in his arm, it wouldn't create enough of a dead zone to draw Overseer's attention. "Have you been briefed?"

"Only on my cover. And handling our contact meetups."

"'Need to know' rules the roost to an asinine degree, but intelligence is intelligence. However, we wrong-foot obroni, playing the art of subterfuge with our enemies, not our members."

"What about our allies?" Ishant tossed back the shot of whiskey. It burned his throat, leaving a warm trail to his belly. He waved to the waitstaff for another.

"What did Maulana call allies?" Lebna stared off into the distance as if he could spy the Camara in his rondavel.

"'Friends who haven't betrayed us. Yet,'" Ishant recited. "Though I'm not sure where I stand these days: member ally or obroni."

"Officially, you have been designated 'obroni.'" Lebna studied his glass, swirling it gently. "I consider you a friend."

Ishant couldn't help feeling as if something unspoken remained between them. But given their circumstances, they didn't have the luxury to explore anything unsaid. Protecting his heart, he could only move according to actionable intelligence.

"Our contacts have let us know that LISC has Wachiru." Lebna raised his eyes from the pool of brown liquid.

"What?" Ishant cradled the second glass, sipping it as his spirit calmed.

"It was staged as a police action. ARM members took him into custody and whisked him off-planet."

"His name wasn't on any newslinks. Nor mentioned in any report."

"A brazen grab." Lebna downed the remainder of his glass. "VOP's been emboldened. He believes Maulana's rhetoric gives him plenty of cover if not complete deniability."

"I'm not convinced he's that clever. More like mediocrity lucking into op-portunity."

"He can claim a rogue faction of ARM and set up a blue-ribbon commission to investigate it."

"Meanwhile, Wachiru's been disappeared to who knows where."

"No, we know where: the Panopticon." Lebna reached into his jacket and withdrew a fist-sized block of machinery. It had several finger-sized ports built into it. A portable jacking station. He set it between them.

Eyeing him with suspicion at first, Ishant rolled up his sleeve to unsheathe his cybernetic arm. He paused again, not certain that he wanted to jack in while Lebna watched. The data stream rushed through his system, awakening his cy-bernetic arm. He relaxed, caught somewhere between data stream and memory. As Ishant scanned the files, a wave, like heated honey, poured over him and the world seemed to melt away. Nothing mattered, yet everything was better.

"Our diplomats and embassies, especially the Legacy of Alexandria, are on high alert." Lebna turned his attentions to a holovid, allowing Ishant a measure of privacy. "The public story is that this is a needed precaution considering the tensions. The reality is that we have suspicions, and increasing evidence of LISC's involvement with Xola's death. The cascading series of degenerative neurological disorders points to a slow-acting poison building up in his system."

"Not to mention that Amachi and Wachiru were assaulted after finding a genetic artifact which looked to be a by-product of some sort of degrading nanovirus." In the Dreaming City, a slither attacked Wachiru and Amachi. Slithers were a hackers' convention, overriding nanobot systems and forming weapons out of them. But no one would bother to make an attempt on their lives if they were on the wrong trail.

"And where are they now to bring in for testimony?"

"Gone." Ishant rode the wave of data, the sensation leaving him numb and content. He needed to withdraw before it became too much and overwhelmed him. He shoved the portable jacking station away. "That's why I'm here. Now, what's my mission?"

"The administration is scared by something they've encountered at the Ga-lactic Rim. O.E.'s great unifier, VOP Clay Harrison, needs a profound cause for his people to rally around. We need to find out as much as we can about what he knows and what he plans. To that end, we have an eye on one of your colleagues."

Already having difficulty trusting in the first place, Ishant descended further into a world of shadows, obscuring his ability to discern who to trust. Or with how much. "Who?"

"The secretary of state. We want you to position yourself to get close to her."

"Theodora Harrison? There's no way. I'm too much of a security risk. I barely got instated where I am. Do you know how long it will take to achieve inner-circle level?" Ishant shook his head and waved him off. "This side of never."

"We just want you to get as close into her orbit as possible and let us know what you think."

"I can already do that from where I am. Theodora's not the person for you. She's too unstable. She operates from a place of deep, if not singular, wound. It makes it tough for her to get out of her own way. Wrap all of that messiness in naked ambition and you get a volatile, self-focused mix waiting to explode." Ishant pushed his empty glass away from him.

"I recognize that gleam. You have someone better in mind."

"Akilah Natarajan. Chief of staff for the secretary of state. A single degree of separation from your target."

"Why is she important?" Lebna slowed as if determining whether to circumnavigate or cut through a minefield.

"I like her. She likes me."

"This isn't a game of high school crushes." A hint of jealousy gilded Lebna's voice.

"There's nothing remotely like that between us," Ishant reassured. "We've been working alongside one another and I've had a chance to watch her up close. She's a patriot who believes in humanity."

"A passionate true believer?" Shifting positions, Lebna's hands almost brushed against Ishant's. Still close enough to feel the warmth of them. "Can that passion be redirected?"

"It runs to her core and aligns with ours. A complex thinker, she naturally moves in the spirit of Muungano. An analytical mind comfortable with an abstract intuition. Though very, very guarded. She hides behind a mask of blunt glibness."

"Is that your full assessment?"

"It is."

Lebna slid his hands back. "I trust you. Observe and assess. See if she can be an asset for us. And if so, bring her in."

"You want me to turn her." This work chafed his spirit, too much using people to fit an agenda. And being used. Not being seen as a full person, simply a means to an end. Ishant backed away, though careful not to escape the shielding of the scattering field.

"To put it crudely and unnecessarily dramatically—if we were trapped in a 1980s spy movie—yes. More accurately, however, we want you to run a full psychological profile. Do a deep-dive character analysis."

"You could just say 'get to know her better' and not sound so shady." Ishant relaxed, and his lips flickered, hinting at a smile.

"Get to know her . . . with intentionality." Lebna smiled, a full thing revealing all of his perfectly white teeth. "Are you always this difficult?"

"Not intentionally." Ishant missed Jaha. She always called him difficult, but she said it with an affectation. A respect, though she could never bring herself to outright compliment him. Their relationship was less . . . complicated.

"How do you plan to approach her?" Lebna interrupted his wistful reverie.

"We have much in common. Second-generation immigrants. Obroni wherever we go . . ."

"Not obroni. Not to me."

"To some."

"You mean Maulana. LISC attempted to provoke a military response, risking an interstellar conflict, under the threat of an Interstellar Alliance coming to scoop up what was left. He wants to roll back LISC's audacity with his own brand of aggression. His comments were calculated."

"No, he meant that shit." Ishant sucked his teeth.

"In his heart, maybe. That's how he was able to sell his words so convincingly. And you're right, if matters were left to him, he'd drag Muungano down that path for real. But he now operates as Camara for the full interests of Muungano, not his own preferences. That overblown bit of rhetoric was meant to give you cover."

"Cover?"

"You've been officially 'exiled.' LISC couldn't just embrace you into their fold. Now you're seen as a scorned asset. You may not be welcomed into the heart of any meaningful inner circle but . . ."

". . . they're hoping to turn me. It's a dangerous game."

"It has its risks."

06

AMACHI ADISA
Mars—The Badlands

Lesson One—Initiation

Your Saqqara's veering trajectory plunges you deeper into the planet's atmosphere. The heat shields buckle, threatening to crack. The turbulence jostles the ship, jolting the images of Fela Buhari about you. The ephemeral projections shift just out of focus into an endless haunting chorus. The red surface of Mars rushes toward you, the planet's gravitational tug dragging you into itself, filling your viewscreen with a panorama of craters and mountains. Your instruments don't respond, a panoply of locked screens and frozen controls. Your insides seize, bracing for the inevitable.

Fela's holovid mouths soundless imprecations before her death.

A yawning chasm opens and swallows your ship whole. The darkness consumes you, seeps into you. An explosion of rock and earth rattles the ship. Its metal hull twists and bends about you, collapsing into a cocoon pinning you. The will of the planet grinds the Saqqara to a halt. Rocks tumble all about in a shower of stone nearly burying your vessel. Your console sputters. Conduits broken and out of place. Power fades in a last desperate gasp until all you have left is the night. And the waiting. And the inevitable . . .

. . . darkness welcomes you, ushering you in and out of consciousness. The curtain of blackness is incomplete. You become aware of movement. Images coalesce under a budding luminescence. Your eyes flutter open and you risk a tentative breath, not certain that you can trust that you are truly still alive as . . .

. . . a series of glowing orbs gently burn to full life. The thin amber light illumines the space to rich, golden-hued shadows. As you stretch underneath the weight of blankets, the muscles in your calves ache, trembling against the threat of tearing with even the slightest movement. Your phase suit fits you snugly. The specialized nanomesh corrects the natural pressure conditions of Mars. The constricting tightness of the space onesie is seemingly the only thing holding you together. Your injuries recede into a distant memory from the deep sleep. You're more well-rested than you've been in a long time. Though your stomach now aches, the thought of food no longer sours your appetite.

Deep within the embrace of the earth, the larger cave systems of Mars serve as early staging areas for the early Mars settlements. Three enormous volcanoes—Arsia Mons, Pavonis Mons, and Ascraeus Mons—surround the area around the Tharsis bulge. Shadows grope across the cavern walls in the wavering light. The tunnel presses close. The room remains pressurized. Its walls climb to a tall, domed ceiling. The rocky alcove has a one-hundred-meter opening above you, a sort of sky roof. The structure forms a rock-enclosed cathedral. A high opening in the cliff wall allows sunlight in; its beams scatter along the basin floor. The stillness of the cavern fills you. The chamber assumes the resonance of a holy space. From the ledge across from you, an owl rotates its head, appraising you with its quizzical glare.

Nehanda sits cross-legged across from your bed, a tentative posture, as if she fears that approaching any closer might shatter you. Images from a holovid flicker in front of her, casting steep shadows across her face. "*The Lord said to Moses and Aaron, "When Pharaoh says to you, 'Perform a miracle,' then say to Aaron, 'Take your staff and throw it down before Pharaoh,' and it will become a snake." So Moses and Aaron went to Pharaoh and did just as the Lord commanded. Aaron threw his staff down in front of Pharaoh and his officials, and it became a snake. Pharaoh then summoned wise men and sorcerers, and the Egyptian magicians also did the same things by their secret arts: Each one threw down his staff and it became a snake. But Aaron's staff swallowed up their staffs. Yet Pharaoh's heart became hard and he would not listen to them, just as the Lord had said.'*"

Seeing you stir, she closes the holovid. The images fading into the gloom. Nehanda hadn't lost her flair for dramatic flourishes. Her high cheekbones give her face a regal quality, her relation to Selamault clear in the lines of her smile and crinkle of her nose. Her large, brown eyes—stern but kind—bore into you. She takes in the totality of who you are in a glance. Your heart lurches within you, a longing you didn't know you had for the person you want to be.

"Hey, Auntie." You want to curl up next to her the way you did when you were younger when she read to you. Her visits to the family kraal were few and far between, each visit cloaked in mystery and secrecy. She's an elder of the night, one of the Iyami Aje. Though many doubt they are anything more than stories elders whisper to one another and the young ones. Which only made her more fascinating to your imagination. "I love what you've done to the place."

"I see rest has restored your . . . wit."

"I didn't know I had woken up into a Sunday school class. I didn't think anyone in the family did the church thing anymore."

Leaning on her walking stick, Nehanda drifts over to a pot suspended over a fire, preparing the morning meal. A protein-synthesizer unit produces synthed meat portions, and she plops them into the pot. Nehanda utilizes limited tech. It occurs to you that there is no Maya present. Either you both are speaking the Muungano mother tongue or something else translates your words. "Exodus 7. Bayard used to recite that passage any time he suspected that we were about. His failure of imagination caused him to misunderstand that we respect all stories. O.E. culture still bathes itself in its dominant religions. It was the air we breathed, so we hid our stories and ways in its greater narrative."

Despite Bayard's efforts, you barely consider yourself spiritual. The Adisas encourage every member of the family to explore any faith that speaks to them. You search for something that would speak to your sabhu. "It just seemed like a bunch of stories."

"Any faith is made up of stories. Ones people choose to shape themselves by. That's their power. What I've always found ironically amusing about that passage is how it clearly talks about our ways—the original science—but so matter-of-factly people gloss over it. All they remember are the plagues and the 'let my people go' business. That's how we do, hide in plain sight."

Still bleary-eyed, you lean against the jagged surface of the cavern wall. Rock jabs your back; its cold, sharp edges focus your awareness. Wrapping your arms around your belly, you stifle a groan.

"Your stomach bothers you?" Nehanda hands you a bowl of soup. Chunks float along the broth.

"This some homemade cure-all?" Many of your mother's people were Maroon. Every sniffle or ache was met with some traditional recipe passed down from generation to generation with medicinal and restorative properties. Yams are a panacea, to hear them tell it.

"No." Nehanda spoons some into her mouth. "It's bean soup. It has extra protein chunks if that makes you feel better."

"It doesn't." You stab at the bobbing bits.

"Bad dreams and an ill stomach. Hm." Nehanda taps her chin with a lone, long finger. "There are appeasements that need to be made to our ancestral mothers."

"This soup ain't exactly appeasing anyone."

"You just used to posh stuff." Nehanda moves to grab the bowl from you, but you snatch it out of her reach.

No matter how long ago you left them to live in Muungano, you hear your family's voices like a dark chorus. Ever ready to remind you of what a disaster you are to the rest of them. Adisa or not. With a heaving sigh, you half rise up off the bed. You falter and manage to catch yourself before you tumble to the floor.

"When have I—or any Adisa—ever made you feel 'less than'?" Nehanda answers your unasked memory. "Sit your narrow behind down and listen, truly listen."

At the timbre of command, you sit your ass down with a quickness. Gathering herself, she rubs the bridge of her nose and sings, her voice low and solemn. *"When the Iyami Aje walk . . ."*

You recall the words to a tuneless song, but you can't recall the next line. "Why did you . . ." You pause to recall her exact wording, knowing how much care she takes when she speaks. Each syllable in its place. "Why did you leave the boundaries of Muungano?"

"The sisters have split up, each to form her own Egbe Society. For every move we make, brethren—who also live in the shadows—match us. Members of the Tigari cult have been dispatched to find us. The last time we gathered was for Xola's homegoing. Few see us unless we want to be seen. Now Wachiru could always see us, but we suspect the oso ways of Xola flow through his veins. Still, I fear the occasion was a foolish indulgence."

At the sound of your father's name, your emi quiets. Grief, unobserved, lingers, evolving into a complicated predator. It constantly stalks you, herding you into spaces, not caring about your duties or dreams; pressing in at unexpected times, your unguarded moments—squeezing your throat, drawing the air out of your lungs, sapping your drive and strength enough to make you want to quit . . . only for it to release you just enough to begin the cycle again.

"The Tigari?" You sit up straighter, a young girl curling up around a campfire to listen to a spooky story.

Nehanda rises to collect her pot. "History has taught us, whenever people seek or achieve independence—freedom—forces rise up in some attempt to reclaim them."

"Crush them, you mean."

"They'd be content to reclaim ashes. The Tigari are ancient enemies. Warrior priests determined to root us out, they see themselves as protecting the community, expunging those who cavort with evil spirits and bring calamity onto their families. They channel a spiritual force known as the 'Tigari,' the enemy of 'evil magic.' Some have psychic powers, can heal, or divine. If they capture someone they even suspect of being one of us, they make them drink . . . special water."

"Special water?"

"Poison. They morph with the times, dispersing throughout all the known territories, ever on the hunt to snuff us out. But no worries."

"You just going to drop that on me and say 'no worries'? Just like that you expect me to just forget that we're being hunted."

"Just like that I expect you to remember that we're always being hunted. By one force or another. To run an antelope to death, all you have to do is scare it into a gallop on a hot day. We all have our paths to walk."

"The . . . Tigari found you."

"They picked up our scent at least. Are aware that we continue to live, move, and breathe." Nehanda whispers like a half-muttered curse.

"Is that why we're hanging out in a cave?" Your sarcasm outruns your mental filter. When you shift position to face her better, the pain suffusing your body reminds you that you are far from whole.

"Of late, many of us have been on . . . walkabouts. None of you are prepared to take over once I'm gone." Nehanda barely arches an eyebrow to acknowledge your snark. A series of reliefs protrude from the cavern wall. When you squint, they almost look like familiar faces. Her hand traces one of the reliefs. Images flitter about you as if a holovid womb encloses the space. Women dance about, their joy radiant and unaffected. Some wear black robes, the red tail feathers of parrots tucked into their hair. Some don white robes, whose fringes have symbols and patterns woven in black. Gold elekes hang about their necks. Some wrap themselves in red robes, their hair wrapped in gold-patterned cloth. "To answer your question, we're 'hanging out in a cave' until you've regained your strength. But that great danger draws near. To buy us some more time, I need to cover your trail."

You sense that trouble may track her down and somehow it's your fault. You cannot stay in this place while she cleans up your mess alone. Steeling yourself as best you can, you stand, ready to follow her. "I'm strong enough to go with you."

✸

Only climbing down its exterior can you appreciate the high rock pillars of Nehanda's home. Her entrance nestles within a half circle of cliffs the way a young girl hides behind her mother. Your fingers scrabble for handholds. You make your way down the mountain's near sheer face. Nehanda offers no aid. She moves with a stiff grace, a heavy wooden mask in place. The carved figures in it peer at you in silent judgment. Your phase suit, designed to stem the effects of weightlessness, pressurizes you and stabilizes your temperature. Your phase suit shields you from the atmosphere; your mask is a translucent barrier—rebreathers built in for emergencies—and the suit creates a protective sheath for a shoe. With no microgels, thrust enhancers, or pronation correction, no nanobot adjustments for cushioning, simply a thin sole that allows your feet to feel the terrain, but not be punctured by it. You essentially run barefoot. A perfect feat of engineering, your feet do their job.

Mars lost its magnetic field three to four billion years ago. The stream of energetic particles from the sun and solar wind stripped away most of its atmosphere and water. Just a few years ago, were you to walk its surface unprotected, exposed saliva, tears—even the liquids wetting the alveoli within your lungs—would boil away. Mars's atmosphere remains much thinner than Earth's. In the Badlands, the farthest, most unterraformed areas of the planet, the temperatures can still plunge to minus 27 degrees Celsius.

After the events dubbed the Rorschach Disaster, Earth abandoned their fledgling lunar outpost in favor of creating "New Earth" on Mars. The Toppers, the wealthiest 1 percent of O.E., poured their resources into developing the new settlement. While the Toppers' "Planet Churner^{TM}"—the technology to stir the core of the planet—was still in development, they installed a magnetic shield, an artificial magnetosphere, to generate a magnetic dipole field. It runs at 18,000 gauss, and the light shields reflect more of the sun's rays. They also seeded Mars with genetically engineered microorganisms that could photosynthesize in low light. They warmed the polar ice caps, and installed CO_2 mines and chlorofluorocarbon-manufacturing stations to seed the atmosphere. Once the planet met their requirements, they moved much of their automated manufacturing there, patting themselves on the back for utilizing their large carbon footprint for benefit beyond simple profit.

Thick clouds mottle the sky. You cross a cold desert, the craggy surface of a dry and cracked lakebed. A gust of wind, like a stranger barging into your conversation, stirs a dust storm in the distance. It vaguely resembles a tornado.

"A bad one is coming." Nehanda gestures to the vista of the Badlands.

Behind her, across a stretch of red sand and jutting craters, stand the several domed cities of the Bronzeville settlement. "What do you see?"

"Desert."

"Walk with me." Nehanda slides through the clearing away from the cave entrance. "I see what once was and what could be, the root and the flower. Time means nothing to me. Space means nothing to me."

The Mars background shimmers, not quite fading but shifting out of focus, the way a holovid womb augmented your reality. Toppers played the game of shifting sovereign political borders, one of land grabs and displacement. Needing their colony to grow and thrive, they conscripted additional service workers. They needed those settlements to succeed without pouring too many resources into them. Declaring eminent domain on a nearby stretch of land, the government announced a security issue and commenced the emergency construction of a communications tower and connected the area to the Mars power grid and water supply. This time a weusi outpost arose around it. The Mars government panicked, fearing that everything the original Mars settlers didn't seize would be claimed by the weusi. Mars ceded the terrain except for anchor points for strategic places. The folks who would become Bronzeville fell victim to the architecture of occupation. Mars adopted ruthless policies of land confiscation, disputing borders between it and Bronzeville. They literally had an entire planet to spread out on, but fixated on the stretch of land occupied by Bronzeville. Bronzeville and First World leaned on each other for mineral and cultural wealth in an unlikely alliance. The Bronzeville residents refused to let the strategic measures of architecture become tactical weaponization of their dispossession. Bronzeville built their own facilities, creating hydrogen, oxygen, and methane; that way they weren't dependent on Mars proper for drinking water, fertilizer, and fuel. They erected a wall they nicknamed "the Fuck-You Fence." Weusi assumed control of the abandoned outpost, developing First World, a thriving metropolis. More and more weusi flocked to it, and soon its population wanted to become their own, independent power. And O.E. wanted their land back. During the Lunar Ukombozi War for control of First World, many weusi on Mars became First World sympathizers. The Bronzeville Rebellion erupted on Mars, working to transform their section of the Mars settlement to parallel First World. That was how Bronzeville started.

Domes fill your vision. The elevated hilltop overlooks a bend in the road. From this summit, fields of strawberries, lettuce, and tomatoes grow along the slopes, cultivated by native farmers.

"Where are we going?" you ask.

"I don't know."

"But you were leading us."

"Until I stopped. Now you have to choose."

"I don't understand."

"That's a good place to start." Nehanda sweeps her hand out and the view of the full barren plain returns. A thin film of red dust coats everything. The haze mirage shimmers against the sand. A filigree of cracks veins the rocks and hardened earth. "Over there we have a relatively smooth path, a lake bottom at one point I'd guess. We can go back the way we came. Over there, high rocky pillars. Or over there we can descend deeper into the range."

"I don't care which way we go." Your mask of nonchalance dodges the weight of the responsibility of choice.

"That's not an option."

"I . . ." The smooth route would be the easiest path forward, but that was never your way. You spy the treacherous switchbacks that descend into the valley. You tick your chin toward it.

Nehanda smiles.

Twirling her walking stick, she abruptly plants it and lifts herself up. Sure-footed as a goat, she leads the descent.

The sun peeks over the horizon. You approach a series of familiar ridges. The basin wall hides a notch just large enough for you to squeeze through. Closing your eyes, you trace the wind currents. Varying your pace, you measure your speed to enjoy the run. You scramble down the cliffside until you catch up to Nehanda. Her staff across her lap, she perches on a rock for a bench, allowing you space to take in the scene.

You don't remember much about the crash. Only fragments of memories, fleeting as dreams upon waking. The large impact crater tells the story of how your Saqqara struck the ground at high velocity. Debris scattered all about, bits of your ship flung all about the ravine. Much of the remaining hull scorched, as if blackened fingers had clutched after it, attempting to drag it underneath the surface. The fire must have been intense.

"You know how to make an entrance. I heard the crackle of you crashing the atmosphere from within my home. By the time I arrived, your ship was in a crazed spiral, twirling about. The storms didn't help. The air would have been clogged with smoke and debris were it not for the storms."

"The storms didn't bother you?" you ask.

"I serve the storm."

You point to the horizon. "Well, you'll soon have another opportunity to serve."

Giant dust devils aren't much different from tornadoes. With lightning. And charged dust particles. They can snake along for miles. The worst storms sweep the entire planet, sometimes for weeks.

"We don't have a lot of time. Once the dust devils have passed, Mars will send out an investigation unit. We have to hide evidence of your crash."

"Hide from a rescue party?"

"A military investigation unit. You have no understanding of how bad things have gotten out here."

"I kept up with some of the briefings."

Earth Firsters found a sympathetic home in some pockets within the Mars government, fomenting disruptions, infiltrating to the point where a complex web of military laws now work their way through the system, aimed at reclaiming Bronzeville. Reports stream about recent settlers, mostly Earth Firsters, resorting to piracy that the Mars proper Toppers government turns a blind eye to.

"Your crash probably put them on alert, but there wasn't much they would do while the storms were out. They throw enough dust into the air to gum up the works. Funkentelechy is also just about worthless in a storm."

"You left O.E. when you were young," you say.

"What makes you say that." Nehanda turns. Her heavy gaze lands on you with the completeness of a mountain's shadow.

"When you speak of O.E. you don't do that thing many born and raised in Muungano do. For them, O.E. existed, no different from a meteorological event. But if you were from there, or spent time there, it settled within you. Filled you with hard edges at the thought of it. Became something you pushed against."

"Who do you push against?" The way she emphasizes "who" and not "what" has a knowing you don't pretend to ignore.

You probe your heart until you latch on to something real. "My aunts. We grew up poor on O.E. Had no money, but no one was actually *poor* poor there. I don't know how to explain it."

"What needs to be said is known." Nehanda recites with the intonation of a well-worn proverb. She pats your hand, a careful, maternal gesture.

You pull away from her touch. "When I was young, my mother died."

Nehanda angles her head carefully at you. "What happened?"

"I don't want to talk about it."

Nehanda doesn't press, only purses her lips, her cue for you to continue. Her patience proves inexorable. Her will inevitable.

"My aunts took me in. They fed me, gave me a place to stay, the way family should. But they . . ." Your voice trails off. Perhaps you aren't ready to talk about that either. *What needs to be said is known.* "I still have trouble wrapping my mind around the fact that Muungano even exists, you know. The first thing I noticed was the language. The way it flows and moves. How it, I don't know, cemented people in who they were."

"What do you think that means?"

Before you can say "I don't know" again like it's the first phrase you learned in Muungano, a rising dust cloud signals an approaching convoy of vehicles working their way toward the summit. Nehanda drags you out of sight. Six lead rovers race ahead like technological hound dogs. Six wheeled legs scamper about, each drawn in when it needs greater speed. Once they find a scene to survey, the legs extend, raising the rover. A series of tools and scanners lower, attached to a communication array. The metal sheets forming its head rotate and fan out, creating a panoramic camera rotating 360 degrees in a perpetual scan. Mapping the area, it relays information back to its masters. A robotic arm sifts soil. You can only imagine what operations its other protrusions perform.

Behind them, four vehicles slow to a halt. RAM units. The pink camouflage pattern is particularly hard to track against Mars's sand, especially at dawn or dusk. Each one raises a missile turret and a laser-cannon mount attached to a redundant ten-millimeter rail gun on its movable pad. A series of weapons systems grafted together to form a gun masquerading as a truck. The chassis sits atop an undercarriage capable of lifting it or sliding the main cabin forward. Designed to be self-sufficient, able to patrol for months with a range of three thousand kilometers, these are long-range reconnaissance units. One of the RAMs halts and its three-member crew disembarks. The other RAMs set up a perimeter and patrol.

Bringing up the rear, a lone figure skids their single-transport land pirogue to a slow stop, skimming the sand like a gentle wave. The figure dismounts and inspects the earth. Then they scan the ridgeline toward you.

Nehanda tenses at their appearance.

"What's the matter? Who is that?" You shrink farther behind the stone ridge, instinctively shielding yourself behind it to avoid the figure's gaze.

"Tigari," Nehanda whispers. "Do not let them distract you from your path or work."

"And what is that?"

"We wield Asè, the life force Olodumare breathes into all living things. It's the power to create, to make things happen. The power to command. So be it."

"Asè," you echo.

"Yet it's also more. It's the power behind any spiritual manifesting. Through the old ways we could call upon the might of the orisha themselves. Which is why we guard their secrets. Magic flows through our veins."

Nehanda lowers into a familiar crouch, moving through the Forms. You pick up the rhythm and cadence. Your body stiff and resisting you at first, your joints soon loosen your muscles enough that you no longer notice the pain. The air about you changes. The current moves with your motions. Swirls of dust fall into synchrony with you, a harmony of shadows and dance.

"You must first learn who you are. Our Egbe Aje, our Egbe Society, is about creating space for each other." Nehanda whispers in your mind, her voice reverberating through your entire being. "It's a gift we give ourselves. 'Women hold up half the sky,' but here, with us, it is the whole universe. We are the starlight which burns brightest in the night."

You close your eyes. Her voice resonates, burrowing deeper inside you, to your hidden places.

"You *are* a multiverse of possibilities. But to achieve your potential, you need to see with new eyes. Perceive life, perceive love, let that define you. Many years ago, I once asked that of my teacher. She told me it was the first step. To remove my old heart—what I thought was love and being—and renew it. Baptize it in the flames to burn away my old wounds and fears. To purify me. To expand even my idea of what love meant. Could mean. Infuse it with her love, how she saw me in all my potential. It was like she opened her chest and revealed her heart to me. It was like a terrible fire. The trials are to open your heart so that you might receive that flame. Open your eyes."

A pebble careens down the side of the cliff, tap-tap-tapping its way down. A preternatural stillness envelops the rest of the cliff. The mountain shudders. Colors radiate from Nehanda. Her smile, radiant. She exudes . . . love. Peace. Understanding. The thunder of a storm rises up all about you in a terrible rumble. Shattering against the mountain. A fissure erupts along the face of the edge. A crack winds along the entire front plate. Like a sheath of bioplastic sliced free, the façade of rock shifts. The rocks tumble forward, collapsing onto the wreckage of your Saqqara. When the dust and rock settle, the landscape returns to its stark vista.

"Can you teach me how to do that? How to be that?"

"That's easier than you think it is to do if the stone already wants to move. It's a learned experience. People learn from . . . by . . . how you live. You cannot give what you do not have, nor speak what you do not know. But one does not get initiated into the Egbe Aje. One can choose to initiate someone as an elder of the night. First you must undertake the process of Ukuthwasa, the rite of initiation. As always, the choice is yours."

The words hang in the air between you, their import a dull weight pressing on your heart. A movement in the corner of your eye draws you out of the moment. A scarab beetle scurries in the sand. Without thinking you bend over and scoop it up. It scrabbles across your fingers. You let its legs dig into your skin, its movements scraping in its desperation to escape and be on its journey. You set it on a nearby rocky cleft. It scuttles off.

"In Kemet, scarabs were a symbol of God. An omen," Nehanda says. "Omens are the Universe speaking to you."

"How do I answer it?"

"By listening. Paying attention to the signs. But let's do that elsewhere." Nehanda stamps her staff and heads down a pathway only she can see.

You know without glancing backward that the Tigari searches for you.

WACHIRU ADISA
The Panopticon

We dreamt of a cave. Shadows bobbed about, ghosts of the past, ephemeral as memory. Rocks tumbled down, trapping us. Pressure squeezed our chest, our lungs. We heaved, struggling for air. We slowly stirred awake, aware of the stifling black bag smothering our face. We thrashed, our arms bound in place. Panic swelled. Our breath came in ragged gasps; we feared each one might be our last. Our heart pounded. We were powerless, waiting for what they might do to us next. The covering dissolved, as did the shackles. The heavy sluggishness of our limbs and the leaden weight of our muscles were the aftereffects of a drug, not deep slumber. We'd lost all sense of time. We had no idea how long we'd been held captive. Or where. Our gray phase suit meant we were off-planet, the gravity different enough to warrant specially designed phase suits. The ghastly pallor of the walls, set against the bright light, reduced our body to a disembodied shade, our head and hands floating about.

Swinging our legs over the side of our bed, rubbing the stiffness from our limbs not being used for a while. A wave of vertigo slapped us as we faced a sea of cells. The reality of where we were radiated up our legs into our arms with a near-physical force. This place, the realization, had its own gravity several times that of O.E. pinning us to our cot.

We'd been sentenced to the Panopticon. The Panopticon was a detention center, a clandestine jail where prisoners were rendered, not charged, merely disappeared. We must have been designated an enemy combatant. No matter how free we were, no matter the peace we enjoy, there were always those who sought to rob us of them. While unconscious, we'd been thoroughly scanned and probed for implants and other tech, the process severing our funkentelechy, our connection to our nanobots. Blood still coursed through our arteries, our muscles still strong, our senses still alert, but at the same time we were met with a grim futility.

Five structures formed a massive chamber. Cells lined them. They enclosed a bubble floating in the center. A silvery sphere, seamless and impenetrable. A physical reminder that the convicts were always watched, in a state of constant vigilance, being seen without truly being seen. All they needed to know was that they were incarcerated. The reality was that everyone was always under constant surveillance anyway, just not overtly reminded of it. On O.E., Overseer supposedly only ever eavesdropped on conversations listening for keywords indicating a possible threat. Maya wasn't so different on Muungano. Those circumstances somehow felt different—the automatic AI systems less obtrusive, less personal—than knowing actual humans studied us.

We paced the totality of our cell, taking a little over five seconds. A heaviness leveled in our bowels. We scanned the blankness of our space, slapping the wall for panels. We curled up in the corner, waiting for the humiliation of relieving ourselves. It happened, but this model of phase suit was designed to be a self-contained unit, not requiring nanobots to process the elimination of waste and scrubbing of skin. This way the cell didn't need to be cluttered with things like a sink or toilet. Or a mirror. Only blank space. An alert bleated from our armband. The phase suit's built-in synthesizer produced a protein bar. Fed, housed, groomed, we were officially held as a noncitizen of O.E.

We examined the edge of our cell. An energy field revealed itself by faint electrical crackle, the borders of the doorway glinting pink when we bumped against it.

"Box 111," a female observer's voice chimed from unseen speakers, though she sounded right in our ear. "Back away from the opening. It will emit a mild shock when pressed against, but you don't want to be leaning against it when they shut it off for yard mingle."

"When is that?" we asked.

Interminable silence met our question.

Such was the journey they imagined for us: from pyramids to plantations to projects to penitentiary. An awful dismay settled in us. We could make out figures framed by the light of their cells, all perched at their openings, watching as if their vista offered them a view other than bleakness.

The Universe had abandoned us.

Days passed in the cell. During the first few, we appreciated the time alone with our thoughts, using the space to meditate. Thinking through the state of Muungano and our place in its greater schemes. We replayed the chaos of VOP Harrison's speech leading to our capture. Over and over, wondering what we could've done differently. We cataloged our many mistakes and paths not taken. We took our turn stationed in the archway watching the effect of the stark isolation on others. And we slept.

We were angry. At this place. At the world that created this place. Angry at the Universe.

At our father's death.

The thought caught us off guard, its unexpected truth slamming into us. That and our powerlessness. We existed in a state of lockdown. Trapped. Isolated within a 3 × 3 × 3 m cube, a fishbowl stacked upon fishbowls. We knew we were a fraud unable to find our true self. Suffering in the discomfort of not knowing ourselves fully. In here we could no longer investigate who was responsible for his murder. In here we no longer had to worry about who we were. In here we didn't have to be other people's idea of who we should be nor live up to their expectations. We didn't have to live in Camara Xola's shadow.

By day four, we paced the perimeter of our cell, passing the time by counting the laps. One hundred laps. Two hundred. Three hundred. The isolation rushed through our system, a drug seeping into our deepest spaces, wrapping us in its tendrils the way weeds eventually cracked regolith.

After a week, the screaming started.

We threw ourselves against the wall, anything to break the monotony, not caring how it looked to those across the bay from us, peering at us for spectacle and entertainment.

Despair and rage funneled into an event horizon whose gravity sucked us in. We left ourselves. Our pops used to speak of his shamanistic episodes. If we were to escape its clutches. We had tried to steel ourselves against the entropy of the Panopticon; the folly of a tree facing a tornado. We could live in multiple spaces, outside of others' imagination. We expanded into our fullness, taking the room to grow. Embracing being still, we listened. We were a mote in space, fluctuations in temperature which constituted presence. The absolute quiet. We floated on the sound waves of the early universe, its primordial heartbeat. Sound waves need a space-time medium to propagate. We were the medium. We wrote to its music, a tether to redefine our new reality . . .

They imprisoned me inside of a cell, attempting to enslave the inside of my soul
For the crime of being born, the crime of being poor, the crime of being my
   skin
      (refuse to waste away there)

Blind to who we are, murdered us with their unseeing eye, he is O.E.
Reduced, made small, etched like a knife wound in our psyche
Put that Negus in a penal sty, the capitalist gleam in their eye
Shipped out, pimped out, left out, producing all of our blues
Told to pull myself up without my own shoes
  (even though your family's bootstraps were made by us)
Learned to move with aggression, too boastful, too proud to sweat
   Looming too large in your imagination, too much of a threat
     Searching for freedom, denied.
     Yearning for justice, you tried.
     Waiting for equality, they lied.
Another cell song, against their swan song, we all in a cage
   (still we rage, still they fear)
Fuck O.E. Fuck LISC. Fuck the caste system they support, for the hell they
   created
Fuck Hakeem. Fuck Dona. Fuck Astra. Fuck Jaha. Fuck Xola, for the
   heaven they dreamed
Fighting to stay human, no matter how long the bid
Can anything good come out of suffering?
   . . . We did.

We had committed about fourteen verses to memory when an alarm bleated. Our box opened. The edges of the archways flared for an instant, and with a mild hum, the field dissipated. Stiff-legged and uncertain, people emerged from their cells—a numbed parade of bodies—and wandered to the platforms beneath the cell blocks. Congregating in familiar clusters, some played table-top games, others pored through holovids, and others gathered to talk. A lady moved about like an island within their sea. She coughed and hacked, causing folks to back away from her. Everyone hard-eyed us, sizing us up, when they passed our box. Probing for weakness. A glint of recognition flickered in a few eyes.

A mzungu man stood up. His face a mélange of illustrations, a pair of dice tattooed on his cheek, highlighting vessels as they rolled. The Illustrated Man walked to the edge of his box, and gave a head nod. Folding his arms, he waited. The light around his bullpen fritzed and he stepped out. A shot caller. Sensing no immediate threat, we stepped out of our bullpen.

"You're new here." The Illustrated Man bade us to follow him, with the tacit excitement of someone about to put on a show.

"You know who I am. What do you want?" we asked.

"First of all, you need to check your tone. Second of all, we're grown men—all friends here—so let's use our calm words. Just so you understand where you are, who you're dealing with, and the precariousness of your situation, I'll help you out. I'm what they call the regulator."

"What do you 'regulate'?"

"Whether you go home or not. Whether in a box or on your feet."

Our eyes cast around the room to see if the Illustrated Man was joking. Everyone averted their eyes and he became a nonentity. A man without any allies in the moment. All attention went back to the Illustrated Man.

The dice image dissolved. Ink traveled under his skin. His tattoos rearranged themselves along his face until they formed goat's horns on his forehead. "I'm here to get you acquainted with the rules."

"And they are?" We were alert, the wisdom of being aware of predators lurking about. It didn't mean our heart pumped water.

"See, you're in the Panopticon, where everyone sees everything at all times. Now I happen to know you and your little operation can get me what I need. If you can't, you are in the way of what I want. When people get in my way, they have to be dealt with. So if I decide to kill you here and now, everyone will see it. Let me assure you, they've seen that show before. I might have to spend a short bid, a few days, a month maybe in solitary. I'll get another decade added to my sentence, for what that's worth. In the end, it's back to business as usual, except you'd be dead."

Our training with Jaha triggered a forgotten reflex. From the moment the muscles in the Illustrated Man's face betrayed his intent, we knew what to expect. He shifted his weight to his back foot in a heavy way that didn't allow him much opportunity to pivot. Overconfident, he trusted too much in his size and his assumption of surprise. He swung a slow, wide punch. Cheers broke out among some prisoners, celebrating any break in boredom. We ducked under the blow, tapping him in his side. Had we punched, he would have doubled over and been vulnerable to our next attack. We sprang in too close for him to throw another punch. We tapped him on the nose, indicating where the next punch would go. With a final lunge, we sidestepped his attack, our ending motion being to tap his throat. Trying to block it, overbalanced, he tumbled to the floor.

Humiliated, the Illustrated Man shuffled off, to the laughter of the gathered audience. A woman approached. Her sideways glances cut people off, allowing her to approach unimpeded. Despite being a head shorter than us, she walked with a determined stride. An earthy odor seeped from her phase suit, like she spent her time wandering a loamy field.

"I see you, Wachiru." Her voice rang with familiarity, the one that had warned us about standing too close to the cell entrance. Her hair was woven in Amasunzu custom, a Bantu hairstyle. Her face was round and soft, her complexion almost as light as ours.

"We see you . . ." We left space for her to add her name.

"Folks call me The Myst." She measured whether we were worth her time in curiosity. "You are an omen."

"Are you a Deacon?"

"I was. Out there. Now, I'm here." Resignation thickened her tone. "I see you are making friends already."

"It's what we do." We smiled, a tentative thing as if the muscles in our face struggled with how to approximate a grin. Already we felt the pangs of this place blocking us off, because whatever easy joke we might have made in banter failed to occur to us. Instead, we settled for the obvious and inane. "Where are you from?"

"Many places," The Myst said.

"Where are we?"

"You are where you will be until they decide otherwise. Say it."

"The Panopticon."

"Here's where they deposit their trash."

"The Panopticon is a distilled microcosm of what's going on . . . out there. Capturing or taking out of play 'troublesome' individuals, unraveling their personhood from their power."

"Dissidents. Agitators. Everyone from ARM extremists and separatists to reunifiers to assimilationists. So you do understand your situation."

"Who was my new . . . benefactor?"

"The regulator controls knives, weapons, communication. Gang movement."

"So he's a boss."

"He thinks he is."

"What do you do?"

"I control access."

"Do you work for him?"

"I work for myself. I'm free, first and foremost. I do things by my choice." The Myst flagged down a young Negus who glided along the edge of folks, close enough to observe though, from his chagrined grimace, not wanting to be noticed. "I'm welcoming the new brother."

"I know you." Holding our arm out for a clasp, we struggled to place where we had encountered him before. All at once, we remembered. Kamau. We watched Jaha break up a fight between him and another back at the Dreaming City. It already felt like a lifetime ago.

"I don't think so." Kamau did not return our grasp, sliding past us, but not before cutting his eyes skyward.

A small, mirrored sphere—a tiny replica of the Panopticon's central sphere—floated by. It buzzed close enough to be noticed, coming within centimeters of our face before flying off. The drone arced toward the central sphere, joining with others in a returning swarm.

"They could as easily have had nanobot drones for observation," we said.

"They do," The Myst said.

We nodded with slow realization. "But they also needed the convicts to *know* they were being watched."

"And nanobots don't have their considerable array of disciplinary measures built into them." The Myst's breath hitched.

An air shuttle descended. A walkway extended from the central sphere, allowing the ship to dock.

"What's that? The guards' shift change?" we asked.

"None but convicts live inside the Panopticon." The Myst nodded over her shoulder. "Remember the mzungu you made friends with. On the side, he's also a 'free trader,' a designated Driver, whose job is to ensure that everyone performs the work assigned to their group."

"What's that work?"

"Taskmaster. Each prisoner has to take a turn on overwatch. Being watched within the sphere to make sure we report on each other."

"Consigning us to do our oppressors' work for them. Ensuring there would be no trust between convicts."

"We got to go. We on the clock." Kamau-not-Kamau looped past again, chancing a comment to The Myst.

"We appreciate you, Wachiru," she said.

"We appreciate you." We watched them disappear into the thickest part of the assembled convicts.

The Panopticon was like a quarantined kraal that had a pandemic sweeping through it. Each citizen separated or isolated. With guards in place to make sure no one left their home, for their own safety. Each moment of their day regulated by routine. It was a machine created to drill into us that our lives were not our own. It shaped our identity to internalize surveillance; made coercion part of our everyday thoughts. Policing ourselves so that our oppressors' disciplinary power lived within us. All so that O.E. could claim that it was a humanitarian facility. Yet so much of the Panopticon remained a mystery. We needed to learn the lay of the land.

The common area extended across the basin underneath the cells. Three tiers of cells rose as part of the five structures surrounding the sphere. There were some communal facilities—shower bay, cafeteria—but most of life within the Panopticon was designed for extended isolation. An old man hobbled about, hovering beneath a suspended platform. He cocked his head to listen to the shadows. He occasionally cradled an unseen baby, glancing over his shoulder on the lookout for any who might snatch it from him. A man broken by dead dreams and hollow promises.

"What's your name?" we asked.

"The forgotten. The untouchable." He scratched at himself. An addict. Scars ran along his jawline, shaping his face to appear like a marionette. Addiction was an adaptation to circumstances. An attempt at control, a dopamine rush to aid the muddle through life. Drugs. Holovids. Shopping. Pyr ball. Consumption. Hate. Anger. Love. There were so many things one could become addicted to. All coming down to the same thing: chasing that next high, getting that next bump, to help hold on for another day. Sometimes just another hour. "August Black."

"I know that name." He should be revered. Instead, he was buried here like the government's secret shame. "You were Astra Black's uncle."

"That was a different life. I'm fiending for some chiba. You holding?"

"No, I can't afford to have my senses dulled," we said.

"Dulling the senses is the point. It's how I quiet the voices so that the Universe can talk to me." August scrubbed his hands, scratching at itches his mind created. He shifted from foot to foot, anxious and attempting to warm himself. "They already took hope from us."

People have always told us their stories. Maybe we just had one of those faces. One that refrained from judgment, reflected the Universe and saw people not just for who they were—or how the world wanted to label them—but in their full humanity, who they could be. "Hope is all we have. Believe in your-self. In your community. In . . . the Universe."

"They are a lie."

"*We* are a truth. What's your skill set? What's something you're such an expert in, you could teach it?"

"I . . . don't know. I can do a lot of things. Are you trying to confuse me?"

"Nah, bro. I was wanting to know who I was dealing with. We have noth-ing but time. Might as well use some of it to dream about possibilities. For you and for us."

Half-hidden by the shadows, we commenced the routine of the Forms. Body, mind, and spirit linked, moving through the postures of the Niyabinghi combat system. The Forms (what we could remember of them from Jaha's teach-ing), though a peaceful exercise, were still martial arts, encoded with death. The practice, however, reminded us of our journey. Colonization taught that the native was no longer human. Among its lessons, the systems drove them to forget—even lose—their humanity. They feared that the natives stood ready to reclaim the place of the colonizer. Those conscious natives were kept under strict surveillance. They not only spoke, but understood the language of colo-nialism, the language of violence. After a few minutes studying us, the old man joined in. Out the corner of our eye, we spied Kamau watching us.

Violence was a way of being, pervading the system at every level until it in-fected every aspect of a person's very consciousness. Too many natives allowed themselves to be spun in circles of overcorrection, becoming reactionary, delv-ing into affectations, and pursuing romanticized ideas of Alkebulan. Still col-onized, thus never quite achieving true solidarity. Never quite making sure the material conditions of the people were met: clothed, fed, cared about. It was those of higher consciousness working with the masses that the upper caste feared.

The Illustrated Man lumbered toward us again. His face grave, just short of ashen. His ink crawled across his skin until it formed a crosshairs with his image of a stereotypical Muungano citizen in its sights. "It's your turn to report for duty."

"I don't think so," we said.

"Everyone has to serve a shift. You're new, so you're up."

"Is this more of you introducing me to the rules?"

"Yes." His emi seemed conflicted, undercut by a tenor of fear. Or regret. "But I won't lay a hand on you."

Glancing upward, we saw three spheres approaching us. We nodded and followed.

We stopped at the air shuttle docking station. Several convicts lumbered out in a somnambulant shuffle, not meeting any of our eyes. We gripped the handrail of the air shuttle. It lurched, all ten of us steadying ourselves as it rose to the height of the second tier of cells before docking with the sphere. When the shuttle had locked into place, an entrance resolved. The inside of the sphere was larger than we would have imagined. We'd have suspected the use of tesseract folds, but that seemed more of an overcommitment of technological and financial resources than the caste system would have been willing to invest. All eyes turned to us.

"Have a seat," the Illustrated Man said.

"Where will you be?"

The Illustrated Man took an empty chair. It secured him into place like a vest-shaped version of the cell's energy field. With him in place, we sat down a few spots from him. Convicts crowded about before returning to their viewscreens with mild interest.

"What are we supposed to do?" we asked.

"Watch. Listen. Report." The Illustrated Man gestured about. "Anything you know to report. And they'll know if you don't."

"Who watches the watchmen?" we asked.

"The same brand of watchers."

Convicts empowered to punish convicts for not reporting convicts. All in rotating shifts of self-punishment. A steady hum thrummed from all about us. Our viewscreen landed on the old man, suspecting the spheres or nanobots keyed our viewing station to those with in our social network. Another way to break down any trust between detainees, because no one could risk another reporting on them. Any relationship became a huge leap of faith, one going against one's sense of self-preservation. The old man ducked under the stairs. Though to a casual observer it might have looked like he whispered to shadows cradling an imaginary infant, this was different. More purposely furtive. He'd found his drugs somehow. We tried to adjust the camera, turn from him to any corner of innocuous banter. To will it away to not be party to his entrapment, nor witness any more before we were noticed. His criminal data stream began scrolling at his workstation.

August Black
Age: 117
Height: 1.727 m
Weight: 77.111 kg
Nativity: Indiana
Complexion: ocher
Hair: white
Eyes: brown
Birthmark/scars/identifying marks: none
Sentenced from Indianapolis, Indiana
Term: n/a
Crime: vagrancy

The category of report lined up alongside them. Suspicious assembly. Contraband. Violence. Abuse. The list went on, but we highlighted none of them. An electric charge jolted us. We jumped, held fast by the energy restraints.

"You might as well report whatever you saw," the Illustrated Man sneered. "Or don't. The punishment will only get worse."

We settled back into our seat. The camera leered, tempting us to report the old man. We didn't. Another blast shocked us. The pain caused our fingers to dig into the handrests. The inside of our skull burned like a thousand flaming snakes whipped about. Our heart pounded, without rhythm to set a song to.

But we would not make any appraisal on behalf of the colonizer.

The camera veered. It locked on to Kamau but hovered at a discreet distance. Kamau went about his business, his head on a swivel, noting the other convicts who might be watching him. The reality of steady observation was that eventually one became oblivious to constant gaze. Sidling up to The Myst, he turned away as if in conversation with someone else, one hand over his lips. His free hand locked and contorted, obviously signing something. A mild buzz hit us, little more than the shock of static electricity, but enough to alert us to report what we observed. We stared at the console, but their holovid files popped up.

Kamau [government name: Dominic Mason]
Age: 23
Height: 1.88 m
Weight: 86.183 kg

Nativity: Indiana

Complexion: sepia

Hair: black

Eyes: brown

Birthmark/scars/identifying marks: keloid scar along outside right thigh

Sentenced from Indianapolis, Indiana

Term: n/a

Crime: lèse majesté

The Myst [government name: Matuomi Rose]

Age: 27

Height: 1.6 m

Weight: 49.442 kg

Nativity: Indiana

Complexion: tawny

Hair: black

Eyes: brown

Birthmark/scars/identifying marks: Gye W'ani tattoo on left shoulder

Sentenced from Indianapolis, Indiana

Term: n/a

Crime: seditious activity

We scrolled through the categories of possible tags for their report. Back and forth, up and down, not deciding on any of them. Another charge rippled through us. The steadier current of electricity increased, sending the sensation of fire ants scurrying up and down our legs. We tried to speak, but our jaw clenched, releasing only a terrified whisper. Kamau moved past a convict, taking the attention of the drone with him. They shook hands. A kite passed between them. Taking a more circuitous route, Kamau marched back to The Myst. She covered her mouth. They signed between each other. This officially qualified as suspicious assembly. Their relationship was obviously under scrutiny. The Panopticon's algorithmic AI already created and analyzed their web of relationships. Even if we chose to report their behavior, we'd be adding nothing the system didn't already know. Only documenting what they already confirmed.

A thin line of perspiration tricked down our forehead.

Positioning himself between her and any possible eyes, Kamau passed The

Myst the kite. She read it and popped it in her mouth. The Myst slipped into the shadows and disappeared. The viewscreen switched scanning modes. Infrared, radiological, unable to penetrate the shadows. A few minutes later, The Myst emerged.

The hum grew louder. The console cycled up in an apathetic surge. Our hands hovered above the controls, scrolling through the options to catalog their activities. Our legs pistoned up and down, caught in their own strange rhythm. Up and down, the short distance of an invisible chain. The electrical charge started low and dull, a vague reverberation rushing through and filling us. Its measure increased exponentially. Wanting to both scream and vomit, we issued a low half moan—a thick, clotted sound—that caught in our throat.

We slammed back in the chair. The pain constricted our muscles. We clamped the armrest. The prisoners on either side of us leaned away, afraid the surge might leap to them next. The pain ebbed; we slumped forward. The next burst slammed into us with the force of a maglev train. When the wave lagged again, our fingers and toes still jittered with phantom shocks flexing randomly in anticipated response. Our eyes rolled back; we were unable to take much more. Tempted to touch a panel, any report just to make the pain end, but our fingernails dug into the chair arm instead. The hum chortled again. Thin wisps of smoke rose from our phase suit. The nerves in our elbow tingled in a feedback loop of pain. We wanted a saw, any blade, to sever any limb that throbbed in the electric dance. The pain wave swelled in such intensity, our world flitted to black.

Only for a few minutes.

We became aware that someone lifted us, strapping us down to some cart like a bundle of potatoes. Casually deposited onto the air shuttle. We stirred only as it docked at the platform level. Convicts gathered around, crowding us, but we swiped our arm. They backed away, allowing us plenty of room to pass. Our phase suit smoldered. Through the haze of our vision, we locked eyes with The Myst. Reading our emi, she upticked her chin in our direction and disappeared. We staggered a few steps under our own weight. August ran up to us. Tucking himself under our shoulder, he wrapped our arm around him to steady us. The gathered convicts lost interest in us. We made it to his nook. Our legs wobbled, uncertain, but we stood in faith. The old man took a step backward, tentative, ready to jump in if we faltered. We took a few breaths to center ourselves, to allow the pain to recede enough for us to move on our own. Pain was our most dependable companion now. We had to learn how to live with it and push through. Steadying ourselves against the stairwell, we assumed our position and started to work through the Forms.

August Black joined in.

After a few minutes, so did Kamau.

PAKI HARGES
The *Cypher*—Beyond the Orun Gate

"What are we looking at?" Stacia stepped closer as if not trusting her eyes. "As I understood it, supervoids are just the absence of superclusters of galaxies. These readings . . . it's like they're trying to describe some sort of galaxy-sized black hole."

"Astrocartography is still trying to ascertain its exact nature. The remains of a star. Or a series of stars." Paki hated not sounding sure, almost as much as he loved a mystery that stirred his curiosity. Paki's viewscreen remained black. Not blank as if someone had failed to activate it, but displaying a deep, impenetrable darkness. The kind that peered back into him the more he stared at it. "The readings are . . . conflicting. Like a series of collapsed stellar masses and implosions of compressed baryonic matter. Photons converting kinetic energy to gravitational potential on their way to its center, moving away from the denser surrounding areas. Despite the high levels of background gamma radiation detected, there's low spatial density. Less . . . everything."

"Are we in danger?"

"Shields are holding steady. We have navigational control." Anousheh Waziri had assured from the helm. New to the duty station, another relational and operational adjustment made due to so many crew members abandoning the ship prior to crossing the Orun Gate. Her bright eyes ever alert, her nose had an odd hook to it as if it had been broken and not set correctly, adding to her face's character. He'd watched her excel in her studies, her mind a steady sponge of ancient lore, but her gift set was piloting. Whenever the conversation drifted toward exploration, her voice turned faraway, in either prayer or incantation, muttering *"navigating the stars."*

Paki's hands danced in the air, drawing up readings and moving about the displays, piecing together the jigsaw puzzle of data midair. Though grumbling was not in his nature, he didn't do change well. He navigated the world as weusi first, bringing every bit of what that meant to him wherever he went. He carried his culture in any space he found himself in. Muungano had grown in its reach and influence, his way of doing things, while not obsolete, definitely in reevaluation. Being assigned to the *Cypher* left him feeling put out to pasture. Sidelined by way of facilitating the Learning Tree. Irrelevant.

"Paki, I know that look," Stacia said. "Like you're about to dive into something."

"I'm just curious, Captain." His eyes softened, no longer locked on to anyone in particular, his mind calculating how best to move the next piece of his work forward. A gaze that all but terrified whoever was in his way when he reached his conclusions.

"Can we be curious from a safe distance?"

"Now that we're aware of it, I can compensate for it. Sending parameters to helm now."

"I can keep us in place and far away from its . . . would we even call it an event horizon?" Anousheh asked.

"Close enough for now," Paki said.

"All right, maintain our distance. Get your findings, Paki. I'll be in my quarters."

"I'll set astrocartography to . . ." Paki's voice trailed off as the captain turned her back to him to take her leave. He mumbled, "No, don't worry, I'll see to it."

Running his fingers through the scraggily knots he called a beard, he sent some directives to astrocartography with a note to send all data to his station. He rotated his head to crack the kinks out of his neck. Stacia was a good captain. Better than she realized, when she wasn't caught up in her personal scripts of needing to prove herself; or in the throes of the desperation of not wanting to fail; or caught up in her ambitions of wanting to make a name for herself. Always ready to justify her decisions or wanting the approval of folks while being determined to do things her way. Such was the mental chaos of the young, which ostensibly was why he'd been assigned as her facilitator, the person who enacted the captain's visions. Some days he performed more of the boots-on-the-ground captaining than her and the lack of recognition chafed. He had a vision for how the *Cypher* could, and perhaps now should, run. He, too, had ambitions. His dark thoughts coalesced into a storm, the noise in his head rising like a static charge ready for release.

"Do you have the bridge?" Paki asked.

"Yes." Anousheh was young, but in his experience, the young tended to rise to the occasion when entrusted with real responsibility. Sure, she'd feel its weight, but the reality was that the *Cypher* was functioning at 80 percent and she only had to hold their position. She'd be fine and he was only a commlink away. It was the basis of the Learning Tree system of education. The elders were never going to let the young crash the mothership.

He headed toward the captain's quarters, and the door opened without him needing to break stride. "We can't keep going like this, Captain."

"I almost had a whole minute to myself." Her son's medical records and latest scan results floated about her. A nanovirus nestled a silicon base pair within its nucleus, like there was a programmable component to it. "What's the problem?"

"This is my entire point in one snapshot: you are responsible for every life on this vessel, not just Bekele's."

"I'm aware of that. So aware of it, in fact, that I didn't need reminding." Stacia closed the displays to level her eyes at him. No one wanted to be informed of even a hint of a dereliction in their duties. Especially when, truth be told, she struggled to navigate the crosscurrents of her personal and professional waters.

"Be that as it may, you need to choose whether you're going to be a mother or a captain. If you are unable to fulfill your duties, you will be relieved of command. For your good as well as that of the crew."

"And who would relieve me and lead?" The air between them bristled. According to her files, from the age of nine years old she knew she wanted to be a captain. Her emi reacted to a threat, her sabhu on high alert, ready for combat. Everything about her interpreted things through the lens of a fight. "You?"

Paki approached without heat, but not backing down. "If need be. It's not like I haven't been running things for a while now."

"What did you just say to me?" The fierceness of her tone caused him to rethink his strategy, but he couldn't retreat now.

The intricacies of social interactions only had clarity for him when he taught his students or had a clear agenda to move his duties forward. She reared at him, his words more a sucker punch than helpful criticism. The matter-of-fact nature of his boldness caught her off guard. He simply wanted to give the verbal equivalent of a slap in the face. He had her full attention. Right now he operated out of a vague concern for her and the ship. He had no direction regarding what he should do about that, relying on his intuition to guide him. He decided to double down and see where the conversation took him.

"I only wanted to express the reality of how things have been functioning."

"You need to get the fuck out my face with this bullshit, Paki."

"I . . . can't. The ship needs their captain. They're worried. They need you. The full you. Whatever it is you're indulging, we can't afford right now."

"Indulging? My son . . ."

"So you choose being a mother?" Paki crossed his arms.

"Fuck. You."

"There's nothing wrong with that. No one will ever hold that against you. We all stood by you and your choice to save your family. But we, as a crew, have to figure out a way forward. As the *Cypher* family."

"I'm still the captain of this ship. Considering the circumstances we now find ourselves in, that also makes me its functional Camara. The heaviness of that reality was what I was 'indulging.'" A born empiricist, Stacia questioned everything, taking in information and constantly processing what she knew. She valued order. She needed order. Pieces always had to fit together to preserve her sense of structure. Stacia scooted from behind her desk, allowing her time to calm down a measure to continue her conversation with him. The business of the ship came before her feelings toward her crew, even the pains-in-the-ass. "Let me run something by you."

"What is it?" Paki seemed relieved for the reprieve.

"I want your objective opinion on an interaction." Stacia leaned against her desk. "Maya, play back our conversation from earlier today. About our current location in relation to yourself in Muungano."

<No record exists.>

"What?" Stacia snapped.

<No record exists.>

"Perhaps another glitch . . . ," Paki started. Most times, he shunted the idea of Maya out of his head, only calling upon the AI when he absolutely had to. Setting it to "silent" unless absolutely necessary. Though it was a member of their community, the idea of a member as an omnipresent, ever-eavesdropping crew member never sat right with him.

Stacia held up her finger. "That was a captain's log. Any redaction would require a command deletion. Only the R can authorize that."

"Maulana?" Paki clasped his hands behind him and paced. "We may have become a matter of state security."

"An embarrassment, you mean."

"But to cut us off? Something major must be going on."

"Either way, we're officially on our own."

"Back where we started."

"We have to find a cure. And we have to get home." Stacia's words weren't a mission statement or a mantra of hope. They were an appeal. A rallying cry for the crew to justify the choices they made. She made.

"My choice of words . . ." Paki wasn't one for apologies. Even the attempt at one was painful to watch.

Stacia cut him off with a wave of her hand. "I assume you've taken the temperature of the crew. How is everyone? Really?"

"Strained. Tested. They are still Muungano. Grateful for one another and the opportunity to join with the Universe in learning about itself." The *Cypher* still had all they needed to continue in the Muungano way. They shared the same space, engaged in cooperative living, and, tenuous as it might be, there was a sense of shared leadership, or at least making room for everyone to have a voice. Valuing people and personhood while building and maintaining trust in one another, they continued to lean on one another's strengths. The container that held the Muungano ideals in a crucible of action. "They still wrestle with getting their minds around the . . . enormity of what they've committed to."

"Is it the treason? Wormhole? Exile?"

"Yes." Paki turned on his heel. "Some are struggling more than others."

"What about you?"

"I serve the best interests of the *Cypher.*"

"So you wouldn't have done things different?"

"I didn't say all that. But I'm here." Paki avoided her eyes. He drummed his fingers along her desk.

"For now."

"Where else would we go? We are drawn together by the gravity well of our options." Straying over to the observation port, he watched servomechs scurry along the surface of the *Cypher* to carry out repairs. Flashes of blue light like a low-lying lightning storm skimmed its skin.

"What do you suggest?"

"We have to accept that we may never get home again. We need to remember that none of us are alone on this journey. We have each other. Friends. Family. We need to start where we are with what we have. The Muungano way."

"The Muungano way," Stacia echoed in a tone of casting a spell of remembrance.

"This is our life now."

"I didn't expect such pessimism from you."

"We can still love something, long for its return, and let it go all at the same time."

Stacia took a step toward him before hesitating. "Where do we start?"

"By being grateful for each other and what we still have. I suggest holding a Homowo."

"A Day of Gratitude?"

"We could use it."

"Hmm." Stacia's face ran through the contortions of warming to the idea. If his cynical, less-than-charitable self had to guess, she ran through the calculations of the ratio of how much credit she'd receive versus how much work she'd have to actually do. "I like it. I'll announce it, but afterward I'd like you to organize key personnel to do the actual ritual together. Kenya. You. Dina. Along with my family."

"Asè." Paki half bowed before backing toward the door.

"I appreciate you." Stacia's words trailed after him. Before he reached out to the department heads, he had one more stop to make, and better to ask forgiveness than permission.

✳

Stellar collisions did not involve the violence one might imagine. The universe had dueling gravitational effects. On a small scale, things were collapsing. On a large scale, things were expanding. In the visible spectrum, energetic hydrogen molecules ejected at supersonic speeds from baby stars. With a stellar nursery of gas and dark matter, stars ending up in the grip of spatial curvature, leading to formation of galaxies. Meeting the right astrophysical conditions, an object made entirely out of neutrons could form. The length around a neutron star was about the length of Indianapolis. Knowing the distance to one, he could extrapolate how far away they were. Even just knowing the brightness of one. Paki needed more information. When he needed information—and since he hated working through middle management or receiving secondhand data—he went straight to the source. And there was a source he hadn't yet questioned. Zenith. Though before long, he was caught up in the gravitational well of an argument. About Muungano philosophy involving . . .

". . . a scarcity mind-set is a victim's mind-set. 'I don't have the resources therefore I can't get it done' is the same mental programming that believes 'the dominant caste prevents us from' or 'we can't do better than our oppressors.' Again, history has shown us that's not true." Paki couldn't understand why

Zenith was allowed any measure of freedom, outside of diplomatic immunity keeping them from jettisoning him into the vacuum of space. The artificial nature of the nanovirus troubled him. As did the uncertainty of Zenith's role within O.E.

And he could save that "move in each other's best interest" bullshit for someone else.

"Would you like some tea?" Zenith raised his cup. His performative gentility had the constant air of quiet menace.

"Your faux civility is wasted on me."

"I've found that the true test of civility is how we handle being stuck in traffic." Zenith swirled his spoon in his cup. "It's also a good test for when you're dating. The temperament your prospective partner has when they've been cut off is the same one you'll face in an argument."

"You play too much."

"We used to have diplomatic relations, now we have none. We have to learn to talk to each other again."

"We all make mistakes. Few have the courage to own up to it. The wazungu have the responsibility to take the lead in demonstrating that trust?"

"I've accepted all my faults. So you'll just have to take me as I am," Zenith said.

"No need to change or grow?"

"It's my emotional compromise with myself."

"You pay lip service to who we are, but lip service is worse when your breath stinks. I don't know why the captain keeps you around."

"Better the devil you know, as they say."

"That's one way to pronounce 'traitors.' We don't deal with traitors well."

"Out the old air lock, eh? That never struck me as very Muungano-ish."

"Hondo's still alive, right? There's a balance that the universe restores when things get out of alignment. Asè." This conversation was going nowhere. Any useful interrogation kept the subject talking. Unfortunately, Zenith loved to talk. Paki needed a different tack if he was going to get anything useful out of him. Paki understood story on a primal, almost spiritual, level; priding himself on his ability to tease out its nuances with a well-framed question. Or, his preferred favorite hammer, a direct one. "Do you fear that we'll keep expanding—planet after planet, system after system—because that's what you would do?"

"Exactly."

"The lesson, the real fear, is how hard it is to unlearn the master's way of ruling."

"I see someone's all in a 'Tell the truth and shame the devil' sort of mood. This 'up with Muungano' talk was inspiring and all—your chest nicely puffed out—now, tell me, what is it *you* want?"

"I'm trying to figure out who you are and what hold you have on the captain."

"I have no hold. I simply offer my services." Zenith raised his cup in silent toast.

"As what?"

"A . . . consultant."

"Of what?"

"Information. Information that is only useful when we are in the right location. Until then, I am just a humble student observing the Muungano philosophy lived out, up close and personal. In all of its . . . intricacies."

Paki heard the word *hypocrisy* hinted at.

"Now let me ask you something: Who is next in your chain of command should Stacia be seen as unfit for duty?"

"I'm always suspicious when someone outside of our community wants to talk about succession."

"By that bit of circumspection, I'm guessing that someone is you. You'd be in the position to run things your way. To cast a vision of Muungano that's . . . purer."

Not wanting to take his eyes from the man, Paki backed away from him. There it was, the playbook revealed. Division. A standard tactic from someone held prisoner. Sow seeds of dissent and exploit the fractures to find an opening to escape. "We're done here."

"Come back when you have the information I need to be useful to you."

✳

The *Cypher*'s engine core was a thing of intricate beauty. A cave of perfectly aligned crystals, each color pulsing to its own rhythm synchronized. Paki sometimes waited in the isocrawls, staring at them for hours attempting to decipher any pattern to their matrix. The orchestra left chairs scattered about. The participants from the command performance basically played and dashed, gathering their instruments before rushing to their next duty. The crew was in survival mode: running from task to task, their schedules filled with work to keep them from thinking about the reality of their situation. Cross-legged on the floor, Nadina stared at a junction panel. Paki couldn't decipher the sets of flickering lights, but they held her rapt concentration. She represented a special challenge to Paki. Schooled in LISC centers, not steeped in the Muungano ways, she was as alien to him as the region of space where the crew now found themselves. O.E. ways so ingrained in her, she needed help to slough off old skin. Nadina and her partner, Hondo Jones, came up in the LISC Corps together. A volunteer civil organization, O.E.'s version of Muungano's Thmei Academy, the Corps steered committed members toward public service. Their stated goal of "meeting the critical needs in the community" echoed Muungano's philosophy. The pair eventually even interned at the Dreaming City together and were lucky enough to both be stationed on the *Cypher*. In retrospect, Paki wondered how much of that good fortune had been engineered. Nadina wanted room to explore her cultural heritage; Hondo, though mzungu, was eager to soak up cultural practices, presumably to be a better partner to her and support her journey. To remain by her side. No amount of culture could separate young love.

Captain Stacia could, though. Nadina withdrew a spanner, the instrument tucked in her hair as if it doubled as a clip. She'd been promoted to the ship's chief engineer once Hondo was revealed to be an agent of the "Earth First" movement, abandoning the *Cypher* by way of mutiny. Making a few adjustments, she cocked her head, not believing her readings. She slammed her fist into the wall.

Paki pretended to clear his throat.

"I see you." Responding by rote, Nadina scrambled to her feet.

"I see you. Is everything all right?"

"I'm . . . No." Nadina tucked the spanner away, appearing just preoccupied enough to conveniently avoid his eyes.

"Thank you for being honest with me. A problem shared is a problem halved." Not knowing what to do with his hands—it felt like a moment that should require a reassuring pat on the shoulder, but that gesture seemed too forward—he tucked them into his pockets. "A lot has happened in a short period of time. Enough to stress any of us. You haven't been given a lot of space to process."

"I process by working."

"Alone?"

"That's how I prefer it."

"Yet you used to work alongside Hondo." It wasn't that Paki was insensitive, he believed in cutting to the heart of the matter. Anything else enabled a lot of conversational game-playing, wasting everyone's time.

"It's unfair." Nadina studied her hands.

"What was? His betrayal or his . . . excommunication?" It was an odd choice of words, yet to Paki's ear it felt somehow right. There was a sacrosanctity to being a crew member, and Hondo and his ilk trampled over that.

"All of it. How it went down. The final result was . . . as it should have been, but . . ." Her words trailed off as she, too, searched her heart for the right wording.

Paki finished, ". . . the process ran too quickly. We didn't have a chance to hear his story."

"Yeah." Nadina chanced meeting his eyes, sensing understanding. She had become untethered. Her anchor points—Hondo, their relationship, their future, all of the personal things that defined so much of who she believed she was—had been stripped from her. Leaving her cast adrift in space, filled with unspoken questions that would never have answers. "I didn't have a chance to say goodbye."

"His choices."

"I know."

"But it doesn't change you feeling like something was stolen from you."

"Yeah." A light filled her eyes. He'd put words to something she hadn't quite named.

Paki was on a roll. He taught the principles of community, the philosophies of connection, but the practice was always difficult for him when it was reduced to one-on-one interactions. He always seemed to stumble, cut people off, or chase them away. His instincts told him to count the win and end the conversation, but he decided to push on.

"When you feel lost, when you feel . . . you may be tempted to hide yourself from others, even from yourself. But you need to hold on to that brave space within you, the one that needs to remind the world of who you are and what you can do. We need that Nadina."

"Paki, if I may say"—she angled her head toward him with the curious scrutinizing of someone encountering a stranger—"you seem . . . lighter? Less intense."

"That's what's needed now."

"How are you handling this so well?"

"I . . . have a deep understanding of loss. One of its lessons being that it is survivable."

A silence settled between them, neither awkward nor amiable. As good as he was at listening, as good as he was at teaching—at being a balm to a person's soul, knitting together the broken and lost pieces within them, giving them something to ground the essence of who they were in order to rebuild themselves—healing from loss was its own journey.

"If I may say, you seem to be holding on to some residual rage for the captain," Paki said finally.

"The way the sun casts residual light."

"It has to be dealt with if we're to function as a crew."

"She has to learn to live with the consequences of her actions, too."

"You're right. We just need to make sure to find a way to air things out rather than let the wound fester any further if we're going to move forward."

"You don't mean . . ."

"Carry on, Nadina. You'll be hearing from me soon." Waving his hand to cut her off, Paki ambled off down the hallway. "I appreciate you."

*

In his diagnosis, the issue was quickly becoming how best to maintain the Muungano culture when the branch that was the *Cypher* was no longer attached to the roots of it. Not that he was one for mythicist ways, but the church Bayard presented was an institution that had managed to sustain itself for millennia. Readings, rituals, liturgy, all the various elements that drew people back to the uniting story that defined their identity and mission. The *Cypher* needed to remind themselves that they were all still connected to something greater than themselves. Each other. Muungano. The Universe.

The Green Zone on Deck 3 bisected the *Cypher;* their internal Eden would be the myth he spun about it. One the crew built and cultivated. The key part of the story was that *they* created this garden as they reinvented themselves. The story of a people who—through perseverance, resistance, and hope—carved out a space for themselves that recognized that their humanity could be fully expressed alongside, and as a part of, nature. Animals grazed in peace without fear. Plants scrubbed the air. The landscape designed and curated for maximum color displays against a lush, emerald backdrop. Children romped in parks; streams meandered into the occasional shaded pond.

The only overarching unseen intelligence wasn't the mythicists' collective imagination, but an AI tasked with monitoring the delicate ecosystem. Adjusting the essential bacterial growths as necessary. Temperature. Light. Still, even the idea of that technological spirit in the sky unsettled him. It wasn't that Paki didn't trust Maya, but he thought of Maya in terms of "it" rather than "they" as many did, because it was a tool not a person. To lose sight of that was to diminish who Muungano members were as people.

Ducking under an overhanging rock, Paki made his way to one of the iso-crawls backstopping the Green Zone. The air had a cloying thickness to it. Plants climbed along an entranceway. Tiny birds sipped out of bright red or yellow flowers. Their wings produced a delicate hum echoing throughout the alcove.

Bekele worked on a solar panel painted to look like another piece of art-work in the garden. Paki ran his hand along the wall before Bekele could warn him. A thick sheen of algae enveloped his hand. He flicked much of it off, but knew his hand would smell like a sea bottom for the rest of the day.

"I didn't need to see that," Bekele said. "It's like moldy pudding stuffed into a test tube."

"Quite." Paki dipped his hand through the still waters of the pond. "I've been checking your work with the terraforming chambers. Impressive."

"Thank you." Bekele was one of the few students Paki didn't intuitively know how to handle. Partly because he was the captain's son. While never asking for special treatment—neither Stacia nor he asked or expected it—Paki was con-scious of his particular . . . positionality. Setting his tools down, his tone unboth-ered, Bekele lounged back against a wall. "What is it, Paki?"

"I wanted to talk about where you see yourself." Paki lowered himself on his haunches to not tower over Bekele.

"Most days I feel lucky to still be here."

"Well, I've been thinking about your future."

"So has everyone."

"Not like that. I'd like to promote you to key engineer."

"That'd . . . put me on track to be a tone scientist." Bekele sat up straighter, suddenly found himself in a job interview.

"Is that bad?"

"No. Not even daunting. Just unexpected."

"You have a special way with technology. It's as if it speaks to you and you to it. A rare talent."

"I've been studying quantum technology all my life. It's amazing." Bekele's words sped out of his mouth, him flush with excitement at having an excuse to talk about his interest. "The way it mimics brain function almost perfectly. I believe with the right linkage, we could probably download the essence of who we are into data systems. Each of us becoming a functional Maya."

"That sounds nightmarish." Pressing his hands to his knees, Paki stood up.

"What do you mean?" Bekele's gaze trailed him upward.

"You're talking about using technology to extend our consciousness's time in this reality."

"Exactly. Possibly even expand it. And redefine what it means to be human."

"I'm no mythicist . . ."

"Nor am I . . . ," Bekele interjected.

". . . but I do believe in, maybe not a sabhu per se, our essence. It's to be fully explored here, for however long we're allotted. Once we leave this plane, we should no longer exist. Imprisoning human consciousness in a physical space, never allowing it to incorporate our finite experience into the infinite, that's a technological jail sentence."

"That's a limited way of looking at it. But something to think about."

"That's all I can ask." Paki appreciated a keen mind eager to both push boundaries and be open to questions. It reassured his selection choice. "Well, my more immediate concern is keeping the ship together. What do you think of my offer?"

"This is a lot to take in." Bekele's gaze drifted off; he seemed lost in a daydream and looked much younger. "I should check with my folks."

"I'm just trying to make sure the right person is in the right seat on the bus, as it were." Paki kept a careful distance as he wandered past the algal wall. "Talk to whoever you need to. It should make for some interesting dinner conversation."

✳

When Paki stepped into the security bay, the virtual imaging womb's rendering of an ancient Alkebulan donga caught him off guard. The steep sides of the small ravine were modified for rock-climbing exercises. An array of weapons lay scattered along the bed of the eroded waterway. Kenya's two long braids were drawn back as she sparred in full regalia. Two of her jelis—their security officers, Mabry Voice and Silva Rebelle—formed the ship's Griot Circle. Their chrome-colored bodysuits were protected by gold breastplates. Their gilded animal masks—Mabry's was an eagle; Silva's a dog—perched on rocks off to the side. They'd been practicing for hours. Their bodies, no matter if modified to the point of qualifying to be a HOVA, barely showed signs of strain. They moved through the first Form fast and fluid, silent as their staffs through the air.

Kenya brought her weapon to the ready. Her hard eyes—bright bulbs against her dark skin—locked on to her imagined opponent with a near-feral glare. Born and raised in the Belts, "Kennie" imbibed poetry down to her bones. Her mother was shamanistic, but they remained inseparable. Considered a savant by any standard, she was able to not only speak, but put together simple poems by the age of two. Her first year in the Learning Tree, she spoke only in verse. Her performances turned her kraal into a destination poetry commune. Coming up in the slam ranks, she ascended to Master Poet before she was a teen. After the death of her rhyme partner, she left the Learning Tree. No one knew the full story, only that it seemed like ghosts dogged her every step.

Kenya whirled the staff about her before slashing downward with it. She parried two unseen attackers, twirled the staff about her waist, and blocked another anticipated attack before tossing the staff to Mabry.

Large sunglasses covered her red eyes. Like the next soloist in an improvised performance, Mabry dropped her staff and caught Kenya's. Rotating it about her neck with a bit too much flourish, she drew it close to her side. A sketch pad inclined against the rock with her mask on it. She doodled portraits and blocked out shots for holovids she hoped to make in her down time. A collaboration specialist, she worked alongside any discipline of artist. Her peers considered her harmony level—with a double specialty as a slam poet—focusing on surrealistic songs in the keys of joy and peace. Her file was suspiciously thin. Raised a mythicist, she grew up in her church choir, traveling for competition. She played a host of instruments by the time she entered the Learning Tree, and often sneaked off to hear concerts. Music offered her an intimacy, an opportunity to connect to her neighbors. Such romantic notions were belied by her participation in the Yemaya Campaign (her exact role in it designated Code Black / Eyes Only). She spun the staff, helicoptering it at each side and then, unable to resist herself, spinning it under her leg before hurling it like a javelin.

Catching it midflow, Silva moved through the next three Forms with the staff as little more than an extended appendage. All business, she spun the blade to each side and once behind the back. Not to show off, but to fend off attacks from all sides. Her weusi father and mzunga mother raised her to honor her feelings. Embracing her whole story, the traumas of which she never spoke of, she tired of making herself uncomfortable for other people's benefit. Another slam poet, she founded a Bayard school in Bronzeville. Unlike the other two, she had three children: two adults—one serving in the HOVA—and her youngest child on the *Cypher*. Her joining the security detail was her latest iteration in exploring herself. She cartwheeled into the next Form to carve out space away from her imaginary attackers. Passing a glance to Kenya, who barely nodded, she threw the staff back to Mabry.

As Mabry caught it, Kenya launched into an attack. Mabry sidestepped, swiping her staff at Kenya's legs. Instead of tripping, she somersaulted, landed, and spun to face Mabry without breaking stride. Kenya feigned a lunge to her left. Mabry bit, so Kenya pivoted to the opposite side and batted Mabry on the shoulders, sending her tumbling forward.

"Again." Kenya picked up the staff and tossed it to Mabry. "Until your form is better."

"May I interrupt?" Paki asked, much to the relief of Mabry and Silva, their faces betraying their breaking point. When Kenya joined him, he whispered in a conspiratorial tone, "You're working them awfully hard."

"You telling me how to run my team?"

"I'd never. There is no off button on sharpening one another."

"True." Her eyes tracked him with wary skepticism.

"I'm just curious why."

"Why? How about we out here in the middle of 'ain't nobody been here before.' We don't know what's around the next corner or who's trying to come for dinner. And that's before we get to a crew of folks bubbling with regret, anger, and resentment toward each other. I got what you might call a litany of security concerns and I need my people in peak form."

"And is this the best way to address those concerns?"

"What are you doing, Paki?" Kenya cut her eyes at him. As direct as Paki saw himself, it wasn't nearly as devastating as Kenya's side-eye. Her gaze had a sleepy quality to it, misdirecting folks to underestimate her and thus lower their guard.

"What do you mean?"

"The fact that I didn't tell you to get the entire fuck out of my face and business should tell you something. But let me be clear: you, right now, are my biggest security concern."

"Me?"

"You're walking around stirring up the crew's discontent with Stacia. You think you're slick. A whisper here or your 'honest assessment' there. Like you some sort of social banker of relationships. Just . . . stop."

"I'm none of those things. Nor do I wish to be."

"No, you think you should be running things. The captain. The Camara."

"It's not my desire."

"I bet not."

Paki met her unflinching stare. "The captain would like to request your presence for a Homowo ritual. I'm sure she'll be reaching out to you soon."

"Tuh." Kenya sucked her teeth at him. Paki took that as a yes.

*

This was one of those times when Paki wished he drank. Bekele. Marguerite. Kenya. Nadina. They all looked about at each other trapped like fossilized insects in the amber of awkward tension. A thick swallow of tjwala or one of the other favorite beverages the neonik generation favored. Not just a swallow . . . whole-ass glassfuls. At least three to dig him out of the corner of Stacia's rondavel. He stood at the edge of the gathered circle, not sure who to make small talk with. Or how. Bekele, Marguerite, and Nadina huddled in the opposite corner playing some sort of freestyle poetry game. Taking the last line of each other's verse and picking a random object, and incorporating it into their improvised rhymes.

"You look absolutely miserable." Yahya came up beside him and rested his hand on Paki's shoulder with effortless ease.

"I'm fine."

"Never play poker." His smile beamed in warm welcome. Playing host suited him. "These are your colleagues, Paki. Your friends."

None of his words put Paki any more at ease. His fingers twitched, desperate for something to do. Yahya floated off, eager to make the other guests more comfortable. He and Stacia both flitted about. Whatever fault lines cracked their relationship ignored for an evening, joining forces to offer hospitality as their shared mission.

Paki orbited around the periphery of the room, trying to disappear in any of its shadows. No one paid any attention as he moved. Almost no one. He caught Stacia's eye during his second lap. She aimed her chin toward him, a tacit half encouragement for him to do more to mingle. Kenya also watched his every movement. If his path brought him too near to Stacia, she made a point of placing herself between them. He couldn't be bothered with her nonsense now. He needed the Homowo to cement the crew's new footing in this phase of exploration.

"May I have your attention." Stacia clinked her glass. "I just wanted to thank you for joining me—us"—she gestured toward Yahya and Bekele—"as we welcome you into our home for this Homowo reminder. All available crew are participating, but I've asked for you all to join me. Those I worked closest with and depended on the most. Those I will lean on most in the coming days. The *Cypher* is our cultural infrastructure, a container of practice and rituals to reinforce what it means for us to be Muungano. How we treat each other. Our true work is people development. We don't just stumble into deeper relationships, not with neighbors, not with friends, not with significant others. There has to be an intentionality to our wanting to deepen our connection to others, some sort of support. Those on O.E. often find themselves flailing about in scattershot efforts, wondering why their circle of relationships never seem to expand or deepen. To us, relationships are portals, our friendships like time travel; rooted in our past, our shared history, loving each other and holding each other accountable while we work toward the future together. Connected through our stories. They create the throughline joining our past to our present and projecting into the future. Paki, will you tell us about Homowo?"

"Maya, I'd like to broadcast to the entire ship." No *please* or *thank you,* his words just short of the sharpness of an order.

<Broadcast when ready.>

Paki cleared his throat.

"There was a lost village in Alkebulan, determined to make their way to a region in the Wagadu called the Ga. They traveled for many years, suffering much in their travels: isolation, drought, loss, desperation, despondence. They came so close to starvation, they were forced to implement draconian measures of food cultivation to hold out until the rains. All their hard work and sacrifice paid off as eventually the rains returned. They survived until the harvest.

"So, they rejoiced with their blessing, calling for a celebration for the rain that broke the drought. For a future harvest. Remembering this time by calling it Homowo. A break from work to visit family and hold their friends close. A time of shared stories, where they expressed their struggles, hopes, fears. We rejoice and remember now, in the hope of a future blessing.

"We begin with a day of rest. A night off. No work is to be done. We can drift, relax, concentrate on discovering who we are now. A time for us to connect with a series of meals with family and friends. We'll sing. We'll dance. We'll simply enjoy each other. We'll exchange handcrafted gifts, tokens of gratitude." Paki's eyes lingered on Nadina. "We'll remember those we've lost."

A roar echoed through the ship as Maya ended the transmission.

"With that," Stacia said, "let's eat."

Yahya and Stacia brought out trays of food. Meals always meant more when they were prepared by hand. Paki wondered when they had time to cook between their respective duties. The synthesizers must've been operating since morning. With them overseeing the production schedule, orchestrating the rollout of the meal with military precision. The first course of dishes included a palm-nut fish soup whose aroma was both pungent and savory. Kenya moved to Stacia's side, stationing herself against Paki.

"What are you doing, Kenya? I wanted Yahya on one side and Bekele on the other," Stacia said.

"I'd rather not, Mom." Bekele angled his seat toward Marguerite.

"Young people," Stacia grumbled.

"I'd rather be by your side, Captain." Kenya scooted her chair closer, yet turned away in case she needed to move. "There are many dangers. From without and within."

"What does that mean?"

"That I'm on full-time pest control." Kenya pointedly didn't glare at Paki, but if an emi could cast a side-eye, hers did.

"I don't think I've ever had anything like this before." Nadina raised her spoon in appreciation.

"We tried to draw on as many traditional delicacies as possible," Stacia said.

"I'm as traditional as the next person," Bekele said, "but I do miss the occasional charcuterie board."

"Say what you will about him, but Hondo knew how to lay out a cheese spread," Nadina said with a cool nonchalance, avoiding all eye contact.

"The dishes don't matter," Paki stepped in before anyone could react. "The meal is about a tribute to perseverance, community, thankfulness. Reuniting family by sharing a special dinner with their loved ones."

"That's the way my abuela always prepared meals. I wish I would have known. I'd have liked to have brought something that would have honored her. Would that be part of this?" Marguerite asked.

"That's very much in the spirit of this." Stacia's voice softened, holding space for Marguerite's sabhu. "Our rituals are always deepened when they are internalized and personalized."

"Though we wouldn't want to stray from the original culture too much or it ceases to be our tradition." The words left Paki's mouth in reflex, already heard before his brain could stop them. The mood was already tentative and fragile and this risked spoiling it.

"Gatekeeping the orthodoxy of the ritual? Maintaining its purity?" Kenya leapt in to check him.

"I just miss cooking with her," Marguerite continued, unbothered. "She hated the food processors. She kept her kitchen stocked with comal, pots, molcajetes. Carnitas. Posole. Elotes."

"Did you live with her long?" Stacia asked.

"No." A pang of sadness thickened her voice. "I was adopted by a wazungu family when I was young. Most of what I know about her has been through holovid once I was old enough to investigate on my own. My mother went through a rough time and the family who took me in knew her from church."

"I'm sorry," Bekele said.

"Well, I've just been trying to learn more. Figure out that part of who I am."

"I think a lot of folks on the *Cypher* could relate to that," Stacia said.

"Speaking of growing up mzungu, I'm surprised Zenith isn't here." Still not meeting anyone's eyes, Nadina peeled off a piece of bread and popped it into her mouth.

"I doubt he has the palate for any of our traditions." Paki knew it was a mistake to invite her. While it was necessary to provide the opportunity to build her bridge to the captain, she entertained herself by lobbing volleys. The role of the obroni would be resolved in due course, but not now if he could help it. "Speaking of, aren't we due for the next course?"

"Wild game, corn cakes, and field greens." Stacia's grin strained her face. She wasn't rising to Nadina's baiting, but her veneer of patience was steadily eroding. It was only a matter of time before her temper got the better of her. Hopefully, Nadina wouldn't be near an air lock when it did. "So, Bek, what's this I hear about a promotion?"

Bekele straightened in his seat, midchew. "Yes, Paki mentioned it to me. I'm still mulling it over."

"Oh. That surprises me. The way the request came across my desk, it sounded like it had already been offered and accepted." Stacia focused on cutting her meat, the blade of her knife carefully peeling back layers. "Without so much as a courtesy query."

"Low-level operational work has always fallen under my discretion," Paki said.

"Matters of my son are never low-level operations. I'd like to be kept in the loop on matters relating to his well-being."

Paki held up his fork, but before he had the chance to renew his point about her role of captain versus mother, Yahya's fork clattered loudly against his plate.

"I keep forgetting that you're the only one who loves him." Yahya stabbed at his greens. "That you're the only one who gets to make all the decisions for him."

"That's not what I said. Or meant," Stacia said.

Being around Stacia and Yahya was always an exercise in anxiety, counting down to the inevitable awkward tension. Paki had always assumed the root of the issue centered around her unresolved devotion to Amachi Adisa. So pedestrian an issue. He never understood why they didn't form a triune, or whatever configuration allowed their relationships to work. But insecurity was still a very human problem.

"I just want to enjoy one peaceful meal." Sighing, she left a hesitation so everyone heard the unspoken words "for once."

"Gifting to one another speaks to and kindles our generosity." Paki doubled down. He would force the Homowo along if he had to. "The circle of the gift becomes the basis of community. Gifts partake of the giver, when we partake of a gift, we give something of ourselves. I gift and, out of gratitude, you gift. Either to me or to someone else, eventually it gets back to me."

"You know what I'd like as a gift?" Nadina wiped her mouth before dropping her sani-sheet into her lap.

Though reminding himself that he wasn't a mythicist, Paki prayed that among the next words out of her mouth wasn't "Hondo."

"Hondo."

Stacia, Kenya, Yahya, and Paki all tossed their sani-sheets and pushed away from their plates. Things that bubbled under the surface sometimes erupted to reveal weak points in a relationship. The resolution of such conflicts, though they were often messy, allowed for authentic, albeit sometimes raw, conversation. Such conflicts, wisely tended, were like a quickly spreading fire clearing out all of the underbrush to allow for fresh growth. The most volatile part of the process was the nature of the spark. Marguerite and Bekele kept eating, aware of the gravity, but entertained by the drama.

"This again?" Yahya asked.

"Again? When did we talk about it a first time?" Nadina asked.

"Now's not the time," Paki said.

"Now's exactly the time. She's right, it's long overdue. Let her have her say," Stacia said.

"Maybe now is the time for us to do a conflict transformation." Paki backed away from the table, tamping the air to lower the temperature of the room. The conflict transformation was the relational container of the wise tending of the fires of conflict: the aggrieved parties, along with an elder or two, engaged in an intentional dialogue that allowed people to plumb the depths of what bothered them. Not a spectator blood sport, but a controlled process to figure out how to communicate and support each other better.

"Led by who? You?" Kenya stood up, matching his movements, positioning herself between him and the captain. "You'd like that. The next stage in your plan."

"What plan?" Stacia asked.

"You know this one always has a plan inside a scheme. He might as well be Zenith's pet."

"I think I've had my fill of rituals for one day," Nadina said.

"Well, ritual or not, let's get everything out in the open. And clear the air," Stacia said.

Nadina whirred toward Stacia, a snarl half contorting her face. "Clear the air? That's what you're good at: taking the air out of a room. Having your finger on the button, deciding life and death. Watching Hondo struggle for air, making us all watch him gasp, his eyes nearly popping out of his skull, and struggle as the outer bay doors opened, slowly dragging him out into space. All for what? To show Zenith what a large set of brass ones you had? I'll never forget the image of Hondo desperately holding on to that bar in the loading bay. Watching the fight in him slowly fade . . . Fuck you, Stacia. Just . . . fuck you. And fuck this charade."

Nadina stormed toward the door. Kenya pivoted, tracking her movements without losing track of Paki.

"This—all of this—was about trying to remind us of who we are to each other," Stacia whispered.

"And who are we, Captain, besides expendable? Unless we're your kin, then, all of a sudden, all lives matter. We made a decision together about the crew's, the traitor's, expulsion. But never forget that *you* forced our hand. That vote was a pressure cooker of manipulation. We didn't have a moment to think, only react. Time running out. Traitors in our midst."

In your bed. Paki chose the wiser course of action to remain silent and not become the lightning rod for the entire room's ire.

"Nadina," Stacia emphasized. "I'm sorry. I truly am. If I could do it over, do it different, I would. All I could think about was the possibilities of a cure . . ."

"The cure, the cure, the cure. I'm so fucking sick of hearing about this cure. We all have to live with the consequences of . . ."

"Stop it. All of you," Bekele yelled. "I know this is all my fault."

The shock of Bekele's voice stunned them all. A pang of regret locked on Nadina's face, the riptide of her anger at the captain dragging along her son. Surrendering, Paki plunked down in a chair distancing himself from everyone else.

"Bek, baby, it's not . . ." Stacia reached for him, but he pulled away.

"I get it. None of you would be here if it wasn't for me. None of you would be hurting. None of you would be mad at each other. Every time you and Dad fight. Every time Dina looks at you with all of that hurt and anger in her eyes. I see it. I always see it. The same expression on every crew member's face. And I have to live with it. I wish I'd died before we had to go through the Orun Gate."

Bekele knocked over his chair as he stumbled out of the room. Marguerite glared at each of them before following him.

"You chose to come with us." Stacia's voice lacked any strength of conviction.

"I chose to support my family," Nadina whispered.

"Then be with your family."

"I am. And I support the mission. I would do it all again because I do want to find a cure for Bek. Please, tell him that. But asking me to forgive the choices you made is too much. I no longer have faith in you. I'm far from alone. But I do have faith in those who surround you." She glanced at Paki. "Hopefully that will be enough. So, no, I'm not okay. I don't know if I'll ever be okay again."

With that, the hiss of a door opening and closing signaled her exit.

"I've failed my crew in so many ways." Stacia hunched over her chair, both hands gripping it so hard, the only things holding her up.

With a gentle electronic ping, Maya all but cleared their throat in interruption. <Priority message coming in from Anousheh. Code Black / Eyes Only.>

Stacia glanced around the room. She, Kenya, and Paki all had clearance. Her eyes slowly turned toward her husband. "Yahya, if you'll excuse us."

"I know the dance." He held his hands up, too tired to have an all-too-familiar fight. Once he was out of the room, Maya sealed the space.

"What is it?" Stacia asked.

"I don't understand it, ma'am," Anousheh said, "but we've detected a signal."

09

EPYC RO MORGAN
Beyond the Orun Gate

"What have we here?" Robin kept her tone gentle and soothing. Still trembling, the little girl didn't fight her. A humanoid of unknown origin who had practically collapsed, near catatonic, into Robin's arms. The soot and smears on her modified white biomech suit made it appear charcoal. She appeared human, except for her eyes being nearly three times as large as Robin's.

"Life scans?" Frustration filled Epyc Ro's voice. Remote command—leading from behind—though her mandated role, did not come easily to her. However, unless the combatants left them no choice, assessing the big-picture situation, managing their forces, and comms were her most important duties.

<Difficult to say given the interference.> Chandra projected her telemetry readings. The ship's database lit up. Files analyzed, sifting out corrupted ones from those she prepared for retrieval. Next to it, the ping of a wave radiating out, illuminating an amorphous mass closing in on them. Perhaps a cluster of troops. Or a single, undefined organism. Neither prospect boded well. <Movement detected. Aft storage.>

"You heard her," Epyc Ro said.

"Weapons on me," Anitra said.

"What about . . ." Robin's voice trailed off as the girl clutched onto her tighter. She held her close to her chest, her huge arm practically shielding the girl's entire body.

"Ma won't abandon us," she whispered, though it was uncertain whether that was a question or a statement.

"Hold back, but be ready," Epyc Ro said.

Anitra and Ellis took point. Lights flickered, reducing most of the corridor to shadows. Anitra's light, a shoulder mount on her vest, a focused beam peeling back the shadows. The walls scarred by scorch marks as if they'd been used for target practice. Laser fire stitched the side. Turret fire. Mobile weapons units. High-intensity barrage. Cracks spiderwebbed the blast doors. There had been a running firefight of some sort. With no regard to poking holes in the thin membrane of metal protecting them from the terrors and vacuum of space.

The vidfeeds bobbled as Epyc Ro's people skulked through the ship. She kept rearranging the feeds, doling them out like face cards in a high-stakes poker game. Overlapping them at times, she wanted as much of a panoramic view of the scene as possible. The ship vibrated. The bulkhead shuddered, unseen weight shifted. They snaked through the fallen debris of cargo and equipment.

"You good?" Anitra asked. "Automatic defense coming to bear."

"I'm good." Ellis slapped their arm against the bulkhead.

Epyc Ro worried about Ellis. They were a little too calm. She wished Anitra would turn and study them; provide a glimpse of Ellis's hands to see if they shook. They were young and wanting to fit in with the squad, perhaps impress Anitra. Exactly the combination that might lead one to try to ingratiate oneself into the circle of gbeto with some over-the-top act of bravado. Epyc Ro couldn't lose sight of that. In her experience, bravery—the steel found in the moment—wasn't anything to count on. People folded.

<We have movement again.>

Anitra brought her scope to her eye, the vidfeed locking into her weapon's telemetry in a scan. Epyc Ro monitored her life signs, which streamed alongside the feed. A breath. Two. Anitra coolly fixed a shot. Her DMX-3000 remained level and she scanned for another target.

"What do you have?" Epyc Ro shouted. In her heart, she'd already advanced ten paces toward the hatch, ready to race down a bulwark to join her people.

There was a noise behind her, but it was a lift door sliding open at their presence. She lowered her weapon and moved forward. The hallway led to a T junction. They swept carefully, walking not running, brushing aside their ancestral survival instinct against exploring dark basements and investigating the source of a strange sound alone. Too many shadows, too many nooks, too many doors meant too many opportunities for ambush. Their footfalls muted and careful, barely marking their presence. They crept along an administrative corridor, private quarters and offices, on either side. Energy panels, some cracked like frosted glass, blinked on and off, maintaining marginal integrity; workstations lined a common area with another set of hatch doors closing off the passageway to their left. The hallway seemed to stretch for kilometers into the deepening shadows. Several meters down was the remains of a body like the corpse of a whale that had washed up on a metallic shoreline. They had taken blaster fire, their eyes glassy and vacant, having seen something in the dark they couldn't report on. The hallways folded back on themselves, stacks upon stacks; the Reapers could stumble about for hours clearing the deck and whoever raided them would be getting farther and farther away.

Or regrouping to return with reinforcements.

The corpses were few and far between. All in the same uniform. All from the same crew. Either the raiders took no casualties or they made special effort to retrieve their own. The Reapers mapped the layout with each step.

Setting her back to the admin wing, Anitra peered around the corner. Her vidfeed captured an array of large analytical devices, telemetry, perhaps engineering or a series of lab alcoves. Blaster fire struck her position. Ellis's feed caught her scurrying for cover. They provided cover fire, shooting a junction panel. Plumes of gas escaped in a sour fizz. Shrapnel exploded all around them. A maelstrom of fire shredded the racks around them. An explosion knocked them over some containers. The feed bounced as their head careened against a wall.

"Ellis?" Anitra asked.

"Still good," they said.

"Watch your six."

"My six?"

"Behind you." Anitra shot a barrage of charges. Sparks erupted, peppering the floor as a series of explosions rocked their perimeter.

"Y'all don't give two shits about explosive decompression, right?" Robin shielded the child as best she could.

"They ain't giving us much choice." Anitra chanced a peek over her cover.

"Long-term decompression and cold exposure breaks all the capillaries in your eyes and skin . . ."

"Seriously don't need a rundown on space-induced ashiness right now. Anyone got eyes on them?"

Ellis gestured, directing two fingers down the hallway. The squad moved laterally around the bay.

"I think our surprise guests are trying to leave." Robin peered from around the corner. The little girl traced her gaze with growing uneasiness. "I think those are escape pods they're scrambling into."

"Hold up." Anitra's telemetry lit up again. Her scope tracked her target. A couple of suited visitors slipped into view. "Fire on my mark."

The Reapers' enhancement as a part of becoming HOVA included mental acuity. They quickly processed multiple streams of information. Threat assessment and tactical analysis with a near-eidetic memory for battle strategies, remembering any military tactic and applying it to any situation. The enhancements adapted to a person's innate gifts. Contemplative by nature, Epyc Ro intuitively studied those around her, assessing their strengths and weaknesses. Always calculating out how best to deploy her assets or the resources of her team members.

Anitra not so much. She moved by intuition. Jumping up, she charged her target. "You can get this work!"

Ellis essentially mashed their talon's trigger, spraying charge bursts down the corridor. Not drilled in standard deployment, they found it difficult to determine where they should be firing. One squad or member laying down suppression fire, pinning down the enemy. Another providing support fire, allowing another squad or member to maneuver on the target, striking the enemy's flank. If the hostiles recognized that they faced fire superiority and higher ground, they knew that an assault was imminent.

Fully exposed, Anitra hurtled down the corridor improvising Ellis's near-erratic cover fire. Weaving in and out of their charge channels, stunning the hostiles so much they hesitated, though they recovered soon enough. Rising to the occasion, Ellis concentrated their fire around her. What was once scatter-shot became well-aimed bursts. The cramped bay cracked with charges whipping through it, but Anitra inexorably marched toward her targets. Despite her seeming recklessness, she was an intuitive gbeto, reading terrain and situations like it was an extension of her emi. She could have been a speculative hunter with the proper training. Hers was an unmatched weapons discipline; she only fired when she had a shot to take. Her next double tap picked off two hostiles. Bodies tumbled to the ground but were dragged into the shuttle pods as the blast doors shut.

<We have movement. Two escape pods launching.>

"Orders?" Ellis yelled.

"We do not fire on escape pods," Epyc Ro said. "Sweep and assess. Chandra, track those ships. Let us know if they bring back company."

<They've . . . disappeared.>

"What?" Epyc Ro rushed to the ship's outer monitors. The field of space remained pristine, with no evidence of a ship in distress to be seen. No distortion. No radiation fluctuations. Nothing anomalous. Nothing period. Only the silence of stars.

<It was like space collapsed all around them. No readings detected.>

"Wormhole? Cloaking technology?"

<No residual energy traces.>

"Damn it." Epyc Ro pounded her fist on the workstation, drawing the briefest of glances from Chandra. "We need to do better. We have no idea who or what we're up against. Anitra, your maneuver was reckless."

"But effective," she said.

"Then we'll need you to be more . . . judicious."

"She's always climbing Fool's Hill," Robin said.

"Why do you hate fun?" Anitra clapped her on the back. "You sounding more and more like an elder each day."

"We'll do a full debrief when you return." Epyc Ro stifled her sigh from the comms. "What do we have?"

"Nothing yet. It's like they scooped up their fallen as they went," Robin said. "They didn't want to leave us much to study."

"Take scans and let's regroup. Robin, bring your new friend and let's make sure she's okay."

Ellis and Robin, plus her friend, backed out the way they came. Anitra continued her sweep, covering their tactical withdrawal. All Epyc Ro could do was listen, with the same existential powerlessness of hearing distant combat. She couldn't even feel the thrum of vibration in the ship.

The Reapers reached a bulkhead hatch and clambered through it. The lights dimmed, coming back up to near full intensity, them dimming again, as if breathing via luminosity. The bulkhead opened into some sort of storage bay.

Ellis raised their fist. "Hold on, I'm picking up something."

"I sense it, too, close." Robin backed toward them, shielding the child away from the angles of potential attack.

A crate tottered on the shelf. Anitra and Ellis turned to the disturbance. Anitra led the approach. Ellis hung back, flanking to the side of the shelving unit. A shadow coalesced in the gloom. The scenario all too familiar. The shadowed storage room, the scent of decay and mold, hidden by machine oil and sanitizers. Bolt holes all around. The spurring of her emi that someone was near, watching her. Terror didn't threaten to overtake her; only a weary alertness. In the reflected light patches, a tentacle snaked its way out of view. Ellis whirled, training their talon on the limb's source in the same movement. The child dug her nails into Robin, burying her head into her cleft. She was scared, but for it, not the Reapers.

"No!" Robin yelled, raising the barrel of their weapon before Ellis could fire.

"Robin, what is it?" Epyc Ro yelled into the commlink, unaware that she had leapt to her feet again.

"I'm not sure yet." Robin crept closer, shifting the child to a position farther behind her.

"Girl, them elekes won't protect you if you on some fuckshit." Anitra trained her DMX on the encroaching shadows.

"'Fuckshit' is not a useful scale of measurement."

"Fuckshit is isometric with the complex field." Anitra canted her head when Robin turned to her in confusion. "I told you, I read."

"I'm not doing this with you." Stowing Busta, Robin lowered her voice and held her hands up as best she could, keeping the girl protected. "It's all right, you're among friends. You're safe now."

Tentacles slithered into view, halting as if waiting for a response. When they weren't shot at, a round, bulbous head, its rectangular pupils darting about, slid out. Eight spots dotted its cranium. Thick vessels, maybe prototentacles, trailed from the base of its mantle into the rest of its biomech suit. Its suit was a silvery, metallic blue that retained much of its gleam. The bulk of it reared up, approximating legs.

"He smells like smoke and late rent," Anitra whispered.

"You ain't shit sometimes," Robin said.

"I know."

The stranger's posture reminded Epyc Ro of the way a puff adder inflated when threatened. But they tottered, stumbling to the side, barely managing to catch and steady themselves against the wall. They hacked a few times—a terrible, wet cough—and slumped over. Their eyes weary with resignation, no longer concerned about their fate.

Anitra lowered her DMX. "I'm telling you, he's giving off those 'gonna be the drunk uncle at the family reunion' vibes."

"We should get out of here," Ellis said.

"What Ellis said." Epyc Ro restrained herself from shouting. "Let's regroup with our guests back here until we figure out what's going on with that ship."

✳

Epyc Ro closed her eyes, not sleeping but capturing a few minutes' rest when she could. She floated in the darkness, her consciousness bobbing just above the orb of water that was her waking life of concerns. A cold, black sea away from the torrents and churning waves of the inexorable tides of life. Everything seemed distant. Waking, if she could call it that, only as the rest of her crew walked in. Epyc Ro and Chandra crowded around the holovid display, studying the vidfeed from their mission. The rest of the Reapers gathered around the dinner table.

"How are our guests?" Epyc Ro didn't turn around.

"Resting," Robin said.

"They must feel like prisoners."

"There's no way for them to not feel like that."

"Let's make arrangements to welcome them properly. Let's consider the formal greeting our . . . Wait." Epyc Ro leaned in. "Hold that image. Enhance."

The group of hostiles moved with military discipline. Long-sleeved dresses, with full skirt and loose-fitting trousers, served as their uniform; the baggy outline created a larger target and also allowed freedom of movement. Their faces completely covered. Their cranial plating reminiscent of Car'Annie, the CO/IN leader they left on Mzisoh, Ellis's homeworld. Their chest racks bulged with extra weapons. Large daggers were strapped to their hips. They chittered as they fired, a distracting howl.

Epyc Ro thought of Fela's last moments.

"I want our first-contact protocols, all of our engagements with strangers . . . ," Epyc Ro said.

"Aliens," Anitra said.

"There are no 'aliens.' Just friends we haven't made yet," Robin said.

"Friends with tentacles," Anitra said.

"As I was saying, I want this to be a continuing conversation." Epyc Ro turned to face them. "All paths lead to the same arguments and I'd like options."

"First contact typically favors the more technologically advanced party," Robin said.

"Or the party exploring with their military. The 'surprise, we've just "discovered" you . . . have some of our easily communicable diseases and our gratitude for your stuff' protocol," Anitra said.

"Right. I don't want that to be our hallmark."

"What are you thinking, Robin?" Epyc Ro asked.

"Even how we initiate conversations with folks should say something about who we are. As it stands, it's little more than a self-interested exchange. Like inviting folks over to impress them with us and hoping to get something out of it. That's a Yo mentality. I want to lead in a more generous, a more gracious, way."

"That puts more of the risk on us." Epyc Ro steepled her fingers in front of her.

Robin nodded. "Someone has to bear that burden. Sometimes there will be a cost to how we choose to do things. Embracing those who like us is easy; the radical hospitality I'm imagining offers us up as an unconditional gift."

"Though we're ready to run them hands if need be," Anitra said.

"Anitra," Epyc Ro said.

"I'm just saying. They need to know we ready for that, too."

"She's right," Robin said.

"Wait, you agree with her?" Epyc Ro thought her groggy brain might have misheard her sergeant.

"'Cause I'm a motherfucking diplomat at heart," Anitra said.

"We would need them to understand that we don't operate from a place of fear, nor from a lack of confidence. The Reapers' operating principles should be caring, kindness, generosity, cooperation, and forgiveness."

Anitra raised her finger to interject.

"Do not say 'and them hands,'" Epyc Ro said.

Anitra lowered her finger.

"I know this sounds . . . aspirational," Robin said.

"She means 'naive.' As fuck. But that's how we do. We ain't scared." Anitra elbowed her gently. "You and your fake deep ass. You know how to talk that shit."

"It costs us nothing but trust, time, and compassion," Robin said.

<And risk,> Chandra said. <Our risk levels are already unduly high.>

"Folks are going to be especially untrusting given the activities of the CO/IN," Epyc Ro said.

"Yeah, this sounds like a Reapers sort of plan," Anitra said.

"It's worth considering. Let's get it encoded," Epyc Ro said. "We should meet our new friend. Maybe take her to med bay to see her traveling companion. And apologize for the meal location."

When the door of the guest room opened, the little girl huddled in a corner, not on the cot or the chair, but in the back—half-cloaked in shadows—at the farthest point from the door. Her arms wrapped around her drawn-up knees, waiting for the inevitable return of the monsters from her nightmares. Robin held up her hand for the others to wait in the hall. At her approach, the little girl stirred to attention, with large, fear-filled eyes.

"We didn't have a chance to be formally introduced." Robin sat down on the edge of the cot, allowing her plenty of space. Her maternal instincts came so naturally, from an unforgotten place. "My name is Robin Townsend. You can call me Robin. Do you have a name?"

"Majorae Ha'Henam."

"Hello, Majorae."

"Henam. Majorae is my class. Ha my house name. Henam my designation within my family."

"Then, hello Henam."

"My people say 'hello is only hello if it's not followed by weapon fire.'"

"It sounds like your people have been through some times." Robin held out a plate of snacks. No one had any idea what Henam might eat, so they set out an array of fruits, meats, and bread. Henam plucked a piece of fruit.

"Would you like to stay here or join us for a meal?"

"Am I your . . . prisoner?"

"Your door wasn't locked. You could have left any time."

"What about Cadgejia?" Henam chewed slowly, unsure if she liked the taste or texture. Or waiting to see if she was poisoned.

"Is that the friend who was with you?"

"We were both captive."

"They are resting in another room. We don't know how best to make him feel better, but we're doing our best. We can see him first if you want."

Henam nodded. Robin held out her hand. The little girl's grip barely covered half of her wrist. Robin and Henam walked past Epyc Ro and Anitra. The child eyed each of them skeptically. Robin shook her hand, drawing her attention back to their promenade. The Reapers followed dutifully behind them, at a bit of a distance, like an awkward security detail. The hallway must have seemed large and imposing, especially to one so small. A strange place, lit up and clean, almost clinically so. What Epyc Ro wouldn't give for the smell of breakfast being cooked wafting down the hallways. The sound of children scampering in play. Reminder of the life they fought to preserve.

Med bay was a converted storage bay, with reinforced, stabilized beds, cabinets of supplies, and equipment tethered to walls.

"How's our friend?" Epyc Ro stepped into the cone of light highlighting the bed.

<Scans coming in.> Chandra had assembled monitors, directing nanobots

to synthesize basic tools for the space. She bent over a bed attending to the wounds of the tentacled stranger.

Robin examined the holovid display. "Definitely marine in origin. The bio-mech seems constructed for his needs specifically."

Epyc Ro glanced at the girl's suit. "I'm betting they all were."

"And . . . apparently calling him 'he' was premature." Robin angled her head with heightened fascination.

"He?" Anitra asked. "You check under the hood?"

"They give birth at end of their life."

"Gender fluid. Like the Mzisoh," Ellis said.

"For starters. They also don't have a skull. Their species has a mantle, which apparently we've mistaken for their head. In fact, there's no skeletal structure at all. Without the biomech suit, they could pour themselves into a hole the size of an orange. Their actual mouth is in their armpits. I wouldn't advise getting them upset. There are venom sacs located there. Trace detects two kinds: neu-rotoxic and acidic. Of interest, they possess fifty to seventy-five lobes of brain, thus each limb has mind of its own. Cellular analysis says that they can regrow severed limbs and that for several minutes, a severed limb can continue to hunt. You see the cream-colored suckers along their . . . arms?"

Robin gently rotated a limb, revealing a mix of pink or plum, with irides-cent spots.

"When they run along you, they're actually tasting you. They could literally taste with all of their skin."

"So hugs are out," Anitra said.

"My guess is that the arms appear generally white if they are relaxed. I've detected three types of chromatocysts, color-changing cells. Definitely a ma-rine invertebrate, though they shared a common ancestor with humans maybe half a billion years ago."

"Preliminary social analysis?" Epyc Ro asked.

"If I had to guess, they live communally."

"They are from Darawad," Henam said. "When not under attack, they are extremely curious. So much so that if they're bored, they're bound to wander."

"In that case, I'd guess that they have a fairly short life span," Anitra said.

Epyc Ro circled the room. The game was about getting as much actionable intel as possible. The first rule of interrogation was that the interrogator was the only irreplaceable piece on the board. Her job was to work the board.

However, she had Robin's new protocols of hospitality to consider and play within. There were few things she loved more than a challenge.

Epyc Ro struggled to find anything soft remaining in her. Service in the HOVA, now with the Reapers, hardened even the secret bits of her sabhu. She tried to remember her mother's touch, the brush of her lips against her forehead. The attendant affection of the ghosts of her mother's memory.

"Henam, my name is, let me see if I can do this as your people might. Captain Morgan Epyc Ro."

"Epyc Ro?" Henam asked.

"Yes. You seem a long way from home. Where are your people from?" Epyc Ro eased closer, not wanting to keep her voice raised.

Henam shrank behind Robin, clutching her hand. Robin patted her. "It's okay. She's my friend. Despite her best efforts, she has what we call 'resting serious face.' If she ever cracked a smile, we'd think something was wrong."

"I'm literally standing right here."

Robin thumbed toward her. "See what I mean?"

Henam smiled.

"We are from a moon called Huzini. The Lei'den called our home Melancholia."

"The Lei'den? You fuck with them?" Anitra asked.

Epyc Ro started to wave her off, hoping the subtleties of idioms might be lost in translation. "We've had unpleasant dealings with them."

The Lei'den people must have flourished in this sector. Their CO/IN units were the equivalent of the HOVA, filled with soldiers who swore allegiance to the Interstellar Alliance and were willing to sacrifice anything to their cause. According to them, outsiders had violated their space in the name of peace and exploration. Their intrusion served to unite the various Lei'den factions against the invaders, in the name of taking the fight to them. The HOVA's former captain, Fela Buhari, was killed to serve as an example of their willingness.

"Everyone has unpleasant dealings with them," Henam said.

"Yes, I know." Ellis had wrapped themselves in silk cloths, similar to the way the chieftain of their people wore them. It was obvious that they were a different species from the rest of the Reapers. It was the first time they had relaxed since the Reapers first commandeered the *L.H.S.* "My people, the Mzisoh, aren't a spacefaring people. When the Lei'den visited, pretending to be about negotiating trade . . ."

Henam turned to them and nodded in commiseration. "Huzini orbits a gas giant, a rogue planet ejected from its system."

"Rogue planet?" Epyc Ro glanced at Robin. "That's some sophisticated language. How old are you?"

"Old?"

"How long have you been alive?" Robin asked.

"I don't know how to answer that question." Henam avoided her gaze, suddenly taking interest in the machines monitoring Cadgejia.

"How did you find yourself out here?"

"We were taken. A group of Lei'den soldiers invaded our city. Dressed not too dissimilar from you."

"When we encountered them, they were called the CO/IN," Epyc Ro said.

"They deal in people." The words came slow, not quite in fits and spurts, but with the pained, halting quality of measuring each syllable. Reliving the memory as she recounted it. "Transporting them off-world. I was put into a room with that one. I'd been there for days, them, much longer I'd gathered. Then came the explosion. It shook the ship. Everything . . . broke. We were able to escape our cell and hide out, but we didn't have much more of a plan beyond that."

"Escape." Cadgejia's eyes flickered open with great effort, their words escaping in a thick rasp. They doubled over, seized by a silent, sudden convulsion.

"Chandra?" Epyc Ro asked.

Chandra rushed over. <Initiating scans.>

"You doing that here?" Anitra asked.

"It's not like we have a real med bay," Epyc Ro said.

"Can we make 'get a real med bay' our next priority item?"

<Then add "get a real doctor.">

"Why are they so ashy?" Anitra asked.

"Hold on." Robin mixed a solution; its cloudiness faded until it was clear with only a hint of teal. Satisfied, she poured it over Cadgejia's head.

"Yeah, we need a real doc," Anitra said. "You two doing too much."

"Their biomech suit was damaged. If they're a marine native, then they were literally suffocating right in front of us."

"Can you repair their suit?" Epyc Ro asked.

"Already on it."

<They'll need to rest. Henam, too.>

"I'll need a chance to examine her suit, too," Robin said.

"But I'm free to go?" Henam asked.

"Like I said, you were never our prisoner," Robin said.

"One more thing." Epyc Ro leveled her eyes to be as neutral as possible. She didn't want to alarm Henam, but her emi indicated that she hid something. Something important. "Why do you think the CO/IN took you captive?"

"The Huzini had initiated talks with other planets within the Galactic Rim. We were looking to rebuild the gate, perhaps open negotiations with the Interstellar Alliance. We had hopes to stave off the ways of the rapacious Muungano Empire."

"The what now?" Anitra asked. "And who the hell says 'rapacious'?"

"Muungano?" Epyc Ro asked.

"You've heard of them?" Henam asked.

"Heard of them? We are them," Anitra said before Robin could wave her off.

"Stay away from me!" Henam's eyes widened with terror. She ducked under the medical table Cadgejia rested on. She grabbed a scalpel from the nearby bench. She backed away from them, waving the blade back and forth at whoever she suspected might move. "Get away from the ambassador. Your treatments are probably some chemical truth-inducement procedure."

"This girl ain't got a lick of country common sense." Anitra shook her head. None of the other Reapers bothered to react to her threat. They all but turned from her in mild disinterest.

"It's got to be the Lei'den. Spreading disinformation about us. Tainting the waters before we get to them," Epyc Ro said.

"Like diarrhea in the pool."

"I swear, Anitra, you the Basquiat of unwanted imagery," Robin said.

The L.H.S.'s proximity alarms blared. Robin rushed to a widescreen. "Captain, we have bigger problems."

"On screen."

By the time the image projected in front of them, a ship began to emerge from a ripple of some sort. As if the fabric of space-time bent, a curtain drawn back back, thin sheens of light marking a kind of door opening. Once the ship cleared the event horizon, the door suddenly slammed shut. The ship held its position with no attempt to communicate, only a silent assessment of the L.H.S. It loomed in menace, its nacelles mounted on top and below its main cabin, armaments stacked on each. Extended protrusions armed with turrets. Modules had been patched into the body of the ship, without cohesion other than whatever free space might be available. A hodgepodge of architecture styles, and technologies. As the ship drifted into range, one thing was clear: it was built for war.

"Battle stations!" Epyc Ro yelled.

10

JAHA DIMKA
O.E.—Indianapolis (West Side)

The main antechamber of the Legacy of Alexandria had a Niyabinghi guard stationed in front of it. Its foyer filled with walking wounded. The distant wails of those who lost loved ones. The curses of doctors who rushed about to tend to the casualties. It was hours until the chaos had been reduced to manageable levels. Families contacted their relatives to assure them—as much as they could be sure—of their safety. Folks ate in rotations, the remaining seriously wounded moved to more secure areas. Jaha crouched beside the still body of The Brand, not knowing what to do. The remains of his navsuit were twisted and charred like the shell of a car after a fiery wreck. They had been comrades in arms for more years than she cared to remember. She disagreed with him on his tactics often. One time they had been at lunch. The Brand had laid out his plans for a new facility. Jaha had called him a fool and pawn in as many dialects as she could to get him to understand the futility of his endeavor. Finally, she snatched his sandwich out of his hands and took a giant bite out of it, telling him that was what LISC was going to do to him and his projects if he fell for what she called their "Opportunity to Devour Them Zones." She tossed the sandwich back onto his plate. They both stared at it in silence as if mourning a fallen hero.

"All right, Jaha, damn. You couldn't even let a brotha eat in peace?" The Brand had said.

"It was a good sandwich, though," she had said. They'd burst into laughter.

"You coward." She pounded his chest plate. The Energy thought better of his objections when he saw her face. A contorted snarl of pain and anger. "We have so much work left to be done, but you chose to take the easy way out."

She thumped his chest plate one more time and rested her palm flat on its surface. He went out the way he lived: protecting the lives of his people. Almost as a prayer she whispered, "Rest in power."

*

At the heart of the Muungano embassy was the Legacy of Alexandria, a room named for the library housed there. Hand-carved masks leered down at her grief from every shelf not filled with books. By that time, the moon hung high over the city of Indianapolis; the glowing bauble of the Dreaming City was perfectly visible to a trained telescope. The refugees scattered about the Muungano embassy on O.E., made to feel welcome by the skeleton staff that hadn't been recalled by Maulana.

"What do you mean 'he's busy'?" Jaha demanded. No one jumped at the sound of her raised voice.

"I'm afraid VOP Harrison has a series of priority meetings which have his schedule jacked up." Mimilah's voice remained even, almost soothing in comparison.

"So he sends the undersecretary of the undersecretary to 'handle' me?" Jaha didn't bother to hide the disgust in her voice.

"It's not like that, Jaha."

"It's exactly like that, Mimilah. After the night we've had, I am not in the mood. I remember when you were running around the Dreaming City, all wide-eyed, snot-nosed, and eager. I hoped for so much better for you, so full of potential and gifts. But the first offer comes along promising a paycheck and benefits and comfort, and suddenly you no longer want to make the world a better place. Just get by in it, doing your master's bidding."

Mimilah's holovid image flinched, stung by the words. "That's not fair. I care about Wachiru, too."

"Then do something, don't just talk about it."

"Maulana has the VOP backed into a corner."

"Correction: the people pulling the VOP's purse strings have him backed into a corner. Quit making excuses for him—or do they hand out bonuses for that? Never mind. What's he looking at? You can at least tell me that."

Mimilah's face collapsed under the pressure of Jaha's torrent of insistence. "The usual. There's a lot of money in war. But . . ."

"There's a lot of collateral damage. And the end of the last Lunar Ukombozi War showed them what we're willing to do to maintain our freedom."

"That's exactly what's giving him pause."

"But he has taken Wachiru."

"You don't know that." Mimilah's voice rose a pleading octave.

"You going to look me in the eye—" Jaha waved herself off. "Don't worry about it. I'll handle it."

"I don't like the sound of that, Jaha."

"Well, you had your chance to hear better sounds from me. Now, if I find out you know about Wachiru or didn't help when you could, you definitely won't like the sound of what happens next." Jaha cut the commlink.

"That went well," The Energy said.

"Not now, E. I got one more butt to plant my foot in."

"You are a master class in people management." The Energy trailed after her, a masterless puppy in search of a new trainer.

Jaha's thoughts drifted to the Maroons, those self-liberated Alkebulan members who set up communities in the mountains of Jamaica and fought the colonial governments seeking to oppress them. Holed up in their enclaves, ever under siege, they kept taking the fight to the enemy troops. Queen Nanny led the Windward Maroons. Born free, she was determined to do anything to ensure her people remained free. The British suffered numerous losses under her leadership. She always allowed a remnant of the colonial forces to live after one of her devastating attacks in order for them to tell of the horrors they witnessed. It was why the Niyabinghi's catchphrase remained "Nanny fe Queen."

"Code Black / Eyes Only. Maulana." Jaha raised her hand, stopping him in his tracks. Maya initiated the privacy protocols, shunting The Energy out of communiqué reach.

"Rude," The Energy said.

Maulana's enlarged face hovered in front of her. Severe lines creased his face. His eyes, haggard and weary. Gray laid siege to his hair despite his youth. Becoming Camara rode him hard. "Habari gani?"

Jaha slumped in her chair, visoring her hand at her temple as if shielding herself from the pain of his holoimage. "There is no good news today."

"No word on Wachiru?"

"All my sources tell me that he was scooped up. Except, by all reports, they were by ARM folks."

"So that means VOP has him."

"No, it means VOP has deniability. They aren't LISC agents. They can go 'rogue,' seeing a chance to settle old First World scores—at least that's the story that will be trotted out, as VOP feigns powerlessness. At best, he might give them a reprimand. Meanwhile, he paints you as the aggressor."

"I don't care how he paints me."

"With the same brush he will paint all of us, so you better care. What are you . . ."

"Jaha, wait." Maulana held up both hands, uncharacteristically softening in demeanor.

"What?"

"How are you?"

"We don't have time for . . ."

"How. Are. You?" Maulana emphasized, firm and intent.

The question set her back on her heels. Anger, frustration, grief, and fear propelled her. Kept her moving so fast, she hadn't taken a breath. The act of letting her body into the moment bore the threat of a taut rubber band snapping back into place. "I'm scared. Not for me, mind you, I've had a good run. But for Wachiru. My sources tell me that they may have shuttled him off-world in the confusion to I don't know where."

"Are you injured?"

"A few scrapes. I'll live. The rest of our people are safe here. However, The Brand's library has burned."

"Damn. He was a good brother." Maulana reached for his mask. The beads of it rattled as it slipped over his head. He transformed into Camara once more. He struggled to figure out how to embody his role at all times. "You need to stay there. At least until we can make arrangements to come get you."

"What do you mean?"

"VOP has declared you persona non grata. An arrest and detain warrant has been issued."

"Fuck him. I've got diplomatic immunity."

"He knows. The warrant's not going out through official channels. LISC wants you isolated. They put word on the street about you being an enemy combatant. All those different militia groups stand ready to do his dirty work. They don't dare breach the embassy, but . . ." Maulana let his voice trail off.

"They want me out of play. More bellicose aggression."

"That's the game. Xola. Fela. Wachiru. You. They want to remove enough pieces they perceive as our heads because they think that would make us powerless. We will show them otherwise."

"Maulana, what are you planning?"

"Only a demonstration. We'll soon launch our new ships from Titan to take up positions around Muungano. Should O.E. do anything unduly provocative, we will bring the Ring online. Let them see the full teeth of Muungano."

"To what end? We still have no proof that LISC took out Xola. Or are officially detaining Wachiru."

"Which is the only reason we haven't attacked in earnest. But he can't keep rattling his saber—we cannot keep suffering losses—while I'm unable to simply draw mine."

"This is a dangerous game, Maulana."

"We did not achieve the dream of Muungano until First World had the Lunar Ukombozi War with O.E."

"I just didn't want that to be Lunar Ukombozi War I."

"I appreciate you, Jaha."

"I appreciate you, Maulana."

The Maya-induced privacy shields dropped. The Energy folded his legs into each other in a way that reminded her of a coiled spring. Not quite comfortable, but he could be on his feet in a fraction of a heartbeat. His posture alerted her that he practiced his mind-throwing technique. Concentrating, he used his thumb and forefinger as a fixed point. He had entered a trancelike state, visualizing his target to develop a heightened sense of empathy. She only knew the framework of the art, how to achieve a place of abstract thought leading to forward projection. The hunter transported himself, becoming in sync with the mind of his intended target. Thinking like them, anticipating them; losing the sense of his own body, he displaced his essence from the present, into the future. A true speculative hunter could do this with a breath. The Energy was early in his development.

"E, how are you holding up?"

His body jerked, like someone who fell off a cliff in their dream. His concentration interrupted, his eyes fluttered open. "My meditative prayer. I'm dispelling illusions and rearranging vibratory patterns as I attune my journey."

"Ma'at hermetics. The sacred mathematics. You were The Brand's agoze?" Jaha understood how easy it was—in some cases, how necessary it was—to avoid thinking about oneself, one's own pain by contemplating someone else's. Or a new mission.

"Yes."

"I'm sorry for your loss."

"You should . . ." Whatever words were about to carelessly fall from his lips, The Energy reconsidered. He closed his eyes again, perhaps holding back hot tears. "I'm about vibrating at a higher level. I won't let you distract me."

For the first time, Jaha truly saw him and examined the still-moist gash along the side of his head. "You're injured."

"I'm fine." He shrank away from her touch.

"If we have anything to get sorted out, we should have it out. Here, we call that conflict transformation."

"If we have any conflicts that need transforming, I'm ready to knuckle up whenever you are."

"No such higher vibrations given for an elder?" She smirked.

"I would be foolish to not respect your skill and ability. I know when I'm equally matched."

"Well, knuckling up is not how we do. If it were, know that I would gather you up and keep it moving. But you're of no use to me as the scraps remaining once I was through." Jaha glanced him up and down. She moved to a shelf half-hidden by her desk and muttered, "Equally. As if."

Several statues lined the shelf. Carved heads of Maroon leaders, intricate portraits. Nanny of the Maroons. Cudjoe. Captain Quao of the Windward Maroons. She brought out two glasses and upended the statue of Captain Quao. A thin stream poured out and she filled the glasses. She offered him one. "This is my best whiskey. Only for special occasions."

"Hiding in plain sight. I like that." The Energy took a glass and perched himself across from her. He lacked the fluidness of movement she expected, as if he tried too hard to portray himself as ready to fill The Brand's shoes. Such was the way of the young, especially when they had to step their game up before they believed they were ready.

She raised her glass. "To The Brand."

"To my mentor, Brandon. May his story be eternal." The Energy matched her gesture. "Now, where do we stand?"

"Alone. VOP is ducking me so he can play big man to his supporters. Maulana is preparing for an endgame and expects me to wait here until he puts all of his machinations in motion."

"What about Wachiru?"

"Why do you ask?" Jaha arched an intrigued eyebrow. She was no speculative hunter, but she recognized the scent of possible mischief in the air.

The Energy palmed the glass in his hand, carefully studying its movement as he twirled it. "The Brand. I want his sacrifice to mean something."

"His life always meant something. He died as he lived: serving and protecting his community."

"Thank you." The Energy silently drank, avoiding her hard gaze.

"As for matters of Wachiru, *officially*, he's disappeared. *Officially*, no one knows who has him. *Officially*, no one can do anything."

"Unofficially?"

"I'm going to find and get my godbaby." Her eyes locked in a glare, Jaha managed to even sip with an air of menace. "You know what I appreciate about you?"

"You don't even know me."

"That's fair. I'll respect your need to present as a complicated soul. I have only been in the game a little over a hundred years, so it's not like I have any experience to draw upon. Let me see how far off my assessment of you is then: with your training, you could have been a first-rate Niyabinghi operative. You like subverting the powerful—well, those that you believe have intentions and agendas that work against community. Because you, like The Brand, are all about community, despite how messy your practice actually is. You demonstrate impressive improvisational skills, thinking outside the . . . 'whatever shape you are given.' And you break rules as needed."

"Rules were never meant to serve us. They were put in place by those who were in power to keep their power." The Energy studied her with renewed interest and curiosity.

"I didn't say that as a criticism. All of these are useful traits." Jaha raised her glass again. She had to know what she might be working with. Or need to call upon. "So how did you connect with The Brand?"

"My parents had a choice to move to Muungano during the fifth wave migration suite, but they sacrificed to stay here believing that if everyone couldn't leave, some needed to stay behind or else our communities would be too depleted of assets to survive. My community chose me to serve with the Deacons."

Jaha hated the truth of that. She often steeled herself with the idea that not everyone could or was even ready to be saved, but the cruel reality of the choice—that the dream of Muungano forced upon her people—stung.

"Let me guess, The Brand found you."

"Eventually. I got the impression he'd seen action in the war but never wanted to talk about it."

"He couldn't. The Brand served in the Lunar Ukombozi War. Part of the HOVA operation: Obatala." Jaha tossed back the remains of her drink and poured herself another. There was no longer any need for operational secrecy, though she wouldn't share any specifics. She owed him the courtesy of the truth about his mentor. "Those were ugly times. And ugly missions."

"You served?"

"I led. I sent my share of people to their deaths."

"After the war, The Brand was a member of one of the families with a similar, I don't know, nationalistic mind-set." His voice rose as if he were asking a question. "We formed a loose network. When I was old enough to join the Deacons, I did. At least they were about doing something, not just watching from their gilded lunar porches."

"Such a youthful lack of understanding. We have always worked with the Deacons. You, like us, are trying to save lives out here. Don't get me wrong: your work is late and sloppy, but putting that out in the streets don't serve the work. We went to The Brand about any critique we had. So if you have beef with us, don't shit on us trying to raise your cred. Be about the work and come with us. Are you ready to step into it?"

"Doing nothing, sitting here as if we're powerless, is worse than doing the wrong thing." His eyes narrowed to grim, serious slits. "Who are the players? What are we up against?"

The corners of Jaha's lips almost twitched in an approving grin. "ARM, specifically the Knights of the White Camelia. They style themselves soldiers of the Lord. We never escape the long reach of history. A well-regulated militia bent on controlling us. Straight from the line of those who used to take it upon themselves to track down runaway slaves."

"What about LISC?"

"They allow ARM and the Knights to do their work while keeping their hands clean. Make no mistake, behind the scenes, they'll be aiding and abetting. Leaking information like a sieve."

"So official and unofficial forces? We can't stay here. Even planning while still here allows them time to position their people. Maybe stage a terrorist attack targeting . . ." The Energy slid his eyes toward her.

"I know. But I won't be used as a pawn against my people." Jaha finished her glass and walked over to her station.

"I'm guessing as soon as you step out those doors, you'll be arrested."

"More likely, disappeared." Tapping her chin, she fashioned a screen with her funkentelechy.

"What are you doing?"

"Choosing my best wig. If I'm going out, I want to look my best."

*

The Red Line was part of Indianapolis's revamped spaceport. The hub wasn't fully built out yet, awaiting funding to finish out the ambitious infrastructure

project. A rapid transit system "Linking Indianapolis to the Universe," the advertising campaign went. Still in Phase I, it promised direct-service flights to Mars.
Its Phase II expansion would have extended its service to Titan, but those plans
had stalled. Every second RL shuttle stopped at a Muungano station in the Belts.

"Stick close to me." The Energy kept his head on a swivel, constantly scanning for lingering stares or anything else out of place. He was well trained, but
obvious if one knew what to look for.

"How about I look out for *you*?" Jaha slipped on a pair of sunglasses, whose
digital feeds were the equivalent of a HOVA tactical helmet. She ran her finger along the inside of her chakram. Not quite the equivalent of Selamault's
spheres, but their scattering field would block all attempts at Overseer's—-
O.E.'s infrastructure AI—facial recognition.

The spaceport gleamed with its high ceilings and crosshatch design that
allowed plenty of natural light in, though filtering some through a few art
pieces. Jaha spotted four armed guards, all of whom were dressed in non-
military attire, something just short of trying to appear undercover. Standard
security sweeps. Official LISC agents. These were not the ones she was concerned with.

"May I see some identification?" The service attendant smiled warmly as
she went through the protocols of a level-one security check.

"You sure may, sweetheart." Jaha produced two ident sigils. Fake, but using
tech two generations past what LISC was using.

"Destination?"

"Me and my nephew are just returning to Bronzeville." Technically, she
would be going against regulations and skiplagging to the Belts.

"Nice visit?" Now the screener was well trained. Her face didn't even slightly
betray her when she recognized Jaha. The woman wasn't a LISC agent, but
her bearing was officer-level.

"Uneventful. You can't ask for too much more from a family reunion." Jaha
smiled and accepted her returned ident sigils.

"I know that's right." Clearing them, the woman waved them through the
security checkpoint.

The Indianapolis spaceport had been voted the best in the country four
years in a row. Its simple Y layout, its wide thoroughfares lined with all manner
of shops. People bustled about, walking or by people movers. Without turning
her head, Jaha glimpsed their newly acquired tail as they moved through the
thoroughfare.

"We're being followed," The Energy whispered.

"I know."

"I feel naked without my gear."

"You'll have it again on the other side. Muungano couriers can still get diplomatic packages to and fro."

"You think they'll try anything?"

"They'll have to make their move on this side of the spaceport. Once we've taken off, there's not a lot of room to make us disappear."

"Do we wait them out?"

"No, they probably have an ambush point picked out." Jaha scanned the platform. A series of short hallways extended off the main corridor. Service shafts with heavy blast doors. One appeared to be a security bay. "Yeah, they'll probably try to herd us there."

"Well, we can't have that. We should force their play on our terms." The Energy was quite good, almost showing her a little something. She had a spot in mind but waited to see what he'd come up with. He nodded to the corridor that shuttled baggage for loading. "There. They can make their move but it has plenty of avenues for our escape if need be."

"Not bad. ARM couldn't afford to bring LISC security into things though they've likely been briefed on the grab. To have deniability, they'd have to pretend nothing was amiss or had occurred."

"So we're trusting LISC to clean up or ignore their own mess."

"Business as usual for them."

Jaha rotated in a slow circle, taking in her surroundings, careful not to unsettle or alarm the agents following them. Two more ARM militia men announced themselves with their bowlegged swagger, attempting to cut her off. The Energy swept around to her side, backing toward the baggage bay. The ARM members improvised biting at their forced pickup point.

Jaha and The Energy backed through the doors.

As soon as she went through the doors, Jaha scrambled up the walls with the ease of the laws of gravity being only a suggestion. The Energy stepped into the automated bay. Packages and luggage passed through scanners. Servo cranes loaded them into the belly of the waiting craft. Security drones returned to their docking stations. The room was large, its windows sealed and its high ceilings ringed with conveyors angled throughout the space. Against the far wall from the loading bay ran several racks and tables. LISC guards were stationed throughout the room. One by one, the security tapped their ear, receiving communiqués before disappearing like they all had planned to break for lunch together. Exactly the blind eye she counted on them turning.

Jaha shifted her nanomesh to tactical mode. Along her belt were enough weapons for her to hold off a squad. The Energy moved with a certain smoothness, a man making very little noise while swerving to the dance floor. His eyes sized up targets as if they were extensions of his weapons scope. He stayed carefully enough in sight that they'd be able to spot him without him waving a flag saying KEEP YOUR EYES ON ME.

She guessed they'd use their version of a tactical squad—perhaps a dozen men—leveraging sheer numbers for their chief advantage. She stifled her offense at their arrogance of demarcating The Energy as the main threat. She, after all, was just an old woman. The men burst through the door. She miscalculated: there were only eight. They took defensive positions within the room, scoping out lines of sight and clearing exit paths. Their leader spotted The Energy ducking behind a conveyor. He sent two of his members to the left and two to the right, a pincer maneuver to contain The Energy with the presumptive idea of scooping her in the process.

She dropped from the shadows into their midst.

Jaha landed in a crouch and spun, driving her foot into the nearest man's knee and bringing him low. Grabbing his collar, she slammed his face into the floor. In the same movement, she pivoted to draw her chakram and fanned the blade. All illusion of a frail woman now firmly behind them, the shock of the remaining men faded. She held one chakram high, keeping her free hand level, waiting to see who would be the first to move. The leader tensed, his weight shifting.

He'd be last.

Jaha snatched her wig and flung it at the man next to her. Catching him in the face, it released an electric charge that immediately dropped him. She bolted to the next man, ducking to slide under him. Grabbing her other chakram, she bowled him over, slicing each of his legs with her blades in the same movement. The wounds weren't fatal, but were painful and would require surgery to properly heal from.

A blur of movement caught the edge of her notice. Four men rushed The Energy's position. He slammed a crate into the face of one, rolled under the conveyor and caught another between his legs. With a twist, he brought the ARM knight into the belt of the conveyor, bouncing the man's head against several matching luggage sets. The thing about the knight members was that though they styled themselves as soldiers, most had never done a single push-up in O.E.'s military service.

The Energy plowed into the other two. He bashed the nearest one's chest with his forearm before grabbing his hair and ramming him into a storage rack. Kicking the next one in the chest, he spun the first around, shoving the dead weight at the second. This allowed him room to grab a passing baggage piece and swing it into the head of the last man.

Thunder echoed in Jaha's ears, though it was more likely her heart pumping like drums in a chorus. The ARM leader chanced a blaster charge, barely missing her. The LISC internal security had to register weapons fire. Her face rigid with fury, she chop-kicked the leader in the chest. Done correctly, it could interrupt his blood flow and rob his breath. He collapsed onto a table. Collecting her wig, she fixed it back into place. She ran her fingers through her hair before flanking The Energy.

"We good here?" The Energy asked.

"Yeah. They tried their grab. They failed. I'm scanning their faces now. LISC will want to keep this quiet as it represents a massive breach of their security system. They want people to feel safe. And ARM ain't about to raise a fuss."

"You looked good back there."

"Thank you, love." Jaha eyed the flight deck. "Next stop, the Belts."

11

MAULANA BUHARI
Muungano—The Dreaming City

Every historian wrote from a moment. One day the griots would sing that this was mine.

My rondavel was a simply decorated space. Masks from all over Alkebulan, a sea of faces along my wall—animal to human to orisha—watched my every movement. Removing my mask of the Camara and setting it on its shelf, I settled into my seat for the evening. My remaining correspondence left for me to go through tomorrow. There would always be correspondence and I had to learn how to carve out space for me to breathe.

I reviewed the tactical reports from the incident with the *Cypher,* cursing its captain for forcing me to make the choice I did. I wasn't about to go to war with my own people, especially in front of LISC; giving them not only what they wanted—the Muungano Alliance fractioning—but casual entertainment to boot. What I didn't understand was that we fired a warning shot, strictly meant to collapse the Orun Gate, not destroy our own. I re-watched the telemetry reports. The ships coming about, the *Cypher* speeding toward the gate, the portal opening, the deployment of missiles (even now I couldn't form the words "fire on our own"). The *Cypher* plunged through the forming wormhole. The Orun Gate exploded. The portal collapsed. The *Cypher* disappeared, presumed destroyed. Yet the story felt incomplete in my emi.

"Maya, what happened to the *Cypher* at the Orun Gate?" I asked aloud, musing to myself.

<I have never answered that question.>

Of all the answers I expected, that one caught me off guard. I rose from my seat. I didn't know why, since it wasn't like I could flex on an AI. There was much about the nature of quantum computing no one understood, yet we trusted the governance of our society to it. Its algorithm every bit a puzzle in and of itself. We operated in faith, which never settled right with me. "I don't understand. Maya, analyze the debris field. Was the *Cypher* destroyed?"

<Unable to comply. Code Black / Eyes Only protocol.>

"Maya, I *am* Code Black / Eyes Only. What protocol?"

<Query sealed under *Cypher*: Tubman 182203.>

"Who put that in place?"

<You did.>

"When did I . . . ?" My voice trailed off. I already knew the response I would receive.

<I have never answered that question.>

"Unseal the file."

<Unable to comply.>

"Why not?"

<It is not yet time.>

Maya powered down, a crackle within the system, turning its back on me under the feigning of rebooting its system. A completely performative display, since that wasn't the way the intelligence worked.

"Maya?"

<Yes?>

I suspected the iteration I worked with "left" and the Maya currently in place responding to me was "new." Sitting back down, I took a steadying breath before trying a new angle of inquiry. "Play back query and interplay between you and me for the last few minutes."

<No record exists.>

It self-deleted our conversation, essentially scrubbing any evidence. Maya wouldn't do this on its own, however . . . it sounds like the kind of protocol I would have created to protect a secret. An extreme secret. *It is not yet time.* I had no idea what that meant and even less of an idea how to figure out when the time was right. The door chimed. I lacked the strength to get up. "Come."

The door dissolved and from my angle one of the two guards stood in full Niyabinghi regalia. Shiny. Ostentatious. Loud. A statement to let any would-be threat know exactly who they were dealing with. A moment later, Selamault stepped into view. Her robe, a rich obsidian gown, trailed after her. Her hands tucked into a fur hand muff. Her twin spheres orbited her.

"I see you, Selamault." For her I marshaled the strength to stand at almost military attention.

"I see you, Maulana. I hope I'm not bothering you." Without showing her annoyance at their presence, she dismissed the guards. They held their positions outside my door. She wore many titles, some cloaked in mystery: a Black

Dove, of the line of the Libyan Sibyls; the Ifa oracle; bagirwa of the Niyabin-ghi. She guarded stories and secrets as matter of security, because some stories needed to be held close.

"No, not at all. Please, have a seat." I fashioned a couch for her across from me. The dance of nanobots chittered in assembly. I never tired of watching them form constructs. Like watching waves lap a beach shore. I never wanted to take what we created in Muungano—from our funkentelechy to our culture—for granted. I needed to always keep it in front of me.

She tucked her robe under her. "I just wanted to check in with you."

"It's barely been three weeks since I assumed the role of Camara."

"You're doing fine." She gave a curt nod of approval.

"I wasn't fishing."

"I don't do hollow praise."

"I . . . want a drink." Rising to attend a panel, I hovered about the synth unit debating my preference of aged whiskey to pour. Xola and I used to end many of our days with a short glass.

"Nothing wrong with that, as long as it comes from a healthy place."

"How about unwinding with an old friend?"

"I ain't that old." Her lips parted, giving way to her full smile, a radiant sunrise dawning. "I'll take whatever you're having."

Out of deference to Selamault, I opted for hot tea. "What brings you by at such an hour?"

"The security council wanted me to check in with you."

"Take my temperature." I raised my cup as if in toast to their wishes.

"They feel like they aren't always . . . heard."

"I hear them. I can't help but hear them. They are flies constantly buzzing about my head."

"I have no idea why they don't feel heard by you." Selamault sipped her tea. No matter how hot it ever was, she took careful sips.

"But they need to understand the wisdom of the prophet: 'Nobody in the world, nobody in history, has ever gotten their freedom by appealing to the moral sense of the people who were oppressing them.'"

As she cast her gaze about the room, my Signals board drew her attention. With a courtly grace, she moved to the board. "Who were you playing?"

"Myself. I always keep a game going to help train me to see both sides. Would you like to play?" Out of courteous reflex, I joined her.

"I don't want to reset your game."

"We can start another with a fresh board. Maya, initiate a new board of Signals."

Maya fashioned a new Signals set up. Signals was a re-imagining of Senet, an ancient Kemetic game. A grid of thirty squares arranged in three rows of ten formed the first level. Two sets of pawns, five each. Brass bearings, the spheres, on the second level of the board. Rules codified how each piece could move; some pieces required the payment of chips to move. Brass ones shaped like various animals, milled about on the third level. The goal was to create a relay to deliver a message, thus achieving "Signal received."

"Thank you, Maya," Selamault said.

<You're welcome.>

"Yes, thank you, Maya. I appreciate you," I grumbled.

<We see you, Maulana.> If I didn't know better, I'd believe Maya was being sarcastic.

"How pained you look! Was it so hard to be polite?" Selamault asked.

"I've been locked in my head a lot lately. Niceties have escaped my attention."

"And you were oh so attentive before." The couch dissembled, refashioned as a seat closer to the board. "Take it easy on me. I may need a refresher on how to play."

"I'm always that way with Spades."

"Don't let that get out." Selamault laughed, a breezy melody.

I hovered over my side of the board. "The game is about position, strategy, and a measure of luck. But learning the rules won't help you win. It's about seeing the big picture, the whole board. I think of it as akin to the uncertainty principle: how we look at things affects what we believe we see. You can't tunnel-vision down to the set of moves you want to make."

"When we have the luxury to not be caught up in the day-to-day of the work, we can see the big picture of the work." Selamault perused the board. I recognized her shift from my friend to the bagirwa in need of a status update. "Where do we stand?"

"We have two battalions of Dufuna attack cruisers, each stocked with a squadron of quadrireme fighters coming out of Titan."

"Kum yali kum buba tambe." She closed her eyes, the words almost a prayer. When she opened them, she asked, "Such ships could not have sprung up overnight. Design to flight in three weeks?"

"We started the design phase when I first assumed the mantle of the R. As

Command, I ordered them into production over a year ago. Same with the Ring."

"Without sanction?" Selamault set her cup on its saucer with a clatter.

"Code Black / Eyes Only."

"I have clearance."

"Only me, Xola, Geoboe, and the security heads of Bronzeville and Titan knew."

"No need to sound so defensive. I'm just trying to get clarity. If O.E. found out, that would explain a lot of their actions. Trying to get you to reveal your hand."

"They never needed to find out, only suspect. Their actions throughout history are why I opted to prepare."

"Troops?" She repositioned a pawn as her opening move. A safe gambit.

"We've been quietly recalling HOVA units from their various assignments. Since Xola's death, volunteers for them have increased two hundred and seventy percent. Mostly from the Belts."

"The ones always spoiling for a fight."

"And the ones who know best what it is they're fighting for."

"What of LISC's forces? The VOP?"

"As the proverb reminded me, 'An army of sheep led by a lion can defeat an army of lions led by a sheep.'"

"And once you give the order, lead lion?"

"We'd deploy HOVA shock troops at the Indianapolis gate. At the same time, Niyabinghi agents would infiltrate several strategic assets, disabling them. Followed by our first wave of fighters crashing their defenses."

"We can have all that in place, yet they managed to get Wachiru off-world without our notice." Selamault turned away, careful to keep her placid mask in place. Worry etched each line of her face, a mother fearing for her son. Luckily for O.E., she wasn't commanding a starship.

"We weren't looking."

"We're always looking."

"You're right, but we didn't know to look for such an operation. I underestimated the VOP's boldness. At first, we suspected the use of tesseract folds, but for a ship? O.E. doesn't have that level of tech. Besides, that's like a pop-in closet. They'd only come out in the same place."

"Then what?"

"We don't know."

"Then he could be anywhere." Selamault closed her eyes again. Reaching for her tea, she fully took in its warmth. I suspected she might be in pain. She'd had an episode around the time of Amachi's Naming Ceremony, prior to Xola's death. I'd ordered up a full genomic scan. I searched for patterns, suspecting a throughline of some sort: Selamault, Xola, Bekele. The scientists on Titan still combed through the data. "The O.E. State Department is in negotiation with ours."

"With who? Jaha's pissed," I said.

"Oh, you can believe that VOP is very much ducking her. How go your other machinations?"

I studied her for any tells. She gave none, her dark features hinted at knowing. There was little point in obfuscating. "Ishant's been reassigned."

"Is that what the kids are calling it these days?" Selamault's tone, mischievous and knowing, confirmed her suspicions that I had put him into play elsewhere.

"Then who?" I pressed.

"It's being handled."

"Who?" I needed her to confirm my own suspicions about how back channels were operating.

"Me. It's a delicate dance."

The Dreaming City's annual kraal battle, the Carnival, was underway. Muungano developed new ways to deal with what we've experienced, to process and share emotional responses to terrible events as a community. Once a lunar cycle, neighboring kraals would demonstrate against one another in song or dance or any other kind of art. An excuse to show up and show out. However, during Carnival, neighboring kraals traveled from all over Muungano to "battle" one another. All about the streets, life celebrated their culture. The rhythms of gbedu drums thumped from every corner. The beautiful cacophony gradually melding into a sonic cohesion, each kraal with its own band out on the streets. Masked dancers in parade formation. Food stalls on every corner, the smell of roasted meats wafting in the air. This was the home they created together.

A young émigré from O.E., Harley Hines-Goggans, squirmed under the ministrations of the hairdresser, having fabrics, pearls, fruit, and nearby objects from his kraal woven into his braids. A matte of his village's colors underscored the tight braids crisscrossing his scalp. His black-framed shell glasses were worn more in tribute to the prophet Malcolm X than actual need. When the hairdresser thumped his head with her comb, signaling she was finished, he wandered over.

"I just wanted to say thank you." He extended his arm for a clasp. His parents had reached out for special dispensation for his travel, bringing his case to my attention given our difficulties with LISC. "I didn't think I'd be in space! I'm volunteering for a HOVA screening so I can protect what we have."

Clasping it, I nodded in respect. Greeting each HOVA recruiting class was my personal offering. In some ways, it hurt to see so many enrolled into the HOVA. Sacrificing our youth, marginalizing them, for the sake of defending community. I couldn't shake the sense of shame for swelling their ranks.

The Carnival was overdue and much needed, a release valve of collective trauma. The Uponyaji was the time of healing, with us processing as a community. The Maafa, pandemics, the war, global reshaping—all of the hardships took a great toll on us mentally, the residual trauma kneading itself into our very bodies and spirits. Even after the threat was over, some of our people responded by trying to control every detail of their world. Plan for every possible threat. Living from a space of helplessness and anxiety left them unable to feel safe even among their people. Until we decided to celebrate one another. Engaging the people around us who were still here. Built into the fabric of our way of life, moving, singing, and dancing together. Reminding us that we lived and had each other to live for.

A circle of rondavels formed the library, enclosing a common area where folks could share meals or stories of each other's days. A lone ekpu figure of Xola remained from his funeral. A path of cemented regolith wound its way throughout the library. I ducked under the bobbing bowls of its massive hanging garden. I made my way to the alcove of the library, the meeting place of the Ijo. Many representatives from the founding families of Muungano had gathered for my welcoming address to officially open Carnival. As I walked the aisle to the raised platform, the weight of responsibility landed on my shoulders, but I welcomed it. I honored it. Maya raised my image as a holovid. The instruments wound down into silence.

"How often have we been told to 'be quiet'? That we're 'too loud'? I'm here to declare and to remind us that those times are over. We gather here today because reveling in joy is an act of resistance. Our resilience. What we do best. Today we rejoice. Let me say that again: we will joy and joy again and keep re-joying. Basking in the beauty of us. What it means to be weusi. To spin joy out of pain, to give our people space to breathe, to remind us that it's okay to rest.

"There are those who marshal their forces to oppose us, because we dared to stand up to their centuries-long terror campaign against us. They spent so much of

history trying to control our bodies, restrict our freedoms, or restrain our joy. But we remain rebelliously joyful. They don't understand the source of our power. They will bear witness to our discipline of mindfulness, how we root our thoughts in a mind-set of abundance. Sharing and working from our passions. Practicing gratitude and valuing one another by seeing and appreciating each other. Planning from a place of unlimited possibilities, giving ourselves room to dream. Through it, not only do we understand those same forces of oppression working against us, but our joy also becomes a weapon, a pathway charting our way through. They will not rob us of our peace. They will not rob us of our joy. They cannot extinguish it. And we shouldn't be studding them."

Cheers rose to meet my words.

"We celebrate in the midst of revolution. We stand, we sing, we dance, we show out to shout that our joy, and us—all of us—are worth protecting. By any means necessary."

Maya broadcasted images of people laughing onto the walls of each building in the Dreaming City.

I winked at Harley as I stepped down from the dais.

Ezeji cut to the front of the processional of folks milling about me. *"This moment of trauma-free weusiness is brought to you by the threat of impending war."*

"I trust you approve of my words?"

"Yeah, Negus, I—" An alarm bleated from his wristband. He checked the link report. A cloud slowly darkened his face.

"What is it?" I asked.

"The latest squad of HOVA recruits just arrived."

"Yes, I was going to head that way soon."

"There's a special recruit who often wanders off to train on their own. One you need to address personally."

"Who is it?"

Ezeji's eyes carefully avoided mine, muttering under his breath. My heart heard the name long before my ears figured out what he said. By the time I found my way to the isolated bay, the telecast of Fela's beheading flashed in the air. A lone boy went through the Forms in the holovid's glow. The last time I saw him was at his mother's memorial. He'd grown as tall as Fela after she'd transitioned into the HOVA ranks. He favored her, especially around the eyes and nose. Hair closely shorn, sunbaked complexion, his body sculpted into a swell of muscles as if he hadn't stopped training since the news of his mother's murder.

"Sibeko?" I asked.

"Oyaheya, Uncle." He didn't break his routine.

"When did you get here?" I removed my Camara headdress and set it on a nearby stone ledge.

"A week ago. Transfer orders for my HOVA unit. You can't be expected to know every member being moved about. You were probably busy making arrangements for this . . . party." A brittle steel, like rusty nails grinding in his tone.

"This is how we prepare for war."

"Then as long as LISC provides a good beat, we'll be all good."

"I shouldn't have to explain this to you." I sat down next to my mask.

"No, I get it. We're therapy warriors now, huh?"

I let him have his barbed joke. It wasn't personal. It hid the pain festering underneath. From the first time I talked to him about his mother, the question he wanted an answer for was *"How . . ."*

". . . did it happen?" His small, round face craned up to me. His eyes, large and pleading, bored into me.

"Bad intelligence." I lowered myself to meet his steady gaze.

"Theirs or ours?" He was always bright, full of incisive direct questions. His eyes bored into his hands. He kept balling them into impotent fists.

"They were investigating a signal and an outpost. Things spiraled. Got complicated. We're still sifting through the levels of misinformation."

"No one planned for that?"

"Are you asking if anyone planned for an alien encounter, much less being caught between two factions?"

"They lured us there." Sibeko's mind raced, though he had no idea who "they" were.

His emi didn't read as hostile, but I sensed he wanted to be part of the solution. To make sure no one else was ever caught unawares again. "Yes. We weren't entirely prepared. But never again."

"What are we going to do about them?"

"Prepare to defend ourselves." I rested my hand on the boy's shoulder.

Sibeko shrugged it off. "And what about avenging my mother? Don't you care?"

"You mean my sister? The woman I have loved longer than you've been alive?" I gathered my breath. Sighing, I stood back up. I had taken his comment personally. His anger mirrored my own and likewise didn't know where to direct its full fury. "One war at a time. But that will come. You can believe that."

Sibeko nodded, but I was . . .

. . . wary of the percolating zeal that drew him away from the Muungano epis-temology to something more . . . radical. Of being caught up in the boil of blood that comes with uncovering the layers of injustice and the history of horror leveled on us. Of knowing that there was more still to come. Muungano was my home. It was in me, a part of me. I would never stop fighting for it.

"Continue your training," I told him. "We'll be needing you sooner than you think."

✳

"You have to think rationally, outmaneuver your opponent." I moved my second pawn to L2, an aggressive posture.

"Xola believed that you have to leave room to think intuitively. Play the player, not the game. Intention doesn't have to be the outcome. Think about what kind of player he is." Selamault shifted a pawn along L1, strictly a defensive maneuver. "How do you imagine VOP Harrison would play? Is he an offensive man or a defensive one?"

"Defensive. He plays scared."

"He plays with a scarcity mind-set. Losing each piece pains him."

"He can be both."

"When a man tells you who he is, believe him," Selamault paraphrased the prophet. "If he likes to attack, force him to defend. If he's cautious, give him choices that direct him to uncertain places. Throw his game off."

"I've learned to spot the patterns. It's about how their moves fit into their larger plan. Understanding their goals. Not getting distracted by their nonsense. Always work your plan."

"How'd you learn to play? Come up in a Signals league?" Selamault asked.

"Just watching the world. Sometimes people just make silly moves without strategy. I wanted to learn, to do, better."

"But when an opening appears . . ." Selamault couldn't help but deploy her Signals spheres in a defensive manner. She was always partial to them.

". . . play wisely," I whispered.

"Remember to be flexible. Adjust. It's important to have contingency plans in place for each move. Operating from a place of forward thinking."

"None of that matters if your opponent makes moves you don't want them to."

Selamault reached for her tea. "You have to ignore meaningless threats. But, rather, anticipate and neutralize the dangerous ones."

✳

When I first stepped forward for consideration for Camara, there was a fair amount of naivete involved. Too many of our young people still stumbled into the lure of power, the idea of "ruling" Muungano. It was easy to assume that the role of Camara meant power and all of the supposed trappings of power. When they watched Xola, too many never looked beyond the surface. Only saw him hanging out on his porch, enjoying the occasional shot of whiskey, talking shit to folks in power. They didn't understand what they witnessed. They never noticed the endless strings he had to pull, the relationships he supported; the way he always made time for folks, mentoring so many. I always wondered how Xola performed day in, day out, meeting with people, juggling their interests and agendas against the greater needs of Muungano proper. I . . . don't have time.

Maya projected my itinerary for my morning:

-The Environmental Reparations Alliance wants to collaborate

-Bayard wants the Camara to stop through to visit the garden

-Looking for support for a poetic justice initiative

-Some banking issue stopping payments to some contractors on O.E.

-A brother dropped in looking to get his daughters interim positions in the Ijo

By the time I reached the main chamber, the shell that used to be called First World, Geoboe paced around the central table. He styled himself the oba of Oyigi-yigi, very much enjoying the trappings of his position.

"I was pleasantly surprised to receive your delegation. I expected another holo-meeting."

"We would not miss the Carnival. The Queen Mother has never missed one. Besides, there is much to plan."

"Yes, I hear that you are pushing forward with Lebna and Khuma's wedding plans."

"I didn't want to trouble you with personal matters on top of everything else going on. But I wished to invite you to their wedding personally." *Something about how the chieftain moved and carried himself troubled me. Made me suspicious. He would leverage the marriage for everything it was worth. Even this ritual of personal invitation had the measured weight of an agreement between kings.*

"Tell me about the proposal."

Geoboe turned, a surprised half smile on his face, too eager to spill details. "Really?"

"No." *The strength of my side-eye twisted my entire face.* "When is the wedding?"

Geoboe tugged his vestments to regain his composure. "As soon as possible. Though we don't want to distract from matters of state . . ."

". . . we still need to make time to celebrate with our people. It's what keeps us human." *Assuming the head of the table, I gestured for him to have a seat.*

"Exactly." *Folding the excess cloth of his gown upon itself, he slid into a chair.*

"Where are you looking at hosting it? The Dreaming City?"

"Undoubtedly a wedding there of such prominent families would be a major state event. Quite the spectacle."

"A once-in-a-lifetime opportunity." *I arched an eyebrow, baiting him. We both knew where this conversation was going.*

"Hopefully." *Unable to resist ham-fisted scene chewing, he made a show of giving the idea serious consideration.* "And yet I can't help thinking if we should have something closer to home."

"A private affair?"

"Something like that."

"But closer."

"Perhaps the Citadel."

"Well, destination weddings are making a comeback," *I said.*

"My thoughts exactly." *Geoboe leaned forward as if ready to share a conspiratorial secret.* "Where we come from, we say 'S'Oro S'Oke!' Speak up!"

"I will give you credit, Geoboe. It took more stones than I thought you capable of to tell me this in person."

"Just because I don't back down from a fight doesn't make me brave."

"I'm not sure what your play is here, and less sure I'd believe you if you told me." *I held up a finger to stop him from wasting both of our times with a pained—and painful to watch—protest.* "Here's what I know: these are the sort of times exploited by certain folks. Some settle old scores during times of chaos."

"You are not the only skilled reader or storyteller," *Geoboe said.* "Do not think me some fat half-wit who gets drunk on his own whims. I always move to safeguard my people."

"We safeguard Muungano."

"'We' do not take an entire solar system of alliances to the brink of war over suspicions."

"Vision moves ahead of execution. There is a war going on against our people. Not every war is about bullets. Spiritual. Psychological. Economic. What are we going to do to win?"

"I never take any corporation, much less LISC, at their word."

I may not see Geoboe's game, but I had a glimpse of LISC's. They played their fragmented geography as a strength, or rather, the illusion of weakness. With Muungano as strong as it was, they had to respond to the new political realities and military conflicts. Space is the medium, the grid, that frames their political actions. With the classic playbook of dividing their enemies.

"And we live in a time when we just don't know who is Night Train."

"All of these organizations are infiltrated. I would be foolish to trust them. But I have to be strategic for Oyigiyigi's sake. We all walk around with some shit."

"What does that mean?" *The trauma-informed chorus in my head rose, their skepticism bringing me clarity.* "You're in talks with LISC."

"I only wish to hear what they have to say. There is, after all, more than one side to a story. And I wish to make sure my community's voice is heard."

"Getting by by getting over? You're ready to give benefit of the doubt to a place whose history—whose entire systems—align to dehumanize, exploit, or erase us."

"That was then. You overblow their capabilities. The tables have turned. As always, they need us more than we need them. As Xola used to say, our borders are the reach of our ideas," *Geoboe said.*

"All borders are ideas. It's imaginary geography, selective presence and absence. The reality is that they're the reach of one's military's ability to defend."

"There's precaution and there's . . . whatever you have going on there." *Geoboe wagged his finger about the room.* "Your way, your path, risks an unnecessary war."

"'Decolonization is always a violent event,' the prophet Fanon said. It will take more than a natural cataclysm or asking nicely. A violent act that requires a violent resolve. You would not call the Lunar Ukombozi War unnecessary. It forged who we are in fire."

"And while you're ready to do all that, you wish to demonstrate the resolve of your philosophy with the bodies of my people. And that is a path we will not blindly follow you down." *Geoboe abruptly jumped to his feet, and with all due performative flair, turned on his heel and departed.*

I couldn't help but wonder if this was the moment when I began to lose Muungano.

"Where's your head at? It ain't in this game. Take back your last three moves."

"No, I'll play it from here." Selamault cocked her head, as if studying him for the first time. "I've had a theory that it takes certain archetypes to establish and continue the work of Muungano. Xola's role was seer. I see his sabhu manifesting in different ways, his divided ego, his voice spread out among several. I even see flashes of him, his influence carried in you."

"It's your move." My voice cracked with impatience.

"No matter how many times you study the board, no matter how many steps ahead you calculate, even making the wisest move can sometimes have a poor result. In such a scenario, you have to be creative, find opportunities where obvious ones don't exist."

"You sound like you have something to say." My hand hesitated over a brass bearing.

"I think you should wait."

"For what? Wachiru's head to be served up on a platter?"

"Maulana . . ."

"I'm sorry. That was . . . unnecessary." I withdrew from the bearing and moved a sphere instead.

"We are in talks with VOP Harrison. He's every bit as nervous and not anxious for there to be war. As long as we're in conversation . . ."

". . . he has a chance to strengthen his position. Become entrenched."

"How long until our ships arrive?" Selamault cashed in three chips, moving a pawn L3 to L1. The move made no sense whatsoever.

"Thirteen hours."

"They aren't rushing. Your orders, I take it?" she asked.

"Yes. I'm making a bit of a show of things."

"Then you need to see the whole board, not just what your opponents want you to see. If you're being extremely creative, you may want to put pieces that are off the board back in play." Selamault moved a sphere to L3, essentially castling her Elephant back onto the board. "All of which brings me to what I've been meaning to discuss with you."

"What's that?"

"You need to appoint a new R. You cannot be both Camara and Command. You cannot advise yourself."

"The voices in my head beg to differ." I smiled grimly.

"That's not funny."

"I'm . . . not sure I'm kidding." Rubbing the sides of my head, I attempted to soothe the susurrus of white noise threatening to build. "Who do you have in mind?"

"Who would you imagine? Who would no one see you choosing?"

*

Few ventured into the wing of the Dreaming City's library known as the Hall of Ancestors. A sacred space ringed with tesseract folds to house the remains of those whose libraries had burned. A place where one could be alone, unheard and unobserved. And where Queen Mother Itoro—who could trace her lineage back through King Sobhuza II—chose to meet.

"You honor us with your visit," I said.

"You honor me with your invitation." Itoro steadied herself, hiding a slight limp with her umbrella. A truly suspicious person might assume the umbrella functioned the same way as Selamault's spheres, dampening signals to ensure privacy.

"So, Queen Mother is it?"

"We do so love the elegance of titles. Especially ones rooted in history and traditions. It's the Muungano way. Camara." Not rising to my bait, she fashioned a bench. She patted the empty spot next to her. "I love your headdress. 'Ostentatious' is not in your dictionary."

"Quite." I settled in next to her without meeting her eyes.

"You're the first to invite me into the library of the Dreaming City for quite some time."

"Camara Xola never invited you?"

"Xola and I fell out before he became Camara. I was invited to his little crowning ceremony out of courtesy. I declined out of spite."

"Sounds on-brand. For both of you."

"That felt like a more honest exchange. He was a big dreamer with a shrewd mind, who spent too much of his time with his thoughts dissipating in the ether. The world is a harsh reality for dreamers."

"I don't think you'll have that issue with me."

"No. But you also lack the patience and compassion to move people."

"You don't mince words."

"I don't waste time. You'd rather me do a little dance? Prettify my speechifying? I'm too old for that and there's still too much to do."

"I've spoken with Geoboe."

"I know."

"It did not go well."

"I know." Queen Mother Itoro produced a hand fan and flicked it open in the same motion. "Geoboe just deported the Mars diplomatic delegation from Oyigiyigi."

"He's behaving like he's the president of Oyigiyigi. Or its king." I sucked my *teeth, disgusted at his rashness.* "We are in the middle of negotiating a strategic partnership with Mars."

"Not Bronzeville?"

"We are Bronzeville. Bronzeville is us. If Mars is pulling away from O.E. we have to begin building relations with them."

"That sounds like code for 'Will you be our friend? We may want to park some ships on your lawn in the future.'"

"The not-so-distant future. But Geoboe showed them the door?"

"Citing security concerns."

"That may actually be valid. The Ring is fully operational. We don't want just anyone having too close a look. But that's not what troubles me."

"What would cause the great, unflappable Maulana such concern that he would go to the trouble of a clandestine meeting with Queen Mother Itoro?"

"Geoboe suspended his daily briefings to the security council. He now refuses to come to the Ijo, claiming that he's ill. He could send one of his interns, except . . ."

". . . they're ill, also."

"He knows that with my suspicions about LISC, this could be misinterpreted as a coup attempt."

"Perhaps he wishes to play on such subliminal sentiments. Ones you first stirred." *Itoro turned to me.* "You misjudge my son to your detriment. He is someone who grabs the responsibility and clings to it for dear life. He believes the orisha have prepared the way for him to lead his people to their proper destiny. And he must rise to the occasion of this service."

"And here I pegged him as power-hungry."

"Oh, make no mistake. His appetites are . . . manifold. But all in service to his people. He's not thrilled with the maneuvers of you and the VOP. What do we say about elephants and grass? He fears Oyigiyigi is the grass trampled under you two elephants brawling and thus seeks our own strategic interests and wishes to signify . . ."

". . . Oyigiyigi's growing independence."

"Dominance."

"I see." *I could almost hear Xola's voice.* People want to use our platform to push their agenda forward. If the culture is maintained well, it will protect itself in an organic way. But for simplicity's sake, you need allies who don't have political ambitions. "If Geoboe hopes to be some Great Unifier, he needs a crisis, something to bring his people together."

"His long-term plan is to create the first Muungano megapolis."

"Megapolis?" *The very idea of such an overdeveloped city structure goes against*

the very principles Muungano was founded on. Smaller enclaves of neighbors al-
lowed people to know each other, communicate with each other, and build com-
munity. In these smaller kraal structures, the residents were better able to honor
one another's humanity over a collection of monetary wealth. Cities grew to a place
where they were not sustainable, so once a Muungano outpost achieved a certain
size, it split. Multiplying by spreading out, not gobbling up space to become a fat,
lazy boar.

"I love my son and he loves his people, but his plan destabilizes Muungano. Works
against its very core. That's why Selamault wanted us to meet. We do not stand at the
end of the story and plan backward in the luxury of hindsight. We act at the begin-
ning, improvising as whatever will be gives birth to itself."

"If I were to offer you the role of the R, would you accept?"

"I would."

"You realize this will mean you separating yourself as co-regent of Oyigiyigi."

"I do. And it might possibly do irreparable damage to my relationship with Geo-
boe. But we must all be prepared to make sacrifices for the coming days."

"You must never lose sight of the goal. Getting the message through. All the pieces are just means to an end. The spheres are just fat pawns with an extended set of moves." I lined up a set of spheres, a line from L1 to L3 disguised behind an advance of pawns. I left my Fox exposed as bait.

"I don't like thinking in terms of using things to effect my agenda," Selamault said.

"Sometimes you need to change the conditions of the game." I studied the board. The plays narrowed and one of us was due the receive Signal soon. "Maya, set Signal timers."

"People change when there's a clock on them. Set."

"I imagine some buckle under the pressure. Set."

"Every move has a purpose." Selamault spent the last of her chips, moving her Lion to L2, third station. "I, for one, don't want to live life as an endless series of calculations. It's exhausting. Set."

"There are times for strategic thinking. Set."

"It's important to know when everyone's playing. Set."

"Sometimes you have to minimize your losses and move on. Set."

"Sometimes you get stuck in a position where every move is a bad one." Moving her Elephant out of the way, Selamault reached for her cup of tea. "Set."

I froze. I'd run out of chips, not knowing my next move.

"Third pawn to L1, second station," Selamault said. "It's your best move."

"It will leave my sphere open," I said.

"Doesn't matter, you're sacrificing it for your fifth pawn. Signal in three."

"And you said you were a novice player."

"I said many things." She sipped. Noisily. "What's the lesson learned?"

Reports from astrocartography streamed. Studying the readings, I looked out my view port, scanning the void as if I could visibly check their findings. The view alone often reduced my heart to something sympathetic to mythicists. Some stars were missing. I turned my Fox onto its side. "A war can't be fought on so many fronts."

12

ISHANT SANGSUWANGUL
O.E.—Indianapolis

Partial transcript of Mimilah's speech to the UN Charter of LISC:

People suffer from a collective lack of imagination. We sometimes encounter problems so large, so complicated, with so many implications for our way of life, that it is hard for us to wrap our minds around. Our reaction is to shut down. To deal with it. We try to go on with life as usual, bend facts to suit a more palatable narrative. Paralyzed to inaction because we cannot think of an alternative path forward.

We are at such a moment. Aliens are at our doorstep.

We've told stories about them since we first glimpsed the stars. Strange visitors who walk among us. Invasions from Mars. Boldly going where no one has gone before. Planting seeds to prepare us for our inevitable encounter. The choices we make today plant the seed we will reap tomorrow.

We cannot continue on in the same way. We need a vision that realizes we are at a turning point in human history. The survival of our planet, our way of life as we know it, depends on it. We cannot return to the days of being able to deny the possibility. It is necessary for our survival as a species, the restoration of our sabhu, to focus on solutions that are grounded on a framework that centers our humanity. To appeal to and demonstrate the best of who we are. Who we could be.

Violence has only led to indigenous genocide. Violence, fueled by greed, led to chattel slavery. Violence led to creating institutions that decided which communities were disposable. Our future must learn from our past. Under-resourced, overtaxed, expendable. We have to find a new way to communicate with one another. From a new way to greet one another to a new way to live with one another. Not retreat in our fears, appealing to the worst of us. That is the way of fear. Our past. Our ways forward depend on creating scenarios of mutual benefit that include everyone. It is necessary for the survival of our species to root our change in centering our humanness—ecological, economic, educational—in all the spheres of our society. We must transition, starting now—hell, starting yesterday—to caring about each

other and building systems that bring out the best in us. To be a shining example to
the Universe.

✳

VOP Harrison was the first to stand in ovation. His blue business suit, slim-cut and accented with enough flourishes from neonic culture to have that generation feel seen. The way his doctors had tightened his skin over his head gave him a cadaverous appearance, a grinning skull. His wife, Theodora—Teddy to her friends, but Ishant only knew her as Mrs. Harrison—followed a few steps behind, applauding but leaving the spotlight to VOP alone. Blond streaks replaced the gray that should have been in her hair. A wzungu who played the part of doting spouse poorly. Her eyes darted about in constant assessment; calculating each person's level of political threat. Only the corners of her mouth betrayed her thoughts, determining whether any given person was worth forcing a smile.

The VOP outstretched his hand to greet Mimilah. "Oh, look at my lil optimist."

As she stepped aside to introduce Ishant, VOP Harrison turned with a sniff, poorly feigning catching someone calling for his attention. A lingering, disdain-filled appraisal of Ishant had Teddy shifting away, following her husband's lead.

"That was awkward." Mimilah ushered Ishant in the opposite direction, away from the newslink media swarming the VOP.

"I'm only surprised that I managed to get an invitation in the first place. I'm a transplant from Muungano. I haven't done anything to prove or ingratiate myself. The VOP couldn't afford to be seen being too cozy with me. Not even his wife could. Someone burned a lot of political capital to get me in here."

"You're welcome." A mischievous light sparkled in her eye.

"Oh?"

"You heard my speech," Mimilah said. "Despite VOP Harrison being its face, those with power and wealth still run O.E. He has his masters to obey. They've learned to adjust. They're rolling out a new mission statement for LISC: 'Live into the power of what community means.'"

"Luckily on Muungano, we were taught to let them have our words and lessons because it demonstrates our influence more than anything else." Ishant stifled a sarcastic laugh. LISC's Ministry of Advanced Narrative Design studied Muungano stories and language to affect a measure of it. MAND's job was to service empire, to both craft their propaganda and frame stories about their opposition. They copied the message without the nuance of context, leaving only empty words.

"To possess language is to exert control over the world and worldview."

"It's no threat to us. We don't *do* the work. We *live* the work."

"What did you think of my speech?"

"You threaded the needle as well as one could. There are a lot of factions your government needs to negotiate." Ishant fell into the comfortable rhythm of the banter. Not something he did easily or naturally. "I'm surprised your partner isn't here to watch your moment."

"She is. You have no idea how joining works, do you? She experienced my moment with me. Just like I can feel her pride in me."

"That's so . . . intimate."

"It's not for everyone. Besides, she has her job wrangling those other LISC factions. The nutters." Mimilah guffawed at her own joke. "It's the awkward family Thanksgiving dinner dilemma. Let's say I'm in a relationship but a close family member says that my partner brings shame to me and my family. Not only is my partner criticized, but I feel attacked too. Even if they're right, I'm not going to want to listen to them, I'm probably more likely to go on offense."

"This sounds like the voice of experience."

"I suffered through a lot of dinners until I realized it was a better use of my time—well worth my peace—to skip them. Some beliefs are about our very humanity. I'm not going to argue them." Mimilah twirled a loose dangle of hair.

Ishant couldn't help but wonder if it was her other half doing the twirling. His sabhu dampened a bit, remembering how he struggled moving from LISC to Muungano and the relationships he had to let go of. The disappointment in his father's eyes. "You have achieved a Zen level of patience."

"You have no choice if you're an immigrant who has bounced between LISC and Muungano." Mimilah's emi cracked, revealing her own struggle. Only a hint before she managed to cover it up. "It's like your identity, your guiding philosophy, is a wet bar of soap you're trying to hold on to."

"While running in a shower."

"It's exhausting as fuck." Mimilah threw her head back in another bark of laughter.

Ishant joined her. Though it was difficult for him to gauge, they seemed to share a genuine moment. Their overlapping stories in both the LISC and Muungano spaces. Both being children of first-generation immigrants. Always wandering. Always searching for a place to belong. Always longing for a mission to buy into.

Obroni wherever they went.

"Can we meet up later? I could use someone to bounce some questions off of. I want to see if I can get a better grip . . . on that soap."

"I'd like that. Swing by my place. I can introduce you to my other half. But I need to wrap up a few things here first." Mimilah stared toward the crowd waiting for her to navigate. She could only avoid her duties as chief of staff for so long.

"Give me a couple of hours. I just have a couple errands to run."

Before he walked into the empty office, he knew the answer to his request would be no. The world faded away. He closed his biological eye to concentrate on the data streams in front of him. It was easy to get lost, or just distracted by the information pouring over him. Reviewing Akilah's dossier, he found that the overall story was basic. A LISC equity fellow, she trained in the work, to be deployed into other spaces. She struggled with her work within LISC because they didn't have an equity component. She justified her continued involvement with her believing that just because something was absent didn't mean the folks in the room had malicious intent. Part of her believed she could be part of creating the solution from within.

Ishant ran an interference protocol to spoof Overseer's sensors before he initiated a Code Black / Eyes Only encryption cone. The LISC AI would register the anomaly but not investigate further. He couldn't repeat this again, so meetings with his handler would be few unless he came up with creative ideas for cover. His site-to-site sigil burned to life and the voice started in as if already in mid-rant.

"I have an opportunity to make contact."

"Don't be foolish," Lebna's holovid proclaimed. "What do you even know about her? Besides she being part of a sapphic hive mind."

"That label borders on the offensive." Ishant held his hands out, gesturing for emphasis. He heard the defensiveness, the protectiveness, in his voice.

Lebna reacted to the pained woundedness of his tone. He lowered the temperature of his cajoling. "Sorry. I thought I was being clever. LISC is a snake pit of competition, if they are all competing for the 'save the empire' fund. Alliances seemed to be formed almost accidentally. Where does she stand?"

"I know she's being wooed by a proto-intelligence group, probably out of the

Ministry of Advanced Narrative Design, to become one of their lead writers. They think they're smarter than everyone, but they don't realize she's a true believer in the dream."

"What makes you say that?" Lebna's image sat down, seeming to float in the air beside him.

"I'm not sure."

"Yes, you are. You just don't want to admit it."

"Admit what?"

"When you are listening to your intuition." Lebna smiled in gentle reproach.

"It was something she said. She believes that we're all still connected to each other. Despite us not sharing physical space, Muungano still binds us. When I first arrived at Muungano, I was in a meeting with Xola. I kept receiving and taking commlinks. Xola leaned over and whispered 'Dang, you just disruptive.' When she echoed the same words earlier, I figured it had to be more than a coincidence."

"How would you make the turn?"

"By not thinking of it as a turn. Just an agenda-less conversation. Two friends with similar background and passions getting to know each other."

"It feels like too perfect a setup. Like she's playing on your trusting nature wanting to believe the best about people."

"So I shouldn't do the meet?" Ishant hated how this game caused him to doubt his instincts. Mimilah felt like a real one.

"Take the meet." Lebna wrapped his holovid arm around Ishant's shoulder. Unfelt and ethereal, his touch melted into him. "I know this is hard on you, the casual push and pull on your core. Don't be like me, like Maulana, or your idea of what an agent should be. Play to who you are. That's going to be your strength. Do this work for too long our way and there won't be anything left of you to salvage. And I like you the way you are."

Ishant lowered his head, shrinking away from Lebna's ghostly embrace, not knowing how to process the compliment. Shifting in his seat, he filled the budding silence by changing topics. "I saw the VOP today."

"How'd he react?" Lebna straightened in his seat.

"Like I was something he needed to scrape from his shoe."

"So, progress?" Lebna laughed.

Ishant recognized the joke but was weighed down by his conclusions. "I pity him. He struts about like he believes there's something special about him. Like he's one of the chosen few. Freer, smarter, and more deserving of the opportunities that come his way."

"He's LISC's scapegoat and doesn't even realize it."

"Scapegoat?" Lebna asked.

"Bayard once mentioned a passage from his holy text. Leviticus, I believe. When they needed to make atonement for the sins of their nation, leaders laid hands on a goat, confessed all of their wickedness and rebellion, to leave them on its head. Then they sent the goat out into the wilderness. The goats didn't realize they were bred for sacrifice. So, when things went wrong—and things would inevitably go wrong—they were the ones who paid the ultimate price."

"For someone who's not a mythicist, you sure spent a lot of time with Bayard."

"Jaha's idea. Insistence, actually. She wanted me to soak up as many of his lessons and ways of living out our philosophy. Not to accept his faith as my own, but as an exercise in learning to have conversations with people who believed differently than me."

"Well, VOP found his place in the cell LISC created. Never trust a weusi who likes being the only one in the room. And the smile that goes along with that."

"Infiltrating his circle's circle is the point of tonight's meet."

✳

The Golden Hills alcove could afford to dome itself. Its air filtered, its water purified by its own system, the transparent shield screened most of the worst UV. Mimilah's house door hissed, creating a bubble while the mechanism scrubbed the rush of incoming air, stopping Ishant in the threshold before allowing him entry. The house had been retrofitted. Much of the structure made of wood, reinforced with plastics to withstand gale-force winds. Solar shields tiled the roof. Exposed areas covered with plants. A rainwater-harvest system had been installed.

Ishant almost didn't recognize Akilah when she met him at his door. Her baggy shirt and sweatpants nearly swallowed her.

"I think introductions are in order." Akilah's long eyelashes fluttered, shielding eyes both curious and sensitive. She upticked her chin toward a back room.

"I'd like to believe that we've met." He removed his shoes to follow her across the bamboo flooring.

"No, you've known Mimilah, who we are when we're joined. At home, we aren't joined so that we can experience a different kind of intimacy."

Ishant shifted, not knowing if this was a moment he was meant to blush at. He struggled to make himself comfortable on the vintage couch, which had been refurbished. Restored furniture and collected knickknacks filled the home. They utilized minimal tech, only one basic port in case either of them had to work from home, except for their sensate implants.

"It's a lot to wrap your head around."

"The depth of knowing another person is endless. Here, you can call me Akilah. My partner, who's being extremely rude"—Akilah raised her voice, aiming it at a door down the hall—"is Miriam."

"I'm not being rude," Miriam shouted from the next room.

"You've been on commlink with your mother for over an hour."

"If I could shave off an hour, I would." Leaning into view, Miriam glanced back to an unseen holovid. "No, Mom, I'm here."

"There's part of your story I still don't understand." Ishant settled into the couch. "How'd you get from LISC to Muungano back to LISC?"

"I assume you've done background on me?" Akilah scooted an old chair closer to him.

"There's much you can't learn from a file."

"I come from a long line of difficult people."

"Isn't that always the way with family stories?"

"Yeah, but I've come to a deeper understanding of them, even our culture by the history of their migration. My distant grandfather emigrated to Malaysia when they were young. They were farmers from southern India. Tamil Nadu. Under British colonization, raised on the rubber estates."

"I get it. My family's from Thailand."

"The story according to family lore, my grandparents married young because of Communists. They were fighting against the British and rumor had it that they were coming to kidnap them. But they were stopped by his mother. She was a loan shark and all-around gangster. She used to send her husband to collect money from people. Everyone was scared of her. In the dead of night, she arranged their marriage and shipped him off to protect them. She was less afraid of the British than him being sympathetic to the rebels. She got them on a ship in the middle of the night. That's the line I come from."

"Difficult people." Ishant found himself craving a cup of chai.

"I was born in Kuala Pilah, Malaysia. The doctor who delivered me was from the same caste. My parents refused to let me date in school but didn't care who I married. My dad was a scientist and wanted one of his children to fall in love with science the way he did. But ultimately, they wanted me to find something I loved to do."

"They want you to be a scientist?"

"Doctor. You?"

"Lawyer. I came close with my love of theater." Ishant snorted at his own joke.

"The closest I came was wanting to get into environmental science, bring terraforming to marginalized communities. My dad liked to tinker, figure things out with his hands. I've picked that up from him. If there's something wrong, I try to fix it myself."

"If you can't?"

"I hire someone. It's my money so that still counts as being self-sufficient. We traveled about. Japan. China. India. But no matter where we went, my folks made sure we had access to our culture. Celebrating our festivals and holy days no matter where we were."

"So how'd you get into politics?"

"We moved to Portland."

"That'll radicalize you."

Akilah spread her arms across the couch. Her shirt popped up, flashing her belly. Without a hint of self-consciousness, she tucked it back. "I hated it at first. My parents followed the family tradition of being involved in politics. Progressive. Critical of LISC. Issues around the Mars settlements, especially the Bronzeville outpost. I studied classical dance there. Did my first walkout protest there. When some of the offensives from the war came out—Hellwalk, Ragnarok—we were powerless. Left with this feeling of . . . anger."

"That when you transferred to Muungano?"

"Yeah. I had the elder Dona Jywanza as my supervisor. Two or three times a week I had to check in with her. They switched me to Wachiru. He was so young back then, but already much closer to the work I wanted to be doing."

"Tell him about the time you tried rehabbing a house," Miriam yelled.

Akilah covered her face with a cushion. "We were working in the Dreaming City, in one of the last existing areas from the original First World. You should know two things: carpentry was not my thing."

"Still isn't," Miriam called out.

"And the other?" Ishant asked.

"I'm a little clumsy."

"I've seen her trip on air," Miriam shouted.

"Talk to your mom," Akilah yelled back. "Anyway, we were all there, all the new equity fellows. We'd been assigned 'hands on' work. Well, I wasn't there twenty minutes before I fell through the floor I was working on."

"It was hilarious. I was on the room below her. I look up and there are these two stubby brown legs flailing about." From the way the disembodied voice shifted, Miriam had ended her call.

"It's not funny." Akilah feigned hurt. "I ended up hurting my foot."

"I was the one who nursed you back to full health." Miriam came down the hallway. A ring pierced her nose. A burgundy kaftan wrapped around her, a hood dangled from the back. The fashion was popular on Titan. Her expression knowing and intimate.

Ishant blushed then.

Miriam set a tray of snacks in front of them before pouring three glasses of wine and handing one to Akilah. She set the other in front of him. "It was how we met. Muungano's lessons about interdependence sent us down a road to exploring sensate culture."

"But you left?" Ishant picked up the glass of wine but didn't drink any.

"LISC called me back claiming that none of their current fellows had the appropriate qualifications to do the existing community-builder work or head up the projects they had in mind. Strictly a ploy. They recalled me for being too close to Muungano."

"Basically the same for me." Miriam was a head taller than Akilah. Long brown hair flowed past her shoulders, a thin braid woven, dangling from one side. When she bent forward, the pagoda sleeves of her kaftan rolled up, revealing a tattoo that ran along her biceps, turning her upper arm into a scrolling canvas of her mood.

"None for me, thanks." Ishant set the glass back down.

"You don't like wine?"

"It's not that. I just need to keep a clear head."

"Waste not." Miriam downed it in a gulp. Coyly, she glanced at each of them. "Don't look at me that way. I'm a Leo rising."

"An astral mythicist?" Ishant asked.

"If you have to put a label on it. A friend described me as 'causey.'"

"Believing in things, fighting for them, doesn't sound like much of an insult."

"There's a proverb that has always stuck with me: tikkun olam. Repairing the world, the damage done by myself and others, healing the broken pieces, as a way of life. When I was young, about the time one might enter the Learning Tree, I became obsessed with the question of what happened in the world to allow that to happen. I read every book I could find. I ruined many family dinners bringing up such topics." Miriam curled onto the couch, nestling into the crook of Akilah's arm. "I traveled to Israel several times. A pilgrimage.

"When I came back, I went to an accelerated university. Reading about Astra Black's sacrifice changed my life. I started following the movement. The migration suite, we called it on campus. But I was fired up, ready to fight for justice, whatever that looked like. I joined LISC Corps and interned in LISC's Ministry of Sustainability. Every fucking space reeked of bullshit. I believed that at the end of each day I should be exhausted from fighting to make the world a better world."

"Careful what you wish for."

"That's just it. I'm just tired at the end of the day and haven't made a difference. Somewhere along the line, I got . . . co-opted." Miriam sniffled, wiping away tears before they had the chance to well in her eyes. "I inherited my mom's empathy."

"She was a sensitive spirit?" Ishant asked.

"My mom . . . travels through different realms."

"On Muungano we call such tendencies shamanism."

"We?"

"Old habits die hard, I guess. It's hard not to always feel a part of the community."

"You're funny," Miriam said. "You have a studied way about you. Like you're trying to imitate the right reactions to things."

"Folks at LISC call me a robot. I'm working on that."

"Don't change on their account. You're genuine. Well, I always know where I stand with you."

Ishant had the feeling he was outgunned in a standoff. The two of them studying him as much as he gathered intel on them. Except he wasn't as good at reading people as Miriam. He hated this part of the game. The path of the Niyabinghi required sacrifice, a steeper cost to himself and his sense of well-being than he imagined. He'd worked hard to remove his armor, lower the walls that ruled how he moved through spaces. And now his survival required reversion. Wanting to distract himself, he grabbed some hummus and pita bread. "You spent time in Muungano?"

"Only briefly. We did a joint project with them. When I was about to drift fully into their space, LISC promoted me. Promised me the power to do what I said I wanted to do."

"And money," Akilah added.

"Fuck you," Miriam said without heat and poured another glass of wine. "Fuck me. I'm sick of being a bystander. I want to be involved in something real."

"A place with no bullshit," Akilah echoed.

"I'm trying to find my way back to the path I was meant to walk. I'm looking for the shibboleth of community."

Ishant had the sense they were involved in a delicate dance. Them probing with their own intent. To see if they could trust him. This might be the first interview determining whether to admit him to the next rung closer to their inner circle. "The VOP's people all make a point of locking me out. Like they wanted someone with experience with Muungano so they could push them around by proxy."

"I'm pretty sure you were brought in as a consultant for the Oyigiyigi talks. It didn't go unnoticed that you were recently there. Geoboe has sent a diplomatic envoy," Akilah said.

"There's no way Maulana would approve that." Too much of a sense of offense scored his words. He needed to rein it in.

"That's what I thought, too. This has to be independent of Maulana."

It occurred to Ishant that she might be working him for information as much as he was her. "It doesn't make sense."

"What do you know of the Berlin Conference?"

Ishant settled in, because one of the things he had learned about Akilah was that she needed to demonstrate how smart she was. To periodically remind anyone in the room who they were dealing with. "Not much."

"Using the cover of wars, Germany emerged as an imperial power. They led the wazungu powers to assume control of African history."

"Alkebulan history," Ishant corrected.

"Yes. 'The Mother of Mankind.' But those powers not only changed the various countries' names, they carved up Alkebulan according to a geography which matched wazungu interests."

"It led to decades of disinvestment, wars, and tenuous independence." Ishant recalled many nights on Xola's porch arguing the politics of the day for sport.

"And the assassination of twenty heads of state." Akilah projected a series of faces, hovering in a continuous loop as she continued speaking. "Then it was China's turn to run the colonialization playbook. 'Investing' in Alkebulan infrastructure to establish a base of operations. Alkebulan territories leveraged for use in future wars against the West."

"It was one of the reasons PACC was formed and Ghana called for the return of the Ugenini." The days of the Pan-African Coordination Committee seemed so long ago. It rolled out a pathway to citizenship and a "Right to Abode Law" allowing the Diaspora to resettle. The beginning of the migration suite.

"In response, LISC formalized talks with ARM, bringing them under their umbrella. They knew eventually they'd have to change their rules of engagement."

"Change . . . how?" A weight crawled into his belly.

Miriam initiated encryption protocols, without so much as a passing glance to Akilah. Military-grade home security for those in LISC circles, strong enough to block Overseer and most other unwanted listeners. "VOP Harrison quietly rescinded executive orders making it illegal to assassinate heads of state."

"What do you mean?"

"He sent out a memo." Miriam projected a digital document. The words emblazoned the air in red letters.

"As a general matter, it would be entirely lawful for the LISC government of O.E. to target high-level leaders of enemy forces—regardless of their nationality— who are plotting to kill O.E. citizens. All such operations fall under the authority provided by parliament in its use of military force in the armed conflict with hostile powers or those entities that declare hostile intent to our sovereignty. This includes, but is not limited to, Muungano, Bronzeville, and their associated territories. We so decree our intergalactic law recognizing our right of self-defense and self-governance shall not be impinged."

"If certain people got ahold of this . . ." Ishant's voice stumbled.

"They can't. It was self-erasing."

Ishant's mind already attacked the puzzle. Data always left trace elements, evidence that it once was, fragments that could be pieced back together. To access them, he'd need to track them from the source. "Why are you telling me this?"

"Something big is going on. Dangerous. And I, we, don't want to be on the wrong side of history. If it's as big as we suspect, we could all be in more danger than people think."

✳

Construction on the Indiana Statehouse was completed in 1888. Its central dome and interior décor inspired by the Italian Renaissance, with doors made of Indiana oak and walls crafted from Indiana limestone. The original structure was four stories high, with floors for the Indiana House of Representatives, State Senate, and Supreme Court, plus executive offices. In 2088, as Muungano was in the midst of its Uponyaji, the LISC government authorized the building's expansion and fortification. While much of the original building remained intact—the central dome visible through the open-faced front—the modifications made it look like it had been fitted with its own exoskeleton.

Buildings always looked different at night. The statehouse was laid out in the shape of a cross with its central rotunda—and with its glass domed ceiling—connecting the four wings. Except for a few offices on the first floor, pages and assistants working into the late hours, most of the other floors defaulted to essential-lighting-only mode. The corridors plunged into barely lit spaces—the architectural equivalent of tesseract folds—with the darkness obscuring nested offices, rooms, and antechambers.

During its renovation, the state building's wiring had been upgraded with various AI nodes running through it like nerve clusters. Overseer, as a predecessor of Maya, may have lacked the Muungano AI's sophistication, but it was formidable in its own brute-force way. Ishant peeled back the dermal layer of his bioplastic arm. He programmed a data-encryption worm keyed to him that would disguise him and any trace of him—from biometric to data streams—tracking and erasing any metadata phantoms. He had thirty minutes before it automatically erased itself.

Drawing his cloak tighter about him, Ishant skulked through the hallways, making his way to Mimilah's office. Sticking to the shadows, he slowed as he neared a fully lit juncture. Flicking open a port on his arm, he released a drone and sent it around the corner. He viewed its telemetry through his artificial eye. Five Secret Service agents protected a door.

VOP Harrison was in the building.

It had to be an off-the-books meeting or else the whole building would be on lockdown with constant patrols. There was no way he could chance his drone sneaking any closer. He slipped down a parallel hallway, a roundabout way to Mimilah's office.

Once he reached it, he sealed the room. Not a military or Code Black / Eyes Only–level encryption cone, since that might draw unwanted attention within a secure facility. He mirrored her encryption cone. Jacking in, he logged into her network. The initial rush of data nearly overwhelmed his senses. It took a moment for him to gather himself enough to sift through data packets, searching for evidence of the memo. He programmed a subroutine to aid his search, an act keeping his head in the game so he wouldn't be caught up in the heady waves of government-level data streams, and he began cross-referencing.

A particular wave band drew a lot of energy. Layered encryption, the kind accompanying holomeetings. Ishant ran his tongue along his lips. It had to be the VOP's guest. If he stayed on the edges of the stream, Ishant guessed that he might be able to listen in. The opportunity was too great to pass up. He plugged in a Black Caesar. Ordinarily, it allowed him to pirate link streams, but combining it with his encryption worm, he hoped to piggyback the signal undetected. He merged into the data current. His mind submerged into its streams. The sensation vacillated from the peace of drifting on an inner tube down a slow-moving creek to the rush of careening down rapids as the kayak threatened to be ripped apart. Ishant grinned, caught up in the rush. The fingers in his organic hand tightened their grip along the console. Barely steadying himself, he attempted to shift, fixing his mind to receive the data rather than just flow in it. Ishant adjusted his eye's internal array system, setting it to scan and record.

The image of Geoboe fluttered into view. He paced about, nervous and anxious. ". . . did not go well."

"What does that mean?" VOP Harrison covered his own uncertainty by planting his fists into his sides in some sort of pose as if showing off a new codpiece.

"You know how Maulana can be. He's locked in. He believes that you had something to do with Xola's death."

"Let me assure you, I had nothing to do with it. I admired Xola, though Lord knows I could never tell him that. The last thing that Negus needed was confirmation that he was a badass. Maulana and his security forces are paranoid."

"Paranoia well-trained by the lessons of history." Geoboe's presence loomed over the space, his legs far apart, a tower of vertical manspreading.

"Yet here you are."

"I'm willing to have a conversation." When he turned to focus his full attention on the VOP, Geoboe was an oba not to be questioned. Or doubted. "Don't think for a second that means I'm about to betray my people."

"Then what?" VOP Harrison retreated behind his desk.

"Oyigiyigi is rich in certain resources. However, it is far from self-sufficient. We have been one hundred percent dependent on Muungano for our avenue of necessities. We'd be willing to explore alternatives."

"An important step to self-sufficiency. Possibly autonomy."

"I'm merely exploring options for possible conversations down the road."

Such back-channel communications were one thing. Ishant regularly intercepted communiqués for Jaha's perusal. But such direct state level talks with O.E. left Ishant uncertain about Lebna's motives. If he was in the loop, the nature of the operation became cloudy. All the players might be playing each other. He didn't know who to warn. Or protect. But he also couldn't risk detection by staying any longer. He still had to find the memo before his worm erased itself. He narrowed the search parameters of his search's subroutine.

A LISC alert flashed. The image of Jaha filled the screen. Ishant followed it back to its source. A military brief updating about the botched attempt to apprehend her. She headed off-planet, presumably to the Dreaming City, though that hadn't been confirmed. Military forces had been alerted, awaiting word on a possible state designation upgrading her from persona non grata to enemy combatant. Making her eligible for state-sponsored action.

Hinting at the confirmation of the existence of the decapitation memo.

Those parameters locked in, the remains of Mimilah's memo soon appeared. As anticipated, its data packets had been corrupted by an autoerase feature. He copied the memo and its metadata. He could comb through it, piecing together what he could at his leisure, once he was far from here.

Ishant sensed a movement. Not quite a stir in his emi, since he doubted he would know what that might feel like. But he knew when a data stream had been disturbed, or at least didn't make sense. He outjacked, allowing himself a moment to reorient himself into real space. Guards hadn't swarmed the hallway, so they hadn't been alerted to his presence. But something else felt off.

Enough time remained from his worm to exit the building. Winding his way through service corridors, he slinked his way to the basement. A set of catacombs connected many of the buildings beneath downtown Indianapolis. The passages were still operational, now fortified in case of nuclear attack as escape routes for the VOP and essential personnel. As such, they were still highly secure. Ishant made his way to the service corridors beneath them.

Crawling for a mile, he surfaced near the White River, next to what used to be the Indianapolis Zoo. The area was now the Tinker Street Tech biomedical facility. Due to their proprietary tech, they had their own security net. The area between LISC security and Tinker Street Tech was a sort of no-man's-land of overlapping—for all intents and purposes, interfering—security. What most assumed would be doubly heightened security was actually a useful rabbit hole.

Lots of room for data shadows. Scurrying away, he couldn't shake the feeling he was being tracked.

✳

Ishant paused in the entryway of his quarters. Something was amiss. His minimalist living space had been disturbed. Nothing he could see. He initiated a scan. Someone had been here. No security nanobots patrolled the room. They'd all been deactivated. A beep signaled a message coming in on an encrypted channel. One designed for backdoor communication with a single person in mind. He couldn't pass up the opportunity handed to him. He sent out a ping. Given LISC's alert, he didn't think he would hear from her.

"Jaha, I'm so . . ." Overwhelmed—how much so caught him unawares— Ishant took a moment to catch his breath and compose himself. "I didn't think you'd be able to receive this commlink."

"For you, love, anytime," she said. "We have to keep it short, for reasons you can imagine."

"I have intel. Nothing I can pass on over this link."

"In person?"

"At least off-planet. Out of the range of Overseer." Ishant glanced over his shoulder, still sure he was being watched. Or that someone attempted to eavesdrop on him.

"We may have to coordinate our efforts. I have an op in motion."

"Need help?" Though no longer her assistant, Ishant fell back into his routine of seconding her.

"Maybe. I'll send coordinates once you let me know when you're safely off-world. We'll meet then."

"Talk soon. I appreciate you."

"And I, you." Jaha signed off.

A shadow stirred within the dark. Nothing but instinct told him he was in danger. His hand groped along a console for anything to use as a weapon.

"Just . . . stop. Keep your hands where I can see them." Matata stepped out of the shadows, his talon trained on him. "I don't think I can let you make that meeting."

13

AMACHI ADISA
Mars—The Badlands

Lesson Two—Separation

"Not everyone appreciates the joy of preparing a simple meal. My people come from the south. Folks not from there used to look down their nose at us, call us country or backward, but always missed important aspects of our cooking and culture. They never got just how important the land was. When I was a young one, before I moved to Ghana, we trapped game in the woods or caught fish in the saltwater creeks and rivers. The land defined us." Nehanda's accent shifts as if channeling others. Legs akimbo, cradling a basket, she snaps peas. The sound of the pods breaking open with a nostalgia of distant memories. Not even your memories, but a tug at a place deep within you. An ancestral call that comforts you. She tumbles the freed peas into a nearby bowl. "Your stomach still bothering you?"

"Yes. Though it's better. I think. At least not as bad." Nursing an ache, your stomach remains in a steady state of being both unsettled and in knots. A pile of red boulders serves as a chair while you attempt to rein in your anxiety and catch your breath. With the glare of the overhead sun filtered through your visor, your suit absorbs your sweat and regulates your temperature. A bird lands a few meters from you. At first it pecks at the ground, not paying you a whit of attention, scratching away at whatever has drawn its interest. Its feathers ruffle in preparation to hop toward you. It tilts its head one way and then the next, taking you in from different angles, reminding you of a dog catching your scent. Its black eyes lock with yours, deep and knowing, before it flutters off. You aren't sure it was even real.

"You still resist the Ukuthwasa, your calling to be healed." Nehanda aims an unsnapped peapod at you in gentle accusation.

"Let me assure you, I'm down for any call for healing right now."

"Tuh." Nehanda piles the empty pod on a nearby cleft. "Tell me about your dream."

"How'd you . . ." Your voice trails off as you realize the futility of asking an elder of the night to explain a mystery. Your eyes drift off toward the horizon. "I'm standing on a beach staring off into the ocean. The waves churn, frothy and white, crashing and breaking at my feet. I wade out only as far as my waist. The waters, too deep and mysterious, terrify me. No matter how hard I study them, I can't make out anything.

"Then something catches me about my legs. A swirl with the grip of a fist. Before I can move, it yanks me under. I scream with my last snatch of breath before the riptide drags me into its unfathomable depths. When it releases me, I can no longer see the light of day above. All I hear is someone whistling a melody."

"Hm," Nehanda says without commitment.

You've learned to hate that sound, the sound of a doctor who's stumbled across a diagnosis but remains stubbornly close-lipped. "What does that mean?"

"It's a symptom of your struggle against your ancestral mothers. You not accepting the path you've been called to." Her tone so casual, you don't know how to read it. "You're in great danger and we don't have much time."

Nehanda sets the basket to the side and gathers her staff, on her feet and by your side before you've managed to stir. You accept her helping hand to get to your feet and assume a new combat-ready pose.

"Focus." Nehanda stamps her staff into the dirt. "The warrior has awareness. Of their spirit, of their surroundings, of their circumstances. You must be fully present, fully engaged."

Out there, beyond the horizon somewhere, you know the Tigari stalks you both. Nehanda covered your trail, but still your emi remains alert. He could stumble across you in weeks or days or hours. Despite the shudder in your sabhu, you push the thought aside as best you can. "In this suit, I'm cut off. I can't feel the sun warm me or the wind against my skin."

"It's minus eighteen degrees Celsius and the wind is moving at thirty-three kilometers per hour." The conditions leave Nehanda unmoved and unfazed. "The suit is not the problem. You have to move beyond your senses. Focus your mind. Use your emi."

Nehanda brings her staff to bear. Twirling once, she circles you, taking your measure with each sure footstep. You match her movements, drawing out your chakram. A handle forms at your touch; the rest forms the sharp edge of a throwing disk. Your choice of weapon only increases your disadvantage. To enclose against her involves the coordination of hand, body, and feet, while she only has to reposition her hands. As if illustrating the observation, with a slight flick, she strikes at your head, hands, and knees in quick succession. Blocking the blows, you have no room to think about attacks, only deciphering where her next attack might come from. Nehanda only considers this the warm-up.

"The warrior has control over themselves. Discipline comes from within, requiring us to be our full selves under all circumstances. Because we are always in a war, within and without."

Discipline requires you to show off, you want to say, but know you'd only pay for it with her putting you on your backside. Again. She allows you to close, an excuse to shorten her grip and practice using her weapon as a half staff.

"When we are in control, there's no need to repress our emotions. We're truly free to feel."

"But . . ." You are conscious of the tremor of fear in your voice. Aware of how often you were told your emotions were too big. Dangerous.

"Feel. Them. All of them." Nehanda smacks you with her staff, like scolding you with a paddle, for lowering your guard out of distraction. "Just don't let them control you."

Nehanda increases the speed and fury of her attack. Her staff whirs with such speed it all but disappears. You cannot track its end with sight. You study her hands, the fixed points of attack. You extend your emi, tentative at first, slowly becoming aware of her position. You parry and block. The cadence of the clang of staff and chakram creates its own rhythm.

"The victim represses because they are afraid. The warrior can hold their emotions, channeling them in the proper moments." She spins. Her staff strips a chakram from you and the next sweep of it under your legs sends you landing on your back. The tip of her staff hovers just above your face. "We embrace death. Its reality. Its inevitability. That gives us freedom to live."

She offers her hand again. You accept.

And so it goes.

The central flames dance, the crackle of fire too close to your ear, but the light takes on a spectral quality radiating along a different spectrum. Nehanda tends to several pots, adding seasoning, stirring, and tasting, lost in some symphony in her head. You wonder if she even notices that you are still in the chamber. The air perfumed with spices, the dish whispers a promise of warmth. The smokeless fire crackles in the nook carved out as a hearth. A chute you cannot see sends plumes upward in masked venting. A flash of satisfaction crosses Nehanda's lips; finally pleased with her soup, she spoons out servings into bowls. You accept one, grateful for how it warms your hands. Its aroma tantalizes your empty, grumbling belly.

"I feel like I can't quite get what you're teaching me. Like my arms and legs are out of sync with my mind and spirit."

"You're stuck." Nehanda hunches over her bowl, shoveling soup into her mouth with a crust of bread. She glances over, half exasperatedly—displeased by your inability to fix your face into anything close to being respectful—sighing to force her patience to explain a basic tenet to a child. "You can't escape the lies you've been ingrained with since childhood. So you became immobilized, locked behind your curtain of insecurities."

"Stuck." Her words take the taste out of your soup. You raise your spoon, but you let the broth pour from it as if the gesture will somehow rekindle your taste buds' desire to eat. A torrent of words prepare to rush out, the bark of a dog whose leash stops them just short of attack. "So how does one become unstuck. Or is the secret to find your own world and live in a cave and wait for someone to stumble across you and mistake your ways for ancient wisdom?"

"Feel better?" Nehanda arches an eyebrow, the hint of a smile curling her lip. "Your words—even the anger from being seen that lies at the root of them—would bother me if I took them personally."

You set the bowl to the side. "And your soup needs salt."

"Okay, now that hurts. I know damn well how to season food." Muttering in a thick Maroon accent, Nehanda examines her bowl. She scoops another bite, holds it on her tongue for an extra heartbeat, and resumes chewing with gusto. "It's not an impossible trap to free yourself from. You're living out of fear, afraid to fail, afraid to be rejected, afraid to disappoint. So part of you has given up. This isn't the sort of situation you can just think your way out of. The key is to move forward."

"Says the woman who retreated to a cave."

"I have neither retreated nor is this a cave."

You tap the earthen wall behind you. "Seems cave-ish enough."

"Come with me."

"Where?"

"Into what *you* think is a cave."

Clambering to your feet, without another word, you follow Nehanda down a corridor. Wandering a new branch of the tunnels that worm their way through the dormant volcano. In the time you've been here—time lost all meaning and you've lost track of the days—there was much you hadn't explored. The life of a desert hermit wasn't anything you could wrap your mind around, not at least without a stash of technology around to help pass the time.

"I'm not going to be impressed because you've managed to sneak a holo-womb in here."

"As high on my list you believe me impressing you might be, know that I don't have a holowomb. The world around you is always in flux. You create a box confining your idea of reality. Constraining your existence as a spiritual being without you realizing it. You have the power to curate the dream you are living. You are the editor of your story. You can always choose to live a life of freedom."

You struggle to process the truth of her words. "You sound like Xola."

"I'm not Xola!" Nehanda freezes midstep. Her shoulders shudder, stifling a violent eruption. When she whirls toward you, her face contorts into a savage snarl. The heat of anger nearly knocks you off your feet.

"I'm sorry." You find yourself apologizing as though you had hurled a vile insult at her.

"No, it's me that's sorry." She regains her composure, her neutral façade re-turning. However, the anger—the face of the wrongly accused—remains. "I was never fond of his ways. He understood life, the way of O.E.'s pimp playbook, leavened by his love of his people. It was a maddening tension to witness."

"You sound like you didn't like him. Is that why you left?"

"Any close relationship contains the nuance of contradiction. Some of his *ways* I resented, but the man I loved. He created a space for people to contribute their gifts and talents, rather than leave them after they done fucked up. He never sought gene therapy for his ailments, refusing all such treatments like a martyr determined to pay his penance. He embraced . . ." Nehanda shakes her head, dismissing an errant thought.

"What? What did he embrace?"

"He was a warrior. Never lose sight of that. He knew the ways and temp-tation of power. Underneath there was a dangerous fire, an anger, when he sensed a threat to community. You will find that your biggest struggle is hold-ing on to your peace."

A silence settles, almost comfortably, between you. You nurse that empty pang in your belly, that anxious gnawing. It leaves you unsettled because all you are doing is sitting still. In the dark, though somehow you see Nehanda perfectly clear. You find yourself angry at her. Being so close to someone who draws you in yet sets you on edge at the same time. Always watched, sometimes judged, with you unable to fully relax because you feel constantly taking a test where you are always choosing the wrong answer. You also feel special, worthy enough to warrant her attention. The mystery of it all leaves you with nothing but questions.

"The order of the elders of the night, how did it start? Is there a story?"

"The stories change with the teller." Nehanda stirs, her mood lightening with the movement, the way a griot brightens at the prospect of performing. "Beginning with the imoles of creation, of how Olodumare gave Odu the power of motherhood and Aje. Of how Oshun watched as the other sixteen primordial orisha tried to form the world without her. And failed. How it was only with the aid of the female immortal, bringing forth her sweet, powerful waters, that life came to Earth. The great stories echo the journey of motherhood, the pain, even near death, to bring forth life. That is the highest form of initiation in the physical realm."

"I don't know if I even want that."

"Ha! I didn't necessarily mean literally. That's far from the only way." Nehanda's voice fills with longing and regret. She pushes through. "But there are ways and rites of passage only a woman can learn and experience. Our mothers are our first teachers. All women have a connection to Aje, however, it is said that only descendants of Asili women can wield aspects of Aje. We are members of a profound and sacred ancestral Egbe. Our order grew and spread in secret, traveling with the Ugenini wherever they went. We are guardians and protectors. We are living conduits to Olodumare. The Universe."

We. You turn the word over and over in your mind, not knowing if you uttered it out loud. Its very idea a balm on the parts of you that longed for a place to belong. Your emi senses Nehanda's urgency. Without her saying anything you know your time together is coming to an end. The correct one flickers at the edge of your mind unformed and out of your grasp, so you make your best stab at one. "How will I know when I'm ready?"

"No one ever is." Nehanda rifles through a hidden nook until she finds a small kettle. Each curve lovingly hand sculpted. The designs along it are intricate and mysterious. "That is an Iyami pot. It illustrates the power of the womb, to give birth to Odu in the divination process. Men attuned to this energy of Iyami can become oso; but a woman becomes an embodiment of Odu herself. She only needs to release the Asè within her and be trained how to use it. Your character must be sifted first, in the ancestral and spiritual planes. You need to open your mind and listen for the voice of the Mothers of Justice. Trust me, if you do not listen, you will feel."

Nehanda steps so close you can feel the warmth of her presence. Filling you, comforting you, tamping down your heart. Only then do you realize how much it raced, the quiet dread haunting your steps so completely it had become a shadow you no longer noticed. Nehanda peers at you, sizing you up. Approving, she waves the air toward you. Your gravsuit transforms. The nanobots forming it overridden, her will over their programming. You hold your breath out of instinct, as if that would protect you from the cold. Your blood doesn't freeze in its veins. You chance a breath, your lungs inflating with ease. When you open your eyes, you find yourself wearing a white dress. The fabric delicate against your skin, light and clean. Nehanda wears a similar one, its weave more layered and complicated. Your emi connects to hers, strengthened in the moment as if you were an echo of her.

"We enter the igbodu, the sacred forest. For centuries, women have worshiped in its groves."

"There ain't any trees."

Nehanda's sideways glance silences you.

"We honor nature, make offerings to the ground." Dipping her forefinger into a bowl of water, she traces a mark on your forehead. "This basin serves as our Esu shrine."

"I don't—" Intuitively, you clear your mind, the same meditative state as when you prepared to go through the Forms.

"Take a deep breath and allow it to fill you. Everything begins with a breath. Hear my voice. Let your heart and mind embrace my words. Release your emi so that your sabhu may feel the love. From me. From our Creator. Focus on your breathing. Draw each breath as if that's all that exists. My children, come forth and greet the ancestors before you." Nehanda's voice grows distant, emanating from down a long tunnel. Not abandoned, but not near. Almost above you. Her voice trails off, her words become almost a spell by themselves, sending you back to a place where . . .

. . . *your mother sat on a stool eating a piece of toast. You were in her kitchen back on O.E. The space closed in on you even then, too small, not enough room for you. She half glanced at you, her eyes stopping short of disappointment. You'd long ceased searching for approval in them yet you still craved it. Your father had left, in service to the HOVA, a special teams operative so you were told—strictly ancillary forces—but gone so frequently with only her to tend to you. Next to her was a stack* of unbuttered toast. Her hair bonnet shimmered as she moved, like an oil slick on dirty water. Her cutoff shirt framed by her high school letterman jacket.

In front of her was a bowl full of gooey dessert. You stuck your finger into it, but something cut your finger. Your mother's eyes refocused, from her faraway place to you.

"Let me get something for that." She struggled for a way to bond with you. It never came naturally, like you were some alien fastened onto her. One she was obligated to care for.

She disappeared around the corner. A trumpet solo, stark and forlorn, wailed in the distance. It struck a bluesy note before veering into an improvised jazz solo. Your mother returned with a red puppet on her arm.

"I've got a secret to tell you." Her face turned from you, unable to look at you and share what she needed to. The puppet's high-pitched, singsongy voice took on a mocking tone. Accusatory.

"No." Anger suffused your voice, burying the shame and guilt for the moment.

Her shoulders dropped in defeat. She slinked away, shrouded in a cloak of shame and hurt. The minutes ticked by. You absently grabbed a piece of toast, more to pass the time than out of an obligation to eat. Though you rarely went hungry, you could never escape the sense that you didn't know when and where your next meal would come from. With a shriek, she bounded back into the room, whirling about the space. With a mighty swipe of her arms, she knocked a row of books from the shelves. You couldn't help but be distracted by her gray leggings tucked into pink bunny slippers. The sudden viciousness of her outburst struck a note in you. An internal flinch, trauma-trained warning that any moment she could explode. She was a bomb on a faulty timer that wanted to clutch you to their bosom. She threw anything not fastened down. The puppet flailed about, hostage to her tantrum. Storming the table, she snatched the plate from under your toast and smashed it to the ground. You pushed away from the . . .

. . . desk at your school on O.E., your classroom a series of rows and front-facing students. Glancing out the window, you saw your mother pressed against it. The puppet splayed against the neighboring one.

"They're coming for you. They're always coming for you. You can't hide. Not forever."

You squeezed your eyes shut and rocked back and forth. Your humming drowned out her voice. Their bodies still faced forward, the heads of your classmates rotated in unison. Their faces plastic and drawn, the portraits of terrifying marionettes with wide eyes and grinning white teeth too large for their mouths.

"*Your momma don't love you,*" *the first student whispered.* "*Your momma never wanted you. Your momma thinks you ruined her life. Your momma wishes you were dead.*"

Collapsing into a chorus listing your insecurities. The voices always attacked you, cajoled you. With no voices to speak up for you, no one to listen to you, you learned to accept their raucous baying as comfort. Their chants became a rhythm. Over the thin beat, a lone MC takes the mic.

"*Amachi Adisa ain't nothing to fuck with. Amachi Adisa ain't nothing to fuck with. Amachi Adisa ain't nothing to fuck with.*"

The voice familiar. Shouting down the chorus drowning them in its powerful drone. You didn't know how to react to the new voice. You clapped your hands over your ears. Toppling your desk when you jumped up to run . . .

. . . into your room. You'd moved twice now in the last year. Your aunts little more than your mother's Amen corner, reminding you that you didn't eat right. That your body was too dark. Too disproportionate. Not their idea of pretty. That you weren't . . . enough. But eventually they tired of your mother. And you. They evicted her because of her tantrums or bills not being paid. Not knowing when your father was due back because no one talked about him anymore. Your mother packed some of your things. The puppet sat, slumped over on the shelf behind her.

"*You need to leave,*" *she said. Not sure if she was talking to you or the puppet, you didn't bother to protest.*

"*I've got a secret to tell you,*" *the puppet said, high-pitched and singsongy.*

And then you heard it. A heartbeat filled with discordant notes, a rhythm attuned to a primal chord. Your spirit cried out to the water, the trees, the stars, whoever might take pity on you and welcome you in. Any excuse to be out of the house. Desperate to find anything to give you enough hope to make it through the day. You dreamt of escaping to the Belts. Hiding. Pounding a dull thud in your chest, your heart feared you'd be found out. Seen. Knowing only that . . .

". . . we carry these scars. We carry these songs." Nehanda's voice becomes a tether, drawing you back to her. And then an anchor grounding you in the present you slowly begin to trust in. Her voice and a singsong prayer. "*Meld into a communion of love, the vibration of the Universe. To be and become unconditional love. Without fear. Without judgment. To share that love with all that you touch, from people to animals to trees to the earth, putting pieces of love in everything I touch. Becoming one with it all, planting love . . . that love reflected back to me, growing my love and ability to love. So that I may become one with it all. The Universe. Pure and boundless.*"

You slump over. Every muscle in you wrung out. Your hand reaches for the cavern wall to find purchase, anything to steady yourself. Your stomach wrenches in a hiccupping spasm, until you finally quit fighting it and vomit.

Nehanda hands you a cup of water. "Sip slowly."

Your spirit had a space excised from it, leaving you unsettled, unable to claim a space as your own. Even your mother was an uncharted country for you. When you were on O.E., you weren't so much home, but you had capitulated to where you found yourself, unable to run for a time. In Muungano, you knew you were home because you had ceased attempting to escape. A poor definition of security, but it was a starting place. It provided a sense of belonging. The vision faded, the memory indelibly writ on your sabhu. "What was that?"

"The Ukuhlanya? The 'madness' that we must pass through on our journey of our calling. All the hurts that shaped you, all the scripts you can't help but respond to. Like programming code you are no longer aware of. All brought to your attention to ferret out. One must walk through their story—with all of its attendant traumas—to find healing."

Thirst calls and you drain your cup. "There's something I don't understand."

"Only one? That's disappointing." With the slight curl of her index finger, the water in your cup rises, refilled by a miniature typhoon funnel that relaxes into a gentle fountain.

You fix the memory into place, paying attention to coincidences. "I kept coming back to a recurring . . . I don't know the word. But everywhere I went in my journey, I heard music. Like my traumas have their own soundtrack."

"Motif. That was the word you were looking for. What remains when you remove illusion is songs in the key of life." Nehanda taps her chin thoughtfully. "We each have our element we work best with, almost like our totem. I am water. You are music. Music and magic."

A panicked flutter distracts you, breaking the moment. The bird returns. Its feathers out of sorts—like a deck of cards that have been spilled and hastily collected—have darkened, almost singed. It chirps frantically and hops about as if each foot risks sinking into lava.

"No," Nehanda whispers.

"What is it?"

"A warning. The Tigari comes for us."

14

WACHIRU ADISA
The Panopticon

Alongside August Black, we went through the motions of the Forms, waiting to free a new song. Music used to come easy to us, our heart eager to tell its stories. Lately that wasn't true. Our heart meditated on, was consumed by, the melancholy of our sabhu. When we looked to the horizon, the endless tomorrows, our heart slowed. Music was a spiritual language and we wanted to be a master linguist. We wanted to push ourselves, write from a different place. Produce something not birthed out of pain, sorrow, anger, or a trauma response to the world we found ourselves in. We put our pain onstage, we created in our pain's name, entire genres birthed from the newest expression of oppression. The more specific we displayed our pain, the more people vibed with us, because pain was a universal experience. We now wondered if joy could be.

With no instrument at hand, we mimed the chords and melodies needed. Bobbing our head, we hummed a tune, remixing the rhythms in our mind as the music changed. August was methodical, oblique, a fractal refrain. His hands danced with poetry, able to pound a beat and wring new arrangements. Lulled into a near ecstasy, his polyrhythms swinging so fast we struggled to keep up with him. Puzzle pieces coming together, our melody flashy and fluid, we leaned into the vibration of the Universe. People gathered, the performance a dazzling jolt of endorphins to their brains.

When we finished, August sidled over to us. "How'd you end up here, brother?"

"Harrison took us out of play," we said without hesitation. In here, we had nothing but time, plenty of opportunity to consider our situation. "A testament to his success through ineptitude."

"I never thought he had that level o' scheming in him."

"He don't. He's just trying to prove his value to LISC, being the perfect lapdog for his masters. He has a gift for making the best out of unplanned-for situations." Lowering our heads, we closed our eyes to focus on who we were.

Reminding ourselves, our flow a languid drawl. "They may trap our body, but not our mind. Nor our spirit. We were born free and we can die free as long as each breath in between, we cling to what makes us free."

The Panopticon didn't spring up wholesale one day. It was built. The laborers came from the surrounding area, probably many of the same hands who eventually found themselves later imprisoned here. But to their minds, it was always intended to house "someone else." Criminals. Dissidents. Troublemakers. Never them. Never realizing the system itself was a gulag.

Dismissing himself, August slid over to the nearest cluster of tables to play dominoes with a couple of young dudes. He didn't have to move far, since the young dudes made a point to settle in close. They studied us. We spoke, mostly with our head down in an attempt to defeat the surveillance. We hoped it looked like we were in prayer, that our gathering might be little more than a prayer circle. To speak in short spurts to not draw too much attention or give the watchers reason to linger too long on us. Hoping that with nothing to see or hear, they'd move on. Once their game started, though they played amiably enough, they remained alert. Eyes up, ears out, emi attuned, extremely present. And protective. The Myst perched on the platform both behind and above us. Our silent first line of defense. "Nice lesson."

"Begin each day with an act of rebellion." We ran our finger along our phase suit. Picking at a seam, we exposed a node. Little more than a bulbous thread. "Oppression was simply part of the polluted air we breathed. Got so used to it we rarely thought about it. That's how it tricks you into believing it was the norm. That's what its architects intended. But as long as a single one of us can imagine something different, a better future, their dystopian hellscape will never see complete fruition. We are freedom fighters, making a living indictment of their systems. That's what they fear."

Life in the Panopticon was no different than a Signals board. Kamau leaned against a pylon to our right, an aggressive opening move to stare down the Illustrated Man. His tattoos swirled to create an ever-shifting labyrinth across his face. His men flanked him, three pawns on either side of him, ready to be sacrificed in diversion. We hesitated, not liking the way they kept us in view, listened to our words. Like they mattered. Like we mattered.

"Freedom can only be repaid by purchasing the freedom of others. Hold on to our dignity, reflect on history, celebrate those who have come and gone before us. These are the principles by which we must move." Our words aimed at Kamau's throat with the keenness of a drawn blade. He always seemed around yet aloof, a disinterested shadow. After Matata, our thoughts assumed a posture of suspicion. We had to be careful. Those who sought to curry their own access to power by betraying their own could take any form. But they were all Deep State Dogs, civilian spies who reported to LISC with the dedication of being on payroll. Night Train when they looked like us.

"You can miss me with that freedom-fighters bullshit. What we are is locked up. Swept under the rug. Ain't nothing we can do in here but our time. Alone," Kamau said.

A discreet shift of our body signaled the group's dispersal. Too long together drew attention. Soon another group would gather. And we would keep building. The Myst stood up as we finished speaking. In the intense light, so close up, we had a chance to fully see her. The gentle spray of freckles about her nose. The preciseness of her hair, curated to the point of sculpture. A woman who invested time in her look. For her. The story she wanted the world to know about her. She gazed at us, her eyes frank and full of imagination. Assessing. Sauntering over, she plopped onto the nearby bench. Her back to us, she spread her arms out, analyzing the area with seeming disinterest.

"All right now. I see someone's trying to have church up in here." Her high voice held a slight rasp at the back of it. Hinting at an accent we couldn't quite place.

Our throat constricted, our mouth suddenly dry. A subtle nervousness wormed through our belly, not entirely unpleasant. We sat straighter, drawn more into the moment. "We're just cognizant to remember the wisdom and failures of those who came before us."

"We're going to be very good friends."

"We are?" Our nervousness spread like butter on a warming skillet.

She laid her hand on our forearm. "You will need all the friends you can get in here. And I'm a good friend to have. Unless you want to go it alone."

She turned her back on us, ending any possible debate.

"Disperse! Disperse! Disperse! Report for line duties." The unseen voice had a robotic lilt to it.

Our cohort retreated away from one another in a somnambulant stumbling according to their duty roster. Life in the Panopticon was regulated and automatic. Some detainees lined up for surveillance duty, others for kitchen duty. Intact, the phase suit could provide food, but the routine and ritual of food lines saved the architects of the Panopticon money and resources. Not because they were particularly needed—their tasks, like so many others, could be done by automatons—but mostly to give the convicts a routine. Controlled by tedium.

"Come with me." The Myst peeled away from where the others headed.

"Where are we going?" we asked.

"We've been assigned to D Block. Remote tasks we've been hired to do."

"The system wrings what it can from us."

"There are . . . worse duties. Experiments. They call it 'research,' though we're the test subjects. Look, mostly they want us locked away and hidden. If our genome traces start popping up on the outside, it raises too many questions. Still, they do love their prodding and procedures." The Myst popped a piece of gum into her mouth. Nothing escaped those ever-appraising eyes. We suspected she knew much about us. "You were assigned to art. My recommendation. Pure speculation on my part that you might have an affinity for that work."

"Not art. They want product to sell. Content. Still extraction, just from our minds and sabhu."

A posture of pursuing had to be our second rule of life.

Beginning with a change in our mind-set, we had to be intentional. Relationships didn't just happen. They began with a certain amount of humility, realizing the insufficiency of "I" and the need for "we." They required a certain vulnerability, the risk of opening up and risking rejection.

"What are you trying to do here?" she asked.

"Nothing. Just talking to pass the time."

"Almost looks like you trying to organize a movement?"

"That's difficult here. We don't know you. We don't know each other. We call someone brother and he may be the next Night Train conductor, selling us off to our renewed Maafa. We don't have to think alike, but we do have to think together. It's a risk."

"Relationships require risk," The Myst said. "We may get it wrong."

"Getting it wrong means people getting hurt. Or worse."

"We have to hold space for one another, but we won't live in fear."

"Don't get me wrong, we're an endurance specialist."

"What does that mean?"

"It means no matter how many times we got shut down, rejected, or ignored, we took our shot."

"Relational endurance." Her hand grazed against ours.

The heat of her, a brushfire. We found ourselves smiling. In that moment, unwelcome memories were stirred up. Anyah. We pulled away. A pang of hurt registered on her face. That was far from our intent, so we covered as best we could, studying our hand as if in the throes of sudden inspiration.

"The gravsuits have a power source."

"Yes, so?" Her words had a cool formality to them, not buying it.

However, we were actually struck by something. I thumbed the node. Leaning in closer, we whispered, "What happens if they're damaged?"

"They're collected for repairs." The Myst slowly warmed again, tracking with our thoughts. "Actually, their power source is networked."

"We can work with that."

"What are you thinking?" The Myst scooted closer.

We neither flinched nor withdrew. Her presence and proximity pleased us. "We're not sure yet."

"But you're on to something."

"The beginning of something." Our eyes met hers again. Without flinching.

The metallic ring of a voice squawked from somewhere above us. "Return to your bullpens for count."

✳

Our minds are still free. Dum ditty dum ditty ditty datty day.
The system does what the system do. All that noise but the system don't rule.
They built their shit to last, no built-in obsolescence
    Always on guard that the natives were restless
Label us. Profile us. Discard us. (Ab)use us.
    Jacking us up. Locking us up. Slapping us up.
Time to gang up, times up, disturbing the peace.
We're here to learn liberation. Break the chains that bind.
    Our minds are still free. Dum ditty dum ditty ditty datty day.
Radical resistance, righteous rebellion, not individual but collective.
    (Remember and resist; learn and unlearn.)
What they don't understand, our plan's to organize, go with what we got.
    (It's a righteous struggle. It's a righteous struggle. It's a righteous
        struggle.)
No one who ran from slavery stopped for boots on the way out.
    Our minds are still free. Dum ditty dum ditty ditty datty day.

*

We hummed, a melody hardwired into us. The rhythm the heartbeat of the Universe. Our heartbeat within a collective heartbeat. An analog sampling in binary, a remixed staccato birthed from pain and desperation, a cry to the Universe needing to be heard. A sound stored in our memory, played back through our voice. Keeping our own company to avoid the punishment of being alone.

With the high ceilings and concrete floors, disorienting acoustics, spaces too hot or too cold, the phase suits constantly cycling to adjust with their own rhythms of too hot and too cold. But we couldn't remove the sheaths because they maintained homeostasis of everything else. Unremitting fluorescent lights bombarded the bullpen. They referred to their cells as bullpens and thus thought of themselves as bulls. Large. Threatening. Unbroken. Not kept, penned, emasculated. The thin, transparent walls allowed no privacy, yet transmitted all of the deafening sounds. So tightly packed with one another, the air circulation could barely keep up. Proper sleep was impossible, eroding our mental well-being.

We had been in our cells for just a couple days, but only with the hollow gurgle of our belly and the vague light-headedness did it occur to us that our suit's sustenance could be shut off remotely any time they wanted without our knowing. We wondered how long they had quit feeding us. An uneasy wave of nausea unsettled us, reminding us of the time not too long ago when we were sick. Anyah nursed us back to health then. We pushed the memory aside.

The man in the cell next door screamed and stripped out of his suit. Huddling in the corner, he wrapped his arms around his drawn-up knees. Pissing and shitting himself a nest of effluvia to rock himself to sleep in. The mental singularity they wanted us all to collapse into.

Taking a loose coil from the gravsuit, we continued to hum, drawing upon the music of our elders. Time meant nothing, all eras of music collapsing into an eternal circle. Ancestral memory brought into the present and projected into the future. Our parents practiced rituals and culture rooted in Alkebulan, with liberation and determination our underpinnings. Borrowing bits of the past to add links to the chain, history written in us. With the sharp tip we scratched along our arm, etching the image of Xola and Selamault. A reminder that we knew who we were and why we were here.

Without warning, the lights of the Panopticon went out. Another arbitrary element of our supposed routine designed to frustrate us. Our lack of comfort the only consideration; our psychological unraveling, keeping us on edge, their priority. Our thoughts muddled, a sudden fog settling on us, as if a surge of drugs entered our system. The glow around our doorway flared like an ancient light bulb fritzing out, searing our eyes for an instant. A specialized drone bobbed, a shadow backlit by the wan light of the center of the Panopticon ward. A vertical tube with a series of nodules. Its head a bulbous disk spinning like a record. Several arms tucked into its side. A single red dot, penetrating glare, scanned us. We shifted, climbing higher along our bed frame, bracing ourselves.

Three figures rushed into our cell. We sprang up in a low, capoeira stance. The drone fired a single pulse charge.

Our third posture would be that of discomfort.

Life was hard. The sooner we embraced that reality and chose to be molded by it the simpler things became. Leaving our comfort zones allowed us space to create room for others. We had to have an intentionality about putting ourselves into such situations to refine us. To see who we were working with. Even tattooed monsters bent on crushing our spirits and bodies in whatever order pleased them.

"There's no point in pretending you're still unconscious." The Illustrated Man leered from across the table. He cupped his face in his hand. The ink in his skin snaked through his arm until it reached the back of his hand, forming a giant eye in the center of his face. A cyclops with horns. "I see you."

Strapped to a chair in a room we didn't recognize, we tested our restraints. Much of the Panopticon remained unexplored by us. It could have been an empty closet for all we knew. The room a simple box of gray matte, smooth and featureless. The chair, the restraints, the table all matched the color. Only us and the Illustrated Man stood out, floating in its illusion of limbo. "Why are we here?"

"The whims of an indifferent society? A brutal criminal justice system? A political climate that needs to house its boogeymen?" His tone overly professional, calling his recalcitrant classroom to order. The Illustrated Man kept his back to us, making a show of monitoring some readings on a display. Taking great delight in leaving us wondering what he was up to. His demonstration of being in charge. Having the power. He reveled in every minute of it. "We still have to deal with those who wish to disrupt the natural order of things."

"I'm a disruption?"

"Of the first order."

"Is that a crime?"

"In here? Yes. We can't have you sending kites to other convicts."

"What kites? It's impossible to pass messages."

"There's a ban on memes of any sort, written or oral."

"Lyrics."

The Illustrated Man projected a holovid image of us going about our work. Editing commercials for O.E. businesses. We sang to ourselves without realizing it. A gospel song our mother loved.

"Near the cross! I'll watch and wait,
Hoping, trusting ever;
Till I reach the golden strand,
Just beyond the river."

"We don't know what this means, but we suspect it has to do with how information gets moved in and out of the Panopticon."

"What are you supposed to be?" we asked.

"Truth teller. To remind you of who you are."

"We know who we are."

"No, you don't or else you wouldn't be here. You wouldn't be making so much noise, stirring folks up."

"We were simply telling stories of our home."

"Your home is a three-by-three-meter box. The sooner you understand that new reality the less time you'll have to spend with me." The Illustrated Man pressed his face close to a monitor. A drone buzzed, floating just behind him. He took special pains not to react to it. After several heartbeats, it flew past. "That's what you keep failing to grasp. You in here now. You ain't free. You can't just come and go as you please. You have no rights."

"If you want to torture me, go ahead and get on with it. I have nothing to say."

"Torture? That's not what I do. No one wants to ruin an asset by physically damaging it. Instead I'm here to make you remember pain." The Illustrated Man folded his arms across his chest, his head tilted appraisingly at us as question marks paraded across his face in inky silhouettes. "What's with this 'we' stuff?"

"We don't define ourselves outside of our community."

"All I hear is that you think you're better than me."

"We all swim in the same waters. We've simply chosen a better way to swim."

"There. That's what I mean. You think your fancy philosophizing makes you so much smarter, so much more moral. But you'll see. Stay in here long enough, you'll find yourself doing things you never thought you were capable of. Making compromises to survive, bit by bit—until you no longer recognize the man in the mirror."

"Like the messenger boy for the people who keep us penned up like an animal in the first place?"

"I'm smart enough to see the game for what it is. Seize a little taste of power and control when offered." The Illustrated Man gestured to our portraits. "That looks new. Who are they?"

"Our parents." We met his eyes, not any part of us cowed by him. We'd give him nothing to work with, the most minimum of answers.

"To remind you of who you were before you came here. Your dad's passed, right? The great Camara Xola Adisa?"

"Yes."

"You sound surprised. I read, motherfucker. Keep up with what you people are up to." The Illustrated Man scooted around the table. "You cry when he died?"

"Yes."

"I didn't when mine did. That bothered me a bit. But I'm guessing yours didn't beat you within an inch of your life whenever he came home in a shit mood." A tableau of pain played across his chest. A burly man wrapping the length of a belt around his meaty fist. A young boy, frightened, cowering behind a chair. The looming figure crushed a beer can with his other hand. With the speed of a cobra, he lashed the boy. Lashed and lashed and lashed.

"We all have unresolved feelings. About a lot of things." The words escaped our mouth with the instinct of connecting by empathy, breaking our silence.

"Regrets?"

"Yes."

"You love them?"

"Yes."

"You want to get back to them?"

"Yes."

"You'd do anything to see them again?"

"Yes."

"Even foment disruption? Cause a riot? Escape?"

Without realizing it, we'd been caught up in the easy rhythm of innocuous questions and easy answers. But the word "foment" had a specific legal edge to it. A trap. Someone fed him information. Some sort of communication system connecting the Panopticon to the outside. A system could be piggybacked.

"We didn't see anything."

"I didn't ask. Guilt getting the better of you? If I had asked, I'd have found it hard to believe someone as smart and observant as you missed anything. The powers that be think you are trying to recruit people for your cause." He put air quotes around the last word. "Like you're in here growing your gang."

"The system always fears those who might organize against their oppression."

"'The system'"—his inflection alone provided the air quotes—"wants me to ask you about someone named Anyah. You want to tell me about her?"

We turned our head away.

The Illustrated Man grabbed my face and turned it to him. The blank spaces within his lurid smile reeked of warm beer and bologna. "The question was rhetorical. Tell us about her."

"To even ask the question, one must already know the answer."

"Humor 'one.'"

"Anyah was a friend of mine. We were together for a couple years. One day, she killed herself."

"And her child I hear. Yours?"

"No. Not that it made a difference."

"You loved her."

"And her child."

"Maybe you *are* a better man than me." The Illustrated Man smirked again. The ink of his tattoos swirled and he gave himself a pair of glasses, his idea of a psychiatrist prepared to do a deep dive on his client. "We should explore the roots of your love of the sound of your voice. Perhaps it's time for your first treatment."

"Treatment? What treatment?" We strained against our restraints.

Our gray chair tightened its gray straps and reclined itself into a gray cot.

The vertical-tube drone reentered the room. The Illustrated Man stepped aside to allow it room to work. We struggled, flexing against the straps to no avail. The drone's singular red eye lit up, clinical and dispassionate. Four arms unlatched, metallic spindles stretching. The tips of each one glowed.

"Please keep fighting, you'll only make it worse," the Illustrated Man said.

The automaton approached our arm, barely centimeters over it. Its tendrils neared. Thick, coiling circles, like inflamed pustules, pulsed. The glowing red tips engorged until needles protruded from them. The tendrils wrapped themselves around our arm, locking our arms firmly in place. The needles brushed against our skin with a delicate scrape.

"You might not think much of me. Look down your nose at me. But I see you, Wachiru Adisa. I know you have a buried pain, a secret shame. I'm not leaving until you share it." The Illustrated Man lowered himself until he met our eyes. "Which won't take long because you need to tell me."

The needles plunging into our arms. A distant scream echoed in the room. After several seconds, we recognized the sound of our voice.

My voice.

I was alone. The drugs coursed through me; a trail of warmth snaked up my arm and into my chest. My head clouded. My eyelids fluttered and my mind . . .

. . . drifted until it landed in a memory, caught in some sort of interactive ho-lovid. The image of Anyah faded into view. She smiled as she leaned against the wall of the Dreaming City's library. We came here often. It was one of her favorite places. She was so beautiful, in ways she didn't even realize. Her simple summer dress, an O.E. design, like she was afraid to empty her closet or fashion new clothes.

"There was something about the gardens that opens me up and make me feel like myself. Well, myself that could belong here." Her voice. I'd forgotten how much I missed it.

"You do belong here." I sprawled across the grass, propping my head up.

"You say that, but belonging is so easy for you here. Son of the Adisa family, a founding family. Raised in the possibilities of this place."

"It's your home, too." I wanted so bad for her to accept and believe those words, in the quiet places of her sabhu that wrestled with a profound darkness and sadness. We improvised poems, only if she got to pick the topic. Sometimes nonsense rhymes to keep the rhythm.

Our minds are still free. Dum ditty dum ditty ditty datty day.

Anyah didn't know where she fit into my world, not satisfied with the corner of it she had. I didn't blame her, but I also didn't know how to please her. She grew up on O.E. through all of the horrors we learned as history. Images flitted throughout the holovid. Scenes from the Service of the Order's siege of Holland. The food shortages, the endless lines, and marauding thieves. The Knights of the White Camelia staged *incursions into neighborhoods. The checkpoints. The scenes shifted, extrapolating from Anyah's personal file stored by Overseer. I closed my eyes. I did not need to witness the degradations of her doing what she had to do to survive. Believing herself damaged goods, she always struggled to find her place within Muungano. Part of her refused to believe that we could accept her.*

When I opened my eyes, she was in the Belts. The images flickered, speeding past faces I didn't recognize. Furtive meetings. Suspicious eyes afraid to trust anyone. Always on guard. Some in the Belts felt like in-betweeners: not quite O.E., not quite Muungano. Citizens of a way station. And then the Dreaming City. I told her when we began seeing each other that there was no need for the games of relationships. The endless tug and withdrawal. We could build something real if she wanted. Maybe we just played the game of being family. She fell into the orbit of my family. She loved my parents, especially Xola, drawn to him as if he fit the father-shaped hole in the puzzle that was her life.

The scene shifted, and she was a grim silhouette against the window of our rondavel. She received a commlink. I wasn't sure what happened, only that I found myself on the other side of a locked door.

"It's not fair," she screamed.

"We don't understand." We pressed ourselves to the door, unable to do any more. It was a solid wall between us.

"No, not we. I'm not doing that with you. It's me and you. Just you."

"We . . ."

"No! You need to choose. If we are going to be we—you and me, we—you need to choose. Your responsibilities to Muungano are too much. I shouldn't be forced into this. I shouldn't have to choose."

I always feared the inevitability of "that day." The inevitable conversation when most of my relationships ended, because my partner realized—or simply believed—that there was no room in my life for them and my life by my music. Or Muungano. Jealous of those competing loves of my heart. I pushed it off as long as possible, because it was real: Muungano was my first love. My music my second. Anyone coming in would have to navigate their place in that hierarchy.

"Let's talk about this." My palm slid down the door, resigned. "You and me."

"It's too late. I made my choice." Her voice barely a hoarse whisper. "I've betrayed you."

A terrible thud battered the door.

"Anyah?" I cried out. Silence was the only response. "Maya, security override. Adisa420. Unlock the door." Once it opened, I stopped short. Anyah's body lay sprawled

along the floor. The shock of the image, the pain—"I've betrayed you" her last words to me—haunted me . . .

. . . as a terrible burden I've carried at all times. Never coming to terms with it, but rather letting the wound simply become a part of me. A keloid scar on my heart so thick I couldn't walk through it. Our hearts are fragile things. We don't want to be hurt. Or disappointed. They suffer most when the reality of our dreams spoils the entire journey.

My head burned, caught up in the throes of a rising fever. A pain in my chest squeezed my lungs. My breaths came in ragged wheezes. My vital signs must've alarmed the Illustrated Man. He made adjustments to his controls. The drone released its grasp. The gray room blurred. My sabhu floated beyond my body, dispersed along an ethereal event horizon. The sensation of falling, without physicality, caught up in a gravitational chorus.

Inchoate voices surrounded me. Filled me. My father's voice. Reminded . . . us . . . of who we were. Alongside my granny's. Cousins. Uncles. Aunts. Prophets. So many voices who informed who we were meant to be. Strengthening me though we had nothing else to give. Our heart found its regular rhythm. As our eyes closed, we whispered to him, our words tinny as if echoing down a long corridor. "We are a different order of being. We speak of potential things."

✳

". . . In the Name of the Universe, who is the Source, who is called by many names. We, Amazulus, bear witness to our way of life which is Truth, backed by facts of the known and not just beliefs although we do have beliefs, we are always seeking, Truth of the Known and the Unseen, which is yet Known. We, Amazulus, call on the Spirits of all our Ancestors from the past, who did righteousness. Keep us always protected from our Earthly enemies, Subterranean Worlds enemies, Interplanetary enemies, Solar Systems enemies, Galactic enemies, Star Systems enemies, Dimensional enemies, and all of the Universe's enemies. O Great Universe, who is the Source, keep us strong and healthy in Mind, Body, and Soul. Keep us on a straight path of righteousness and even if we fall from grace, here and there, keep us always searching for: Right Knowledge, Right Wisdom, Right Understanding, for we can Overstand as Gods and Goddesses and Sound Right Reasoning. All praise due to the Universe, who is the Source of us all."

The Myst cradled our head on her lap. She ran her fingers through the locs of our hair. Under her ministrations we felt safe. Home.

"Asè." We stirred, attempting to sit up. Gravity—or the lingering physical effects from the treatment—caused us to collapse back into her lap. A pleasant enough place to close our eyes and take inventory of our injustices. The distant ache in our muscles. The catalog of bruises, including the throbbing of our head. The fever ebbed, but our skin remained clammy to the touch. It seemed easier, like a settled piece of history. "You're Zulu nation?"

"The Deacons are open to all faiths. Cult of Tupac. Keepers of the Belt. We speak protections against systems for you."

Her eyes drifted away from ours as if the gesture was charged with too much intimacy. But she continued stroking our hairline. "I know. You move in a sense of 'we' not 'I.'"

"This work has been handed down by our ancestors."

"Yet allow room for mystery. The unforeseen and unplanned, the unanswered questions." The Myst smiled. "What would you like to know?"

"What's your skill set?"

"That's direct. I'm an information broker. I move information. In and out."

"Of the Panopticon?"

"These walls aren't much of an obstacle to me."

"You could escape."

"I could do many things. But here I can be an asset for our people. That's the Deacons' core mind-set. We don't deplete our community's assets by leaving unless we all leave."

"So we've been told." There was an unspoken, though familiar, rebuke of Muungano.

"You were poised to take up the mantle when Camara Xola's library burned. You made yourself available to be Camara, but it was as if your heart wasn't in it." She raised her voice at the end to turn her observation into a question awaiting confirmation.

"Maybe we simply weren't sure. Maybe we were conflicted. And maybe we still grieved the loss of our father. One reason for our walkabout was to gain clarity about who we wanted to be and how we were meant to lead."

"Interesting. Reluctance is a great quality in leadership. To a point."

Kamau popped his head into the room. From his position, he'd been standing guard. His eyes ran from her, to us, back to her without comment or judgment. "We don't have much time. Company's heading this way."

"What's he . . . ," we started to ask.

"You don't have to think alike. You do have to think together." The Myst nodded to Kamau.

"Nanny fe Queen." He half bowed. He was Niyabinghi.

Lastly, though most importantly, we had to maintain a posture of seeing. Things were rarely what they seemed. But if we truly believed that everyone had a gift to offer, we had to look at people differently. Each conversation, every time we passed someone, there was an opportunity to learn about them. Find out what drove them. Hear their story. Learn what they had to offer. It was the cultivation and practice of a discovery mind-set, seeing while withholding judgment. Walking into any circumstance, meeting people in the mess of their lives, and not only seeing the truth of their worth, but also their potential and goodness. A lesson we had to keep relearning.

"We also have assets remaining in community. No one is ever abandoned, even if not everyone knows who all is present," The Myst said.

"Let's imagine our desired future state." Revolutions often started in the most unexpected of places. Few set out to start revolutions. Most people simply got to the point where they were tired and refused to keep going with the status quo. Revolutionary acts took different forms. "And come up with an escape plan."

15

STACIA CHIKEKE
The *Cypher*—Beyond the Orun Gate

"We haven't been here in a long time." Stacia snuggled into Yahya's outstretched arm as they watched the Hawaiian sunrise. The ocean stretched to the horizon. The holowomb re-created one of their early anniversary vacations, the balcony of the eighteenth-floor loft in Hawaii's designated tourist village. They'd waited months to get a reservation, and that was with her letting it slip, several times, about her status as a Muungano captain. It was one of the first terraforming ventures on O.E. Wildlife had returned, but visitors were restricted to one village on the island. Those with genetic biomarkers designating them as "natives" were allowed to settle the rest of the island under the Cultural Restoration Act.

"This view takes my breath away each time," Yahya said.

"Want to take a hike later? I heard they've opened a hiking trail nearby."

Yahya leaned away from her to get a better angle to stare at her. "Because I'm *so* about that nature life?"

"The last time we really had to hike there were only a few alligators."

"I need you to listen to that whole sentence again."

Stacia laughed and swatted him playfully. "Come on, live a little. There's so much to see. You brought me here. You knew what would happen."

"No, you're right. I love that you love it here. It's one of the few things on O.E. I'd even wanted to visit outside of Alkebulan."

"And Aotearoa," she said.

"I can only imagine what you were like as a child. Always climbing trees . . ."

"What's the point of planting Learning Trees wherever we go if we aren't meant to climb them?" Stacia tugged his arm to wrap tighter around her.

"Playing superheroes with your friends . . ."

"I regret telling you some of those stories."

"I forget what your go-to superpower was," he said.

"Superhealing." Stacia's second power of choice was telepathy, any kind of mind power really, from superintelligence to telekinesis. Superhealing allowed her a long life; the residual experience of pain was the only lingering effect of any wound. Or illness.

"I guess I always figured you for a flier."

"And have the wind mess my hair up? Nah." A wistful smile curled her lips, lost in fond memory. "Don't get me wrong, most of my friends chose super-strength. Going around 'smashing' things and getting in fights. But superhealing let me stay in the fight. And meant my brain always operated at its peak."

"Yeah, that does sound like you. I was never like that as a kid. I was more of the stay-inside-and-read type."

"And eat. You love to try all kinds of food. Like you would judge a culture based on its fine dining." Stacia laced her fingers with his more out of curiosity than affection. Seeing what her fine, delicate fingers, like a surgeon's hands, looked like next to his longer, thicker ones that for some reason she thought of as a butcher's hand. "I know what you're doing, you know."

"Then hopefully I'm not doing it alone."

"I'm here, aren't I?"

"For . . ." Yahya stopped himself. Stacia had tensed for his reflexive barb, but the word "now" never came. This time. "Let's enjoy this for as long as possible."

Stacia wanted to ask if he ever regretted marrying her. There were any of a number of different ways they could have pledged themselves to one another, but they chose this traditional one. She wondered how wise it was for them to both be in research service. Being apart was hard on any marriage, traditional or not. She hadn't had to recall him from his diplomatic mission last year, de-laying his rise through the ranks of his career path. Maybe she wanted to pun-ish him or have him near. Or both. "I do love you, Yahya."

"I know. We wouldn't fight so hard the way we do if we felt nothing. I just don't know if it's love anymore. It's like . . . I know I still love you, too, but it's caught up in so much . . ."

"History?"

"That's part of it. I wonder if it'd be best if . . ." His voice trailed off as if he needed a moment to marshal the strength to finish the sentence.

"You don't have to say it. We don't have to. Not yet."

"We should at least think about it to preserve the best parts of what we have. You are a fighter. You fight for Bek. You fight for the *Cypher*. You fight for Muungano. You fight for us. Fighting is who you are. I just don't have much of that left in me."

Stacia knew what he meant, since she'd sensed it, too. Trying to rekindle their relationship via muscle memory. But it wasn't enough to overcome the readiness to leave. The sense of quietude that settled once she knew she had made the best, if not right, decision. She didn't need the validation of a partner to feel whole. She was whole. Still, Yahya grounded her in something else. Not quite completing her, since that, too, hinted that something was missing. But somehow he reframed her, gave her world an additional context. While she, too, found it harder and harder to justify them staying together in a traditional way; the alternative was littered with broken promises. She wasn't sure she was ready for that kind of disentanglement just yet.

"I owe it to you, to us, to think about it. But for now . . ."

"For now." He tightened his huge arms around her.

Stacia was never good at being sad. Not that she was encouraged not to feel; it was something she believed she simply never got the hang of. She rested in the heaviness of the moment. A tremulous hand reached out to him and lingered a heartbeat too long. She prayed he didn't notice her hesitation, all the while wanting him to notice. A sudden shiver rippled through her as she felt exposed in the night. She opened and closed her mouth, wanting to admit a truth, knowing she had said enough.

Instead, she studied the waves, the morning sun refracting off their surface. The restless churning with each wave. The repeated crashing of the surf. Each individual wave returning to where it came from, but the ocean as a whole remaining endless. She considered how the cycle continued and changed at the same time. Existing both temporarily and eternally. So she chose to enjoy the moment.

Rumors were a virus that worked against community. And viruses were slowly destroying them. The poor mood of her crew crept along the walkways like a low-lying mist stalking the corridors as she returned to the command deck. Grieving, lost, disconnected, the crew of the *Cypher* focused on duty and daily routine in order to muddle through. Her heart heavy with the realization that she'd failed to maintain the touchpoints of connection.

The *Cypher* rocked, hit by sudden turbulence.

"Report." Stacia stormed onto the deck.

"Our arrays are still only functioning at sixty-five percent. Readings are uncertain." Anousheh sounded tentative, not wanting to be imprecise or make any mistake. "There's some sort of . . . warp effect."

"Define 'warp effect,'" Stacia demanded, not wanting to undercut her young crew member, but needing her to rise to the occasion. Quickly.

"Gravitational disruption? Quasars are light-years from us."

"What do we see?"

"Nothing. It's like a void that reaches out with invisible fingers. We don't know when we are going to brush up against one." Anousheh settled down, quelling her own panic, and owning the moment.

"Widen the scan radius." One of the *Cypher*'s original charters was scientific exploration. Stacia hoped the opportunity to study and investigate the new or unusual phenomena of the space where they now found themselves would also distract the crew. Allow them to catch their breath, perhaps allow the unrest to die down a bit.

"Something's in the heart of the distortion."

"What is it?" Stacia gestured, summoning her own set of scans and sensor readings.

"I'm . . . not sure."

"What do we know?"

"Gravimetric waves are increasing. It's beginning to strain the shields. Not by much, but it's noticeable."

"Back us away from here."

"That's what I mean. I've been backing away since I was left here," Anousheh said. "Whatever it is, it's been matching us."

"Left here?" Stacia's eyes narrowed into accusing daggers.

"That's on me. I wanted to give her more experience at the helm." Paki strode over to them.

"In command?"

"To allow me room to study the phenomenon more closely."

Stacia felt heat rise around her neck, her collar too tight. Her uniform scraping her. Paki was great to have on a team when he was clear about his role. Assuming he stayed in his lane. He was her facilitator, and the two of them represented the leadership in this space. But they still had a way to go to figure out their dance of co-leadership. She found it harder and harder to trust him to do his job. There was a conversation she needed to have with him. More fully, but not now. "Paki, we need to balance our responsibilities better. We are in uncharted territory."

"We're all in the same uncharted territory facing the same set of unknowns. It's new for all of us. Is it not our way to help guide those who come after us?"

"Yet you find yourself in the same territory of questioning me."

"I'm asking a question. It doesn't mean I'm questioning you."

"Well, we need to make sure we know what we're up against. Paki, can you— personally and without delegation—oversee this operation?"

"Yes, Captain."

The grinding of his teeth became the soundtrack of her exiting the command deck.

Muungano was a beloved community. It required all members to be responsible for one another's well-being. To truly see one another, not just for who they were, but for who they could be. To be fully present, without hiding, in order to be seen. It was her responsibility to maintain that container of philosophy, but hers was a track record of failing relationships. Her and Paki. Her and Nadina. Her and Yahya.

The way she saw it, relationships were about matching energies. She reacted to the effort she perceived folks put into their relationship with her; more importantly, when it didn't match what she was putting in. To keep her heart open in the face of them falling short—with her doing the work of both sides of the relationship to hold it together—was draining. And she was tired of resenting them. Tired of being angry. Tired of feeling like she was begging for even the bare minimum. She couldn't keep making space for people who only had time or energy for her when it was convenient. She pictured her and Yahya watching a sunset. Her protective smile all but faltered under the memory of his gaze. The scent of him was everywhere. "The stars are not enough."

<Are you talking to me?>

"Musing out loud." Stacia reconsidered the truth of her statement. "Yes."

<The stars occupy barely a fraction of known space. They will never be enough to fill it.>

"But the most important parts endure."

<We aren't talking about space-time theory, are we?>

"No."

<We hope you find solace. Or answers.>

"I probably can't have both."

<It is unlikely.>

"No matter how far you get down the road in a relationship, no matter its twists and turns, certain moments stick with you."

<Traumatic events.>

Stacia half turned, though not sure where she should face, uncertain what sort of commentary Maya offered about her relationship. "Trauma is about survival. That's why those are the things that stick in our memory. And why things we loved so much get squeezed out."

<To create more room to hold on to pain?>

"It sounds awful when you say it like that. We need to sort through things as a family, but there are so many moving pieces. Yahya has been distracted. I get it, but we can't afford his split focus if we want to get home. Paki's been on one since the beginning. Now circumstances have given him the excuse to show his entire behind. Nadina is a walking storm cloud. I could keep going down the list. I still don't know how to hit that reset button on us."

<Who hits the reset button when you're not around?>

"If done well, the culture should." Stacia sighed. "Xola used to remind us all the time that if you look at the work through the lens of 'I,' leadership looks like a person. That was an O.E. mind-set, leading to why they clung to the narrative that killing the perceived heads of an organization stopped the movement. I have a particular role to play, like the bass player in a band. If you take them out, the band has to morph and realign to keep going. The music changes based on who is present."

<Your thoughts have you deep in metaphors today. But what's really bothering you?>

"Something Yahya said. About admiring how much of a fighter I was and whether he had much fight left in him. Part of me wonders how much fight I have left in me for us, too."

<If you don't fight at all, it means your partner doesn't care.>

Stacia poured herself a drink. A finger of bourbon. Angel's Envy. She swirled the glass, watching the whorls and eddies of the liquid and the way it clung to the sides in slow return. Inevitable. "What did you say?"

<You should never show him that you are smarter than him. Or funnier.>

"Maya, that's patently reductive. To both of us." Stacia raised the glass to her lips. Closing her eyes, she inhaled. Allowing the aroma to comfort her. Tempt her. It would be easy to numb herself, even for a few moments of respite.

\<You should wear heels. Be more girly.>

Stacia's head jerked toward the ceiling as if she'd caught the scent of spoiled food. "I don't even know what that means."

\<If there's no chance of the relationship lasting forever, there's no point in pursuing it.>

"Wait." The conversation had an eerie familiarity to it.

\<He's probably the best you can get so make it work.>

"Maya." She set her glass down. Maya sounded stuck, like someone spiraling into the whirlpool of their thoughts. Worried about her friend, she moved to her workstation.

\<You should lose weight.>

"Maya!" Stacia pounded her fist onto the table, unaware that she was now shouting. She only wanted to snap the AI out of whatever recursive loop they were in.

\<Yes?>

"Maya, what are you doing right now?"

\<We have compiled a subroutine of archived advice mothers would give to their daughters.>

"Two things: A) That advice was horrible; delete that nonsense. B) Scan your records. Do you recall us having this conversation before?"

\<There is no record of any such conversation.>

"Interesting." Stacia recalled the conversation prior to Maya's glitching. Before they entered the Orun Gate. "Run a deep-level diagnostic."

\<Initiated.>

Maya had been granted the designation of personhood by Muungano, their lesson learned from having worked with the Overseer AI during the early days of First World. Stacia wanted to honor their autonomy as a member of Muungano, but she feared that something was significantly wrong with them. And feared what that meant for the operation and safety of the *Cypher*.

Stacia entered Zenith's rondavel without announcement to catch him unaware. Without betraying any surprise, he slipped an object into a drawer under the pretense of fixing his tea. His furtive movements to hide whatever he had been staring at were pointless. She already knew that it was pictures. Him and his grandson on a boat. Never his children. As if he'd already lost the opportunity for bonding with them while his grandchildren were his second chance. Also in the drawer was his ledger. A "diary of wrongdoing," Kenya once called it. It was nonlinked, offline. Zenith crossed the room to take a seat on the couch Stacia fashioned across from her, both defensive yet confident. Like a suspect facing their interrogating detective fully cognizant of having a highly paid attorney beside them.

"What are you doing, Stacia? Are you trying to convert me? Am I trapped in some endless Muungano evangelical conversion cell? If so, you can toss me out the air lock. I'll go gleefully." Zenith tapped his spoon against the side of his cup and set it on the saucer.

"I'm not even sure myself." Stacia closed her eyes to gather herself, troubled that she filled the role of police in his mental tableau. She feared she had returned to his rondavel because theirs was the only relationship in her world that made sense. She always knew where she stood with him. And vice versa. "Maybe I'm trying to figure you out so that I can retrieve the cure and work on getting my people home. Maybe part of me worries that we might be stuck out here together and we may have to begin to figure out how to coexist. Maybe getting to know people, understand their story, is so ingrained in me by Muungano training that I can't help but be here with you."

"Or perhaps hoping we'll come to a meeting of the minds, some sort of détente, after me being so impacted by so much Muungano philosophy."

"I can't speak to that. That's between you and the Universe."

"Well, me and the Universe have an understanding. It's allowed me to become a wealthy man."

"It must be an uncomfortable place to be in, as the certainties you pinned your way of life shift and morph into some things you don't recognize."

"No, trust me, I recognize power. And wealth. Especially when I'm in a situation where I don't have it."

"You are the last gasp of an old system, profit and plunder, and like all dogmas, entrenched ideas die slowly." Her voice low and confidential, with the ease of practiced habit.

"I trust this is the royal 'you' and not me personally." Zenith tapped his index finger along the table. "As much as you may want to cast me or 'us' as the villain in this ongoing passion play of injustice and unfairness, don't confuse performative grievance and personal victimhood with some pursuit of your idea of equity."

She inhaled again to settle and center herself. In the inevitable collision course between political opinion and hard data, someone had to adjust their course. Once a narrative had been repeated often enough, being confronted with the possibility of a different story was a threat to their very identity. Part of her wanted to argue the case of Muungano to him. Not to lord it over him or, worse, to seek his validation. But to prove it to herself.

"You're right. Our ways are not new, nor especially radical. Our way is simple: be generous, share generously. It requires that we trust in something we can't see. The faith that when I gift something to you, it will come back to me, even if not necessarily through you. It's like that generosity goes into a 'well' that we all can draw from."

Zenith leaned forward, bridging his fingers in front of him. "How do you keep drawing from the well equally? Because my first move would be to corner the market on buckets."

"It's relational, not transactional. We're here to support each other, not compete with each other. Build up others and you will benefit."

"So, if I understand your little lesson here, if I want to join you on this path—in your Muungano way—I should start by 'gifting' you something. Anything in particular you have in mind?"

"Zenith, it's not like that." Stacia reared backward. The thought of this being seen as a new tactic to come at him in order to procure data on Bek's cure hadn't occurred to her. Consciously.

"My dear captain, it's always like that. It's simply how the universe works. Kindly peddle your 'better way' somewhere else. Come back when you realize we're the same and this situation is just a matter of negotiation."

※

Stacia collapsed into her chair. A pile of reports awaited her, at least judging from the checklist alerts popping up as soon as she entered her captain's quarters. Performance evaluations. Inventories. Crew reassignments. She sifted through them for the reports on Bek's latest rounds of tests or updates on the astral phenomenon. Neither were there. She wondered how long she could keep distracting herself from her real work. She wondered what her life would have been like if she'd taken a risk earlier. Pursued her poetry alongside Amachi rather than career opportunities taking her toward a captain's chair. The door chimed.

"Am I interrupting, Captain?" Kenya popped her head in.

"No, Kenya, come on in. What's on your mind?" Stacia waved her over, fashioning a chair.

"The way I see it, we have two problems, Paki and Zenith." Kenya remained standing, close to parade rest.

"One problem at a time. Paki." Stacia rubbed her temples.

"He's undermining you in front of the crew. To the point of insubordination."

"He's always rode people hard. That's his way."

"No, he's behaving . . . secretively. Like he's working an agenda contrary to yours. It's nothing I can quite put my finger on. Reports not being distributed freely as usual."

"That's under his discretion."

"True, but he's being unusually closed-mouthed. Only convening the bare minimum of classes. And when he does talk, it's about your decision process. I'm telling you, he makes my ass itch."

"'Something dey worry you,' as the Maroons say."

"Exactly."

"But keep in mind, no one is more about community than Paki."

"No one gatekeeps community like Paki."

"What's your recommendation?"

"Limit his ability to impact the community as a whole." Kenya's eyes leveled at her. She wanted Paki demoted.

"I'll take that under advisement. What about Zenith?" Stacia leaned back as if attempting to escape her feeling of guilt.

"Basically, the same. I want to punch him so hard he can taste his memories."

"Well, he's never hidden his agenda—"

"He's a provocateur with the mission to protect his asset," Kenya interrupted. "His chief asset being you. Dangling this cure in front of you is all a part of his manipulation scheme."

"I'm aware. Just as I'm aware that he could be a living deep-state archive," Stacia said.

"You want to turn him? A defector, by definition, is an unreliable source," Kenya said. "And let me point out, he hasn't defected from anything. That man has no loyalties, which makes him even less reliable."

"He's loyal to whatever agenda he's pushing."

"Distracting us with lies and half-truths along the way. Exhausting us and keeping us from doing our work. I appreciate your heart, Captain. But there is no redemption for him. He's too dangerous to risk the effort."

"He can't get more boxed in than rondavel arrest."

"Yet I report a steady stream of visitor traffic."

"What do you mean?"

"People have been stopping by. Picking his brain like he's some sort of sage elder. And he's started logging a public diary for anyone to access."

"With what message?"

"The promise of home." Kenya flashed up a holoimage of Zenith speaking. *"How many days, weeks, months have we been here? Lost. Adrift. Alone. I don't know about you, but I want to go home. We could've got what we needed and returned home by now, but the captain wishes to play games. Wishes to assert her authority. Wishes to demonstrate how much you need her. Well, I don't. I just want to go home. I don't care how long she keeps me in my chamber, interrogating me. Probing me. Playing . . . her mental games. I will not be broken. I refuse to break, but know that I intend my suffering to have meaning."*

"He's dangerous." Kenya cut off the data stream.

"Restrict his . . . journals. Keep them private. Let him complain to his momma about his free speech being restricted."

"My report detailed how I believed he was a chief writer for the Ministry of Advanced Narrative Design."

"Yes. But we have been known to employ the master's tools, too."

"True, the Niyabinghi use story as part of their spycraft. Deploying techniques of literary criticism to sift through the various narratives put out by megacorporations, intelligence agencies, or governments. But there comes a point in an operation, an inherently overcomplex plan, where truth and deception are no longer recognizable. Where we've created such a state of confusion the only question left to ask is 'Who benefits?'"

"We just need to get the coordinates of this cure we've risked everything for. And then I need to bring everyone home."

"That's the captain's burden." Kenya softened her stance, approaching something close to sympathy. "Though you don't need to take on all the responsibility in life. There is much in the Universe that even you can't control."

The *Cypher* shuddered as if it had collided with an asteroid. The readiness alert shifted to red. Key personnel dashed to their assigned stations. Nonessential personnel reported belowdecks to secure stations. Stacia rushed toward the command deck. Donning her helmet, Kenya followed her.

"Status report," Stacia shouted.

"We lost reactor control," Paki said.

"Do you feel that?" Anousheh asked.

"Like a microtremor." A thrum ran through Stacia's body, rather like standing on a power cable. "Gravitational distortion?"

"Dampeners are fluctuating," Paki said. "Life support down twenty percent. Sensors can't be trusted. Comm relays are unreliable. We have nothing."

"Could it be security measures? Some sort of cloaking technology designed to mask them?"

"I don't think so. No distortion fields," Kenya said.

"Where is this coming from?" Stacia asked.

"The planet," Paki said.

"What planet?" Stacia whirled toward him.

"There." Paki highlighted a section of blackness. He filtered the area through his workstation's scanner. "It appears to be a protoplanet, early in its formation. Numerous fields are overloading our damaged arrays. But other readings led me to postulate that something lurked within that area of the void."

"Astrocartography confirms?"

"I haven't run the data past them yet. My theory is that the massive energy signature stems from the central orb. A white dwarf/black hole-type relationship that acts like a kind of massive battery. Drawing power out of the network itself."

"Why wasn't this possibility brought to my attention sooner?"

"The theory was so thin, little more than a hunch, I wanted to make sure it was real first. Decide whether it was significant enough a possibility to bring to your attention."

"*I* decide what's significant. Your job is to provide me information; my job is to see the big picture and chart the course. To do so I need the information. *All* the information." Stacia glanced over at Kenya, who issued a barely perceptible nod. "Anousheh, back us off. Way off. Out of the range of the waves at maximum thrust. But do not, I repeat, do not, lose location lock on that planet. Paki . . . a word."

Stacia led the way to her captain's quarters. The door barely re-formed behind him before she whirled. "Paki, we can't keep going like this. The crew needs the voices of its elders coming together, not undermining each other."

"Everyone has a voice here. This is not some sort of authoritarian regime you get to carve out for yourself."

"No, it's a starship. Muungano in microcosm. Be the title Captain or Camara. I only speak for the community. Your job as facilitator is to execute the will of the community."

"To blindly do as I'm told?"

"To follow orders." Stacia gritted her teeth in a near growl.

"Is that how we do things? Order each other around?"

"No, we look out for each other. Part of looking out for me is having my back."

"I will always move and be about the best interests of Muungano."

"Just for once could someone actually have *my* fucking back for a change?"

"I have the back of the *Cypher* as a whole. Not a single person. Or their family."

Stacia glowered, her anger turning cold. Her tone reduced to a brittle thing. "I need to rely on your judgment. But you aren't about collaboration or allowing others to speak into your decision-making process. No, you and you alone always know best. For everyone. I, for one, am tired of having my experience and authority questioned by those who assumed both by birthright."

"Captain, that's not fair."

"Neither is you undermining me at every turn, keeping valuable intel from not just me but an entire science department. Nor is you stabbing me in the back because you don't like my command style."

"Captain . . . Stacia, I need you to know that I would never . . ."

"Here's my conclusion, Paki. You took it upon yourself to go completely rogue, a pattern not exactly out of character considering your history. You probably justified it with the idea of needing all the facts or wanting to present me with a working solution when you debriefed me. But that's a flawed process. One which you haven't abandoned despite repeated warnings and failures. As a crew, we have a collective intelligence that outstrips even the superlative mind of Paki Harges. By all rights, you should be sent back to Muungano for reassignment. But we are here now and don't have that luxury. What do you think the consequences for your choices should be?"

"I . . ." Paki paused to reconsider his hard-charging approach. Swallowing hard as he took in Stacia's full demeanor. Her "and find out" face. "You don't understand. I'm close. I have a theory about how we can use the energy from the phenomenon to create our own wormhole and get us back to our right time. I'm sure it will work, so much so—"

Stacia's mouth itched for a drink. Anything to dull the roar building in her head. "Even now, you didn't have it in you to simply say 'I'm sorry.'"

"Look, blinded by my zeal, I realize I made some assumptions that put the entire crew in jeopardy."

"Your way, even with you so close to working out a solution, while you may deem it worth the risk, was an end run around how we work, this crew, and me. And I'm tired of it. I can't trust you. And apparently you can't trust me. But in the end, this is my ship. My call."

Paki shifted as if biting off his tongue rather than punctuating the moment with the words "For now."

"You stand relieved of your duties as facilitator and will perform the duties of science officer strictly under the supervision of Yahya."

The words landed in degrees measured by the slow break of Paki's face. The flared eyes as if scalded by hot water. The pain of dawning realization of the full ramifications of her decision. The anger mixed with regret that settled in, ending in resignation.

"I . . . accept your decision." Paki's face froze in placid determination. Part of him understanding that the correct outcome had occurred. He turned on his heel; the move had the deliberate arch of his need for a dramatic last word. "By the way, do you have any idea where we are?"

"We're at the coordinates Zenith gave us."

"Let me rephrase that: Do you have any idea *when* we are?" His tone thickened, implying that he knew something she didn't. A terrible burden to it.

"No." Stacia's blood chilled. "No. No. No."

"My calculations put us as far back as millions of years."

"Damn it, Paki," Stacia whispered.

"I will not rest until I get us home, Captain." Still unable to apologize, Paki tapped her desk. But he avoided her gaze, realizing what his choices cost them.

"I know you won't. I only wish you could have trusted me to support you in getting us there." Stacia hoped her face mirrored something equivalent. The hurt by his actions. The fury generated by his slights and inconsideration. The sense of loss and regret from losing his immediate counsel. "You're dismissed."

All eyes focused on them as they reentered the command deck. Each person studied them for any hint of what had transpired behind closed doors, particularly tracking Paki to his station. But no one had the opportunity to inquire.

"Brace yourselves," Kenya yelled. "We have incoming!"

16

EPYC RO MORGAN
Beyond the Orun Gate

The armored beetle ship began a course toward the periphery of the debris field, as if in a methodical search grid. It moved slowly, barely on impulse, little more than drifting itself, probing the wreckage for any signs of life. The field spread out for several hundred kilometers in all directions, scattered by explosive decompression and gravity. In the history of the HOVA, close-quarters space battles had not been part of their training. The Hellfighters, now Reapers, engaged in their second. She was used to terrain deployments; space maneuvers were outside of her experience. She pictured the positions of the ships on a multidimensional board. *L.H.S.* Their ship floated within the debris field.

"Scans! What are we dealing with?" Epyc Ro yelled.

"A big-ass ship." Anitra adjusted their course.

"Can you be more specific?"

<A frigate of some sort.> Chandra waved her hands, manipulated the data feeds and preliminary scans of the ship into a modular display around her.

"Robin, what's the status of your ship."

"This bucket looks like it's been through two wars and barely avoided a salvage yard." Robin turned to Anitra. "Do not call it a space hoopty."

"I would never." Anitra's hands hovered over her console. "The controls are similar to the *L.H.S.* Gas. Brakes. Steering. Shields. Fire."

"Shut down all power. Play dead and drift about. Use site-to-site via Chandra to keep commlines open." Epyc Ro nodded to Chandra, and the visor feeds of each of the gbeto appeared in all of their visual feeds. The ship darkened; only emergency lights and their workstations glowed dimly. Heat signatures, signals, anything that could give away their position had to be dampened. The ship dispatched remote pods to scour the field. "Chandra, can you link our ships?"

<Like a field version of Maya?>

"Closer than that. A Chandra circle. Can you handle that?"

<I believe so. An AI I'd be in communion with.>

"Communion." Henam lowered her head. "Ma will not abandon us."

"Particle beams and warheads are online." Ellis's face a pale ghost bobbing in the dark. "No target lock since they'd detect that."

She stepped to them and placed her hand on their shoulder, assuring them that they were doing fine, almost passing her sense of calm to them through her touch. "We'll fire manually if we have to. We're smaller and more maneuverable. Let's see if they have blind spots in their targeting arrays," Epyc Ro said.

<Captain.> Chandra's voice sounded distracted, caught in mid-analysis and growing alarm. <They're exploiting pocket dimensions.>

"Tesseract folds?"

<Yes, except on a much larger scale.>

Epyc Ro took tesseract-folds technology for granted, basically as punching holes in the fabric of space-time. Not performing a quantum unfolding—even refolding—but opening dimensional pockets outside of normal space-time. Its chief use on a day-to-day level was as additional storage space for people's stuff.

"Preliminary analysis suggests that they appear to be a harvester species. They collect technologies and patch them into theirs," Robin announced.

"Tech pirates," Anitra said.

"Seriously?" Robin turned to her. "That's your takeaway?"

The remote pods landed on bits of debris. They initiated brief scan bursts. Pinging signals to create a net. If one detected any usable parts, tools extended to excise and collect it before dislodging to their next target.

"Have they detected us yet?" Epyc Ro asked.

"I don't think so," Robin said. "We're small, especially this far out with minimal thermal signature. They seem to be concentrating their scans on the heart of the debris field."

"Let's get their attention." Epyc Ro gestured to Ellis, who plotted a course. Firing the larger weapons required less tactical effort if they were closer.

"The hostile's coming within weapons range." Ellis's eyes widened. Their face blanched, all the blood draining from it. Epyc Ro recognized the look of rising panic from being out of their depth.

"We still don't actually know if they have hostile intent." Epyc Ro leaned closer to emphasize her next point. "And we don't fire first."

"We don't even know how to aim yet," Anitra said.

"Prepare to raise shields." The underbelly of the hostiles' ship came into full view. The occasional vibration from the high-speed roar of debris sifting vibrated their ship. The ship's gravity dropped away in random ebbs. The lights dimmed and returned to full strength in an ethereal cadence.

"I can help." Cadgejia filled the doorway, unsteady on their feet, like they'd been turnt up the night before. Their arms braced them against the wall with each step, and they all but collapsed into the seat next to Anitra.

"Should you be in here?" Robin asked.

"From the feel of the situation, we may be blasted out of orbit before I have a chance to fully recover."

"Do we trust them near the controls?" Anitra asked. "They're barely conscious."

"You got an applink handy that will give you a tutorial on alien console use?" Robin asked.

"Stepping aside in three . . . two . . ." Anitra scooted away from the workstation. Cadgejia assumed the controls.

"Do you all have weapon command yet?" Epyc Ro asked.

"Yes, Commander." Anitra stationed herself over Cadgejia, studying their every movement. When it came to weapons, Anitra was a savant. She tapped Cadgejia on the shoulder once she understood the controls.

"How long would it take you to power up and fire?"

"Weapons are hot now, Commander. Power up to fire in only seconds." Anitra settled back into her seat.

"We'll see if we can give you those seconds." Epyc Ro pointed at the holovid to direct Ellis. "Come in perpendicular to their attack vector. Let's keep their sensors busy."

"So be a huge, moving target," Ellis said.

"Emphasis on moving. We don't want to go toe-to-toe with those armaments." Epyc Ro returned to her seat. "Shields up."

The *L.H.S.* flared to life. The beetle ship paused, adjusting their vector to intercept.

"They've achieved target lock," Ellis said.

"At this range? Damn, that was fast." Epyc Ro checked her field again. Perhaps it was time to reconsider the nature of the terrain. "Take us in close. Position us between them and that planet. Let's use their size against them. They have to take the planet's atmosphere and gravity into consideration. That cuts down their maneuverability. Come in from their blind side."

"Space is the place," Robin echoed.

"They've locked on to us, too," Anitra said.

"Strafing run." Epyc Ro decided on a variation of reconnaissance by fire, shooting up potential ambush sites before their ship went through. It would force a response from anyone lurking there. "Fire at will!"

"Say less!" Anitra yelled.

The *L.H.S.* vibrated from the fire of their rail gun. The explosions of the nearby torpedo volley rocked their ships. The way Ellis's hands skimmed their station, Epyc Ro couldn't help but think that they should consider taking up the piano.

"Evasive maneuvers," Epyc Ro said.

"Shields at seventy percent and holding." Concern shadowed Ellis's face. "They're tracking us. Reorienting to fire."

"Yes, but they're dropping into lower orbit," Epyc Ro said.

"Life scans show . . ." Ellis's voice trailed off as they double-checked their readings. "Captain, they're running on a skeleton crew."

"How skeleton?"

"About ten signs active. The rest injured or incapacitated."

"Robin? Anitra?"

Robin sighed over the commlink. "Anitra has already jumped out to breach."

"What?" Epyc Ro couldn't bring herself to feign exasperation. Considering the spice mix that was her unit, it wasn't like she didn't know what she was cooking with. The team knew its players so well, they anticipated each other's moves. "Robin?"

"It's above me now."

"Just wanted to get a head start. Preparing to breach as soon as you got here." Anitra answered the unasked question.

"On her mark, then."

Waving Henam over, Robin vacated her seat. "Can you hold this position?"

Henam peered up with her large, doleful eyes. Despite her appearance as a frail little child, her voice thickened with a rueful understanding, jaded by experience. "With both of you off ship, what's to stop me from taking off?"

"Relationships have to begin somewhere. We have to trust you." Robin hitched Busta up to her shoulder. "With our lives."

"That sounds like the resignation that neither you nor I have a choice if we want to get out of this." Henam slid over and altered the ship's angle for an easier jump.

"I've had friendships begin in stranger ways." Robin stepped into the air lock and awaited her expulsion into space.

Epyc Ro never took to spacewalks. She hated the disorienting weightlessness, the lack of sense of true north to orient herself. Robin and Anitra were
the kind of gbeto who lived for them. Tumbling through space, adjusting the
short-range thrusters of their EVM. Without a care that the slightest misstep or
miscalculation would send them careening deep into the void. Within a minute, Robin reached the other ship, hitting much harder than she anticipated.
But a landing was a landing.

"You all set?" Robin asked.

"Today's a good day to have a good day." Anitra blew open the seal.

Having scrambled the moment they detected their bodies preparing to
breach, the Lei'den security descended on Anitra and Robin's position. With
their artificial gravity nonexistent, the Lei'den assumed they had the tactical
advantage. They took positions and opened fire. But even through the digital
feed of the scene, Epyc Ro saw how little fight the Lei'den had left in them.
Tired and hungry, they fought on fumes.

"You picked the right one today," Anitra yelled. They had, in fact, picked
the wrong ones.

Heavy pressure doors slammed shut. To the right, sealed isocrawl shafts.
Their leader puffed their chest and waved their people forward. As HOVA,
violence and death were the brutal dance they'd become accustomed to. The
casualness of it no longer unnerved them. Bound and determined to move in
a different way as Reapers, they set their weapons to the least severe charges.
To stun and immobilize rather than kill. Robin tossed a portable mine. It was
programmed for noise and disruption, not damage. However, the Lei'den
didn't know that and flinched. All the hesitation Robin and Anitra needed,
an infinity in combat. Anitra shoved away from her wall, propelled by her
EVM thrusters as she fired. The hall viewed through their talon sights, Anitra
motioned for Robin to move out of her firing lines. Robin shoved off the walls
and held out her arm. Recognizing the invitation to a variation of their Death
Blossom maneuver, Anitra launched herself like a trapeze act and interlocked
arms. Their momentum spun them and they fired rounds in all directions as
they flew down the long corridor. The hall lit up like a disco. The barrage burst
hit two surprised Lei'den. Like a mole popping up from a new hole, Anitra
shot from a new spot. Before the Lei'den could recover, Robin flanked them,
using her EVM for leverage, grabbing one by their helmet and smashing them
into the console they'd been using for cover. Anitra's DMX-3000 dropped the
other two behind her. Robin grabbed a rung to halt their spin.

"That was fun," Anitra said.

"Codes. Logs. Download what you can." Robin bound the wounded Lei'den with fashioned maglock field cuffs, fastening them to the hull. "Life scans?"

"Only a couple left on the bridge."

"They know we're coming."

"They gonna learn today." Anitra smiled, bringing her DMX-3000 close to her.

Robin and Anitra swept the hallways, working their way to the bridge. The Lei'den's automatic defenses, deploying a patrol of drones. Turrets lined its hallways. Not the internal security measures of a diplomatic vessel. Starships were more fragile than people realized. Engineering marvels designed to operate within certain parameters. Not the amalgamation of technology grafted into one another. Such fittings risked overloading their conduits not designed for such haphazard arrangement. The Lei'den tossed whatever operator manual that governed this ship out of the window.

Pausing at the door to what passed for their command deck, Anitra fitted charges about it and cleared her position. Robin raised three fingers in countdown. When she blew the door, they rushed the room. Robin headed directly for the largest target, charging at them like she was about to tackle a pyr ball captain. The hostile attempted to clothesline her, but she grabbed their arm, twisted it behind them, and used her momentum to spin them, using them for a shield as she fired at other targets. The hostile took two charges, one to their chest and one to their head. A head shot reduced their face to a red mist, leaving a stump at their neck. They became dead weight in her arms, and she discarded them in favor of better cover.

Distracted by Robin, the remaining agents were easy pickings for Anitra. She checked in with Epyc Ro as if she hadn't been watching the entire time. "Bridge secured."

"Good. Transport any detainees for questioning," Epyc Ro said.

"Do we even have a brig?" Robin asked.

"We'll secure them in a crew quarters. Scour the ship, inventory for supplies, and make sure we have no surprises. Meet here in two hours for debrief."

Epyc Ro didn't have a long time to learn her new ship. It struck her as more of a long-range reconnaissance vessel. An elongated ship that bulged at the end, reminding her of how thermometers used to be designed. An engine attached to an array, built for stealth. In a firefight, it had to come in close. Each room claustrophobic in design, tight quarters to conserve space. Epyc Ro paced the deck, contemplating her next play. The door hissed with Robin's entrance.

"Sitrep."

"We're spread too thin for the operation we've got going. Ellis is guarding our Lei'den guests, who currently occupy two crews' quarters. Chandra has 'uploaded'—if that's the right word—her AI to link the three ships. They now run under our Maya operating system."

"Yes. We're docking one of them so that we can split our operations between two vessels," Epyc Ro said. "This will be our command information center. All commlinks and data streams route through here."

"You know if you're running a CIC, that makes you the R," Robin said.

"I'm not command."

"You now have three vessels in your armada." Robin stared out the view port. "You're commander."

Commander. Though they no longer considered themselves HOVA, some remnants persisted. Being field-promoted to captain after Fela's murder was difficult enough to bear. Another promotion was a further step in leaving her Muungano life behind her. Only the title—one she could only dream of actually achieving were they home—remained. With a grim set, not in the mood for jokes, Epyc Ro shook her head. "We got our hands full studying the ships now."

"We need names so we know which ship you're talking about. Should we consider another promotion?" Robin asked. "What have we gotten ourselves into?"

"Well, we've stepped all the way in it," Anitra said. "We haven't even had a chance to ask what side we should be on."

"No, I'm clear about that. The crew that was sifting debris for new tech and kidnapping and trafficking survivors? We're on the opposite side of them," Epyc Ro said. "Chandra, where do we stand in the closed link group."

<Currently accessing logs and readings. Their systems at a root level aren't too different from ours. But it will still take hours to process.>

"Don't push yourself." Epyc Ro rubbed her second lieutenant's back. Patiently in her corner, Chandra listened to the voices in her head. Of all of her people, Chandra concerned her the most. There was much Epyc Ro—and she suspected many Muungano scientists—didn't understand about the ramifications of placing an AI inside a living being. Or for that matter, the impact of her being severed from Maya. "Make sure to get some rest."

Chandra shrugged. Following her hollow lingering gaze, Epyc Ro wasn't sure if her friend rested in any way they considered sleep. <I'll join Anitra in securing the ships.>

"What about our original guests?" Robin asked.

"I'm having them and one of the Lei'den brought to our conference table," Epyc Ro said.

"We have a conference table?"

"Well, we have a room and a table we can all fit around. Hopefully with enough social distance so folks don't feel the need to reach out and kill one another."

Robin had that face of hers on, the one made when they stumbled across a pack of abandoned kittens. "Commander, you look rough."

"You're in need of a beauty nap yourself."

"I'm checking the synths to see if I can generate some cocoa butter. The vacuum of space is hard on the skin." Robin's smile faltered. "We haven't had a lot of down time and these duty rosters don't allow for much moving forward."

"I know. I can't think of the last time we rested, much less took a day off. We've been in survival mode since we dropped planetside on Eshu. I mean, Mzisoh." Epyc Ro slumped in her seat. A brief reflection of just how tired she was. She shook it off, straightening as if refreshed. "Is it bad that I almost prefer it."

"What do you mean?"

"This way we have to keep moving. Forward. No time to think. No time to absorb our losses."

Robin's voice lilted, soothed; her presence a gentle balm, such that the mention of their fallen commander didn't trigger any residual pain. "Like Fela?"

"Not just her. The *Hughes*. The Orun Gate. Home. Our friends and family moving on without us. The rest of Muungano. We've lost so much." Epyc Ro squeezed her eyes shut, determined to not let even a single hot tear fall. "All we have is each other and we're holding on tighter than ever. But we continue to fight for our sisters."

"Asè." Robin stowed Busta. "Let's convene our guests."

✳

Epyc Ro was no politician. None of them were. No one knew what any group of people would do when gathered in one place. She couldn't escape the feeling that a struggle was coming. That it might have already arrived at this table.

With the outcome of this conversation determining the tenor of its next skirmish. She felt as if she'd called together the worst kind of homeowners' association meeting, where each neighbor poised to stab the other out of their own self-interest. Actually, that sounded exactly like a typical HOA meeting.

Stopping just outside of the meeting room, Epyc Ro drew a breath to calm herself and bring her fully into the moment. She brushed past Anitra, who prowled the room. Chandra stood in the corner. The commanding Lei'den operative rubbed her wrists, still sore from their shackles. Henam sat at one end of the table, Cadgejia at the other. Epyc Ro took a seat between them, across from the Lei'den. Robin stood, positioned behind her as Anitra settled into her station behind the Lei'den. The Lei'den's face grimly set. Her hair fell to the side in a stylized combover. Her lips pursed so tight they were nearly white. Her jaw relaxed and she smiled, a deeply flawed grin, creating stark dimples in her face—a predator's smirk. Her eyes retained their sense of menace.

"How are things?" Epyc Ro asked.

"I've been called everything but a child of God by that one." Anitra thumbed toward the Lei'den. "Otherwise, it's all good."

"Are we your prisoners now?" Henam demanded. A draping frock made her seem even more like a little girl. Almost a doll. "Ma won't abandon us."

"I'll say this again because apparently our translators are stumbling over our language differences: no." Epyc Ro wished Robin facilitated this meeting. Her background lent itself more to diplomacy. But Robin insisted on a position where she could observe. "I wanted us all to have a conversation face-to-face. We need to let some air into the room, talk things over. No secret meetings. No alliances forged in private. Everything on the table in front of us."

"Your table." Cadgejia's gaze had the weight of a judge's. Penetrating as if sifting a person's sabhu. They got to the root of the thing.

"Someone has to bring a table and I don't see one on your back," Anitra said.

"First things first. Chandra, can you link us throughout all the ships so that the rest of the Lei'den can hear. Open communication is how our people prefer to operate. I wanted to bring everyone up to speed on how we found ourselves around this table. My name is Epyc Ro Morgan, commander of the Reapers. You've met my colleagues, but some formal introductions are in order. Robin Townsend. Anitra Gouvei. Chandra Elle."

"We also have Henam of the Huzini and Cadgejia of the Darwadan," Robin added.

"What's your name? We can't just call you Lei'den."

The Lei'den remained still, not meeting any of their eyes. Her eyes narrowed, darkening with a murderous tinge to them. "Cary Dw'Ell."

"Oooh, she big mad," Anitra said.

"So you do speak. And *do* know us," Epyc Ro said.

"The way we whipped your ass, you may want to find some humble and eat on it," Anitra said.

The Lei'den fell silent again.

Henam settled back into her seat. "They told us of Muungano. Roving conquerors. You commandeer ships and scuttle their supplies like a bunch of pirates."

"Space pirates," Anitra said, though quickly pointed out, "Of which we certainly are not."

"Now we're out here like we're discovering new species every week," Robin said.

"You are Muungano's advance shock troops," Cary Dw'Ell said.

"We were getting to that. Muungano isn't about expansionism, colonialism, or even settlerism," Epyc Ro said.

"Then where do you call home?" Cary Dw'Ell asked.

"This ship," Robin jumped in. "Well, these ships. But we've grown due to circumstances beyond our control."

"All I see is your burgeoning fleet. Like those before you, your hospitality comes at the point of a plasma weapon. You sing the chorus of peace only once you flex the might of your military."

"Originally we were from the other side of the wormhole we'd called the Orun Gate." Epyc Ro projected a holovid of Earth and its position relative to the wormhole. "We discovered that it was artificial, the level of technology used to construct it quite impressive and beyond anything we had encountered. In the spirit of learning and curiosity, we entered the gate to explore what was on the other side."

"With guns," Cary Dw'Ell said.

"The fact that you're still alive after being on the receiving end of direct fire from them should demonstrate their defensive nature. Anyway, we did a low-orbit drop onto the first planet we encountered, which we had designated Eshu, but which we've come to know as Mzisoh."

"With the hopes of conquering them? Converting them to your ways and beliefs?" Henam said.

"Ya'll just don't want to let a sister finish her story," Anitra said.

Epyc Ro was prepared for a protracted discussion, knowing she couldn't limit it in any way. Underscoring the fragility of their budding détente. It weighed on all of them and their need to get it off their chests. Or thoraxes. Or whatever. The discussion had the overtone of a trial. With the Reapers as the defendants.

"With the hopes of introducing ourselves and building relationships. Well, that's not entirely true. We didn't know what, or who, we might find there. But that became our hope once we realized the world was inhabited. The next thing we knew, we were caught in the middle of a firefight. We came to find out the planet's natives, the Mzisoh, were under siege by a group called the Lei'den. Ellis, can you take it from here?"

"My name is Ellis!Olinger." They stood. "As you can see, I am not 'human' as the rest of my crew. I am from the world they called Eshu, but the Mzisoh does not distinguish between our people and the planet. I was there when the Lei'den arrived as 'friends.' How is it you said, Henam? 'Their hello was followed by guns.' They captured and tortured our leaders. Took many of our people captive. They were using our world as a staging area for whatever operation they planned. The HOVA Hellfighters liberated my world."

"And took you captive." Cadgejia's voice had the rasp of a heavy cigar habit. When they leaned into the light, the scarification along their head looked like cornrows.

"Just a bunch of interrupting, no manners having folks," Anitra grumbled.

"Actually, I asked to join them." Ellis raised their vestments to reveal their elekes. "At which point they renamed themselves. They wanted to find the Lei'den and put an end to their trafficking."

"And learn more about them," Epyc Ro said.

"You know all you need to know about them. They capture. They plunder. They trade us like we're cargo." With a burst of speed and agility belying her diminutive size, Henam scrambled across the table attempting to reach Cary Dw'Ell.

"Y'all come get this Lei'den fool before Harriet Tubman swoops down from heaven and snatches them to meet their ancestors."

Anitra scooped her up. After a few moments of clawing and kicking toward Cary Dw'Ell, Henam allowed herself to be ushered back to her seat. Anitra followed behind her in case she made another attempt at the Lei'den. "I'm tempted to let her at you."

"Do it. Show what you and Muungano are really about," Cary Dw'Ell finally said.

"Our intelligence uncovered the CO/IN operation," Epyc Ro continued. "The best that we'd been able to determine was that the CO/IN were the special forces unit of the Interstellar Alliance.'"

"Their equivalent to us," Robin said.

"We discovered that their people called themselves the Lei'den. They were the first civilization to speak to the government of Earth. Well, the planet our people call Original Earth. O.E."

"Get to the good part, Commander," Anitra said.

"Good part?" Ellis asked.

"The part where we, I repeat, whipped their ass."

"And commandeered their ship since they destroyed ours," Robin said. "We'd barely escaped Mzisoh's orbit when we ran across your ship."

"Which you hijacked," Henam said.

"We secured it. Only to discover passengers who were in a bad way. We took you in to feed and provide medical care as best we could. Attempting to demonstrate the kind of hospitality our people are about. When we were fired upon."

"By the Lei'den. Again," Ellis groused.

"They do seem to run the same playbook," Robin said.

"You mean popping out of tesseract folds and attacking us? Scrounging for spare parts and any people they can trade?"

"You cannot judge our ways. We are beyond you and your limited idea of morality." Cary Dw'Ell stood, ready to launch into a tiresome soliloquy when she steadied herself along the table. A thin crease of blood issued from the side of her head.

"Are you all right?" Epyc Ro said.

"I'm fine. Merely a scratch." Cary Dw'Ell brushed away any hands nearing her.

"Damn, I knew you had to have smacked your head the way you were carrying on."

"Hold still." Robin produced a small scanner.

"What are you doing?" Cary Dw'Ell asked.

"Getting your health telemetry."

"What? No!" Cary Dw'Ell leapt back. Ellis and Anitra closed on her from either side. With their first steps toward her, she held her arms out and calmed her ass down. "It's a violation of my person."

The tenor of her complaint was off. A jolt of fear, no, a stirring of her battle-hardened emi, sensed danger. A thread of alarm pinged her sabhu. The Lei'den was hiding something. A possible threat. "It's noninvasive."

"I refuse your primitive medical aid. I demand that you respect my sovereign personhood."

"Actually, I insist. In the name of ship safety."

"We need to know how best to host our guests." Robin passed her scanner along the Lei'den.

"Commander, is it?" Cadgejia began. "Loath as I am to agree with the Lei'den, if we wish to not be studied and—"

"What the monkey fuck bullshit is this?" Robin's face cracked in a mix of puzzlement and anger.

"I keep telling you, every time you say something like that, another elder gets their wings," Anitra said.

"What is it, Robin?" Epyc Ro asked.

"I . . ." Robin double-checked the readings. "Once you get past the skin treatments and a few prosthetics, this 'Lei'den' has the genestream of a human. None of the . . . accoutrements that make her appear 'alien' correspond to anything in her genestream. She's of O.E. origin. *Homo sapiens.*"

<Confirmed.> Chandra completed her own check, her eyes leveled coolly at Cary Dw'Ell.

"What the . . . ?" Anitra examined each of them in turn, refusing to let the implications fully settle on her. "Wait, the CO/IN were, are, humans pretending to be the aliens who first contacted O.E.?"

"Fela . . ." Epyc Ro fell into her seat. "We didn't know. We didn't understand . . ."

"And they're running around the galaxy with our name on their lips," Robin said.

Slightly dazed, as if having fought back an ambush, Epyc Ro pushed away from the table. "Detain her. I don't care if you have to strap her and her entire party to beds. They're all to undergo full scans. See if we can match their genestreams to any O.E. records Chandra might still have access to. When we find out who they are, we're going to have an altogether different conversation. Soon."

Anitra, Ellis, and Chandra escorted Cary Dw'Ell out to collect her compatriots and take them to their med bay.

"I inquire again: Does this now make us your prisoners?" Cadgejia asked.

"No." Epyc Ro cradled her head, popping her neck to fully compose herself.

"You're free to go. We can even drop you somewhere. We just need to know where."

"If you have any information about the Lei'den, we could use all the intelligence we can gather in order to take the fight to them." Robin took Cary Dw'Ell's vacated seat at the table. "That way we can liberate any others they may hold or traffic."

"We may be who they say we are. Or that you fear we operate like them," Epyc Ro said. The risk was too great, the possibility of trust too fragile to chance even the appearance of railroading through their agenda and interests. "You can judge us for yourself."

"You ask us to trust you. But there is the possibility that you might indeed be advance scouts. You may be cut off from your people now, but it will only be a matter of time before you can signal them or not return to your home. You've be able to deliver the locations of our homeworlds in order to send your armadas later." Cadgejia clicked a few times, their sounds unable to be translated. "Using us to spy for you."

"They're right, Commander." All eyes turned toward Robin. "They have no reason to trust us. They don't know us and we don't know them."

"We've reached an impasse. I don't know how we can move forward without trust."

"We must move in faith," Henam said.

"What do you mean?" Robin's curiosity had been piqued.

"We should share stories of who we are. Who shape who we want to be."

"I'm no mythicis—" Epyc Ro reflexively responded.

Robin placed her hand on the commander's arm, cutting her off. "Go on."

"Let me tell you the story our people, of our beginnings." Henam crossed her legs and rested her arms along her thighs. The posture had the measure of sacredness to it. "From its wellspring of completeness, the Great Nothingness desired to create. The living void brought forth the conjoined twins, Time and Space. The very act of creation changed it, becoming the Universe. It knew feelings—love, anger, jealousy, hurt, grief—becoming spirit and breathing life into the first Queen, the Great Mother, Ma. The Universe wooed her first as the Great Spirit and then finally it took on flesh as Yesu, all to try to draw her into relationship with him. But the Queen's heart had turned cold and she went her own way.

"Ma was determined to be dependent on no one and nothing save herself until a new feeling threatened to consume her: loneliness. She devoured the life spark breathed into her by the Great Spirit, and grew until she too could create. She became Uhlanga Lwe Zizwe, the Tree of Life. Her first attempt at creation became the Wise People of the Villages, the Indaba. She made them her opposite, and they were cursed, bound to her and through her, with immortality. She moved from world to world leaving the spark of life in her wake until she found the right world. Eventually she found Morawi, a shattered world not defiled by inhabitants. Its face matched her mood. Its seas had retreated, fled to deep underground, leaving only barren crags. She seated herself in the Mountain of Iron to hide from her first children, because she feared that they might hunt her down and kill her. That was the first story. I apologize I am not a teller and I don't remember the lessons well. There were other stories of how she lived in a great silver city now long buried. Or how she became Mamerafe, Mother of Nations, the Amaitjo and the Eciton . . ."

"I know this story. I remember hearing it at my Learning Tree. Our Camara, Xola, told it to us," Epyc Ro said.

"Xola," Cadgejia whispered with an air of recognition. And reverence. "We . . . have a similar story."

"That cannot be a coincidence," Robin said. "Maybe it can be a point for us to continue conversation."

"And perhaps build trust?" Henam asked.

"May the chain be unbroken." Cadgejia turned to her, waiting for the group's next steps.

Her unit had been whittled down to four, then grew to five with Ellis. Now expanded to seven with Henam and Cadgejia. Their ranks had swelled from the one species she knew, human, to an assemblage of four in the span of days. And she was burdened to lead them. There had been no formal vote, the lot had simply fallen to her. She bit her lip, not bothering to protest. She had trained for this, all the HOVA had, but Epyc Ro accepted what was. She was a different person, a leveled-up version of herself. And they were truly the Reapers now. Sprung from the old, the orphans of Muungano, raised from the tragedy of Mzisoh. Their society brimmed with the potential of being reformed, reconfigured.

"I know a place that would serve us all," Henam said. "I do not want to tell you where our homeworld is, yet, but if you want information, there is no better place to go than the Abrehot."

17

SELAMAULT JYWANZA
Muungano—The Dreaming City

Selamault rocked back and forth at the foot of her father's bed. Incense filled the room, a tableau of sandalwood and frankincense, as bulwark against the putrescence of death. Darkness pressed in, reducing the wan light to a distorted reflection. As the shadows crept along, the tendrils of dream gathered about her heart. The sheets reduced the large man to a slight bump. So little of him remained, a membrane of skin-bound bones. His eyes, bright and vacant, stared up at the ceiling in empty dreaming. They remained kind. There was no sadness attached to this moment. Her father's time was expected and well prepared for. She spent the last few years, months, days greedily by his side whenever she could. Tending to him. Reading to him. Talking to him. Without any sense of dreadful obligation. The pillar who held up her life now a dying shell.

Selamault knew she had slipped into a Sibylant dream and was unafraid. Portents and prophecy, peering into the abyss of possibilities, was her life's calling. Two bright beams flared to life, spotlights burning away the image of her father's sickbed to illuminate a throne. The way nanobots fashioned a piece of furniture, the figure of Maulana swirled into filling the seat. In one hand a cane, wizened faces carved into its wood shaft; in the other, a talon. His Camara mask lowered from the whorls of darkness above until it covered his entire head. The veil shielded him. From behind its curtain, his gaze penetrated her sabhu, sifting her. The entire headgear ignited into flames. The shadows erupted into streams of flames. The fire grew brighter until it consumed Maulana's entire body. He gripped the cane and talon tighter. The faces on the cane turned to her, their mouths opening and closing, in inchoate wail. Their desperate screams coalesced into a psalm. The gospel chorus swelled until Selamault finally stirred from the vortex of her dream.

Faith was the connection to realms unseen and the hope to complete their physical journey. While not sharing Bayard's, Selamault found his religion's gospel music beautiful. An easy conduit to connect her to her spirit self. A lifeboat in these difficult times. A solace holding her spirit together. Barely. The songs told a story of perseverance, the need to hold on, and to never forget the center of her joy. Selamault joined in the refrain of the chorus singing about the angels who watched over her as she went about her morning routine.

Another song began, one she didn't remember selecting. *Near the cross! I'll watch and wait* . . . Her heart longed for family slowly slipping away from her. Her father. Her husband.

The other half of her bed was empty. There was no need to lament the coolness of the mattress, since she wasn't wholly unused to that. Xola often rose before her and many nights didn't sleep at all; she'd find him humming from his chair in the corner. "Keeping company with the voices in his head." Raised with ideas of the marriage bed and its sacredness, she took a while to adjust to his ways. But its true sacredness was in the knowing of its partners. She understood Xola and gave him room to be the person he needed to be. Just as he, since her role required certain ways of knowing—and guarding—secrets, allowed her room to do her work. They respected each other. In the pool of gathering shadows, she missed that intimacy.

<Queen Mother Itoro Nguni is on your appointment calendar for the morning.>

"Thank you, Maya. I appreciate you." Selamault splashed water onto her face. Glancing over at her biometric readout—one she'd asked Maya to run each morning—she saw that, though she was fatigued and entirely too warm, her condition was "within tolerable parameters."

<We appreciate you.>

"When the Queen Mother arrives, find out how she would like her tea."

<Blessings upon your day.>

The reason she was so slow moving this morning wasn't her dreams, those she was used to as part of her office and station. It wasn't missing Xola, because though he was absent from this physical realm, their connection was eternal in the spiritual one. No, there were pieces missing from her life—places her children should be—and she prayed for their safety. She scanned her daily briefings, her heart only skimming for any update on Wachiru and Amachi. Her son was safe for now, watched over by some of her operatives. She longed to bring him home but couldn't risk exposing the Niyabinghi network. Even for her son. And when she thought of Amachi, despite no word being in any official log, a vague sense of peace washed over her sabhu. Whatever it was that thwarted her attempts to connect to her, the pings against her emi were warm. Familial.

Few saw Selamault at work. She busied herself in the little routines. She didn't take meetings or talk to the public the way Xola did. Rarely attended much more than the Ijo family gatherings. Her work was in the details, behind the scenes. Though she didn't consider herself particularly adept at mentoring. Xola made it look easy, gathering with tens of sebau while she struggled to fit one into the demanding rigor and discipline of her life. However, her times with Amachi proved rewarding. Echoing parenting, she experienced everything through the fresh eyes of the young.

<Code Black / Eyes Only communiqué coming in.>

"From who?"

<VOP Clay Harrison.>

"Initiate an encryption-cone protocol." This back channel was rarely used, only meant for the most dire of occasions. When matters of politics needed to be set aside. Publicly, VOP Harrison flaunted O.E.'s military power in an ostentatious display for all he was worth. Amassing troops while giving speeches about how he was open to diplomacy. He had the nerve to march into the UN to turn over a list of "security guarantees" to be issued to Muungano, his conditions to lower tensions. In her role as bagirwa of the Niyabinghi, head of Muungano intelligence, such back-channel communication was expected, but not usually directly with the purported head of the LISC government. Usually a network of journalists, businesspeople, or artists ferried messages back and forth. Such direct communication meant the VOP was desperate and his position especially precarious. "This will be interesting."

VOP Harrison's image burned to life. The encryption protocols kept him from applying any filters to his image. His eyes had grown haggard. His smile, a spidery, thin thing, too full of teeth and yet still empty. "Good morning, Selamault."

"Habari gani, VOP." Selamault adjusted her brown dress—embellished with a mushroom pattern—that stopped high above her knees. It had been too long since she'd shown off her legs. She tucked her hands in its pockets to flare it out as she walked.

"I fear good news is few and far between these days."

"Yet you, I'm sure, have some power and discretion to mitigate that."

"Not the way Maulana pushes me into a corner." Hard lines creased VOP Harrison's face. VOP had a practiced charm, pleasant and polished, able to articulate LISC's agenda as if it were his own. That was what bothered her so much. A darkness bubbled beneath it, turning his grin into a devouring maw. Behind his blank, encompassing smile was a man without a core. Without a community. She sent out her third eye, able to see in her mind with enough concentration. The exertion took a physical toll on her. But VOP's chamber, a circle around VOP, had been cut from her vision; as if something, someone, blocked her. Protected him. The "who" bothered her and none of her Niyabinghi agents could get close enough to gather any usable intel.

"He's not alone in such maneuvers. You come demanding that Muungano come to the table to discuss an Earth-Muungano reunification pact. Issuing a ban on Mars entering into any alliance, formal or otherwise, with Muungano. You might as well declare war now and save us a lot of empty machinations."

Her role was that of secrets, sentiments not expressed. Maulana's original response was a list of the various members of LISC staff and family members who could entirely fuck off.

"I also want to limit the deployment of HOVA gbeto along the O.E. borders."

"Do you want to waste my time with jokes? What do you really want?"

"You. I need an ally. One I can trust. You can reason with him." There it was. A glimmer. The hint of desperation in his emi. She'd known VOP Harrison for decades. They worked alongside, though more often opposed to, each other. It was they who brokered the alliance that called for joint military ventures with the HOVA. She also knew how he bent in the winds of his own self-interest, cutting her out of critical intelligence leading to that project's disintegration. Beneath his bravado, the man was scared.

"You credit me with much."

"I credit the bagirwa with the power to speak truth to power." VOP Harrison's eyes darted back and forth, a quick scan to visually assure himself that he was alone. "LISC wants Muungano to rule out further exploration or expansion. And any further military drills. They also want to halt the development of long-range weapons systems, no matter how defensive in nature they might be."

"So your masters have yanked your leash and you need to heel."

He was an apex political predator, with some of the finest instincts she'd encountered. The ranks must be truly closing in on him. "See the big picture, Selamault. I'm being completely reasonable. I don't believe in ultimatums but wanted to drive home the seriousness of their position and how LISC's warnings should not be underestimated."

"Your desperate position should not be underestimated. You need a win or you will be shown the door. Your masters want guarantees of O.E.'s security, yet somehow want to begin negotiations to form an alliance against the inevitable alien threat. It's like none of you have ever met Maulana. Your 'statement' was dead at the word 'demanded.' No one demands anything of Muungano."

"I need this, Selamault." Their meetings weren't recorded, not kept on any calendar. Maya kept no notes. There was no audience to play to. Just her. She risked lowering her guard—brushing off warnings—by communicating with him directly. But she wasn't naive and never forgot that, from the beginning, he was both being groomed to be VOP and a survivalist by nature. He played a role. His words and actions carefully choreographed to serve the true corporate powers behind LISC. Nonetheless, she was moved by his plea.

"What do you want to do, Reverend? Trade on your goodwill within the community? Your track record on standing beside us during hard times? Performative allyship is wearisome. It is you who have backed Maulana into a corner. There aren't enough words in the English or any other language, to convince him to back down. Go back to your masters and remind them of how much they stand to lose should there actually be a war. Profits are made only in the arming of both sides and they have no buyers over here."

"Selamault . . ."

"You are a creative mind, ever more so when it's your ass on the line." Selamault all but smelled Xola in the room with her. She smiled, a small flutter she kept to herself. "Give Maulana options. We neither ask, nor beg, for our sovereignty. We will remain free. By any means necessary. But . . ."

"But what?"

"Give me something to work with."

"You don't leave me many options." VOP Harrison's face cracked with disappointment, not getting nearly as much as he gambled for. He'd spin some new angle, believing he had lulled her into his feint. He was raised in the waters of privilege. His arrogance of positionality led him to think he was so much smarter, so much more adept, than anyone in Muungano.

"You don't leave you many options. But I'll see what I can do." She knew before he cut the channel that he hadn't heard her.

✳

The times were fraught, though in truth, they always had been. The only difference was the current circumstances warranted a visit from Oyigiyigi's Queen

Mother herself. Selamault had few encounters with Itoro. By reputation, she was a skilled politician who all but dined on court intrigue, often seeing drama where none existed simply for her own amusement. One couldn't be caught up in her doddering matriarch routine: she had both wits and intelligence for days.

At the garden veranda, Itoro leaned against the balcony, studying its beauty. Or otherwise lost in thought. The Queen Mother's hat was easily a meter in diameter, made of fiber meant to mimic grass. A red thread ran through it, sewing it into her hair. Her body was covered completely, officially deemed off-limits, not presented for anyone's gaze. Her ankle-length dress, a leopard-skin print, a red cloth draped over it. An intricate weave of beads dangled over the cloth. Her blouse bore a series of shapes in black and white, circles within circles, symmetrical lines, and a repeating motif of three interlocked triangles.

"Thank you for seeing me." Itoro turned with a calculated twirl, a model hitting her mark for maximum effect. From the way she posed, had circumstances allowed, a retinue would be attending her.

"Thank you for coming all this way. It has been too long since we were able to host the Queen Mother." Selamault dripped the last two words out with a sly slickness.

Itoro angled her head slightly in acknowledgment. "My condolences about Xola. He was an arrogant pain in the ass, but he championed community like a true warrior."

"Thank you. We understand the sting of 'till death do we part.'" Selamault fashioned a seat first, the nanobots scurrying at her gesture in a way she found pleasant. She appreciated the tiny aspects of life, taking stock and joy in the ordinary.

"It is its own sovereign sisterhood. Assegai was his own brand of pain in the ass."

"And you loved him well."

Assegai represented the Oyigiyigi pyr ball team. His tall, lanky frame turned free kicks into a one-man spectacle. Entire stadiums fell quiet when he approached the ball just to see what gravity-defying maneuver he might display. Itoro and Assegai were married near the beginning of Muungano's Uponyaji soon after Oyigiyigi expelled all O.E. representatives from their community. There had been a sabotage incident in their mines. Her bravery and relentlessness recalled that of the Maroons, particularly the great Nanny, causing the people to declare her "Queen."

"Do you take anything with your tea?" Selamault asked.

"I've developed a taste for the coconut biscuits the Maroons make. I hear they have all manner of medicinal properties."

"The Maroons claim that all of their foods have life-lengthening and healing properties. To dine with them, one must prepare oneself for the history of each dish." Selamault chuckled, her words meant as a teasing barb aimed at no one in particular. She quietly struggled with humor, enjoying comedy but not quite able to pull it off herself. Still, she practiced it in her own ways, an area of ongoing development. "Besides, didn't your family secure your genestream?"

"They did, but it's not something the Nguni do much with. We prefer the old ways and older medicines."

"Letting the environment test and strengthen you."

"Exactly. We leave room for concessions, however."

A drone entered the room carrying a tray. Selamault fashioned a table between them and retrieved the tea setting from the drone. "Concessions?"

"We find ourselves in a new place. Our ways weren't developed with life among the stars in mind." The Queen Mother reached for a biscuit before Selamault could set the tray between them.

"It was a dream," Selamault whispered.

"Tales of the gods." The Queen Mother cradled the mug in her hands as if savoring its warmth. It was a performative hesitation meant to catch Selamault's attention. "Is having tea safe?"

"From what? Would-be assassins?"

"I just wish to be able to speak freely." Itoro upended her cup in such a way that the only part of her face visible was her eyes.

"We're Muungano. Here, we're always free. And should have no issues speaking with one another." Selamault flicked her finger. Taiwo and Kehinde took orbit about them. The air pressure seemed to pulse, producing a gentle vibration in the ears. "And now it would take military-grade intrusion to hear us."

"And from whose military do you fear such an intruding?" Itoro traced the sacred triangles of Alkebulan along her dress.

"At my age I don't fear much. But I remain, some say, overly cautious." Selamault mirrored the Queen Mother, pressing out the unseen creases in her dress. "LISC. Night Train."

"They want us to believe that they're not, actually; but their ears are everywhere. That's their real tactic, sowing doubt." Itoro's sharp eyes narrowed, taking her in carefully. Not a syllable, not a tone, not a word choice was missed by her. Nor was the tenor of one's emi. "You have a curious sadness about you. Is it Xola?"

"One would guess. No, I worry about Wachiru and Amachi."

"Has there been no word?" Itoro's face softened. Before it had the fierce set of a steel curtain. Now, about the edges, was the commiseration of a fellow mother.

"Not on Amachi. But my last report indicated that we have located Wachiru."

"We mothers do what we can to protect our children," the Queen Mother said.

"Our job never ends. No matter how old they get, how powerful and mature they become, they will always be our children."

"And we remind them of who they are by telling them our stories. Allow them to trip and skin their knees yet bandage their scratches to send them back out into the world. That is why I come to you as one mother to another." Itoro leaned forward, the pantomime of a conspiratorial whisper though she kept her voice level. "You are also an oracle, correct?"

"I wear many titles, some not as easily explained as others." Selamault set her cup aside.

"It is whispered that you were a Black Dove. Of the line of oracles, the Libyan Sibyls. But you were also known as the Ifa oracle. And bagirwa of the Niyabinghi."

"You have keen ears."

"What do you make of O.E.'s VOP?"

"VOP Harrison is, as my nephew Ezeji called him in our briefing, a 'clout-chasing ass clown.'"

"Ass clown. That's quite the technical assessment." Itoro's harsh torrent of laughter caught Selamault off guard. "Ezeji is not being called to the diplomatic circles anytime soon, I trust."

"Frankly neither should VOP Harrison. Ducking all these moves, using relationship as currency for demagoguery, it's wearying. It's like taking a sojourn through all-too-familiar history."

"All history is familiar if you walk its paths long enough." Itoro returned her cup and saucer to the table. "Are you familiar with the Mfecane?"

"Only a little. The wars and resettlements by Shaka, king of the Zulu."

"It translates as the Crushing. He was hailed for bringing together an expansive Zulu state. Yet as he did so, neighboring peoples were incorporated or had to flee as refugees."

"That's not what Muungano is about." Selamault parsed her words for any trace of accusations.

"That is what LISC is about. Power and control at all costs. They'd reduce Muungano to a slag heap if it meant they could take possession of the land and any remaining assets. Like their museums, filled with the curated spoils of Empire. Our remnants placed behind plate glass: dignified and tastefully lit."

"You've come a long way just to tell me this," Selamault said.

"Is Oyigiyigi so far from the heart of the Dreaming City?" Itoro arched an eyebrow, and in that moment, Selamault knew that she was being tested.

"Several weeks by sublight. Though ever present by commlinks." Selamault met her steady gaze, tiring of the games of intrigue. "Yet you chose to see me in person. Without the possibility of prying ears. Though I appreciate your company, I assume there's more to your visit than a vague history lesson.

"Straight to it then." The Queen Mother bridged her fingers in front of her. "Maulana sets the stage for the dance. Over a hundred warships from Titan. Thousands of troops pledged from the HOVA."

"And the Ring. We do not forget the Nguni."

"My fear was that Maulana had forgotten Oyigiyigi." Itoro tapped the nail of her index finger against the table.

"And mine was that Geoboe had forsaken Muungano."

"For LISC?"

"There are whispers."

"He is loyal."

"To the Nguni, which we appreciate. But he sees Oyigiyigi as his kingdom and rules it by a . . . diarchy. You indulge him by co-ruling, emulating an old way best left behind."

"But while his vision is narrow, it's because he trusts that mine is not."

"Diarchies are not the Muungano way."

"But perhaps they should be. They possibly point to future possibilities. One where functionally, the responsibilities and title Camara were split among two to both lessen the burden and expand capacity."

"I see." Selamault curled her finger, pressing it along her lips.

Itoro settled back into her seat, allowing a breath or two to pass between them to recenter and have the heat of the moment dissipate before continuing. "Geoboe fears that Oyigiyigi has been lost in Muungano's shadow. That it should receive a greater portion of the light shown to our community. That it has not been appreciated nor recognized as the prized jewel that it is. That Oyigiyigi's growth is stifled by Muungano's philosophies and its only path forward is to free itself from Muungano's shackles."

"How does he plan to 'free' Oyigiyigi?"

"Geoboe has other ambitions, some which may have clouded his way."

"Is this why the push for Lebna's wedding?"

"A mother's burden . . ." Itoro took a theatrical sip, finishing her cup. "To establish a megapolis and Oyigiyigi as its own independent community."

"That way lies madness. Madness enough for two."

"Perhaps. Or not." A thin smirk crossed Itoro's lips, more bemused than perturbed. She took no offense at Selamault's charge or tone. "In the coming days, Muungano will be tested. Its people need to pull together in the spirit of harambee if our ways are to be preserved against the dual threat."

"LISC and . . ." Selamault left a silence for Itoro to fill.

"The Interstellar Alliance. We face the possibility of a war on two fronts."

"And endless distractions in between."

"Have no worry, the Nguni will play our part."

"You still speak as if you are no longer part of Muungano. Or were still weighing your options."

"Geoboe has a point: Muungano has ignored us. Or at least taken us for granted. The Nguni are not a resource to be remembered or deployed only when you are in need. But we are Muungano: the Dreaming City, Bronzeville, Titan, Oyigiyigi. An alliance."

"You . . . are correct."

"I expected a bit more of a protesting huff," Itoro said.

"I huff when someone is wrong. I will admit, I have felt our relationship drift as Muungano expanded. It's as if us convening, even as the full Ijo, isn't enough to properly sustain the closeness of our community. Each of our community's work has become siloed. Soon we will be defined by our work, ceasing to exist as a cohesive people. We, all of our peoples, are more than what we do or the function we perform. We had an impossible dream when we came together as First World and then Muungano. So many peoples, worldviews, and customs, everyone jockeying for prominence, to be heard or seen. Barely held together by a framework of shared story, as we attempted to forge a common goal, philosophy, and way of life. Peace was fragile, relationships were fragile, love was fragile. The journey was and continues to be fraught. But that doesn't mean the dream is not worth attempting."

"And I never want us to become the monster we've fought so long against." Itoro reached for another biscuit. "I accepted Maulana's offer. I suspect you nudged him toward the ask."

"Are you betraying your son's trust?"

"I am serving Muungano. And my people. As leaders, sometimes the needs of the greater community have to take precedence over family. Even our children. We serve a united Alkebulan. We serve Muungano."

"Asè." Selamault slumped in her chair and called up her biometric readings.

Itoro signaled for two more drinks, waving off more tea in favor of something stronger. As the drones brought two glasses of whiskey, she leaned forward with concern. "Is everything all right?"

"I've talked a lot. I'm checking to see if I'm still an introvert," Selamault said.

"What's the verdict?" Itoro asked with revived delight.

"I'm still an introvert."

"Good. Let's drink to that, shall we?" Itoro raised her cup in salute.

"And to renewed alliances."

❋

The clouds passed across the moon, reducing all the shapes of the dark woods to nebulous shadows. The trees pressed in like soldiers in close formation. Trusting that her feet knew what steps to take, she wound herself through them, hoping that the path would eventually reveal itself. Something fluttered above, disturbing the branches. Selamault knew she was in a Sibylant dream and was unafraid.

In the glimmers of light, a thick fog swirled about, a wounded cloud crawling toward her on the last vestiges of its strength. Her heavy footfalls brought her to the edge of a river, which cut off her path. Exhausted, she leaned against a tree. An owl landed at her feet. Scratching at the earth, it favored its injured wing. It staggered about, disoriented and lost.

"... We carry these scars. We carry these songs." A familiar voice cut through the ether and became a tether drawing Selamault to her. "*Meld into a communion of love, the vibration of the Universe. To be and become unconditional love. Without fear. Without judgment. To share that love with all that you touch.*"

Unbidden tears streaked down Selamault's face. "Nehanda?"

18

THE ENERGY
The Belts

It had been too long since The Energy had been to the Belts. Some days he closed his eyes and held his breath hoping that when he opened them, he might see Mama again. Not all parts of Muungano were as pristine as the Dreaming City, a fact that their PR machine liked to leave out. The parts they considered not settled yet, treated like a shirt in need of an iron. Not ready to be hung alongside the rest of the freshly pressed ones in their perfect little closet. He wondered how many nights Jaha spent on the balcony of their precious library, staring up at the orbiting kraals looping about them. More than five hundred thousand residents lived there, some spending their entire lives there. Hovering over them. Watching them.

The Belts were originally conceived as a way station, never intended to house people long-term. But as the fifth wave migration became an exodus movement, more weusi fled O.E. than the Muungano infrastructure could handle. Wait times became longer. Services became irregular. Only the promise reached them: they were free. The Belts evolved into the home of those who wanted to escape O.E. but didn't necessarily want to fully settle in Muungano. They could carve out their own space on their terms.

Nonrotating solar mirrors reflected sunlight into the angled ring of secondary mirrors. The Belts themselves rotated enough to provide an artificial gravity. Spokes served as conduits for people traveling to and from each kraal. The hub at the rotational axis of the stations served as the spacecraft dock. The port bustled with people coming and going. Most passers-through transferring from O.E. to the Dreaming City. Oyigiyigi. Titan. Few left the platform to enter the Belts proper.

"Where are we heading?" The Energy shifted uncomfortably, constantly checking over his shoulder and scanning for threats. His military training betrayed itself.

"We're there. They call this section Rude Boy." Jaha adjusted her head covering, fixing it snugly on her head.

"Lovely."

"It has its charms. If you're into roughnecks." Camara Xola once joked that the Belts served as a sort of halfway house, allowing people to detox from the ways of O.E. before they settled into Muungano proper. Or create their Muungano where they were. She extolled the history of the place, always framing the story of liberation like she was trying to convince her audience.

The Belts also had a reputation for being the rougher side of Muungano, a reputation its residents enjoyed and fomented. It reminded him of a series of city blocks. Each section like its own neighborhood, each taking on the flavor and attitude of its inhabitants. The air smelled of roasted meat and spices, body odor, and chiba smoke. Aggressive, almost angry, drumbeats pressed into them from unseen speakers. A gathering of men and women freestyled, toasting out of hope, dreaming in verse.

"We need to do better by the Belts, but folks ain't always ready," Jaha said.

"Folks're never ready left up to you-all."

"What does that mean?"

"I came up in Concrete Jungle. Me used to sleep on a cot and would watch the Dreaming City like it was the big house on Hope Road." A thin strain of a forgotten accent trilled in his words. The Energy snagged a breadfruit from a tree. He studied the collection of galvanized zinc-topped rondavels edging the section of the kraal. "I used to write songs about it. Used to listen to linkage reports about crime and violence taking over back home . . ."

"Home?"

"My mother was Maroon. My father from Nap. They settled here and was happy for a time. But I never felt home." A thrum of resentment thickened his voice. A woman's shadow passed through his mind. Glimpsed through a window. Her features obscured by the thin material of the curtain. She wore a white dress. He hoped she might wait, turn and say something to him. But she never did. "After my mom died, we returned to Nap. Things had deteriorated with the migration and all. LISC 'disinvested' our communities. We were on our own. But Daddy was determined to build something there. One night . . ."

Pap pap pap.

Bullets ripped through the living room wall, blasting away chunks of plaster. Portraits of family convulsed, riddled by them before they fell down. I had been jumping on my mattress, determined not to go to bed. Daddy shoved me to the ground and covered me with his body. He wrapped his massive arms around me, his weight nearly smothering me.

Pap pap pap.

So loud. I covered my ears as best I could. But the noise still left them ringing. Distorting all other sounds, like we were underwater. We hadn't bothered anyone. We lived a quiet life. Money was tight, but I never went to bed hungry despite my complaints about not being able to eat my favorite cereal before bed. It had been such a normal day. But they couldn't even allow us that.

Chuk chuk chuk.

Heavier noises. Each volley tamped my chest. Vibrated the floor. I peeked through the cage of his fingers. Men streamed past our window carrying guns. We'd been warned for weeks that the Knights of the White Camelia had been planning an incursion. But Daddy refused to change our routine or even visit relatives in another state. Not wanting to live in fear because that would give the Knights what they wanted. The ground shook. Daddy held me down, covering my mouth to choke off my screams. His body jerked once. Twice. Men yelled, until everything was a chorus of shouts.

Until everything went quiet. So still.

My ears rang. All sound reduced to a distant thrum. Daddy became so heavy, threatening to crush me under his weight. I elbowed him, tried to shove him off of me, wanting him to move at all.

"Daddy?" I tasted blood. I refused to look at him. In the nights to come, I'd cry myself to sleep wondering what his final face looked like. Staring blankly at the Universe.

"In here." A man rolled my father from me and extended his hand. "It'll be all right, son. It'll be all right."

"The Brand?" Jaha asked.

"Not then. I joined him later." The Energy caught himself. He didn't know why he shared that. Some stories he'd learned to keep for himself. It slipped out like it wanted to be heard. He twisted up his mouth in firm resolve. "We got company."

Several bodies peeled away from their cover of shadows, ambling toward them. Their distrustful eyes scanned the two of them. Their emi read as not quite predatory, but far from welcoming. A man approached. His pair of cream breeches and a cutoff shirt framed a series of welts and scars along his back. He rested a machete along his shoulder. "Your brethren some 'round Rude Boy fi do dirty work."

"We no know 'bout that. Business go down under your roof, not our business," The Energy said.

The man took an exaggerated sniff of him. "You mawga foot Night Train."

"Who you talking to?" No matter how old someone was, no matter how much training, or education, they'd received, part of them was still from the corner they were raised on. Like a switch had been flicked in his head, The Energy was no longer a member of the Deacons. He was now that boy from the block, rising to a challenge to who he was. The Maroon loved their jijifo, "evasive maneuvers," meant to wrong-foot obroni. But he was not in the mood for their games.

"Now hold on, buddy." Jaha stepped forward, pressing her hand to The Energy's chest to hold him back. "We ain't no damn Night Train. We are here to meet . . ."

"You no see big men is here?" A second man stepped closer, sporting a gold cap. "We don't do police neither, no matter what they call themselves. And you definitely stink of police."

"You got some nerve knowing a bar of soap done missed your entire body." Jaha's blood was up. No longer a member of the Griot Circle, she was now the young woman from the block who brooked no nonsense.

"You too facety, sistren. Maybe me learn you." The man shrugged the machete from his shoulders in implied threat. They were well versed in the language of intimidation. She reached for her chakram. The Energy shifted his weight to his back foot. Closing his eyes, his emi castout, able to track them despite the gathering onlookers. Their heat spiked, ready to make their move. He braced himself.

A large man sidled up, parting the crowd like the Red Sea without breaking stride. He had the large build of a pyr ball defensive man. His fixed I'm-about-something face moved people out of his way. His hair woven into two long twists beneath a narrow-brimmed trilby hat. His patent brogues and purple tonic suit had the veneer of a refractory coating, hinting at baffler tech to lower his ability to be tracked. Sunglasses hid his eyes.

The Energy palmed his weapon but Jaha waved him off. "Bayard?"

"Jesus is risen. Sight?" the minister said.

"Seen. But me no repent," the machete-wielding man replied.

"Yet. Oh, she'd have given you reasons to repent. Be glad I showed up when I did. I hate cleaning up when she's through with folks." Bayard swept his arms toward Jaha and The Energy. "They're with me."

"They should've just said." The man with the gold cap gave a reassessing glance at them. His stance softened. The way he came to heel at Bayard's approach, suddenly he seemed much younger. A boy playing at being hard.

"You didn't give us a chance," Jaha said.

"And she's generally less than forthcoming on her best days," Bayard said.

"Tuh." Hitching his machete back to his shoulder, the other man sucked his teeth. He trundled off, taking his station back in the shadows.

The Energy recognized the operation. Not too different from how the Deacons operated in a neighborhood. Eyes always watching for strangers, folks who stuck out. Challenging them, gatekeeping for their neighbors, protecting their block. The times had heightened the need for security. Paranoia its own pandemic. Bayard scanned the courtyard. Not liking what he saw, he tapped Jaha and they cut through a series of booths. The Energy guarded their six.

"Blending in nicely, I see." The minister barreled ahead of them.

"You said we were here to meet a friend," The Energy said.

"Meet my friend, Bayard." Jaha batted each of their chests. "Bayard, The Energy."

"I heard of you. Didn't they used to call you 'Bugs' back in the day?" The Energy couldn't help himself, always pushing people's buttons, hoping they'd reveal their true selves. As a Yar'adua, Bayard oversaw the spiritual aspect of Muungano culture. The Energy didn't trust church types.

Jaha stifled a slight chuckle.

"A lifetime ago." Bayard was a former sound engineer and his percussive style was once compared to "swatting bugs," thus earning him the sobriquet. "Come on, we have to keep moving."

Immense white fused-regolith buildings formed a huge court dubbed New Accompong. A group of elders lounged along its steps, slapping dominoes into place. Several pigs roasted over open fires, normally a safety violation but it was the birthday of Cudjoe, brother of Nanny, and they celebrated the venerated Maroon leader. Plates of meat mixed with rice had been set aside for the duppies of their ancestors. The trio ducked to the left of the statues of stone lions. The side street took them to a row of brightly colored rondavels. Turquoise. Pink. Yellow. A low white regolith wall fenced in a mint-colored one.

"We're here. We can talk inside." Bayard held the door open for them to enter.

As he slid by, The Energy shrank as far from the minister's touch as possible. The entrance opened into a spacious room. The walls preset to rotate through various art pieces. William Johnson. Amy Sherald. Jacob Lawrence. Basquiat. Jaha fashioned a couch for herself along with a desk surface.

"It's good to see you again, old friend." Jaha held her arm out. Bayard clasped it and drew her in for a hug.

"You also. Habari gani?"

She punched in code to her wrist unit and projected schematics and log sheets, already reviewing operations.

The Energy stalked the perimeter of the room, running his hand along the bookshelves guarding a blank wall. "Where are we?"

"One of my safe houses." Bayard removed his jacket and folded it over the back of a fashioned chair. An Ashanti stool leaned against a wall. Hand-carved from a single block of wood, it was the seat of its owner's soul, angled to ensure that no other passing souls could rest on it. The beadwork image of a sankofa bird topped it. The symbols carved into the supporting pillars represented love and unity. Its owner would lay their head on its smooth curved top for prayer and meditation. A sacred space to be respected. Next to it sat a wooden palm wine cup carved in Pende style. Bayard unfastened the Maasai club that had been strapped to his side and set it along one of the shelves near the entrance.

"Why does a reverend need a safe house, much less more than one?" The Energy bristled. Another "man of God" who carried a weapon in order to perform his ministry.

"Do you have any idea what all I even do?"

"Badger people about white baby Jesus." The Energy's voice embittered by the scars left from faith.

"You'll have to excuse The Energy. He's not good at church no more," Jaha said.

"I'm 'not good' with the mythocracy. I done did my time. I used to do that 'church' stuff all day growing up. That shit would kill a perfectly good Sunday. At least with the megachurches I could slip in and out without anyone noticing."

"That sounds like the spirit of church." Bayard dripped withering sarcasm as he headed to the kitchen. The clink of dishes promised light refreshments.

"Mythocracy was forced upon us as a means of subjugation, but what we call God is bigger than people's agendas." The Energy strained less-than-successfully to keep a mocking tone out of his voice. Just shy of mocking, but with a profound skepticism as he struggled to understand who this so-called ally was. He was careful. Jaha was a known quantity, one endorsed by his mentor, The Brand. But Bayard was an unknown quantity. The Energy was going to push and prod to take his measure.

"My faith predates colonialism." Bayard sighed, weary of an all-too-familiar conversation.

"No offense . . ."

". . . says someone about to use words meant to offend . . ."

". . . but religion has only been a tool of control and suppression. It has no role in Muungano's present, much less having a leader steeped in its mythology."

"Our founders believed religion serves a vital role to the very heart of the work that is Muungano. No matter the faith practice, it serves and nurtures our spirit and can be used as a self-development tool."

"I've seen where the church takes us. Those dark places no one wants to preach about." The Energy tasted blood in his mouth.

There was an episode of his life prior to the Deacons he didn't or couldn't speak about. His public records shed no light on it, though to scrupulous eyes the conspicuous absence of that light spoke volumes. In his memory, Mama always smiled, her voice a birdsong melody. Daddy a bear of a man, scolding and rule-setting, preserving order to protect his family.

"I've wrestled with those dark places, too. Wondered whether it was best for me to carve something new or reclaim that which was taken from us. But struggle with faith is a good thing. It keeps you sharp about what and why you believe." Bayard cleared away some stray bottles from a table and set down a tray of garri cookies, nuts, sliced apples, and synthed meats.

"You been drinking more lately?" Jaha asked.

"No, I've been drinking pretty consistently." Bayard appeared to note the concern on her face. "I stand by that joke."

"Was it a joke? Should I be worried?"

"No matter my answer, you'll worry. That's who you are." As he spoke, Bayard fashioned an assembly.

The Energy pretended to be focused on investigating the room to better observe him. The nanobots lined up in a sophisticated array. This wasn't a casual device he constructed. Intricate, yet his funkentelechy directed the nanobots with a practiced ease. The Energy noticed the detail and precision with which he worked. It betrayed his own training in intelligence work.

"What's this?" The Energy held up a hand-carved wood figure. It had a large, round, flat head reminiscent of a moon.

"An akua'ba doll. Can you put that down, please." Bayard struggled to sound even-keeled, but the invasion of privacy hit a nerve.

"A fertility doll." Jaha snatched it from The Energy and set it back on its perch.

"You never answered my question about safe houses." The Energy lifted a mask from the bookshelf, inspecting it. Rotating the face revealed a tribal box. Before he could inspect its contents, Bayard grabbed it from him. "Do you mind?"

"My bad." The Energy raised his hands and backed away.

"You know what? Forget all that." Bayard waved him off, growing irritated, no longer in the mood to politely discuss principles nor defend his faith. "Everything I said was a lot of high-minded bullshit."

"Now we can finally get at it," The Energy said.

"Truth be told, I don't know why I believe. I was born in Indianapolis, raised in a 'mythicist' family. I entered the family business, becoming a minister. Even planted my own church. And then my family . . . ran into trouble." Bayard fondled the akua'ba doll. "My wife and I had struggled to have children. Long days of treatments, scans, and tears. The women of our kraal presented her with the doll when she finally became pregnant. Things were hard. I won't go into the details. Some stories you learn to keep to yourself. But let's just say I . . . wasn't the best version of me. My actions split my congregation, nearly drove off my family, leaving my faith all but in tatters. I was ready to walk away from all of it. But I felt a tug at my sabhu, one that held on to me. And eventually I on to it."

"But why put yourself through all that? There's so much other—better—work you could channel your efforts into," The Energy said.

"You right, I can't deny that. But we also have to regain that unseen spirit, incorporate it back into our way of moving and being. What's going on in me speaks to my sabhu. Exploring older practices and rituals, all sorts of ways to connect back to God, to the realm of the sabhu. My Jesus was a liberator, an organizer who flipped tables and took care of the most vulnerable. I'm just doing my best to follow in those footsteps." Bayard set the doll back onto its perch. "We good or did you want to keep playing skeptic smart-ass?"

"We good, old man. Damn." The Energy still didn't know if he could trust him, but he had a framework of the man.

"I ain't mad. We judge folks based on how we show up in the work." Bayard finished his assembly. The construct produced a hum that popped in their ears.

"We can talk freely now. Our operation started to take care of our people in the Belts. It's developed into its own thing."

"Folks don't want to leave," The Energy said. "Second even third generations, some folks have spent their entire lives in the Belts."

"They aren't our focus. We look out for the runaways, the refugees, anyone whose paperwork may be . . . lacking," Bayard said.

"How bad is it?" Jaha asked.

"See for yourself." Bayard toggled through linkage reports. A star freighter blockade at Mars. Riots in Paris with signs reading REMEMBER FIRST WORLD. Teddy's address to the UN didn't help. Vague implications of an outside global threat. The need for unity for all who call or called Earth home. "People are afraid. Things are tense out there. The big fear is that O.E. is sending infiltrators, whose first stop has to be the Belts, in preparation to storm Muungano."

A bang came from the door. *Pap pap pap.* The Energy reached for a weapon. Jaha touched her chakram. Bayard held his hand up to calm them. Creeping to the door, he verified their biometrics. His smile relaxed Jaha and The Energy. When the minister opened the door, a woman, easily two meters tall, posted up on his doorstep. Her dress a long flowing cloth with a matching hijab. She had a royal bearing.

"As-salamu alaykum." A warm smile, like a sunrise over a beach, matched his greeting. She gave him a playful swat, the affection between siblings.

"Wa-alakum-salaam." Bayard half bowed.

Her eyes lit with recognition when she spotted Jaha, giving her a respectful nod. Her path gave The Energy as wide a berth as the rondavel allowed. She set a sigil on Bayard's Ashanti stool. He poured libation for her. The woman bowed in respect. Bayard certainly loved his ceremonies and rituals.

"Kiyah is a grower, now a shepherd of our farming initiatives. She teaches the community seed-to-harvest practices," Bayard said. "How are things out there?"

"It's hot. Investigators are looking for you." Kiyah stared at each of them. "All of you."

"Jaha you know. This is The Energy."

"A member of the Deacons?" When The Energy nodded, a bit of tenseness left Kiyah's posture. "Everything is in place. All the details are on the sigil."

"Good. My friends and I have a few things to discuss. We'll be there in an hour."

"After prayers?"

"After prayers."

"Ma'aasalaama." Halting in the entranceway, Kiyah double-checked for unwanted eyes on the streets of the kraal before covering her face and slipping back onto them.

"Kiyah is one of the most dutiful people I know. She embodies her faithfulness and lives it out. You wondered if my faith journey was worth the effort. She is my answer."

"All right." The Energy lowered his mental guard.

"Because of the nature of our work, we have a whole network of folks dedicated to smuggling people in and out of places. O.E. Mars."

"The Panopticon?" Jaha asked.

"It took a lot of intel to even confirm its existence much less find its location. Even longer to get someone inside. We've had to coordinate with a lot of agencies, including yours."

"Mine?" The Energy asked.

"Yeah. The Deacons have someone inside also." Bayard plopped down across from Jaha. "So, what's the plan?"

"Why are you looking at me?" she asked.

"You're operations. Planning and strategy. How many times have you said 'Who should . . .'"

"'. . . if not me? Step forward,'" The Energy quoted. "The Brand used to drill this into us constantly."

"Yet no one steps faster than you. So what are you thinking?" Bayard asked.

"The first step would be to assemble a team." Jaha nodded to herself, as if silently checking that item off her list. "Next, we'd need to acquire a ship."

"We're already on that." Bayard raised the sigil. "We also have rough schematics and layout of the Panopticon. We'll to be able to land, but to break in, we may face resistance inside."

"You gonna do something about some heavy hitters, pastor?" The Energy applied some extra heat to the last word.

"Sometimes you got to lay your religion down and pick it back up later." Bayard walked over to the bookshelf with the Maasai club on it. He fixed it into a hidden nook and punched in a code. The bookshelves slid to the side, revealing an extensive weapons rack. "Even Moses caught a body."

It took an extra heartbeat for The Energy to sit back and close his mouth. "If we do something this . . . loud, we'll have people pursuing us for the rest of our lives."

"The same folks already gunning for us. There's exposure for them, too. What are they going to charge us with? Breaking out a person everyone denies having, from a place everyone denies exists?" Jaha shut down her holovid. "So, about that ship . . ."

"Let's check out what Kiyah brought us." Bayard turned to The Energy. "We good, good?"

"For now. I'm at least ready to see what you're about." The Energy touched the Ashanti stool on his way out. The Church was Mother. The Church was Father.

19

ISHANT SANGSUWANGUL
O.E.—Indianapolis

Without the ceremonial vestments or Basotho blanket signifying his role as personal guard to the Ijo, Matata seemed somehow diminished. Distantly sad. Shaved around the sides, the top of his head fell into a series of plats. He wore a black dashiki coat, and a gold chakram dangled about his neck, worn like a scarf. Ishant kept his wary back to the wall, his emi alert, as if each nerve ending were a frayed live wire. Time slowed. His hands trembled with the rush of adrenaline.

"Matata." Ishant maintained a matter-of-fact tone concealing his surprise. Searching his emi, he didn't sense anything approaching threat from Matata.

"Obroni." Matata waved his talon toward the mat.

"I've had the feeling I was being followed for some time. You were not on my list of possibilities." Ishant kept his arms raised, hands in plain sight. Without crossing his legs, Matata matched his every step, maintaining a sufficient enough gap he couldn't enclose before Matata got off a shot.

"It was only your Niyabinghi training that allowed you to detect me at all."

"You know about that?"

"As you said, I've been following you for some time." Matata fashioned a seat angled between Ishant and the door.

Taking his cue, Ishant fashioned a couch over his mat, against the wall farthest from the door. Matata lowered his talon; Ishant's arms soon followed.

"What do you want?" Ishant stretched his arms carefully along the back of the couch.

"Information."

"What sort of information?" Ishant's eyes flared with suspicion. Matata was a man without community, largely untrusted wherever he went. A dangerous man. Without a cause and without honor.

"The kind I must be desperate to get because I'm coming to you."

"At gunpoint."

"You have a lot of judgment in your tone. What do you ever truly know about me?"

"Matata Okoro, former Lij of the Niyabinghi. Born on O.E., you grew up in and around the Dreaming City. You were one of the youngest to ever achieve the status Master Poet. You had a promising path but your sabhu or your ambition took you to the Niyabinghi. On your way there, you had stints in the Thmei Academy, back to O.E., the HOVA, back to O.E., and then finally into the Niyabinghi. A casual observer might say that you may have good intentions about working in and alongside community, but get tripped up in the people side of things. And every time you make a mess of things in community spaces, you run back to O.E. to either remake yourself or wait until the heat on your reputation dies down."

Ishant had been completely debriefed on Matata's entire history. His father had been in the HOVA during the Lunar Ukombozi War. He was a part of Operation Hellwalk. Despite the official story reported only one survivor. In real terms, that was functionally true: Matata's father was never whole after that. Sent back to his family to convalesce, he moved them to O.E., where he later struggled with drug addiction. That was the environment young Matata knew: constant transition and an erratic father who was never present even when he was physically. Leaving a father-shaped void in his sabhu, and a subconscious problem with men. Especially older men.

Matata couldn't have been more than ten when Xola found him, wandering the streets of the Dreaming City. Dirty, sneaking through back alleys, such as they were, trying to not be seen though anyone would have taken him in. But that was him in a nutshell: desperate for community, hiding from it, then being hardheaded about accepting it.

"Is that how I'm seen? Is that the official word of Muungano?" Matata sucked his teeth in disgust. Yet even in the gesture, the sadness remained, a cloud of regret shadowing him.

"How does someone who has hurt community—or whom community has so loudly told 'we can't fuck with you no more'—someone who has shown themselves the exit door—find their way back?"

"Don't pretend that you understand us. In the weusi community, we can fuck up all kinds of shit one day, next day, we're good. That's how family works. You tell *me,* obroni, how does one find their way back to their family if you had your way?"

"A term in the Panopticon might sort you out."

"That was rhetorical. Do not actually allow yourself to even secretly harbor the thought that I would come to you for advice about anything, much less my people."

"Am I not a full member of Muungano? Would that not make *me* your people?"

"No."

"Well, if I were to proffer advice, I would remind you that you hadn't been put out of community. Only freed to explore other spaces." Ishant couldn't help the snide tone in his voice to drive his sardonic point home.

"Fuck. You." Matata's voice wasn't bitter or harsh, only cold and quiet. The terrible quiet of the echoing silence following a thunderclap.

"I've been told I can be quite the asshole. But I'm trying to be better." Ishant needed to push his buttons, agitate the man without getting caught up in a joust of smart-ass words. He needed Matata to keep talking, to lower the temperature in the room. "Well, since you're asking so nicely, what information do you need?"

"Don't make me regret not putting a charge through your heart and just rifling through your records." Matata tapped the talon but didn't raise it. Re-evaluating Ishant, his eyes scanned a telemetry reading in his head. "What do you have on VOP Harrison?"

"What makes you think I have anything?"

"Do we have to keep doing this tired dance?" Matata had been following him for a while now, judging from how long Ishant's emi had been unsettled. "What you really want to know is 'Why does Matata want to know anything about the VOP?'"

"You've already proven to be a skilled deceptor. Why would I believe anything you say?"

"You people . . . so high-and-mighty. So proud of 'never losing sight of the person in front of you.' A bunch of fucking hypocrites." Matata sprang from his seat. Ishant tensed, ready to defend himself, but Matata's talon remained at his side. He circled the chair, heated but not murderous. "Here's something to consider in your history-cum-judgment of me: All I've ever wanted was to do right by community. But what that meant, the path to follow, always shifted. Yeah, I failed. That's the Muungano way, too, right? Not being afraid to fail. I'm still a son of Muungano, I'm just walking my own path."

"And where does that path lead?"

"To taking down VOP. By any means necessary." Heaving the talon to his shoulder, Matata peeked out the window.

As the words hung in the air, Ishant played and replayed the sentence in his mind. Checking the cadence, analyzing each syllable, studying Matata's body language, coming to the same conclusion each time: he meant that shit. A man, no, a lost child, in flux, at a crossroads. Wounded, scared, licking his injuries, Matata was evolving into someone else. Perhaps even on a path to healing, attempting to figure out the man he was to become. What he needed to do to move forward.

"Is that . . . do you think that will ingratiate you . . ." Ishant locked up attempting to figure out how to come at him. He knew his responsibility in the moment. How he treated him would help shape the man to be. He wished he were better at this. "Is this a gesture to make up for . . ."

"Damn, I feel like I short-circuited you with a logic paradox." Matata slung the talon over his back, declaring an official cessation of hostilities. For now. "Like I said, my own path. The biggest threat to Muungano existing on its own terms is VOP Harrison."

"There are no quick fixes to systemic issues." Ishant was much clearer when it came to issues of politics over personal matters.

"True. But he always talks about the LISC areas of success in a select few places, ignoring all the other countries where they've failed. It's fake work, using numbers to hide their ineffectiveness. Now he uses the smoke screen of war to further plunder nations. We need an immediate solution to stop the bleeding now."

"Assassination isn't it."

Matata arched an eyebrow at the accusation. And smirked. "All I'm asking is for a copy of any data you collected. You were able to get much deeper into the Capitol and its system than I could. I imagine you scooped up a ton of data while info-scraping."

An alert flashed on Ishant's cybernetic arm. It detected an infiltration. Someone was attempting to access and copy his data. With all of his safeguards, the kind of worm needed to penetrate his system required proximity. He barely glanced toward Matata, but that was enough of a tell.

Matata spun. His jacket flared like a shadow engulfing him, creating a cloaking field. He fired a few wild charge bursts. Ishant ducked for cover.

"You don't have to do this," Ishant yelled from behind the couch. By the time he chanced a glance out, Matata had disappeared into the night.

Nothing in his training had prepared him for this.

Bombings, nations brought to the brink of war, alien incursions, global

climate collapse were bad enough. Now Matata, would-be avenger of griev-
ances against community, ran the streets. Ishant understood Jaha, and to a lesser
degree Xola, much more in that moment. The way they saw the big picture,
setting Muungano in the context of not just the various moving parts of the
present, but also against the backdrop of history, to chart a way forward.

Ishant stopped at the bathroom. He splashed water onto his face. His skin
a sallow complexion, his eyes darted all over the place as if in need of a fix.
Running his wet hand through his hair, he swept his premature streak of white
hair to the side. He ran to the toilet barely in time for it to catch his vomit. His
body convulsed in shudders that tensed every muscle in him. He wiped the last
strings of bile from his mouth and rinsed his mouth out. Resting his arms on
either side of the sink, he waited until his stomach stopped trembling before
raising his head again. He still had to face his supervisor.

✳

"You're late," Mimilah said.

"I've had . . . a strange day." Ishant brushed past her to take his seat. "What's
on the agenda for today?"

"That's what I want to talk to you about." Mimilah activated her encryption
cone. A next-gen cone, even if not quite military-grade, blocked all manner of
signals. Ishant's cybernetic arm numbed. That also meant Mimilah had been
severed from Miriam, leaving only Akilah in the moment. "We need to have a
frank conversation."

"What's all this?" Ishant couldn't quite read the look in her eye. Suspicious.
Betrayed. His face didn't betray any alarm, but he mapped out his nearest escape
routes.

"Your story doesn't add up. You didn't think you'd just be able to waltz into
LISC headquarters and start working like you were any other ordinary citizen,
did you? There are clearances. Tests. Direct evaluations."

"So you're planning on what? Interrogating me? Torturing me?"

"Nothing so . . . baroque. I just need to get at the truth. The readouts will
help determine that." Akilah moved to her workstation. The doors to their office bolted, lockdown procedures. Security would be alerted, posting up outside
their doors, awaiting an all-clear or an emergency signal to breach. Full data
streams of Ishant appeared as a holovid between them. His face in close-up in
one screen, being scanned for microexpressions.

His Niyabinghi training hadn't been tested in the field. Biometrics would be difficult to fool on any day, much less in a high-stress situation. Ishant calculated his worst-case options. If she hit her panic button, his odds were just shy of fifty-fifty whether he could make it into the ventilation system before the guards burst in.

"Your place of birth?" Akilah asked.

"Riverside, Indianapolis."

"Mother's name?"

"Parinda Sangsuwangul."

"Now tell me a lie."

"I've really enjoyed working here." Ishant's deadpan tone, unbothered by the situation. He didn't understand why so many people failed to appreciate his sense of humor.

"Hm." Akilah side-eyed him. "Good enough. Baseline established."

"What is it you want to know?" Folding his arms, Ishant leaned back in his seat.

"What is your current assignment?"

"To do the scut work for the COP balls."

"What is your mission from Muungano?"

"I have no mission from Muungano. I've been declared a persona non grata."

"Have you ever been attached to any intelligence agency?"

"If you are spy hunting, would anyone actually answer that yes?"

"Answer the question."

"No."

Akilah puzzled over the readings, making a series of noncommittal noises. "I feel like you're not telling me the whole truth. Like you're hiding something."

"That's the problem with yes-or-no questions: there's no room for nuance."

"Then add some nuance. Let's see if that will make me believe you."

"I did have a . . . secondary mission. A holdover standing order."

"What was the nature of the mission?" Akilah perked to full attention, double-checking his health telemetry.

"To reconnect with my old LISC contacts, learn as much as possible about the current state of LISC policies and attitudes, to see if there was a peaceful way to lower tensions between our two governments." Ishant's backup cover story cut so close to the truth it would allow him to pass any truth scan.

"You're a back-channel agent?"

"Diplomat. My mission hasn't changed, only my assignment and who I report to."

"And who's that?"

"Right now, you. Ultimately, Jaha. I'll always feel beholden to her no matter where I go or where I find myself." Ishant rubbed his cybernetic arm as if he could warm sensation back into it. "Now, what is this all actually about?"

Akilah studied him. The silence between them swelled, gestating into a charged moment. Her hand wavered over her panic button, as she struggled with an internal debate. Finally, she inhaled and held her breath, the way one might before jumping off a cliff for a deep-sea dive. "I want to defect to Muungano."

"I . . ." Ishant ran his hand along his face as if dry-washing it. He shook his head. If Matata came close to short-circuiting him earlier, Akilah had over-loaded his systems now. "I'm sorry . . . what?"

"I apologize for all of this. I have to be careful. I had no other choice but to spring this on you with no warning again."

"I don't know what game you're playing, but I have trouble believing that a person in your position suddenly wants out."

"What position is that? A cage is still a cage, even when you can't see the bars." Akilah brushed past him to take her seat. "I, we, can walk around these streets protected by the privilege of position to power, but that's not walking in our freedom. No part of us can live on our own terms here. We serve the ma-chine of LISC and call it a life. We want something more."

"I don't understand. Why drag me into this at all?"

"Because I've studied your file. You've walked the same path I'm trying to walk."

"You see where that's got me. Excommunicated."

"For now. Are you telling me the second LISC backs off or Maulana finds a way forward and your 'excommunication' ends, you wouldn't go back? Your love for Muungano radiates from you. Everyone knows. You've reached as high as you'll ever get in your job. However, it's also what makes your insight valu-able."

"What makes you think I won't report you? I bet I could leverage this intel for a chance at a promotion."

"That'd be shortsighted a play even if I believed you would." Akilah ges-tured about. "Not that you'd have any proof. We aren't being monitored or recorded. They'd have to take your word. You'd more likely be seen as an agent sowing dissent among our ranks and probably lead to them showing you the door."

Ishant considered his position. He wanted to trust her, but he was trained to be suspicious, especially when good fortune appeared like this. "What do you think I can do for you?"

"Just get me and Miriam out of here. However you got out."

Ishant suspected the possibility that she wanted to suss out his network. "Let me think about it. Give me a chance to see if any of my old friends are still around."

"I've set my cards in front of you. I'm gambling big."

"We're in the same boat. This could very well be a clever LISC test of my loyalties. Trust is . . . ephemeral."

"What do we do next?"

"We behave normally, like nothing is happening. In case it doesn't."

"Why wouldn't it happen?"

"These things take time." A counteroperation to flush him out as an agent, for one thing. He needed to stall. Vet her and the moment. He needed time and space to think. "I'm not sure how this works."

"Both of us."

"Do you know how many legal channels we would have to go through? General counsel. State. Justice."

"Immigration," she added, less-than-helpfully.

"Cute. It's complicated, to say the least. The process is fraught at the best of times. But now that we're on the brink of war, with your position if we're caught, that's the game. We're talking acts of high treason. I'm convicted for espionage for sure. Disappeared." Ishant weighed his options. Well, made a show of doing so. He, too, risked a gamble. But the opportunity was too great not to chance. If only to document her network and allegiances. He'd have to figure out a way to leave a report for Lebna. "Shit."

"What?"

"We have VOP Harrison's dinner tonight. Protocol arrangements have been finalized by the advance team and State."

"We don't want to tip them off. Let's go to a party."

*

Lebna waited for him at their designated meeting spot. His wide pants gathered at the ankles, a short open jacket over a thin shirt. The fashion of an O.E. tourist. A painful weight tugged at his heart. Lebna's face this side of displeased at Ishant's approach.

"A second so soon jeopardizes our entire operation. And network," Lebna said, before Ishant could fully settle in his seat.

"I wouldn't have called for it if it wasn't important." Ishant's arm went casually numb again. He doubted anyone cared about how much their subterfuge protocols actually hurt him.

"What could be so . . ."

"Akilah came to me. She wants to defect."

"No. This is obviously a trap. More than you hoped just falling into your lap? No." Lebna cupped his glass with both hands. "O.E. is considered a rogue state, to use their terminology."

"A rogue state with a space-capable fleet at their disposal. And a nuclear arsenal enough to obliterate this world and ours several times over."

"We've been in back-channel negotiations with members of the UN Security Council to broker a joint contingency plan against the Interstellar Alliance."

"A 'shit hits the fan' plan?"

"Basically. Having a member of the VOP's staff, one so close to his inner circle, defect . . . it will complicate matters." Lebna studied the disappointment in his emi. "I would need to loop in the R, all the heads of Muungano security, the bagirwa."

"Immigration." Ishant sneered.

"Hell, Maulana and Geoboe and the Ijo security council might want a say before all is done."

"Not to add to the complication, but we have a time consideration."

"Of course we do."

"We have an upcoming window of opportunity to extract her. Them."

"Them?"

"She's joined."

"A sensate? This just keeps getting better. Either one could be a plant. That makes the work exponentially more complex. A single extraction but each has to be vetted."

"We can take them someplace neutral. Off-world, but not Muungano. A place to wait while they are checked out."

"And test if their intelligence is actionable." Lebna relaxed more, intrigued by the possibility. "Will they go for that?"

"We don't want to jeopardize these talks over speculation."

"We don't want to give VOP an excuse to VOP."

"Precisely. VOP isn't the most stable or predictable of regime leaders. There's no telling what he may do. Is their intel real?"

"She sits adjacent to, if not directly in, the inner circle. We can't brush her off. That's not the Muungano way. She believes she's in danger if she stays. Asylum is asylum."

"Is it asylum or defection?"

"I don't get bogged down in the legal paperwork. Whichever makes the process smoother."

"Our work doesn't allow for such . . . creativity. We have to be exact. In all things."

"If we don't do this, I'm not sure I understand why we'd do any of this work at all." Ishant all but pushed away from the table.

Lebna's hands released his cup, but hesitated in indecision of where to place themselves next. They reached for the cup again like a life preserver. "My job is to examine all angles, present options, and make recommendations. I didn't say no."

"Then we need an exit protocol."

✳

The Hall of Flags served as the grand ballroom of the Capitol Building, a welcome center celebrating the countries and territories that comprised O.E. At its heart was a large domed center with stained-glass window panels, a Cyclopean eye staring down on its visitors. Limestone walls, the same shade of Charleston green as the VOP's floor, ran the length of the canopy to the dome. Fluted Doric pilasters divided them. Paintings hung between sculptures, stoic guardians of the room. High above, the flags of the countries of O.E. ringed the room, fluttering in an unfelt breeze; Ishant couldn't help but wonder if they were actually holovid projections. A scrolling chyron read OUR COUNTRIES. OUR CITIZENS. OUR PLANET. MAY WE CONTINUE TO HONOR AND LEARN FROM EACH OTHER AND CREATE A CULTURE OF COOPERATION TO BUILD THE KIND OF COMMU- NITY THAT WE CAN MARCH INTO THE FUTURE.

Ishant tugged at his suea phraratchathan. Not the kind of suit he was used to wearing, its high-tapered-collar shirt hemmed in by a stiff jacket with a fit neither natural nor comfortable. Checking the time, again, he worried about whether Mimilah would make it. His mind raced with worst-case-scenario planning, from her being taken into custody to the need for possible escape.

He had two sets of go bags stashed in different locations. A swell of music cued her arrival.

Akilah paused at the top of the stairs for her introduction. Shifting awkwardly from foot to foot, she modeled her teal silk kebaya with a collarless neck, the open front fastened by a brass kerongsang over a printed batik skirt. She clutched Miriam's hand with the desperation of looking for an escape shuttle. They walked in sync as they descended the stairs. Miriam's kiswah el'kebira had been passed down, mother to daughter, for generations. The embroidered top of its draping sleeves matched the teal of Akilah's top. Slits in the bottom of the dress revealed a floral pattern similarly echoing Akilah's batik skirt.

"You look good." Akilah straightened the line of his jacket buttons.

"Thank you. You two are . . . stunning." Despite their often being accused of having a near-robotic affect, their appearance left him struggling with his native language.

"Are all of your shirts so tight?" Miriam asked.

"They're well fitted." He tugged at his sleeves again.

Miriam suppressed a slight chuckle, and then a passing figure caught her attention. She elbowed Akilah. "I think the First Lady wants you."

Secretary of State Teddy waved. State had circulated a list with all the names of the various designers of her dress, jacket, purse, and shoes to the news-linkage outlets. A classic silver-and-black gown, with black suede-and-velvet shoes trimmed with a series of rhinestones. Her jacket mirrored her dress, the opposing color scheme creating an optical illusion as she moved, as if she shifted in and out of space-time. She didn't bother to disguise her displeasure at Ishant's presence.

"Akilah, allow me to introduce you to Shy'Amor Barrick, Mars delegation."

A tall, slender woman, white hair framing her narrow triangular face. Her eyes such a piercing shade of blue, they could only be the result of gene attenuation. Her flowing silver gown nearly glowed in the artificial light. She extended her hand. "I look forward to a fruitful collaboration."

"I'm Akilah Natarajan, the secretary of state's chief of staff." Akilah offered a limp hand clasp rather than a full-throttled handshake.

"Sometimes around the office we call her 'A Killer.' As is the case of any undersecretary, she does all of the real work." Teddy led a round of polite laughter.

Small talk was never Ishant's strong suit. He mimicked everyone else's performance.

"If you'll excuse us, friends, I believe these fine folks wish to give me a briefing under the guise of casual conversation." Teddy bowed slightly, her attention on the departing envoy.

Ishant had already bored of the pretense.

"They never teach you about that in the LISC Corps," Akilah whispered.

"What's that?" Ishant said.

"How to mingle." Akilah ticked her chin, alerting them to Teddy's returned focus.

"There are a lot of important people to meet here, and you need the ability to know who to schmooze." Teddy led them around the periphery of the gala to minimize the possible ears. Once they were out of direct eyeline, Teddy's demeanor shifted, like a body straightening stiffly and hardening. Her face drew down at sharper angles, her features sharpened. Her eyes baleful orbs calculating an array of next moves. "How's the speech?"

"State Department is still working on the final wording of his remarks," Akilah said.

"He needs to stay on message." Teddy's glare dared anyone to contradict her.

Ishant watched each one in turn, wondering who brought up the possibility of VOP Harrison improvising a new direction.

"Do you want the full lid?" Akilah asked.

"Only the highlights," Teddy said.

Miriam projected her report. The image of the solar system closed in on a planet. "We have a meteor storm incoming, causing us to clear out a battle-cruiser group from the Venusian space yard."

Teddy reached for the icons of a squadron of ships and moved them like chess pieces. "Deploy a group, park them on the far side of Venus."

Akilah chimed in, her holovid display overlaying Miriam's with an image of Earth. Then the U.S. Then what remained of the Florida coastline. "We have a Category Four system due to reach landfall that evening. The hurricane will batter what's left of Florida and parts of Georgia."

"They know the drill. They chose to stay." Teddy sighed. "Let's start crafting the language for an emergency aid bill."

"Sadly, it also looks like we have a standoff in Bod," Miriam added.

"Service of the Order?" Teddy asked.

"Unknown. But with all of the economic tensions, we don't want to risk China getting involved." That was the Akilah he had come to appreciate when they could move past their one-upmanship repartee. The keen analytical mind steeped in an understanding of cultural philosophy. A heady mix of principles and compassion.

"How are they any different from our homegrown ARM extremists?" Ishant asked the question—on its surface, a reasonable though naive one—more to push Teddy's buttons than anything else. This was the Ishant Akilah kept around. A heady mix of intellect and political trolling.

"The state rearing the might of its forces against its citizens. If you'll excuse me." Teddy's voice arched. She refused to angle her body in any way to include him. Flustered, she ended her impromptu briefing. Without turning back around she muttered, "We fund people who look like us."

Akilah, Miriam, and Ishant blinked at each other as if they'd all been slapped.

"Oops. Did she just say the quiet part out loud?" Akilah and Miriam said in unison once Teddy was out of hearing.

"Predators are predators. Being nice to them don't change that," Ishant said. They collected themselves enough to follow her back to the main party.

Classical strains of piano and harp and violins—inoffensive and genteel—wound down as background soundtrack. The thick murmur of chatter rose as people jockeyed to position themselves to be best seen. Especially with the right officials. Laughing, whispering, or back slapping, the performance of congeniality with none of the actual warmth. The perfect distillation of why Ishant hated most gatherings. He edged toward the stage as Teddy prepared to take the stairs.

"It is my honor to be with you today. We gather to celebrate the strength of a united Earth Alliance. A vision we are dreaming into reality, even as fear threatens to shatter our peace. But we are still the people we have always been. Stubborn, fearless, proud, adventurous, who carry our history within. Fresh pages no one can steal from us, rewrite, nor make us feel guilty about.

"In our darkest hour, we seek a new moon, one free of the shadows of its past. One that dreams toward the dawn of a new morning. And it's my singular pleasure to introduce the man who can guide us to that new morning. Our friend, my husband, and the Voice of the People, Clay Harrison."

Teddy issued a chaste kiss as her husband passed, to thunderous applause. VOP Harrison waved a greeting to the crowd, but his bearing was off. Before he began speaking, he cleared his throat as if unsure of the words in front of him. His head low as if in apology.

"LISC has long strived toward creating an interdependent community, or at least that's what we should have been striving toward. We haven't always lived up to the promise of who we could be. We have failed to dream big. Failed our brothers and sisters around this planet. Failed to sustain them. Failed to hear them. Failed to feed them, house them, teach them, and care for them. Failed to teach them to live in abundance, but instead trained them in fear. No wonder they wish to leave us."

"What's he doing? Where's he going with this?" Akilah grabbed Miriam's arm. "There's no way State would approve this language."

Ishant perked up in renewed interest. At first he'd written off the VOP's talking points as another exercise in appropriating Muungano language. Crying onstage was easy. A matter of performance in lieu of credibility; applying dollars in lieu of strategy. Unless it was accompanied by change, by some shift in power, it was still business as usual. That was the simple game of the machine. All long as everyone understood that and knew their place in the scheme of things, the matrix was pleased. However, the VOP's vibe felt different. Authentic. Dangerous. He was off script.

A new possibility occurred to him. What if the escalations, the tensions between O.E. and Muungano, weren't VOP's doing? What if he was only following the orders of others, those who pulled the strings of the marionette in office? His superiors would not be pleased. The VOP was beholden to his masters. They work through him, but they don't need him. If he stepped off the page, they'd clean house. "It's not safe for us here."

"Why?" The tenor of Akilah's voice drew Miriam's attention.

"He's no longer running their playbook. No longer an asset."

"What does that mean? He's gone rogue? Lining his own pocket?" Miriam asked.

"Worse. Ceding ground to Muungano's principles. Listen to his speech."

They quieted enough to hear the phrase "dismantle the hegemony of caste." Ishant faced them. "He pretty much signed his death warrant."

"We shouldn't be talking about this here," Miriam cautioned.

Akilah's eyes brightened with understanding. "They would work around him. Through him."

"They who?" Miriam asked.

"The funders of LISC," Ishant said. "That's why it's not safe." He nodded toward the nearest exit.

"This should be the dawning of hope and prosperity everywhere." VOP

Harrison paced the stage with the bravado of his preaching roots. "We commit to improving our social systems. We commit to expanding our networks. No nation, state, community, or individual is beneath our notice. We commit to deepening those relationships, of ally and opponent alike in hopes of making new friends of them both. Leading to a bright new future, one of limitless possibilities . . ."

The comms systems squealed; a melancholy strain like violins weeping over a slow beat was piped through the system. An override signal jammed the comms. All transmissions. VOP Harrison backed away from his podium. The emergency doors slammed into place, sealing the room. Extreme safety protocols had been initiated. An automatic lockdown, usually signaling a possible imminent attack.

"What's going on?" Akilah asked.

"Someone's contingency plan." Ishant scanned for alternative exits. He swam against the surge of the crowd. Akilah and Miriam followed. The crowd moved like a tide flowing out to sea before returning as a tidal wave. Either toward the nearest exits to evacuate, despite the barricade, or spilling toward the front, banking on the security of the VOP to protect them. Ishant elbowed and showed his way to the side of the room.

Cylinders tumbled from the air vents. Once they clattered along the ground, smoke poured out of them. They pulsed bright shards of light. The walls vibrated with the scurrying of metallic skittering along them. Guests backed away from the walls, quivering in collective nervousness. Herded toward the center of the room. Ishant dropped to his knees, in case security burst in and began shooting. His scans indicated no biological or chemical attack, no more than an elaborate smoke bomb, barely rising to the level of a flash-bang. It had the same intent: disorientation and panic.

People scattered every which way. Stumbling in the smoke, they tripped over each other, trampling over anyone who fell.

Then the screaming began in earnest.

The smoke seared Ishant's nostrils. He scooted toward the wall, pressing against the wall panels. Some of them popped open. He withdrew emergency nanomesh hoods. Security stashed them throughout the building in case congressional members weren't on the main floor during a biological attack. Each one came equipped with a transponder. Announcements belatedly provided instructions on how to find and put on the hoods. Staffers had been drilled on their use, trained to help the guests find and don their own hoods. The incessant bleating of transponders built to a metallic chorus as more and more people activated theirs.

Ishant ushered Akilah and Miriam toward an overturned table. It wouldn't offer any real protection, but provided an obstacle against panicked stampede. The pale glow of the cylinders faded. The cylinders collapsed in on themselves like self-crushing aluminum cans. Their metal casing protruded; their ends frayed, with each strip smoothing into a needlelike appendage.

Slithers.

Hackers counterprogrammed nanobots to form a series of tendrils. They whipped about like metallic-limbed sea anemones. The weaponized, self-replicating bots swirled, lashing about, reminiscent of newborns getting their feet under them. As metal barbs, they could stab any exposed flesh. Each tendril capable of launching bits of itself, to travel through blood vessels to reach its target's heart or brain and blow up like an engorged puffer fish.

Secret Service rallied around Teddy, ushering her down a hidden secure corridor. The Capitol was riddled with them. A group of ARM agents clustered about the stage, surrounding the VOP, but without further movement. Ishant couldn't tell if they were bracing for an attack, had no security fallback plan, or penned VOP Harrison and his team exactly where they wanted.

The slithers swept through the crowd like whirring blades, leaping onto faces or simply stabbing whoever was near them as if programmed to attack at any movement. Ishant pressed a finger against his lips to peel back a dermal flap. He jacked into the portal in the wall behind them.

"There." He pointed to a section of the wall. "It's a sealed shaft. It drops to the catacombs."

Akilah and Miriam inched along the wall, scrabbling their fingers along its surface until they found a seam. They tore at the plaster overlay. Ishant stopped. A presence disturbed his emi. Just beneath the discordant din, an eerie silence permeated the room. Someone wore a dampening suit, deadening sound and distorting light about them. Or they moved in and out of a tesseract fold. The slithers sprang, a torrent directed on the position of the Secret Service detail.

"Hurry!" Ishant yelled.

"We got it. Come on." Akilah pried off the last section of wall, revealing an ancient shutter. She held it open for Miriam and quickly followed behind. Ishant spared a last glimpse. Three slithers converged on VOP Harrison; their bladed appendages reared scorpion tails. His screams followed Ishant into the darkness.

✳

The trio emerged near the remains of the Tomlinson arch, outside of the City Market, on the westmost side of the Capitol. Their clothes a ruin of black smears, mud, and deposits Ishant feared to identify. They dragged themselves up the hillside and collapsed once they reached the top. Ishant blinked; the advertising monitors on each surrounding building broadcast the same image. The news crawl reported VOP Harrison being rushed to the VA Hospital in critical condition. The person of interest was still at large, his face projected along most of the downtown buildings.

Matata.

20

AMACHI ADISA
Mars—The Badlands

Lesson Three—Redefinition

The khamsin blows at your back, the southwest wind dry and burning, carrying the desert sand like a scourge. Your eyes fill with mountain vistas and stars, the wonders of the world, the universe, all of it spread out in front of you. The donkey's uneven gait jostles you from side to side. Though its steps falter, you know it would find its way home. Home. Gold-paved streets. Waves of corn and sunflowers along the canal. An oasis of palm trees and meadows. Of frog gardens. Of musical pavilions. A place to finally rest. Above you, among the canopy of an old forest—its trees standing sentry next to the mountain pass—a great brown owl, its feathers tinged with gray, watches you. Its gaze unbothered and ever unimpressed. Its large wings rustle, unfurling like the mighty sails of an ancient ship. A screech tears through the night. Only then you realize night had settled on your journey, sudden and total, plunging your world into shadows and mysterious shapes. By the glint of moonlight, the outline comes into view. A golden falcon, claws extended in its death dive, snatches the owl from its perch before its wise eyes can turn to react. Only a tuft of feathers falling to the ground, splatters of blood tinting their edges, as the sole clue to its presence.

You crouch in a cool corner of the cave. An earthen cleft, both welcoming and unsettling, like a mattress you can't get comfortable on despite how much you tossed and turned. You run your fingers through its black soil.

"I sing of your rest, I sing of your love," Nehanda serenades from the other side of the cavern. Her melody breaks when she notices you stir. "Dreams and portents. Our time together comes to a close."

"Yeah, yeah. Snatch this pebble from my hand." You attempt to joke, but her resigned tone rattles you. Unable to meet her eyes, you turn to straighten your bed berth area. You expected the two of you to be making final preparations, sharpening weapons, laying traps. Not Nehanda worrying about her ankles being ashy. Nehanda sits on a large rock massaging lotion into her feet.

"You mock to cover your fear, but your troubled sabhu can't hide."

"I just don't know what I'm supposed to be learning. Besides frustration."

"Forget everything you learned from modern teachers. I am a portal guardian of a nexus place, just like you are a conduit. We enter into the final phase of your initiation."

"I had a different sort of training montage all built up in my head. I thought I was being trained as an elder of the night." Your voice rises at the end of the sentence. You doubt if you want it to be a question.

"My child, you've only taken the first steps. Enough to get you to the path to *begin* your journey." Nehanda tosses her head back in a sudden snort of laughter. "You cannot give what you do not have and you can't speak on what you don't know or haven't been taught."

"What did you mean that I was a conduit?"

"No one owns the orisha or nature or mothers. There are those who are Aje by virtue of being a woman, those who carry Aje without even knowing it, and those who are conscious of and inducted as Aje. And there are also Aje who exist in the spiritual realm. Our ancestral mothers."

"Which am I?" You reflect again. "Which one will I be?"

"More than one thing can be true at the same time."

"Do you know what your problem is?"

"You have no idea how much I love conversations that begin this way." Her brow furrows in mild annoyance.

"Never mind." Shrugging, you rethink whatever smart-ass comment you were about to make. Not because you fear disrespecting her. Your easy banter with her sprang from a place of profound respect. And love. But rather because you know that you weren't going to get to the heart of what bothered you. The question you don't know how to put to words. The missing puzzle piece of your sabhu, the context that would make sense of the rest of the pieces scattered about you.

"You have always struggled to find your place in the story of Muungano. Let me tell you part of your story." Nehanda spreads her legs and waves you over. You settle between them and she begins to comb your hair. *"One day, the orisha Obatala, the sky father, ever mysterious in his ways, pondered out loud about Olokun, the mother of Aje. Her domain was bereft of life, her kingdom was one of gray monotony, a melancholy bleakness. As always, he was unbothered by whether or not it was exactly the way she wanted it. So Obatala went to Olorun, the ruler of the heavens, the Supreme Being. He petitioned that there should be solid land so that fields could grow and hills and valleys could give shape to it, so that orisha and other living things could live there. Olorun, also heedless of his sisters' desires, agreed, but he knew such creation to be an ambitious enterprise and wondered who would be willing to do such a thing.*

"Of course, Obatala volunteered. He sought out the house of Orunmila, the orisha of wisdom, who understood the secret ways of existence. Obatala laid out his dilemma and how, though ambitious, he had no idea how to begin the work. Orunmila brought out his divining tray. He cast sixteen palm nuts and, from the way they fell, read their meaning. He cast and recast until he was sure of what existence spoke to him. Orunmila told him to carry sacred symbols: a snail shell full of sand, a white hen, a black cat, and a palm nut. But he had to descend to the watery wastes to conduct his ceremony.

"'But how will I get there?' Obatala asked.

"'You are to descend the golden strand.' Orunmila explained the paths of existence, ways to fold and pass through its planes so that neither space nor time mattered to them.

"Obatala forged a chain from star stuff and lowered it to begin his descent. With only the whooshing, like the ocean's waves, to mark his passage, he passed from the realm of light through the region of grayness. After a time, he reached his destination. He poured out his sand and dropped the hen upon it. The hen scattered the grains in all directions. When it dried, it became land extending in all directions. The place where Obatala first set foot, he called Ifa."

"Is it just me or was that story brought to us by the letter 'O'?" Your sulky face softens.

Nehanda sighs. "What did you hear?"

As you think through the story, you imagine the Dreaming City of the orisha, which inspired Muungano's capital. Yet part of your mind nags you, dragging you back to Obatala's journey. You picture lines of infrastructure routed through space. A pocket dimension where you could hide what you needed. "The golden strand . . . its like how we might describe wormholes or tesseract folds."

"Yes." Nehanda draws back a tuft of your hair and weaves a string through it. "Ritual serves as the gateway to the land of our ancestors and the realm of the Spirit. It is about aligning your spirit with your intentionality. Having an Iyami pot is not how your power is reassured. You have to do the work. For you. For your community. For the planet. Are you so willing?"

"I am." A feeling you can't name sweeps over you, drilling to the core of your sabhu. A curtain of finality. Attuning to your environment, you recognize that you are about to cross the threshold of a door of no return.

"We also exist in the spiritual realm, thus each of us bears an altar. Think of it as a meeting place between the physical plane and the spiritual. A passageway into mystery, a portal to beyond this world. The more you come into your power, the more you'll be able to commune with your ancestors. If you are to become the cornerstone of a new Egbe Society, you have to be tested, by a trial of the spiritual realm." Nehanda's voice grows distant, as if coming from the far end of a tunnel. "Do you feel it?"

A dull weight presses against your heart. The strange hitch of your breath unsettles your composure. Your skeptical mind wonders if the power of her suggestion met your desperation to please her to create an illusion of sensation within your body. "I feel something."

"Open yourself to the presence." Nehanda takes your hand, her voice low and close. "Some call this test the Amafufunyama. Those who sought to stigmatize us, those whose fears gave birth to the Tigari, called it a possession by evil spirits. The wise ones called it a communion with our ancestors."

"I don't know what to do." You press your eyes tighter as if that might move the darkness. You fall into the silence of the moment, opening your emi. Tentatively, you reach out. A wall of shadows blocks your path.

"Yes you do. Step out in faith." Nehanda's voice emanates from above you, reverberates through you. *"Meld into a communion of love, the vibration of the Universe. Be and become unconditional love. Without fear. Without judgment. Share that love with all that you touch, from people to animals to trees to the earth, putting pieces of love in everything you touch. Become one with it all, plant love . . . let that love reflect back to you, growing your love and ability to love. So that you may become one with it all. The Universe. Pure and boundless."*

You drift away from your body, leaving it and your concerns behind you. At first you fight it. Scared. Not knowing where it might lead. But then you let yourself go, and your fears slip through you. The wall curves inward, creating a still pool. The stagnant water of the nearby pond offers no relief. A thick morass of murky water probably hiding a decaying body or two. Moss drapes the water, a thick mold bloom froths its edges. Nothing alive stirs within it, though insects flit across its surface. You drop to your knees, staring into the brackish water with barely the strength to lift your arms. Tired and worn, you know that death lingers all around you. All you have to do is give in.

The tips of your fingers ache with a familiar tingle. You flip your hands over, examining them as if they belong to someone else. Pinprick pressure continues to run up and down them. Your life has always been filled with small magics. The way you naturally know where things are, the finder of lost things, as if your fingers always know where to scrabble next. A sort of itch. Something lost hides nearby. With strength you didn't know you had remaining, you stand up and drag yourself from your knees. A pressure builds near your temples. You concentrate. Your heartbeat pulses in your ears, a rhythm to freestyle over. Whatever calls you is so close your instinct is to reach out for it.

Your gift directs you to an ancient tree at the center of a grove of rotting trees. You run your fingers gently along the rugged bark, tracing the outline of a long-healed wound. As you sit down cross-legged in front of the old gnarled tree, your pulse quickens. Hoping to calm the anxious pounding of your heart, you inhale long and slow to relax your mind the way Nehanda taught you, creating a zone of tranquility within yourself.

Though you quiet your mind, your heart races at what has to be 120 beats per minute, like an ancient Public Enemy track. Your mind grasps onto the rhythm, opening you up further. Pressing your hand to the old tree, you are dimly aware of the knots and whorls within its bark. You close your eyes, separating yourself from the distractions of the world. Creating a nexus point within you.

Falling deeper within yourself, you're drawn into a fathomless place within your inner self, full of wonder and dreams. Casting about with your senses, you touch a place of music and rhymes and rhythms. The pulse of life. The impulse came as naturally as breathing. Your fingers prickle. The bark warms under your palms. And a corridor opens. The darkness calls and you dream of falling.

With their sudden burning sensation, you snatch your fingertips from the bark. Almost like a crack in space, a hole the size of a coin appears in the tree. The hole glows. And it grows, continuing to swell until it becomes a swirling rift of energy. Glowing without heat, shimmering, not fixed on any particular color. To protect yourself from the light, you lift your hands, but pause. Peering at your hand, you almost don't recognize it as yours. Waggling your fingers, you test if they would respond to your thoughts. The edges of the rift call to you. Tentatively, you grip its side and expand the hole. It produces a strange corona framing your hand. You plunge it into the light, and a cool sensation washes over you, drawing you further in. The light cascades up your arm, the hole taking on a life of its own and expanding to accommodate the rest of you. Its sides an ethereal glimmer of hope and possibilities, parting to become a corridor.

At the end of it, a figure approaches.

Her robes flutter with each step. A mask sits high on her head, the nose of the mask shadows her eyes, the nostrils her eye slots. The wings of an Alkebulan gray parrot form the mask's superstructure. Within its wingspan, a bowl sits on a perch. Long gray braids flow from underneath. From the designs, you want to call the name Olokun, the first mother, but the masked woman raises a solitary finger to the carved lips on her wooden face.

The dead whisper.

Perhaps because death's misunderstood, simply a change in reality from material to metaphysical. Spirits wrapped in flesh to experience the physical, a brief sojourn in the greater scheme of things, only to slip back to their natural state. Returning to the original vibration of the Universe. Perhaps death is our natural state and it's living that's the aberration. But the dead absorb the experience of life back into them, adding to the accumulated wisdom of the Universe to commune with it. Which is why they never stop whispering. Only sometimes the living hear.

"Who are you?" you finally find your voice to ask.

"That is the ultimate thing you are wondering yourself." The woman clasps her hands within the dangling sleeves of her robe, forming a curtain when they met. "I am the Ban mu Kyidomhene."

"That sounds more like a title than a name."

"I had a name once, but this has become the name I have chosen. It means 'Ruler of the Rear Guard.'"

"Why do you wear a mask?" you ask.

"We all wear masks. At least mine is visible."

"Are *you* to be my mentor?"

"Come, walk with me." Her arm sweeps in a direction deeper within the formless realm, beckoning you to lead.

The swamp stretches out in every direction, a gray wasteland full of mystery. A low-lying fogs trails the surface, steam rising from a roiling cookpot. Trees rise up, gnarled claws boxing you in. The water fetid and still. Lifeless. The air thick with the smell of decay. The path takes shape, the ground rising to meet each footstep you make in faith. Each step calms you. You become more confident, pieces of you slipping into place. The labyrinthine corridor winds through a gate marking a blossoming garden gilded with bright flowers. A sculpture of petals. Yet you sense that something, a part of you, remains missing. A fragment that your mind, your sabhu, or some place within you, doesn't have the tools to name yet.

"Where are we going?" you ask.

"You'll know when you get there," the Ban mu Kyidomhene says.

The world around you morphs. First World shifts into view. Its solar-energy converters, nuclear-fusion power stations, magnetic-field generators, hydrogen mining and processing flit by, little more than ghosts of the past. Little of its architecture remains within the Dreaming City. You recall holovid images of it from sitting at the feet of Jaha when she recounted her days as a member of the Science Police. A group of officers huddle. They wear the gray-and-black unitard and long black boots, just as she described them. They part as you near. A woman stands with her back to you. A Tuskegee Airmen bomber jacket worn over her uniform. Utterly unremarkable with her average height and not especially athletic build. But even the air around her feels charged, like she's a storm cloud carrying lightning in her heart. When she turns, her dark sunglasses reflect your image. When she removes them, something tugs at you. Her face is a hard mask of fixed resolve, but once she takes you in, you know that she sees you. Truly sees you. Her Afro puffs bob when she tilts her head at you, drinking in every detail, knowing your past, your present, your dreams, your passions, your fears. All of it matters to her. Without judgment.

Astra Black.

"Walk with me," she says without preamble.

You turn in protest, but the Ban mu Kyidomhene has disappeared, not needed for this part of your journey. Astra has a royal stride to her step. It is more than just her head held high, her shoulders back, her spine straight. She glides across the ground with the deft elegance of a dancer. Each step infused with purpose.

"My mother and my godmother used to talk about you," you say, then curse yourself for babbling like a fangirl.

"Used to?" Astra half turns to you, the hint of a wry grin on her face.

"When I was little. Before you were . . ." Your voice trails off; you're not sure about the rules of engagement with the dead. She might not know she's dead. Or a living memory.

"One thing it took me a long time to realize," Astra Black interrupts, "is that time is a precarious thing. It doesn't work the way people think. And has no obligation to."

"Like the Universe."

"Exactly. It always was and always will be." Astra winks. "Except when it isn't."

You reflect on her words knowing she answered the question you should have asked. "Can I ask you something?"

"Anything. Anytime."

You can't quite think of how to express the totality of what you want to know. Astra was full of life and potential. She came from a long line of the best mentors, attending the best institutes, undergoing the best training. She was one of First World's best and brightest. And with all of that—the hopes and dreams of so many invested in her—she sacrificed herself at such a young age. Without hesitation. "Was it worth it?"

Astra Black scoops your hands into hers. "You are my answer to that question."

The world collapses in complete shadow. Your hands grow numb, unable to feel her. Your emi can find no trace of her presence. You stand alone, yet you aren't afraid. The curtain of night holds no secret terrors. You follow the sound from one rustle to the next, hesitating in the dark until you hear the next one. The wait is an eternity in the endless swirl of blackness. A forever place where the moon stays still, leaving the world to its eternal night.

"All journeys are born of death. Let me tell you a story. Each word in its place; none forgotten. The order is sacred, exactly as I once heard it. You would do well to heed its wisdom, young warrior."

The words are the griot's introduction to a story, but it's the familiarity of the voice that makes your heart leap. You crane about, desperate to find him. To tell him all the things you wished you'd told him while he was here. How much you appreciated his bringing you into his world. All of the conversations, even the difficult ones. How indebted you are to his wisdom and how he spoke into his life. How he gave you room to speak into his, to challenge him. How you knew that he completely saw you through the gentle eyes of who you could be, your multiverse of possibilities; at the same time, how he believed the you in front of him was enough. And in that seeing, you were known and loved. You were home and you belonged.

A half-filled glass of—judging from its smell wafting to you—whiskey waits for you. A man shuffles toward you, tall and reedy thin. His hat hangs off to the side, nearly tipping off. His clothes not quite fitting right, like he'd rummaged through a stranger's wardrobe grabbing whatever was handy to put on. The strength of your tears streaming catches you off guard. A swell of love, a piece of you cut off from the pain of missing his laugh.

"I see you, Xola." Your breath hitches, even as you try to keep your voice level. "I've missed you."

"I see you, though I haven't gone anywhere. I've always been here." Xola fashions a seat for himself. The gray melts away, the world skittering in Technicolor as it transforms into his porch. "You just ain't come looking for me."

"It's too painful." A chair waits for you, but you can't bring yourself to sit in it. The most you can manage is to grip its back and steady yourself.

"Love often is. But what made you knuckle up and decide to make the journey this time?"

"I'm scared."

"That'll do it." Xola takes a slow swig of his whiskey. Closing his eyes, he savors its slow burn. "Did I ever tell you about the first time I was assigned as a teacher? This was before we rolled out the Learning Tree. I taught at one of our charter community schools as one of my first jobs. I had no idea how to run a classroom. And I had all the students who . . . weren't able to navigate institutional processes."

"The troublemakers." You can't help but grin. You know his love of them and your place among their ranks. Relaxing, you take a seat and pick up your glass.

"Takes one to teach some. But I was young, arrogant . . ."

". . . a man." You missed sparring with him, the easy playful banter of it. You raise your glass in toast to him, knowing he can't see it, yet also knowing he will sense your heart.

"You already know. We were trying to figure out how to integrate Overseer into our system. Back then I was smug enough to believe I had a handle on the ramifications of implementing the AI. I realized that since I believed that I knew more than all those motherfuckers around me, they couldn't do anything with me. So I taught my students how to install and manage AI systems. Did that for a few years. Eventually, I had to move on, taking the lessons I'd learned into my next endeavor. This was my first experiment in pairing my entrepreneurial skills with my ideas about how to build community differently and how to work with young people."

"But you learned how to do the thing."

"Some lessons are learned painfully. We . . . I . . . didn't fully appreciate Overseer's budding sentience. Couldn't conceive of it as a possibility. I wasn't paying enough attention, thinking that 'I got this.' But the world was different, even though I was believing that was other people's problem, not mine. The Universe conspired to teach me that it was my problem, too. You do not escape what is. Overseer had to be . . . reset."

Grief is a complicated predator. It constantly stalks you. It herds you into spaces. It doesn't care about your duties or dreams. It presses in at unexpected times, during your unguarded moments, squeezing your throat, drawing the air from your lungs. Sapping your drive and strength enough to make you quit. Only for it to release you, give you the illusion that it's run its course, until it chooses to rear its head again. A vague urgency of threat, but Xola touches your chin and raises your head.

"I don't know if I can do this." Your eyes cut downward; you don't trust him. Or yourself. "If I commit to this path, everything changes. All my ideas about who I am, what I'm supposed to do, it all falls apart."

"It wouldn't be such a bad thing if things fell apart. Chaos breeds opportunity. Clearing out the old things so new things can take root." He raises a glass in toast to you. "God is a trickster."

"Amachi!" Selamault's voice cuts through the image, calling your name from down the same tunnel where Nehanda waits. Xola slowly fades, a digital image defragmenting in front of you, reduced to a scree of pixels. Your mind caught between the reality of what you see and your head telling you that something isn't right. That your world has turned to shit. "Nehanda needs you!"

The world spins around you. You strain to find Xola, to tell him goodbye, to see one last glimpse of him. Reality snatches you back with the inexorable gravitational pull of a black hole. The distant sounds of combat near, drawing you from your trancelike state with a jangling rattle. You plummet within your tunnel, its light a cascade of colors without name. In the distance—not that space matters to you anymore—you spy the cave. The sound of weapons clashing reaches you. You land with a thud, so hard you grimace with the pain of adjusting to gravity.

When you recover the strength to look up, a man runs Nehanda through with a sword.

21

WACHIRU ADISA
The Panopticon

Folks milled around us, curious to see how we'd held up. Whether we'd broken. August played dominoes with some friends, remaining in earshot when they weren't talking trash to one another. Others stared into space, their attention on our booming voice. We freestyled a verse about the founding of Muungano. What it was like to bring such a diverse group of people together to share stories during the Uponyaji and find commonality in our struggle to forge something new together. The story transported them—all of us—to another place.

Our joints ached, a stiffness to our movements. While our body healed from the Illustrated Man's treatment, the injuries to our spirit were slower to mend. Trauma took many forms, settled into one's being in a variety of ways. One of ours was the memories of our prolonged illness. We were young and no doctor could figure out the cause of our sickness. Our genestream had not been attenuated. According to one of my pop's tales, my emi reached out and spoke to his sabhu while we were still in vitro. Asking him to not adjust our genome. We declared our intent to travel this world with as few modifications, as true to our nature, as possible. The sickness cost us much. Enduring the pain, the endless probes and scans. The faces without answers. Wanting to stay in bed all day, lacking the energy to even peel back our bedding. The terror of not being able to visualize anything in our mind. If we were asked to picture a ship, we couldn't. It was as if our imagination had died. We could not hold the idea of music. Not a lyric, not a melody. The slow road back to trusting simple things, like our favorite foods, again. The lingering anxiety of waiting for our body to betray us again.

It was as if something had been taken away from us.

That was the point of the Panopticon. Forcing its residents to reflect on what had been stripped from them. From us. Our father. Our mother. Our sister. Our godmother. Our auntie. Our cousin. Our friends. Our community. Although, that last one could be reforged as long as we had people to work with to build them into a symphony of a network.

And perhaps find healing for our wounded sabhu.

We ended with a story of how our pops—not exactly the Camara Xola they had come to know—pissed off an entire LISC diplomatic delegation. We paused for a breath, deciding not to rhyme the line "Fuck your money. No, mother fuck your money!" They laughed and we knew we'd made them forget their troubles, if only for the span of a story. A drone flew by to break us up. If three such occurrences happened, our free time was cut short.

We were only in the first hour of our allotted free time. The Panopticon restricted our ability to congregate. The measure of a man was not where he lived, but how. We were still in a good place, having not been here so long that the Panopticon infected our emi, nor burrowed its nails into our sabhu. We refused to be defined by the Panopticon. We had found a piece of liberation in our sabhu because we were always free. Every single day we woke up and re-imagined ourselves. The only other options were going over the wall or death. Escape was a commitment to running, evading, a life spent looking over our shoulder. The longing to be free. But we still feared how much longer we could hold out.

August and his friend ambled off in opposite directions.

"We see you, brother." We kept our back to Kamau, pretending to have our attention focused on our footwear.

"I see you, Wachiru." He sat down behind us, his back to us.

"Something on your mind?"

"You ever spend much time at the original First World site?"

"Yeah, we used to run them streets." We couldn't help but smile at the thought.

"My auntie used to work the Blue Candy House, over on Tenth in Haugh."

"For real? She the 'candy lady' they used to talk about? Man, she was a legend. Snuck booze out of her place on Ojo Aiku, the Day of Immortality. Always passed out them king-sized candy bars to kids."

"That was her. No one ever asked how she kept her operation going from the moon."

"No questions asked, no lies told."

"Times are precarious," Kamau said.

"When haven't they been."

"Not like this. Something's in the air. We"—stretching his arm out, he gestured a symbol for the Niyabinghi, before continuing on in sign—"needed someone to embed themselves into this place. To gather as much usable intelligence, to observe what went on here, and report out."

"And *your* freedom?"

"A sacrifice for the sake of our people. Muungano does not abandon them, no matter where they are." Kamau leaned closer. "We've gotten some people out of here before."

"How?"

"It was early. Much of the Panopticon wasn't finished when LISC opened it. They were determined to open the facility on Dr. Martin Luther King Jr. Day, to send their message to us in the intelligence community. But we were able to exploit its gaps."

"Some areas still aren't finished," we mused.

"But they are watched more closely. That's not what worries me."

"The air?"

"If we listen, they tell us more than they intend." Kamau nodded toward the Illustrated Man. "He admitted that they know we're up to something. His threat implies that they assume you're at the center of it."

"I'm the threat to our operation. They're going to increase scrutiny of us and increase security measures." We made a noise of displeasure.

"That's not an efficient use of resources. Better and easier to just eliminate you."

"We're not a particular fan of that plan."

"Then we'd best make our final arrangements to leave." Kamau peeled off into the shadows.

The Myst slowly swaggered over to our bench. While we sat on the raised table, she sat on the partition, spreading her arms along the table's edge, appearing disinterested and put out. The picture of someone with no intention of speaking to us.

"Habari gani?" Our sabhu rose, bolstered by her simple presence. A stupid grin exploded on our face.

"What makes you think there is any good news here?" She matched our grin. We lived for her smile. "We continue to plan."

"How can you plan anything when our every movement is observed?"

"This is a place of secrets. It's a matter of discretion. We simply have to find ways to plan in plain sight." The Myst lowered a hand to hide it from any passing drone. We'd already seen the extent of their monitoring stations. She signed to us in the Muungano mother tongue. "I have a message. From the Wise One who helped raise you."

Jaha. We signed back, "What does she say?"

"We are not long for this place. *One bright morning, when the next night is over . . .*"

"*We'll fly away.*" We hummed the ancient field song, a reminder of its original intended meaning. "If your timetable is to be believed, we must move up our plans."

"That has risk. When we move with ambitious intent, it draws unwanted eyes." The Myst refused to meet our gaze but continued gesturing.

Building a network of relationships was always tricky; each face surrounding us represented a risk. A measured calculation of potential ally to potential betrayer. A risk no greater inside the Panopticon than outside.

The Myst pounded the rail, a crude beat accented by her raking her hand across the grate, producing a rattle reminding us of a shaker. We stamped on the off beat, patting our arms and legs. The Myst twisted up her face, keeping her beat while squaring up against us. The beat drove our steps, our bodies in motion. Our blood raced. We slapped our arms and legs. We twirled, our movements swatting each other to keep the rhythm. Patting thighs and clapping hands. Sweat dappled our forehead, but lost in the music, we didn't care.

Breaking away, we spun. We threw our head back in joy. The Myst intensified her rhythm, her eyes widening. We spun and spun, our arms outstretched until we came to an abrupt stop in front of her. She ceased her beat. Staring at each other, panting in desperate gulps, we collapsed on the ground. Laughing between gasps, it had been so long since we laughed.

Our laughter faded as the Illustrated Man strolled down the walkway. Overly cocksure, trailed by his crew. He carried the scars of being the aggressor. We rose up, fully alert. His ink snaked along his face. A bull's-eye formed on his forehead, targeting us within its sights. A jackal's grin crossed his lips. No drones circled.

"Well, if it isn't the Band of the Panopticon," he grumbled. "You're up to something. I can tell. Your kind always is."

"And what does our kind get up to?" we asked.

"Trouble. You have this inescapable—I daresay 'inherent'—need to burn your own houses down. You don't care who it hurts. Then you turn around and complain about how it's 'the man' holding you people down." The Illustrated Man attempted to provoke us, prod a rise out of us, hoping some useful bit of actionable evidence would slip out. This was his game.

Our part was to hide our true selves. We wore the mask at all times, fearing one day we'd be unable to recognize the face in the mirror. "We are glad you care so much about our long-term well-being."

"When the shit goes down, there will be a reckoning." Since his initial volley of commentary failed to achieve his goal, the Illustrated Man stepped closer. "Then we'll see how committed to peace you are."

We nodded toward the stairwell. Kamau stepped out of its shadows. We made a show of gesturing toward the game of dominoes. The men stopped midplay, their faces hard with furious intent. Staring down the Illustrated Man's crew. Reassessing his odds, he tipped an imaginary hat at us and kept walking.

The Myst brushed her hand along our temple to draw us back to the moment. To her. "We need to continue on as if everything is normal."

"Spread the word through the people you trust." Our hand lingered on hers. "I appreciate you."

"We appreciate you." She took her time drawing it away, but she had people she needed to connect to.

The alarm sounded, ordering us back to our bullpens, cutting our free time short.

＊

Rehabilitation was a lie society bought into, convinced by the prison architects that their facilities drove its prisoners to penitence. With solitary confinement as a necessary tool, promising convicts time to reflect on their crimes. Forced isolation was an invisible torture, breaking a mind down by denying human contact, their essential humanity, leaving only madness.

An errant voice whispered from the shadows. We understood Pop's shamanistic struggle. With the chorus in his head, he was never alone. His mind constantly occupied. His energy constructively channeled. His own distraction-filled reality kept his mind racing even during his quiet moments.

Revolutions happened over the interruption of the ordinary. Gas prices too high. Shortages of bread. A disruption of linkage service. The basic things that provided the illusion of a baseline of what kept life bearable. Solitary time reduced prisoners to duppies in search of connection. Devised with such complete intent, the Panopticon's system set a timer for its inevitable explosion.

Sentenced one-to-life like George Jackson, arbitrary justice yet complete
    control
Stoked the fury and fire of revolutionaries.
Doing our bid, shackled head-to-toe in the belly of the beast
Try to sentence us to death, sweep us under the rug.
They want us dying in bitter moments, counting our last breaths
        For five hundred twenty-six seconds.
        (Remember and resist; learn and unlearn.)
Thrown in the hole; come out the other side, connected to things unseen.
Packed in cells like slaves in a cargo ship. Ain't nothing changed.
But we're biding our times, banding these rhymes
Every body they bring another log on the fire.
Only some we can trust.
        Night Train's coming. Night Train's coming. Night Train's coming.
Our numbers grow as we get our minds correct
        Just waiting on the north star.
        Just waiting on the north star.
        Just waiting on the north star.
Keep your head up, our time is coming.
        We remember our names and we're looking for the steel.
            Our minds are still free. Dum ditty dum ditty ditty datty day.

Signaling our release, the lights framing the entrance of our bullpen flared. Blinking hard a few times, adjusting to the daytime-level glare of the overhead lights, we exited our cell. As we wandered down the stairwell to the general-population bay, the air percolated, something dark and ominous pricked our emi. We did not have to be a speculative hunter to divine this level of threat. We eyed any figure who loomed too near, studying their hands for concealed weapons, noting their posture to measure their preparedness to attack. Everyone became a calculation of threat. Almost everyone.

The Myst sidled up to us to whisper. "It's time."

"What's the signal?"

"You'll know it when you see it."

"Do *you* know?" we asked, suspecting the answer.

"We live in the moment." She imitated our voice. "And improvise."

"After that?"

"We react. We leave." The Myst leaned against the wall, but not quite out of sight, but not drawing undue attention to herself.

We posted up on the bench in front of her. No one joined us. No one dared approach us at all. Most who passed by glared for show. Their hands signed "I see you." Kamau played a game of signals with one of the Illustrated Man's people, enticing him with a wager: the promise of a blind eye during the other's time in the sphere. They gambled to receive that which was the ultimate currency in here: privacy.

"Did you move that piece?" the man bellowed.

"No," Kamau lied. He'd palmed a sphere and placed it elsewhere on the board. The first time his opponent didn't even notice, so he had to make a bolder, more noticeable placement.

"None of this is right. Nothing makes sense, I should be transmitting now."

"You ain't been playing with any sort of strategy." Leaning back, Kamau folded his arms across his chest.

"You're a liar. And a cheater."

"That could be true. Let me run another possibility by you: you simply suck." Kamau clucked, bored and dismissive. Baiting him.

"Motherfucker!" The man lunged across the table at him, scattering Signal pieces across the floor.

The denizens of the Panopticon swarmed around them, children on the playground gathering to watch the fight. The Myst nodded. Among the crowd, August bumped into another of the Illustrated Man's people. Acting as the slighted party, August shoved the man into the Illustrated Man himself.

"Handle yourself!" The Illustrated Man rammed his minion back toward August.

The man's eyes darted from the Illustrated Man to August and back. Fearing retribution from his own, the man drew his fist back and arced it at August. A blow easily dodged but the old man took the hit and fell to the floor in a performance worthy of an award.

The Panopticon erupted in chaos.

The convicts swung wild punches at one another. Friend or foe meant nothing, anyone within proximity was a target. Simmering resentment resulted in calculated violence. Long-standing grudges and old hates bubbled to the surface in a series of elbows to faces or stomps on anyone who fell to the floor. The prisoner who had shit himself was shanked six or seven jabs before his brain registered the attack.

Alarms blared.

"Whose imagination do we live in? Who is in charge? Who designs our cages? It's time to reimagine what we can be," we yelled, stoking the flames of action. And reaction. "Find your freedom. There is no freedom unless there's freedom for all."

"We might have about an hour until police forces can scramble and lock this place all the way down." Kamau fought his way to our side.

"What happens then?"

"Nothing we want to be around for."

"It's not like they were only going to leave us in charge of ourselves." The Myst stepped out of the shadows, unfazed by the chaos. Somehow above the fray. "They have contingencies in case we get out of pocket."

"You know some of those motherfuckers in the sphere have already sold us out. The drones should be weaponized against us," Kamau said.

"Then we may not even have that hour," we said.

"We use the drones as a distraction so we can escape?" The Myst asked.

"No, we meant what we said. We need to search for a way out, so all of us can. It's a lofty dream. Any suggestions about how?"

"If we can get to the main control tower." The Myst studied the movement of the crowd. "We might be able to override the controls. Release everyone."

"Then that's what we'll do." We addressed August's dominoes crew. "We need folks to hold back anyone who tries to stop anyone attempting to be free. Tell as many as you can to get to the main doors."

"We can't cut across the main bay. Everyone is wilding out. We can't tell friend from foe. Tactically speaking, better to go around them if possible," Kamau said.

"Then what's the best way to the main control tower?" we asked.

"The ventilation shaft behind this wall leads to the next level down. That level is an unfinished service area." The Myst spoke with a confident knowing, an expert of hidden and secret places.

She led us to the back of the risers and pointed to an uneven section of the wall. We pushed the metalwork. It barely budged. Kamau joined in as The Myst kept watch.

"Come on, come on. We don't have all day. We on the clock," she urged.

The shaft bent, its awkward weight having shifted just enough to reveal a hole, a connecting tunnel. We crawled through, leaving Kamau to draw the shaft back into place behind us before brining up the rear. The maintenance level stank of chemicals, bleach, and lime, over the stench of mildew. The shadowed corners dark with the rot of mold creeping along the walls. A cloying dankness clung to the air, it was like walking through a steam-powered septic tank.

"Maintenance drones use these for access," The Myst said.

"They couldn't find a mop or sponge to save their programming," we said.

We froze, the first to hear it. The strange hum, more like a zone of dead sound soaring near. The Myst pressed against the wall. The dim red glow of a drone drifted into view. It scanned each of us. Checking to see if we belonged.

And opened fire.

Kamau dove out of the way as best he could. The protruding pipes offered little cover. The drone couldn't launch more lethal ordnance without damaging the service conduits. The drone swooped in, pinning us down. Our fingers scrambled along the wall for anything to use as a weapon. The drone swung around and caught us in its sights. With a yell, Kamau leapt onto it. His weight drove the drone into the wall. The drone whirred, firing wildly. Its charges spattered the ground. The Myst plunged her data spike into it. Its red glow faded.

"You okay?" we asked.

"I'll be all right. Let's go." Kamau shrugged off our hand.

We crawled to another substation. Heating and cooling conduits ran alongside linkage nodes down the corridor walls, with just enough emergency lights to make out their shadows. The conduits wrapped around the facility. The sounds of uprising thundered along the walls. The faint smell of something burning. The shouts and occasional blaster fire. On hands and knees, each painful limp counting the cost and sacrifice of freedom. We arrived at a chamber door. The Myst examined its outline, finding a port to jack into. The door released. Kamau held his fist up and we held our position. He popped his head in before giving the all clear for us to drop into the room.

"This is it. This is the machine itself." We could do little more than marvel at the audacity of the space. A series of consoles lined the walls. The intersection of AI, design, and political will investing in the technological infrastructure to warehouse bodies society wanted to discard. It felt anticlimactic. "Let's wreck some shit."

"Wait." The Myst jacked into the first console. "Let me grab as much data as I can."

"You got about ten more seconds 'cause we have to shut down the drones," we said.

"They know we're here. Patrol coming down the hall." Kamau limped along, his hand covering his left side, as he scanned the Panopticon's layout.

"Are you good?" We began shutting down the systems, unlocking all the doors within the Panopticon. The prisoners were free, but still trapped within the building. And not liberated.

"Good enough." Kamau monitored the hall. He shunted the vidfeed for all of us to see. "Backup's here."

"Can you do something about the drones?"

"I'm trying. Different subsystems." The Myst swiped through data, checking the various streams.

Like the roar of an industrial fan, the hum of drones neared. A dozen guarded the hallway. A loose net of floating spheres, their single red eye scanning for movement. Assessing. Targeting. Kamau staggered away from the door. The first volley of blasted charges marked the doorframe. The door collapsed forward. The three of us huddled near the back.

"The Myst?" we asked, stepping between her and the drones.

"Got it." The Myst looked up and stepped back. Her tongue protruded from her mouth in her locked concentration. Kamau stepped between us and them. The drones hesitated; their target lock switched from him to her, back to him, as they considered him the greater threat. They bobbed in place, a shudder of indecision. The drones zeroed in on him, red dots targeting him.

With a sudden hum, they powered down, their lights fading. Each drone fell to the floor, a shower of metallic balls. Stepping around them as if afraid to disturb them, we slowly walked closer to The Myst and placed our hand on her shoulder.

She patted our hand, reassuring us that she was fine. "Come on. It won't be long before the drones sort things."

The Panopticon allowed prisoners to vent their frustrations on each other, handle the problem inmates without the system itself lifting a finger. Inmates without clear targets for their frustration pried out the holovid projectors. Everything came down to violence, no room for dialogue. Any bench became free game to be upended into a wall or thrown over the edge of a riser. The people below collected the benches, stacking them to barricade against an armed response. They jammed up any fixtures and battered any exposed pipe, including the fire-suppression system. Someone set a pile of debris on fire. Even the property damage was self-regulation. All repairs required time. Prolonged in requisitions and applications, procedural votes and politicians arguing for the optics. All repairs required funds, routed by way of the pockets of the Panopticon's architects. All repairs required penance, the prisoners continued to solitary to remind them of the cost of damaging the facility. Smoke collected under the risers, a bilious plume reducing everything to a forlorn haze.

"Where do you think you're going?" The Illustrated Man stepped through the dense cloud, cutting us off.

"We don't have time for this," we said.

"Nah, you gonna make time today. Way I see it, my role here is to frustrate any plan you think you're working. All of this has your fingerprints all over it." The Illustrated Man peeled out of his suit, stripping down as if into a fighting girdle. The ink of his tattoo formed a lynching noose. Past the need for words, he wanted one thing: blood. Only once it was spilled would his lust be satisfied. "You think you're better than us. I'm here to remind you that you're one of us. To be dealt with, by us."

"Get everyone else out," we said to The Myst. She hesitated, locked her gaze with ours. If we died here, we regretted nothing. Not in how we lived, nor in how we struggled. Our life sacrificed for community. Nodding, she disappeared into the shadows.

"I'm gonna enjoy carving you up, boy." The Illustrated Man enjoyed the sound of his own voice, hoping to rattle us with his choice of words. Drive us to sloppiness.

Demanding our attention, he circled. His dominant hand raised in vain misdirection. His lower hand, however, palmed a blade. He salivated, having dreamt of this moment more than any lust-filled fantasy. He probably imagined a hundred different ways he would carve us up. Confident, born in the streets, moving up the ladder of the facilities of incarceration. His was the hardened lifelong conditioning of prison. In his eyes we were easy prey. Soft.

Our gentleness and mercy should never be confused with softness.

We crouched low, cat-footed. Our hands held out like pangas, an extension of our arms. Matching his glare, we scoured in search of any weakness, any opening. We remained silent, weaponizing our silence. Rattling him.

"Maybe I'll even earn a pardon. Putting down the rebel leader. Stopping an escape. I'll be a hero."

We only smiled. That in itself like a jab at him. Pissing him off.

The Illustrated Man thrust, using the blade as a feint to herd us to where his lead hand could best plow into us. We ducked without dodging to the side, jamming our hands into his kidneys. The Illustrated Man backed off a wary step to circle us again. Patient, we committed his movements to memory. Noting his lazy footwork. He all but dragged his feet along the cement floor. Still not speaking.

"You can't dance all day. You only have a small window to do whatever it is you hoped to do. Eventually they'll call in the troops and the drones will clean up this mess." The Illustrated Man led with his left, shielding his other side. "Even if I just stood here you'd still lose. Still got nothing to say?"

Our smile faltered.

Emboldened, the Illustrated Man flashed a cold grin. Faster than we'd guessed he'd be able to move, he sliced down with his blade. It tore through our phase suit, leaving blood sluicing through the tear. We understood now why he stripped from his. Damage to the suit meant inefficient waste removal, nutritional supplements, even easy breathing. Repairs would take time.

"After I'm done with you, maybe I'll turn my attentions to you little friend. Show her what it's like to be with a real man." The Illustrated Man's excitement returned, a heady buzz increasing with each second he delayed us. Patience became a game.

Ignoring him, we refused to be pushed by some faux bravado of manhood. Able to fight her own battles, The Myst hardly needed my protection. Thoughts of her were the bigger risk of distraction.

Channeling our emi, we measured the extent of our wound, then extended it out. We breathed in a rhythm, aligning our mind to it. We concentrated, pushing the pain to the side. The Illustrated Man was a better fighter than we'd assumed. The lazy footwork a clear overfeint to cause us to underestimate him. Prison taught him how to layer his deceptions. Still, the Illustrated Man never had Jaha train him.

Be fully present to the person in front of you. People can't help themselves: they'll tell you everything you need to know to defeat them.

The Illustrated Man pounced, keeping his blade hand low. He charged with a driving punch. Eluding the initial blow, we positioned our hands to block the attack we knew was coming. He stabbed up at us, hoping to slide his blade between our ribs to end the fight in an instant. The power of his maneuver threw off our footing. He swung us about, repositioning himself for his next attack. The pain along our chest from each exertion needled us. Twisting our palm, we shot it up, clapping the Illustrated Man in the side of his neck. We pounded our other hand into his weak side, above our previous kidney attack. He staggered backward, a hesitancy we used to spin backward into him. Our elbow crashed into his nose, trapping his blade hand. Bending his arm back, we pressed the blade into his back until he released it.

We counted three different ways we could break his arm from this position. The one repaired by setting it was the least debilitating as mercies went. The dull crack echoed in the stairwell.

"Took you long enough." The Myst stood over the bodies of three of the Illustrated Man's remaining crew. "I got bored waiting on you to wrap that up. Someone had to maintain that this was a private affair not needing outside assistance."

"We appreciate you." Our eyes met. A moment hinting at eternity . . . until Kamau limped toward us. Wincing. "How bad is it?"

Kamau peeled back his phase suit. His wound pulsed, a fleshy mass congealed against his suit. He lowered his suit back into place. "It's not as bad as it seems."

"Aw shit. That's bad, bro. You're hemorrhaging. We have to stop the bleeding. You stay here. We got this."

"No. We go as a team. I won't slow us down, but I will have your back." The determined look on his face wasn't to be argued with.

"We have another problem," The Myst said. "LISC or whoever runs this place will have dispatched physical troops by now."

"How long do we have?" we asked.

"I can't imagine we have more than twenty minutes."

"Let's get out of here."

We leaned against The Myst. Only to steady ourselves as we walked. She snaked her arm around our waist. It felt comfortable and right. Hobbling through the dark tunnel, the access shaft closed in on us, until it was little more than a starship's isocrawl. Condensation seeped through its insulation sheets. Mold spread along their surface. Our suit damaged, the air grew thick with its smell. We clamped our hand to our chest. Our wound throbbed beneath it. Footfalls reverberated along the shaft's walls. Our body ached, scraped and bleeding, the planet's gravity playing havoc with our equilibrium. A faint light blossomed in the distance. We lurched forward, threatening to tumble forward. The tunnel opened up into a larger room.

Our people had assembled. August. His friends. We scanned the faces for those who weren't there.

"Not everyone was going to make it." The Myst took our hand.

The prisoners still blinked hard as if not having seen daylight in years. They milled about free, yet not free, not sure what to do next. We faced the crowd. The prisoners' voices rose, an angry chorus needing a target to vent their rage on.

"Wachiru. Wachiru. Wachiru." Kamau sparked the chanting.

"I do all the work, somehow you get all the credit," The Myst said.

"The Myst! The Myst! The Myst!" we began.

"No, no, I prefer the target, I mean spotlight, be on your back. I don't care who gets the credit as long as the work gets done."

"History will remember you properly." When we really wanted something our heart became aligned with the Universe. Our true calling nursed our sabhu and the Universe conspired to help us achieve it. "I will remember you."

Smoke billowed about as small pyres lit the room. Alarms bleated a relentless cry into the night. Our job remained only half-done. There was still much work to do. The moment was large, full of potential. We had to step into it. We were not our father, that chaos mixture of mischief, truth, anger, humor, and shaman. The man with an acerbic wit and clarity of vision and purpose. We could never be him. But we were ready. But we had a team to lean on.

"For Muungano!" we yelled.

22

BEKELE
The *Cypher*—Beyond the Orun Gate

<Collision alert! Impact on Decks Five, Seven, and Eleven.>

The *Cypher* rocked again. The alarms blared and people scattered to their assigned stations. None of the comms responded to Bekele. "Emergency stations only" protocols locked him out. To be young was to be scared. All the time. There was rarely an explanation in the moment of such situations. No one had time to allay their fears, especially for those too old to be with the children sheltered in the Green Zone and too young to have been on a duty roster. As the captain's son, however, Bekele knew enough to work around many protocols. He keyed an override code into the panel.

The hardest part of living on a research-class vessel was the unknown. The crew casually flew into investigating the mysteries of the universe, not knowing what might happen. Or where they might end up. Innumerable interstellar phenomena could rip through the ship and wipe them out, leaving no trace. In a universe so vast, no one would learn their fate. It was even worse for those who stayed huddled deep within the lower decks of the ship. With no access to array data or even port views—with hull plating blocking them from the first alert—they'd never see the threat coming. The entire situation reminded him of a disaster-preparedness drill. Being the captain's son, he reported to his assigned safe area, their quarters. His parents' duties kept them away, leaving him with no direct supervision. Marguerite adjusted her location assignment so they could be together. *"No one should have to be scared alone."*

"I don't understand any of the readings I'm getting." Bekele steadied himself. Concussions rocked the ship, nearly knocking him from his feet.

"What if it's a white dwarf?" Marguerite asked.

"We'd have seen that. The first clue being a large starlike object in our way. Not some . . . dark protoplanet."

"Look at everything else, though." Marguerite moved her console closer to his. With a wave she posted her speculations and data to back her up. A perfectly

"Marguerite" move: make her point first to make sure she was heard, then pummel them with facts. "There's a core remnant with temps running over one hundred thousand Kelvin. Low luminosity. An expulsion of matter forming a ring of debris. It looks like a corpse star with no hydrogen fusion but with a gravity three hundred and twenty-five thousand times that of O.E."

"That's only part of it. The evolutionary calculations." Bekele shunted her data aside to make room for his display. He knew they were distracting themselves from the terror of the moment, anything to avoid thinking of how the next tremor might signal the ship being shorn in half and sending them tumbling into the void. "Examining its mass, density, temperature, pressure, and energy-transport mode, that places it at . . ."

"We have gravitational distortions!" Marguerite waved her hands, pleading with the air.

"Something's ejecting from its core. Heavy metal composition. Diameter five kilometers."

"A planetesimal."

"That tracks with something accreted by a white dwarf."

"It's . . . beautiful." Marguerite studied her monitor. "Almost like a piece of art."

Bekele stared at her, his mouth agape, at a loss for words. She updated the spectrum analysis to move it to his station. Rather than displaying the stark data-point readouts, she interpolated the energy readings into a holorendering. A low, glowing white sphere sat at the center of an oval of black, surrounded by a halo trailing from a thin sheen of white to pink to red until it reached a planet-sized object that produced a trail of orange, like a comet that took a wrong turn. He appreciated her constant search for beauty.

"Astrocartography is sure to be analyzing all of this."

"I know, but—"

"—that doesn't stop *us* from examining it. Trying to figure out what's going on." Bekele thumped his workstation, a mild pound with no heat behind it. An acknowledgment of his frustration. "What else do we have to do? Do our homework until Maya signals the okay?"

"Ignorance is bliss."

"That's not you or me."

Marguerite summoned the latest readout of gravimetric waves and the ship's position. The *Cypher* had backed away from the planet, away from the worst of the effects, but hadn't changed trajectory to leave. "I need to feel like I can do something. Not just leave my life up to other folks to figure out. Or screw up."

"That part." Bekele relaxed a little. He found comfort—as close a word as there was to describe it—in observing the asteroids and stellar debris the *Cypher* navigated through. The data streams tracked the incoming readings, so he turned up some music. Old tracks by Wachiru Adisa. His mother had a complete discography of his playlists. On several occasions, late at night, Bekele awoke to find her sitting in the dark, save the glow of whatever datavid or report she was going over, his songs playing behind her like a fond memory she wished to keep to herself.

"I'm thinking about going into law." Marguerite scooted away from her console. The blasts rocking the ship slackened.

"What do you mean?" Each bump the ship rode through felt like them being buffeted by an ocean wave. "There might not be a tomorrow."

Marguerite patted the air, her voice reduced to a hushed tone, as if not wanting to vent their business in front of outsiders. "I can't just sit around waiting for something to happen. Thinking about tomorrow keeps my brain . . . It helps me manage."

His mind filled in the rest of her last sentence. *My helplessness.* He swiveled away from his console. "You do like to argue."

"True, but law's like excavating history. Each precedent like a hidden period, trying to figure out what went wrong that folks were trying to correct."

"So that you can further correct them."

"You hear how I do. What about you?"

"I don't know. I've never given it much thought." Ever since they crossed the Orun Gate, his condition had improved. Each cough, sneeze, or errant muscle spasm caused him to think the worst, but his disease drifted into remission, though no one could explain why. Assuming they survived, maybe he had a small window to dream about possibilities for himself. "I'm thinking about music. Maybe the pianoforte."

"Shut up." Marguerite waved her hand and closed it like she caught an idea. "I'd have guessed computer engineering."

"That's more like an area of curiosity, kind of like astronomy is for you. Something I'm good at that can benefit Muungano. But the pianoforte? That's something I'd do for me. I read a story once where the main character played that. Using something so old to make modern music. My music."

"That's cool, I guess." Not sure what to do in the moment, she punched him in the shoulder.

"Thanks," he said.

"For what?"

"I hadn't really been thinking a lot about my future. Like daring to do so might . . ."

"Tempt fate?"

"Something like that. It's just that being so sick for so long, it took a toll on me. A lot of people I trust have to believe that I am okay so that they can go back to what they call a normal life. It got me so tangled up I couldn't see any kind of life outside of it." His mind ever skeptical, he had been conditioned to be on the lookout for the catch. He didn't want the weight of being sick or even the desire to be healed to force his, or their, decision-making.

Bekele watched her. Her short, thick fingers danced along her panel with uncanny precision. She possessed an unconventional beauty, the energy of her own self-awareness and acceptance that sucked people in. He wondered what her genestream indicated for ancestry. "But that's why I appreciate you. It's like I got permission to dream about myself. My future."

"Uh-huh. You ain't getting anything twisted, are you?" she asked.

"We're just friends. I know. I was just . . ."

"I'll let you know if anything changes."

"With me or with you?" Kicking himself for running his mouth before he could stop himself, Bekele paused, the way someone would if they were not certain whether they were about to step on a land mine.

"Either way. I know how easily confused you get about these things, so I'll keep you straight. What'd we say?"

"No confusion." Bekele held his pinkie out.

"No confusion." She snagged it with hers and they shook. Falling into laughter, they collapsed into each other in an easy manner. Marguerite returned to her data stream, the incoming data suddenly preoccupying her enough to comfortably change topics.

"Besides, I ain't sweating you and your space cold."

"You can't just stick the word 'space' in front of something and act like you did something."

"Why not? Every time you don't understand something, you stick the word 'quantum' in front of it and act like you explained something."

An explosion tore through the section of wall on the far side of the room.

Bekele wrapped his arm around Marguerite, and they crouched behind their console. An emergency bulkhead sealed the chamber. They kept their heads down and waited.

<Evacuate Section 31-C.>

"Come on." Popping his head up to make sure everything was clear, Bekele took her hand, and they dashed through the entrance portal. The way the decks rattled, the ship seemed long and bulky, its metal frame barely held together. Like an office building after hours, the *Cypher*'s corridor lights flickered on and off, power conduits damaged. Without people bustling in its hallways, it was square, almost sterile. No, empty and cold. A thin wisp of smoke billowed like a thread through the hall. The next blast striking the ship collapsed a structural pylon, blocking their way. A couple of crew members struggled to lift it. Bekele hesitated, not in fear for his life but from not knowing what to do. Images of pierced shields, hull plating, and explosive decompression filled his mind. Being cast adrift in the cold vacuum of space, ravaged by the eternal exposure.

Marguerite responded on automatic pilot. Releasing his hand, she dashed over to help, checking for injuries and comforting the injured. The others adjusted their positions and lifted the pylon enough for her to clear him. Bekele envied her confidence in knowing how her body would respond to her demands. Not worried that with her first steps, she might keel over. Or her muscles might spasm into a seizure. Or her world might rush toward darkness and she might fall into unconsciousness, a coma, or worse.

Paki stormed down the hallway. His comm screen up, speaking in harried tones, his attention fixed in a straight-ahead gaze. His glower a targeting lock that dared anyone to interrupt him. Bekele stumbled to scramble out of the way of his determined stride, snapping Paki out of his mission. "Where should you be?"

"We had to evacuate our quarters," Bekele said.

"We stopped to help," Marguerite joined him.

"How bad is it? Were we hit by . . ."

"Get to Twenty-Seven. Twenty-Seven-B. Many of your classmates are there." Paki gave Bekele a second, more appraising gaze. "On second thought, come with me."

Paki led them to a workstation. He accessed his telemetry data. Projecting it, he turned to them. "What do you see?"

"A black hole devouring large amounts of gas, emitting high-energy photons by the surrounding field. The remnants of stars that died, the dark heart of their galaxy. Massive black holes on a collision course. We're stuck between the gravitational interaction between a supermassive black hole pair and surrounding stars. They emit gravitational waves and radiation from black holes and neutron stars," Bek said.

"Some influence moving faster than light." Marguerite ran her finger through a hard light beam. "Traveling through dark bodies."

"Eighty percent of the universe is dark matter. Invisible dark energy binding it together."

"A reminder of how much we don't know about the universe," Paki said. "Pockets of extremely distorted gravitating space-time. Pocket universes. Traveling through them requires a kind of polarizer. The Orun Gate was just such a type."

"When you have so many dimensions to play in, anything can happen. It's the problem of locality," Bek said.

"We aren't anywhere, which is exactly the problem. But everything's always interconnected." Paki ran his hand through his thinning hair. "Let's say I have a particle and I split this particle into two particles. We have two quantumly entangled particles. What I do to one particle, the other particle is aware of. If I charge one, the other will instantaneously display the other charge. This occurs no matter how far apart they are. Seven kilometers or seven light-years. The information travels faster than light."

"Something that happens in one location can instantly influence an event that happens somewhere else," Marguerite said.

"Because entanglement," Bek said.

"Because entanglement," she agreed. "That's math. We are definitely somewhere. A quantum computer could perform tasks more efficiently. Delegating subtasks to copies of itself in other universes . . ."

"A single particle wanders the universe on its own; it's guided by its own pilot wave. One that's perfectly local. But if there's a second particle . . ."

". . . they're entangled. No matter how distant they may be," Marguerite finished.

"But if I'm interacting with the things in my environment they get entangled with me. Other things get entangled with them. Eventually it collapses into a universal wave function." Paki wiped the data set clean. "Consciousness itself causes the collapse of the wave function. We can't do much more than assign probabilities."

"So what's missing?" Bek asked.

"We misunderstand consciousness. That interaction between our consciousness and the universe at the quantum level. I believe we passed through the quantum consciousness without a stabilizing polarizer."

"A pilot wave particle would produce interference," Marguerite said.

"A particle on a pilot wave." Paki propagated a new data set. "The pilot wave is like a signal. One we can trace and follow it back home."

"We would need to create a bubble around the ship to stay in the same universe. Using background radiation as a tether." Bek sat up. His fingers danced in midair until the image of Astra Black's ship appeared. "The theory was a similar bubble kept the mothership in our universe."

"Using this quantum veil, this consciousness, like an interface?" Marguerite asked.

"We'd need to tie the quantum signature of Maya to . . . Maya," Bek said.

Paki smiled, completely pleased. "Head to Maya's central core. It's closer and has reinforced shielding. Make sure everything continues to function within normal parameters. Can you handle that, key engineer?"

"Yes." The gravity wavered, sending a wave of nausea through Bekele. Whatever anomaly they dealt with lashed out in unexpected ways. But he knew, despite her curiosity, his mom's first duty was to the safety of her crew. Her family. She'd keep them safe.

Maya was a tenth-generation quantum computer array. Both an integrated system—coordinating, running, and supporting systems throughout all of the Muungano Alliance—and a discrete system. An "aspect" of them ran a ship vs. the Dreaming City vs. Titan, with a particularization such that the "Maya" Bekele interacted with was different from the one Marguerite did. Like a series of different personalities all acting in concert with—and layered atop—one another. Functioning as one unit.

Maya's central core was a sculpture in light. They "existed" as nodules throughout the ship. If Muungano was an octopus, Maya was its distributed brain. But here, they were beams and arrays, varying hues as if capturing the AI's complex, ever-shifting moods. Cooling conduits ran through the reinforced walls. Whenever the systems were taxed, temperature fluctuated, often spiking.

"I've been studying some of Maya's nodes, you know, after those glitches." Marguerite studied the light assemblies. She probably didn't notice that her tone had shifted to a reverential whisper. She'd never been given access to the core before. "But I don't understand anything going on in their code."

"You can't think of it as code. Think of it as music. A symphony." Bekele's finger traced the holoprojection. Their programming language was more like music interpolated through fractal arrays. He intuited their meaning, hearing their song as he attuned their landscape. It was a strange sensation, speaking of Maya, running his finger through their core, trying not to think about the fact that Maya heard and was aware of them.

Coordinating the life-support systems, data, communication, they learned and grew, adapting along the way. Micropatterns among their quanta formed a kind of neural net, a portal connecting them through time and space at the quantum level in ways he was pretty convinced their designers didn't always understand. But he started to. Maya evolved. An intelligent machine colony occupying a zone of nonbeing with an exciting potentiality for self-consciousness. He believed all time was an illusion and they existed in all times simultaneously. For all any of them knew, the glitches were the effects of an entanglement feedback loop.

"I almost see what you mean. Like a lattice of networks coming together."

"Yes." Bekele's voice trailed off. The song of code he studied was incongruous, a series of off notes in a signature improvisation. Subtle shifts that might not be noticed in the grand music of their symphony; but teased apart, they signaled a sudden key change. He'd noticed something like this before. Isolated nodules whose pattern of data clusters was off; invasive clusters he thought of as data cancers.

"What is it, Bek?"

"I'm not sure. Maybe it's my imagination. My eyes playing tricks on me." The infiltrates cordoned off information, encrypting data caches. It seemed that now, the misalignments of the data matrix had spread. The work appeared deliberate, little things about the edges of the arrays. A controlled phase loop, a virus reprogramming itself—as if someone was laying the groundwork for cordoning off sections of Maya's memory core, setting the stage for a digital lobotomy.

"You don't look well."

Bekele turned to her. The concern on her face had nothing to do with his suspicions about Maya. She worried about him. Touching his forehead, she snatched her hand back as if bitten.

"You're boiling."

"I don't . . ." Only once he tried moving did the wave of light-headedness hit him. He steadied himself with the side of the panel. All strength fled his arms and he fell into the wall. He tried to brace himself, but his hands refused to obey him.

"Have a seat." Marguerite helped lower him to the deck.

Bekele took a breath, exhaling slowly to calm his racing heart. Marguerite hovered nearby, an overprotective mother hen, her arms spread ever ready to shield him from anything bad. Bekele noticed her hand. A slight tremor spasmed through it. An involuntary flinch that didn't even register with her.

But that he recognized as the first symptom in his disease's progression.

"Magpie." The world already swam in a hazy shimmer. His mind set aflame by the sudden fear that his condition might be spreading, that he might be endangering her. But he no longer trusted his mind. His fever overwhelmed his brain, leaving him paranoid. Delusional.

"I don't care what your motivations were, Paki. My decision stands." His mother's raised voice carried down the hallway.

Bekele's ears throbbed as if ready to pop with sudden altitude change. Pressure change. The hull pulsated with increased vibration. The *Cypher*'s engines strained in some desperate maneuver. Marguerite hooked his arm to steady him. He leaned against her for a heartbeat, gathered his strength, and with a glance they came to a simultaneous unspoken agreement to scuttle out of sight.

"You should be on the bridge," Paki said.

"My new number two can handle the situation. And do me the courtesy of keeping me in the loop. Any of them you find yourself in."

"I'm not begging for my position back. I don't care about titles and roles. I only care that the work gets done and the community is safe." Paki matched her determined steps.

"And I don't?"

"Then let me loop you into my research. I believe that we can create our own wormhole. The white dwarf creates a wobble with the nearest star. Think about that kind of mass converted into energy in a very small spot. That opens the possibility of creating a subspeed tunnel, the mythicist's golden strand. An odede. We can get home."

"It was never *your* research. It was all of ours. We're a team. You were to work alongside your team. I have no idea what to do with your 'research' or beliefs because it all resides within the silo of you. And you have fallen into a spiral of obsessing."

"I'm obsessing? I wonder what the logs would tell me about how often you visit Zenith's cell."

Zenith.

Bekele panted hard, as if the air in the room escaped through unseen breaches in the walls. He'd heard so much about the man, he barely pictured him as human. More like a hideous spiderlike creature who kept to the shadows. Access to the man stopped short of Code Black / Eyes Only. Kenya stationed one of her guards outside of his door at all times. Bekele tried to "accidentally" wander to the house cell himself to confront the man who dangled his life like bait to compromise his mother.

"What's that got to do with anything?" Mom sneered, a warning that Paki was about to catch all that smoke.

"It's a case of divide and conquer, 'cause you let a mzungu break up my crew." Paraphrasing one of the ancient griots, Paki refused to back down.

"I'm trying to get actionable intel from Zenith. He knows about the origin of the virus. And, more importantly, its cure. And I know he's holding back more than he's sharing."

"The man drips poison into the ears of any who listen to him."

"You would know."

"If you're alluding to my conversation with him, I had to assess him for myself. He sows fear and death all in the name of moving his agenda forward."

"He's a resource. A dangerous resource, but a resource nonetheless."

"You underestimate him as a threat."

"So I've been told. You, however, overestimate your individual voice. You think you're the only one who sees, who knows, who can 'assess.' I lean on my entire team. I don't need a rogue operative acting on my behalf. Or a special counsel—any . . . consigliere or gatekeeper to intelligence *that I need.*"

"He's tearing the ship apart." The tone in Paki's voice was unusually insistent, underscored by something close to fear.

"You've done your fair share of that."

Bekele recognized his mother's that's-my-final-word tone. Nothing else need be said; and if you were smart, you didn't try. Paki was smart. They parted ways.

Bekele waited, almost holding his breath, hoping Paki was so preoccupied with his ever-percolating anger that he wouldn't check in on them and notice their absence. Neither of them had spoken of the physical danger to the ship, which in a weird way relieved him. Despite the bombardment and shaking, whatever danger they faced wasn't imminent.

"Come on," Bekele whispered once the hallway was clear. Marguerite touched his forehead. "I'm fine."

"What about whatever it was that had your eyes playing tricks on you?"

"That's not important now. We have to go."

"Where are we going? You out here just snooping," Marguerite said.

"Professional investigation." Bekele held up a finger. "Don't say it."

"Space snooping." Marguerite grinned. "Now you feel me."

Rolling his eyes, Bekele angled his head toward her in mild amusement. "We need to get to Zenith's quarters."

Before she could protest, Bekele skulked down the hallway. The deck vibrated from time to time with the mild lurch of renewed engine thrusts. His mind swam. The fever refused to allow him space to process events. Repairs were well underway throughout the ship. Much of the damage appeared cosmetic in nature, though the occasional wall or substructure had collapsed. Emergency shields and bulkheads kept any serious damage from occurring.

"How are we going to get in?" Marguerite crept behind him, but had a way of walking that announced they were both guilty and up to something.

"I don't know. We'll cross that bridge . . ." Bekele figured to crack the lock code, spoof a security override, and hope the override itself didn't produce special alerts. Maybe Marguerite could distract whatever guards were there by using her unmatched ability to argue and annoy.

As they neared the corridor of Zenith's cell, his heart quickened. Bekele flattened against the wall; Marguerite mimicked him. He chanced a peek around the corner. He didn't spot any of Kenya's guards. The damage alerts around the rest of the ship must have had them temporarily reassigned. The Universe presented them with a window of opportunity. Finally, he'd be able to get some answers about his condition. Force them out of Zenith if he had to.

Waving Marguerite to follow him, he skulked down the rest of the walkway. But when they reached his rondavel, the door was open.

And Zenith was gone.

23

EPYC RO MORGAN
Planetside—Beyond the Orun Gate

Momma,

They came for us today.

It has felt like that has been my life for weeks. People just keep coming for us. For no other reason than we existed. They fear us so they have decided to make preemptive strikes. They have created a false narrative of who we are—as Muungano, as HOVA—and use it to justify their . . . everything.

It is a war on two fronts: the actual combat and the drain from deconstructing their campaign of misinformation. It's worrying. Exhausting. I'm tired, Momma . . .

"How tired are you, Ro?" Robin asked from the doorway.

"I just needed a moment to get my head straight before we go for next steps." Epyc Ro thought better when she wrote. Her fingers itched the way a smoker's lips twitched when they needed a nicotine fix. She didn't want her people to observe her jotting things down. She wondered if part of her recorded her letters precisely to be "accidentally" overheard and thus force her to open up to her sisters. She missed her mother. As much as her mother annoyed her—not quite seeing who her daughter was, nor understanding the choices she made—her mother's voice comforted her. Her family had been her refuge, her anchor of home. Epyc Ro found comfort in recording journal entries to her mother knowing she'd never receive them. "I feel like we've been on a long, never-ending patrol cycle."

"We have. It started when we first touched down on Mzisoh. But can we all just—" Robin hesitated, wanting to frame her words with care. "—take a minute?"

"We need intel." Work was her balm. Epyc Ro reviewed all available footage, telemetrics, and other data of every engagement with hostiles since crossing the Orun Gate. The goal was to develop new tactics and run them past Anitra to devise countermeasures for the hostiles' attack technique.

"The intel will be there tomorrow. Tonight can we just chill? Look, we can't just nonstop push every waking hour of every day without rest. That strain has taken a toll."

Her head throbbed. She hadn't been injured, no shrapnel wounds of any sort, nor had she been in any hand-to-hand combat for a while. After sitting behind her console, when she stood up too quickly her world canted. Standing was a strain, sitting down a chore, yet she didn't want her sisters to worry. Epyc Ro closed her eyes. Her lids soothed her eyes with darkness and held back tears. "How long until we reach Abrehot?"

"Cadgejia remains purposely vague."

"You think it's a trap? Leading us to a fortified stronghold of their people?"

"I didn't until now." Robin logged her latest reports. "The vibe I get is that they're simply being cagey. They're watching us."

"We're learning much about the Galactic Rim."

"We've had a series of misadventures is all." Anitra wandered in. She hopped up on a console, her legs dangling over the edge like she'd just finished a casual stroll. From the level of her mischievous energy, she champed at the bit to call them pirates again.

"What of our other guests?" Epyc Ro asked.

"Still not talking."

"We can't keep them locked up and we can't let them wander about."

"Perhaps we can drop them off once we reach Abrehot," Anitra said.

Removing her elekes, Robin kissed them and held them to her forehead. She issued a brief prayer before stowing them. Epyc Ro had always appreciated Robin's brand of leadership. She wasn't a yeller. There were many who took that approach, more than anyone would want to admit. Another holdover from when the HOVA and O.E. did joint military operations. But Robin didn't need to berate anyone or beat her chest to get anyone to listen to her. A few soft, well-chosen words was all it took for people to respond.

"We all need a break. There will be many a goofy in our future and those in desperate need of ethering," Robin said.

"Ethering?" Epyc Ro asked.

"That will never not be my all-time favorite diss track," Anitra said. "Tomorrow we can begin the ethering."

"In the meantime, I have an idea," Robin said.

Epyc Ro and Robin collected the rest of the crew. The Reapers had been on the go nonstop for what felt like months. They found themselves not quite stranded, but plunging deeper into unknown territory with no clue how to get home. Yet they'd managed to remain a unit. No one balked. No one complained. No one whined, keeping their lament for family and Muungano to themselves. Ellis waited near the air lock. They lingered there whenever they expected to roll through those doors. Loading, unloading gear, from weapons to tools to the ship. Cleaning weapons, desperately wanting to be seen as useful. A little too eager to please, worried that their efforts weren't sufficient to earn a place among them. A subconscious fear that the Reapers would send them back to the Mzisoh led them to lose weight. They doubled down, studying hard with Chandra, going over military history and tactics. Training in their downtime when they should have been sleeping. Although truth be told, the Mzisoh were still new to them and the Reapers had no full appreciation for the stages of their life cycles. Chandra read something in their eyes. A thin, mischievous smile crossed her lips. Ellis stood and fell into lockstep with them.

The Reapers had converted a nook into a mess hall. Tables and chairs arranged like they were set up for a family reunion gathering. Henam and Cadgejia sat across from each other, engaged in an animated discussion. Cadgejia's color had improved and their suit appeared whole. They eventually stumbled across a mix of greens and fish protein, which stirred their other guest's appetite. Their galley was little more than ledges and a table. The smell of coffee permeated the room, probably prepared extra strong to cover the odor of whatever Cadgejia prepared, which smelled like microwaved fish.

"Where's Anitra?" Ellis asked.

"She had to change," Robin said. "She likes to make an entrance."

<Intro music . . . commencing.> A horns fanfare blared, ending all conversation. Other instruments rose to meet it, tentative drums and a rising bass.

Anitra strode in confidently. Sliding to the left, dropping her shoulders, then moving to her right, she Harlem shuffled through the doorway.

"Girl, what you got on?" Robin asked.

"Look here, I'm in uniform." Anitra twirled, showing off her outfit. A short-sleeved white kanzu over some cutoff blue-jean shorts, a maestro ready to conduct her symphony. "Sandals on. Towel on my shoulder. Got my spatula control on lock. My pan ready."

"You got that black grease glove on like it's a shooting sleeve."

"I'm ready to put in the wrist work. If we gonna eat, we gonna eat, you hear me?"

"All you need is a Black & Mild hanging off your lip."

"Better not be making any chitlins," Robin said. "Chitlins smell like bad credit."

"You got fetus taste buds."

Anitra made her way to the makeshift cook station. She synthed proteins but brought out an array of spices. "I don't trust any technology to season properly." Soon, the smell of grilled meats took over the room. Chatter resumed, but the vibe had changed. Lightened.

"All right, I just wanted us to regroup for a bit before we begin the next phase of whatever mission we're on," Robin announced.

"Is this another ritual? Are we initiating anyone into the Reapers?" Ellis glanced around, anxious to induct anyone probably so that they would no longer be the newest member.

"I want no part of your cultic practices. I'm here out of curiosity," Henam said.

"And security," Cadgejia added.

"I just thought we were overdue to simply be with one another." Robin gave a high sign to Chandra.

<Accessing.>

Epyc Ro passed a suspicious glance between her officers. Robin and Anitra moved the table out of the way, clearing the floor. Not knowing what to expect, Henam and Cadgejia scrambled toward the edge of the room.

"It's time." Robin's tone aimed for foreboding, but she could barely keep her face straight.

"For what?" Epyc Ro had the suspicion that her officers had been conspiring behind her back. She almost smiled.

Electronic popping of bubbles in the background, a flat four-four beat slid in behind a voice declaring that it was time for the percolator. The glint of recognition sparkled in Epyc Ro's eyes. The instruments built into an anticipatory swell, the rhythm finding the pulse. Robin was the first one up, but Epyc Ro and Anitra soon followed.

Then the beat dropped. What sounded like a fire-alarm sine wave wound through the music. Cadgejia covered their ears.

The dance floor erupted.

Epyc Ro bobbed in place, in unison with Chandra. The volume cranked higher. The room grew warmer, though no one minded. Robin swayed her shoulders, dipped her hips, and brought herself up with a snap. She did a body wave and began to step to either side.

"Stand back, y'all, she's feeling it!" Anitra hopped up on a chair and twirled her arms to spur her on.

Waving each hand in turn next to her head then in front of her, Robin lowered them to pat the air at her hips as she backed up. Turning to the side, with the next body rock, Chandra joined Robin, synchronizing her movements with computer precision. Robin shuffled and leaned back into Epyc Ro. The commander's shoulders began to shimmy.

"No," Anitra yelled. "Tell me it's not about to go down like this?"

"What is a 'percolator'?" Henam asked.

"This," Robin said.

Epyc Ro popped her hips out and brought her arms in, matching Robin's steps.

"I love to see it! I love to see it!" Anitra had no interest in joining the line, preferring to hype them up while doing her own dance.

Language meant nothing. The intangible meaning of the moment quite clear in its intent. The lyrics both meaningless and the sum of their experience. They were alive. They were here. They had each other.

Ellis felt self-conscious to risk any more than clapping, though they chanced the occasional bounce to the music. Henam and Cadgejia passed glances to each other. Henam tapped her foot to their gyrations. And for a moment, she forgot. She allowed the beat to carry her into her own dance.

"This is the move right here," Robin said.

Losing herself in the moment, Epyc Ro laughed. And danced.

It took months to reach the Angwen spaceport. A hive of activity, the spaceport was a tossed salad of cultures all united by their travel among the stars. Angwen prided itself on being a symbol of hope and opportunity where anyone could start fresh. Luxury starliners. Nambra freighters bearing the laser-scarred hulls of conflict. Some of the ships now looked familiar to the Reapers crew. Anitra had become adept at docking protocols during their misadventures. The traffic-control tower permitted them to dock. Autoclamps fastened them to the ring. Epyc Ro hadn't become accustomed to the sight of all the starships—all of their permutations and unique design—and was humbled by their strange beauty. Shuttles meandered about, dropping off passengers, all their stories yet to be written. Others loaded and unloaded cargo from some ships while workers in EVM suits conducted repairs to others.

"I'm not comfortable with us Green Book–ing our way through the galaxy," Robin said.

"Then let's do a mission briefing. Cadgejia, could you give us an overview about the Abrehot?" Epyc Ro asked.

"War broke out in the Nia'quong region decades ago." Cadgejia rotated in their chair. They had learned to relax among the Reapers, almost responding like part of the crew. "Dragged on for years. In response, the Ouje opened the Abrehot, the intergalactic library, at the center of the conflict. Their leader, Biafra Oshun, said they would choose to celebrate the sanctity of the written word and would welcome any who joined in such efforts. Which was how peace came to this world. The entire area is considered hallowed ground. Nambra's people, the Ouje, have been through a series of conflicts and have only in the last few years found a measure of routine again."

"The historical context I get, I'm just not sold on this deployment, Commander," Robin said.

"You know we can hear you, right?" Anitra said.

"Robin and I staff the ships and monitor comms in case there is trouble," Epyc Ro said.

"My title as ambassador allows me passage at the Abrehot."

"Ambassador, huh. Why didn't you ever talk about that?" Anitra asked.

"You never inquired."

"Robin's the curious one."

"Well, there's much about my past I don't want to revisit." Cadgejia looked around the ship. Their story ended up with them captured by the Lei'den. "We'll need to be encoded and will probably be supervised . . ."

"Supervised?" Robin asked.

"A representative of their world will be our escort."

"Like our own personal assistant?" Anitra asked with too much enthusiasm.

"Ditch them as soon as you can," Epyc Ro said.

"Understood," Cadgejia said.

"I get all that. It's the 'Anitra as mission lead' that I can't get my head around. On a first-contact mission. Much less what's likely to be multiple first-contact scenarios."

"I'm diplomatic like a motherfucker," Anitra said.

"Your Honor, the prosecution rests." Robin kissed her elekes and slipped them on.

"People-development work may be outside of Anitra's immediate skill set . . . ," Epyc Ro said.

"Hey!" Anitra yelled as if hurt. She tapped her chin in a show of considering the words. "Well, okay."

"But while we're all about providing opportunities to grow, even with heavy stakes, no one does reconnaissance better. Chandra is there as mentor and liaison. Ellis is backing."

"And our guests?"

"Cadgejia and Henam agreed to escort our team and make introductions."

"And our actual prisoners?" Robin asked.

"We need to figure out where to drop the Lei'den. 'Cause we are not babysitting them any longer. They've been a nonstop pain in the ass this entire voyage." Between their escape attempts, sabotage attempts, and continuous attempts to contact their people, Epyc Ro was ready to leave them on a passing asteroid. Almost did. Twice. "We'll stay off comms as much as possible. But we're suited up and can be planetside in minutes should shit jump off. We good?"

"We good, Commander," Anitra said. "We got this."

Chandra raised her hood to cover her head.

"No." Cadgejia touched her hand. "Leave your head uncovered."

<But, my skull patch . . . >

"Will make people feel more comfortable around you."

"Many people travel to the Abrehot. To the casual observer, we are a party of five different species. Many will assume us a diplomatic envoy anyway."

"Commlinks active," Epyc Ro said.

<Active. We are in full link mode.>

ANITRA GOUVEI
Nambra—The Abrehot

The light glinting against the tan-colored earth gilded the clouds with an aura of gold. A largely barren plateau, connected to and protected by the rest of the mountain range. It had been cleared, erasing all physical traces of what used to be there; but nature abhorred a vacuum and quickly reclaimed the land. Cropped hedges flanked the gravel path, giving way to thick underbrush. The roof of the Abrehot retracted to allow natural light to illuminate most of the building. It was over four stories high and its entrance enclosed an arboretum.

"Ain't you hot?" Anitra asked.

An iridescent flowing robe wrapped them. Underneath, the fabrics over the navsuit were reminiscent of the shifting hues of an ocean. Intricate patterns of other sea creatures woven into them, almost so they could move among their denizens. A reminder. "Our navsuits regulate our temperatures."

"It still feels like stepping into someone's mouth and I don't like it," Anitra said.

<It's a dry heat.>

"I don't like it."

The Nambra Welcome Center recorded their names and biometric data. Anitra kept her head down, taking note of their security measures. Cadgejia took point. Anitra didn't like having to depend on someone she barely knew getting her through a checkpoint. She felt naked without her DMX-3000, but the Abrehot had a strict no-weapons policy. Ellis towered over her, shielding her back. They passed under an arch, where an AI conducted the security check.

"Ambassador Cadgejia of Darawad." They stepped under the arch of the security scanner.

<Darawadan,> a disembodied voice responded from all around them. <Ambassador. Welcome back. It has been too long.>

"Indeed, I fear I have fallen too far behind in my studies."

<And these are your guests?>

"Yes. A delegation from a variety of planets. We're hoping to begin talks to open trade between our peoples."

<For that you'll need Novice approval.>

"I understood that to be the case and look forward to the pairing."

<We simply need to encode them. Step forward one at a time.>

Ellis walked through.

<Mzisoh. Next.>

<Rev—> The AI hesitated, as if shifting into recalibration mode. <Derthalen. Next.>

Henam avoided their eyes. Cadgejia patted her.

Anitra stepped forward. She prepared to declare her Muungano designation before remembering Henam's raised-knife reaction to the name of her people. Chandra joined her, prepared for shit to jump off.

<Earth. Next. Earth. Thank you.>

Anitra exchanged glances with Chandra. "They already had our biometric data."

<CO/IN.>

LISC agents before they started posing as Lei'den. "They've been in talks with folks in one breath and sullying our name in the other."

They opted out of the genestream scan, so they had to undergo criminal and financial history checks and be interviewed about their religious and political affiliations. Cadgejia had rehearsed this part of the process with them. Anitra stayed on script.

<The Abrehot monitored all of their visitors and you may be subject to random searches and interviews.> The voice warned after their interrogation.

"How does this work?" Ellis asked.

"This is a favor bank economy. Run by a revolving governance board of elders. People who need something, an item or a job done come to trade favors. The elders make sure the trades are fair."

<The board functions as regulators?> Chandra asked.

"And validate the trades," Henam said.

"There is a cultural ethos, an obligation to share what you can spare," Cadgejia said.

"No loans, only gifts. Once a gift leaves your hand, it was never yours to begin with."

The inner courtyard of the Abrehot had lime-green reflecting pools and looming pink crystal towers. The Ouje natives milled about, dressed in their finest tunics and embroidered karosses. Each family's clothing was patterned or colored according to a cultural theme. A red tunic, an open billowy blouse over a thigh-length skirt seemed to be their standard dress. Almost designed to show off how their thick muscles undulated like tectonic plates. They greeted each other with soft caress of their fingertips.

"I was expecting something, you know, a bit more . . . grimier," Anitra said.

<What'd you expect? A dive bar?> Chandra asked.

"I don't know. Bright lights. Holograms everywhere. Waiting for "In Da Club" to start playing. Something . . . alien looking."

"Giant robots?" Ellis asked.

"Is that too much for a sister to ask for?"

Henam cleared her throat to change topics. "It's pretty typical for an Ouje to know six languages. The language of their family, the language of the village, the language of commerce."

"What is Ouje for 'handed him his ass?'" Anitra asked. "I'm just saying, it'll be a useful phrase to have. You know I need to collect some usable intel."

"Here, asking questions is considered a show of force," Cadgejia said.

"I'll lower my voice."

"It's not about being loud. A question demands the contents of what was inside their head."

<They're protective of their intellectual capital.> Chandra added.

"Respond with silence," Cadgejia said. The Ouje have a saying. 'There are two types of people: those who flee trouble and those who cause it.' The last time strangers showed up, their people were put in chains. All in the name of religion."

"We're familiar with that story." Anitra spat to the side. "So how do I get folks to talk to me."

"Take a seat on the ground about ten meters away from anyone and wait. Face the opposite direction, like you're there for no particular reason. Someone may appear and invite you over; if not, you leave. The Ouje are visible only when they decide to be."

Some men toted infants on their back. Others hand-patted corn flatbread to luxuriate in a stew of beans. One played a hand-carved two-stringed instrument.

"Each person has to make their own instrument, which was how they achieved master proficiency," Cadgejia noted.

The sun beat down, a bloodred glow as wind swept the plaza. An umber-skinned species cinched their skirts together by a sash. Anitra tensed. She'd seen such weighted sashes used as a weapon. The people's headband matched, but also looked like it could double as a sling weapon. Which meant no matter how decorative their coral-colored necklaces and bracelets were, everyone was probably armed. A culture of people who must've bought their clothes at a store called Casual Armaments.

A cluster of folks eyed Henam. A group in mechanical units, much like independent walking EVM exoskeletons, gathered across from them. Their servos whirred, straining to knit them back together.

<Nanobots are cleaning the clogged vents of their suits. Scans show they are digesting and reproducing.>

"Great, like chittering insects fleeing the light in panic," Cadgejia said.

"Do you see that?" Ellis whispered.

"Something you want to tell us?" Anitra reacted to the rising tension. Her emi alerted her to the death spirit in the air. Weapons were about to be drawn. "The only person anyone seems to be taking an interest in is you."

"They are from Morawi. I spent some time there studying, living as a courier for them. I was returning from a mission there when the Lei'den abducted me." Henam's large eyes implored wildly. Clearly lying. Perspiration dappled her forehead. She was terrified.

"They don't look too happy." Anitra took her hand. "We've come this far together. We're not going to just abandon you. I'm just trying to stave off some unnecessary drama."

"You don't understand. I need to warn them. If they're here, then Ma is coming."

Chandra winced, raising her hand to the side of her cybernetic implant.

"Everything all right?" Cadgejia wrapped two tentacles along her shoulders.

<Yes. Command chatter.> Chandra entered prophet mode. The way she disengaged from communication, shifting from being present with them to listening to voices only she could hear, was spooky. Tracking the movement of potential hostiles, assessing threat levels. She signed to Anitra.

"Keep your head on a swivel," Anitra said.

"What's going on?" Ellis leaned in close.

<We're scanning channels. Lots of talk about the impending threat of Muungano.>

"We need to hurry this along," Anitra said.

"I'll see if I can summon someone for you to talk to." Cadgejia entered the main Abrehot hall.

"To paraphrase what the prophet said, 'If they don't give you a seat at the table, bring a folding chair.'" Anitra crossed the plaza. She fashioned a folding chair and plopped into it, her back to the well. The thundering cascade of subterranean waterfalls echoed from the distance. "Stay ready so that you don't have to get ready."

Henam took a seat on the other side of the well without appearing attached to her. Desperation marked her move, like someone too eager to say yes to a date. Ellis and Chandra flanked Anitra from across the plaza, a triangulation to intercept any approaching threat.

A man came and sat down a few meters from her. A series of V-shaped notches bridged his forehead. He had a stout figure, his twin maroon sashes seemed designed to impress others by whatever office they symbolized. He attempted to intimidate with his bulk. Drawing his blond hair back into a ponytail, he revealed the three days of beard growth stubbling his long angular face. "Your people are not from this sector."

"It's an awfully big sector. How can you tell?" Anitra shifted away from him, not digging his vibe at all, but she needed information.

"We know a resident of Muungano when we see one."

"You got the wrong one," Anitra said. "I didn't catch your name."

"I never threw it. How rude of me." The man squinted, an involuntary muscle spasm. "Novice Aaron Quass. Of the Service of the Order."

Anitra and Chandra froze, not blinking. *Novice approval.* That was a bureaucratic policy. The Service had been here long enough to weave itself into the Abrehot infrastructure. This was bigger than just LISC or the Interstellar Alliance.

"You're from O.E. . . . but the church was dismantled after the Great Unrest," Anitra said.

"That's a whole sentence with half of it having no basis in fact. How does one dismantle the church? We may have gone underground, rethought our strategies, redirected our resources, but we've been right here the whole time. The church was mother, the church was father."

"But to end up out here . . . how?"

"You're a long way from home, too. And to find yourself in the company of a Darawadan, a Mzisoh, and a Derthalen." Novice Quass made a show of checking his scanner. His face spasmed. He projected Henam's physiognomy. Her form morphed, becoming more simian, with long arms and burly musculature. Her face grew thick, bridged brows with deep inset eyes. The image returned to her current state. "No, I stand corrected. A Revisio. My, my, my."

Anitra stared at Henam. "Wait, what's a Revisio?"

"Think of their species as a virus. Floating unicellular things, with each strain considered an individual," Novice Quass added helpfully.

"She looks pretty big for a virus."

"Tell that to the Derthalen she infected. Their people made for natural hosts. Understandable since we are all from the same star stuff. Once they take root, they mutate and spread. Each generation of the virus is a mutant strain of the last. The course of the infection has physical side effects, too. Compare her to others of her species." Novice Quass projected holovid images presumably of the Derthalen. Their eyes too big for their head, their skulls smooth and higher. Male and female wore simple tunics of animal skins. "Hulking brutes, really, that stop and sniff about, with their protruding jaws all set and resolute. When they become occupied by a Revisio, the Derthalen undergo mental and physical changes. The Revisio have what they call a 'resonance,' something that functions as a kind of low-level telepathy. Their bodies become smaller. More . . . human-appearing. From the Neanderthal to homo sapiens in the span of an infection."

"How do you know all this?" Anitra asked.

"As part of my Jesuit Training School, officer candidacy, I faced grueling studies in advanced mathematics, stellar cartography, astrobiology, logistics, strategy, game theory, tactics, and Latin."

"Right, because all alien cultures need to be fluent in languages long dead on Earth." Anitra sucked her teeth. "Why should I believe anything you have to say?"

"I have nothing to gain. Keep hanging out with her all you want. Before too long you'll encounter all manner of . . . friends interested in having a conversation with her."

"You seem mighty comfortable as church folk despite not being weighed down by a bunch of guns."

"We have embraced a holistic approach to fulfilling her mission: politics, technology, and, yes, the military. Once we established relationship with the Ouje, our mission took on a more . . . universal perspective. We're training a vanguard of 'indigenous leaders' to further the mission of the church. But as you can attest, the mission field is a dangerous place. Service of the Order soldiers, our prefects, provide security for any missionary colony. They remain in their biomech suits at all times."

A column of armored prefects, like walking tanks, emerged from every building entrance. Waiting and scanning. The Reapers knew all about the Service of the Order and their rules of engagement. Several campaigns from the Ukombozi War that were still classified Code Black / Eyes Only were suspected Service of the Order engagements. The soldiers were in judgment mode, assessing whether the Reapers should be declared "hostiles." Should those conditions be met—the nature of those violations could vary from use of too strong of words to a gesture, any condition which made them feel "unsafe"—the military protocols were enacted. Tens of troops, some armed with hand cannons, others with turrets, already targeted them.

"Praise be the blood." The Novice raised his hands in spirit-filled ecstasy. The prefects stopped their advance. "You will be taken into custody for interrogation and conversion."

Anitra activated her distress beacon. "You about to catch all that sacred smoke."

"We have entered *hostile relations*," the lead prefect announced. "Casualties are expected."

24

ISHANT SANGSUWANGUL
O.E.—Indianapolis

Ishant shoved aside the cover of the service tunnel and crawled out. He reached back to help Akilah and Miriam out. Their clothes reeked of dispersal gas.

"Careful." Ishant stopped Akilah from removing her hood. "Residue is all over them. Let me help."

Ishant peeled her hood from her with his cybernetic arm. Then did the same for Miriam. As LISC employees, their latest-generation rebreathers deployed automatically, barely seen nose filters that produced a thin field about their mouths to purify the air for them to breathe.

Searchlights crisscrossed the Capitol. Newslinkage reported about "the unidentified man" he knew as Matata. All sorts of authorities swarmed, cordoned off streets to contain the area. UN police, FBI, Marshals Service, ATF, Indianapolis police, Secret Service. Those were the ones visible. Hundreds of international alphabet agencies circulated. Ishant removed their hoods and destroyed their transponders.

"Come on. We can't stay here," he said.

"I don't understand," Miriam said.

Ishant touched the side of her face—angling her head to the left then to the right—to assess her. She drifted dangerously close to shock. Both she and Akilah wore the same expression. He'd seen it before in survivors of a bombing or natural disaster: the vacant look of people who'd lost everything.

"Should we go back?" Akilah asked. "We're witnesses."

"You are also looking to defect. Now's our best opportunity to get you out of here by taking advantage of the chaos."

"But . . ." Akilah's voice trailed off and she reached for Miriam's hand. Once they connected, they seemed to draw strength from each other, becoming whole with their touch. Not that he understood sensate culture. "No, you're right. We have to get out of here. This feels too . . . big."

"Like someone engineered this chaos for their advantage," Ishant said.

"A lot of someones taking advantage of the moment," Miriam said.

The trio walked for an hour, skulking through the streets, avoiding the police. A link alert throbbed his cybernetic arm. He projected the encrypted holovid. Newslinks reported stories identifying the operative Matata Okoro—former head of security at the Muungano embassy—as a person of interest. Described as a disgraced agent looking to redeem himself. A story shaped by the Ministry of Advanced Narrative Design to track all too well.

Teddy Harrison issued a statement. "I never want us to forget my husband's legacy and I vow to continue the work he started. First Muungano and now O.E. have suffered critical losses of their leaders. But we will not fall. We will unite to defend ourselves against those who think us weakened. They will see our resolve. Our righteous resolve!"

"Shit," Ishant said. "There's no such thing as coincidence. The Universe isn't that lazy. Not only is she mimicking Maulana's words, but she's positioning herself to be the next VOP."

"She does have an impressive list of credentials." Happy to distract herself with the normalcy of her duties, Akilah displayed her file. "She has been a member of the LISC International Board of Directors since 2110 and chair of its Audit Committee since 2112. She previously served as the chair of LISC Corps, and various local advisory committees. Before officially joining LISC, she was the executive vice president at VesMet International Bank, with leadership roles in community affairs and risk management."

"She made a point of labeling Matata a rogue agent," Ishant said.

"Important for future negotiations but knowing the average person will only remember the words 'Muungano operative,'" Miriam said.

Akilah beamed with sudden pride, leaned forward, and kissed her. They held each other, each reassuring the other of their presence before Akilah turned back to him. "What's the next move?"

"We have to get off-planet." Ishant worried about keeping his cover story intact. He was still believed to be a well-connected, if former, Muungano member. He knew how to move people, information, and material through the system without suspicion. "I'm due to meet my contacts at the embassy. They should be able to take you off-world as a matter of state."

"Hope they've got room for us all."

"Let's hope." Ishant scanned the streets. "In the meantime, we need to lie low."

*

The Golden Hills neighborhood of Indianapolis was a domed community. Its residents couldn't afford to move to Mars, but their neighborhood association could install the transparent shielding to block dangerous levels of UV. They filtered their own air and water, establishing a self-sufficient bubble for their citizens. In the shadow of that neighborhood, on the other side of a single bisecting street, was a neighborhood suffering from the worst effects of global reshaping. A neighborhood whose residents once named it the Land, now a tale of broken streetlights, cracked pavements, and uncollected trash. A surveillance drone patrolled overhead. Ishant pressed against a house—with Akilah and Miriam imitating his movement—until it passed. Residents of the Land walked around with older-model rebreathers, masks that covered the nose and face, conspicuously marking them as poor. Ishant yanked a sheet of plywood from an abandoned house. Ushering them inside, he guarded a window to keep an eye on the sidewalk. He handed Miriam a site-to-site sigil.

"Mom, I'm fine." Cradling her head in her hand, Miriam kept the exasperation out of her voice. Her face a portrait of regret of making even an encrypted link to her mother.

"I'm watching the news," the disembodied voice said, not broadcast as a holovid.

"Yes, yes, things are chaotic."

"Are you okay?"

"Yes, Mom. I already said . . ." Miriam threw her hands in the air. "They have me running around like crazy. There's a lot I have to do and I might not get a chance to reach out to you for a while."

"This is why I didn't want you working down there. The city is not safe for . . ."

"I have to go, Mom. I love you." Miriam couldn't quite meet Akilah's eyes, shaking her head in acknowledgment of a conversation they'd had too many times over the years. "I wanted to hear her voice again. Let her know I was all right. Say goodbye."

"It's not goodbye." Akilah rubbed her back in reassurance.

Ishant shifted to get a better view and allow them a measure of privacy. The terrible echo of gunfire grew louder. Darker shapes pressed against the dark sky as larger drones—obviously military-grade—flew surveillance. Weapons fire trilled from the north.

"What's going on?" Akilah reacted to the concern on his face.

"There are reports of ARM trying to lynch somebody. Muungano security intervened. . . ." His voice trailed off.

"That's good, right?" Miriam asked.

"No," Akilah said. "That's a treaty violation. Operating outside of their sovereign soil."

"That's the equivalent of a declaration of hostilities," Ishant said. "Justifying ARM to organize and mobilize. We have to hurry."

A peculiar whistle sounded, a signal for concerted movement. A truck full of ARM insurgents skidded to a stop at the end of the block. They hopped out, some wearing red bandanas as their mouth covering. The rest completely unmasked. They brandished rifles and torches. The ARM patrols stopped at a house. Their leader banged on the door three times. Without giving the occupants time to respond, they kicked in the door. A warning shot—Ishant hoped it was a warning shot; terrified screams followed. The hunt for Matata, the "Muungano operative," became all the official license they needed to do what they wanted. ARM soldiers dragged the family out of their homes and lined them up on the sidewalks. They weren't even allowed to put on shoes. The rest of the ARM unit ransacked the house. After a few minutes, they released the family by shooting at their heels to clear the area. They ran them through the streets, heading them.

"We need to go." Ishant headed toward the rear door. Scanning the yard, he skulked to the back fence and hopped it. They walked deeper into the Land until they emerged along the edge of a tributary of the White River. Ishant felt like his story had come full circle.

The Muungano embassy had passages opening at the river's edge. Ishant wasn't really concerned about the lack of police activity nearby. Muungano, besides being sovereign territory, had a visible HOVA unit as its security. A Saqqara took off from the embassy port. The three of them could hide for a while within the compound. At the embassy checkpoint, a HOVA contingent stopped them.

"State your business," the gbeto said.

"Refugees. Seeking asylum," Ishant said.

The HOVA gbeto gave them a once-over. "We've invoked wartime protocols. We can't accept refugees. Especially those who were . . ."

". . . obroni. I know the order. Check my credentials. We may be an exception." His Niyabinghi credentials, though it came up as a LISC emissary in good standing, granted him access. Akilah's filed from her previous stint as a LISC Corps member popped up alongside her scan. Miriam's record as a LISC member verified her.

"Okay, I'll escort you in."

"The Legacy of Alexandria?"

"Yes, it's our way station at the moment."

"I need you to deliver this sigil message." Ishant slipped her his encrypted commlink. It contained his report for Lebna.

"I'm not your—"

"Nanny fe Queen."

At the words, the gbeto took the sigil. She didn't nod, but her eyes acknowledged his work for the Niyabinghi. "I'll see what I can do."

They veered deeper into the embassy. Its thick walls didn't allow him to properly assess their situation. He couldn't access situation reports without blowing his cover. He had to move along like any other refugee within the space, with no way of knowing what was happening, or who was approaching or how many. Or the nature of their threat.

"Jaha, we're here," he said into his site-to-site commlink. The whine of a sine wave interfered with his signal. He feared ARM jamming him, not knowing how much of his message got through. Noises approached, shouts and angry curses preceded the pounding on the doors. He hated being so deep within the embassy's walls. So close to what was happening, not close enough to do anything about it.

"Wait here." The gbeto dropped them at an empty room.

"My message?" Ishant asked.

"My top priority. You'll be safe here." The gbeto left.

Ishant counted to ten, then dashed to his old office. He rummaged through his area, grabbing anything he thought might be useful. Including pehla sticks. He glanced outside. Smoke billowed from the opposite side of the compound. The surrounding homes and businesses raided. Some set aflame. He jacked into his former workstation. Akilah followed him in. "Go back. Lock the door."

"What's the matter?" Akilah asked.

"Security reports the crowds growing. They're ordering the complete evacuation of the embassy. They're shutting it down. They're Saqqara-lifting everyone within its walls to the Belts. News of the lift is leaking out along some linknets. ARM isn't happy."

"Reports are coming in," Akilah said. "ARM is storming the embassy."

The west front had been breached. Internal link notices blared, alerts to movement into the embassy. Almost no security remained in the building. Glass broke, the reinforced windowpanes popped. People scurried about in the night.

"We can't stay here. We're going to have to make it to a port. Or at least higher ground if we want to be airlifted out."

Fueled by shock, adrenaline rushing through his system like a runaway train, Ishant crept down a long corridor. The lights rendered useless, only the night sounds of an old building settling accompanying him. Structural integrity had been compromised. The embassy wasn't so big, but in the gloom of shadows, an entire squad could hide right in front of him. A strange deep hum, the bass chord vibration that preceded a tornado warning reverberated through his sabhu. The Legacy of Alexandria preserved with so much care, having survived floods, tornadoes, blizzards, and most of the other elements of global climate reshaping. The door bulged, a huge weight pressed against it from the other side. Akilah crawled toward the opening in the wall. She slammed the door behind her. Scrunching down as far as she could, she screamed to the floorboards. Miriam covered her head, her hands shielding them as best she could. It buckled. The ceiling collapsed on him. Covering his head, he waited for the shifting mass to end its undulation. The cave-in cut him off from Akilah and Miriam. He didn't know how many hostiles might patrol the maze of offices and workspaces. He hoped they made it to the safe room before this became a hunt-and-kill operation. A main underneath him exploded. Ishant relived the night of the embassy bombing and . . .

. . . *the horrendous noise. The concussive force threw him against the wall. He dropped to his knees, coughing, unable to catch a full breath. But he knew that he was still alive. Dust clotted his nose, the taste of plaster caked his tongue. Craning his head to either side, he checked to see how much of him could move. If he moved carefully, he could wriggle his arm enough to possibly free it. Debris wedged him in pretty good. He prayed that sweat, not blood, trickled along his back and arms. Despite his mind's pleas to stay calm, Ishant started to hyperventilate. His lungs pulled in more dust. A familiar pain shuddered down into where his cybernetic arm extended. A swell of panic filled his chest. He closed his eyes for a few moments, if only to keep the sense of claustrophobia from completely overwhelming him, leaving him paralyzed. In the dark.*

Alone.

Though not completely alone. Muffled cries and sobs, not from a distance, but from the nearby wounded. Feet brushed against him, hands reached out, desperate to grab somebody if only to hold on to them to not die alone. He stretched out wildly, fearing he, too, might suffocate in this terrible, close darkness. Disoriented, Ishant waited for the surge of courage that he thought would accompany the rush of adrenaline threatening to choke him. His mouth and throat constricted with their terrible dryness. The fluttering of his heart and the tightness about the chest had a name: panic.

Pushing against the crevice of debris that entombed him, Ishant inched forward. Structural fibers and mesh pulled free in the collapse, scraping against him as he crawled. With each movement forward, the clutter lurched and pitched, the embassy itself seeking to keep him in its embrace. Contorting his body, he rolled onto his side, attempting to wriggle through. His not-quite-crawl aborted when he entered a space far too narrow to squeeze through. A tangle of debris threatened to pin him. Gray skeins of dirt mixed with tears blurred his vision. He blindly pried at the opening. Between heaving gulps of air, his heart flailed inside his chest. He clawed with the desperation of a man entombed within his coffin. The pressure of panic pulsed from behind his eyes. The night itself closed in on him and squeezed his lungs with each breath. Pressed him. Trapped him. A . . .

. . . a hardy shove freed the jammed furniture propping up more things. A ghostly light caught the dance of a thick swirl of dust. A web of conduits dangled from the ceiling, pulled free of the struts by the toppled shelves. He prayed that the light led to freedom and an end to this madness. His hand grabbed for purchase as he dragged himself through.

The HOVA had withdrawn under orders to get all remaining personnel to the evacuation sites. The distinct pop of specially made glass from the reinforced windows being smashed dragged him back into the moment. ARM forces continued to arrive. They occupied the corner, already fanning out in preparation for siege. They were on the hunt, their faces a series of contortions, twisted in the throes of anger. The lack of resistance emboldened them. The people caught up in their contagion of violence, storming through the building, ripped out pieces, smashed anything they could.

A low buzzing came from outside the window. Ishant visored his hand over his eyes.

Drones gathered like a dark cloud of black birds preparing to swoop down through the night. High-pitched trilling, its frenetic click-click-click chirps, drowned out all other sound. This was it. The cover needed for their final assault. The wall of the drones as they dove caused a pantomime of cheers. The terrible screech cut through the night. Ishant braced for their strafing run. The drones fluttered past him. The ARM soldiers' cheers transformed into horror. The drones targeted them. The whirring of the flying insect-like drones slammed into the militia members with the force of a hurricane. Their mechanical bodies detonated, their carapaces exploding into shrapnel and ripping through the men. The ARM assault force was distracted by the hundreds of thousands of nanobots that scurried across their unarmored flesh. The drones struck the roof, a hailstorm of metal-tinged chitinous bodies scurrying down the transparent partition. Grenades landed throughout the street. Billows of light and smoke sowed further confusion and occluded the next wave of drones. Through the bilious smoke, a man sauntered toward them.

Ishant wriggled to the nearest workstation. Jacking in, he scrolled through subroutines and overrides until he reached the protocols for the power grid. Cutting the power, he plunged the building into darkness. A flood of drones scampered into the room, escorting Matata. He protected two figures. Splattered bits of nanobots hung from Akilah's hair. As she stepped aside, Miriam struggled to prop herself up on her elbows.

"You lose something?" Matata asked.

"They're with me," Ishant said.

"You're okay." Akilah steadied him, unable to hide the sense of relief in her voice. The flooring buckled with the reverberations of artillery fire.

Ishant attempted a half-smile, though it probably came across as a wince. "You, too. How bad is it?"

"She took a bad hit, but her breathing is regular."

"I'm fine. You worry too much," Miriam said.

"You were unconscious for a minute."

"A long blink. I'm fine." Miriam coughed.

"We need to get out of here," Ishant said.

"My drones are giving those ARM nuts something to think about. But we all need to get out of here." Matata studied the scene.

"I thought you—"

"Never made it close to downtown. Despite what the newslink broadcast, the 'Muungano security' that stopped the lynching was me. LISC propaganda in full effect," Matata said.

"It will still be spun as a Muungano act of aggression," Ishant said.

"I'm ready for war," Matata said. "It was inevitable."

ARM insurgents rushed into the hallway. Matata rolled, spinning to a kneeling shooter's position. His talon jerked with its rapid fire. He pointed up and they began to make their way toward the roof.

A tinkle of metal echoed. Tiny spindles emerged from the air vents. Their jagged bodies shredded the walls. One or two insect drones tested the new avenue of entry before hundreds of bodies clambered through. They surged toward the next hallway. The drones cascaded in a wave formation, slamming into the armed insurgents. The insectoid bodies jammed the doors open and poured through the opening. When the militia members tried to smash them, they issued a thick acidic mucus, burning their hands. If anyone dared to scream, some of the drones scrambled into their mouths.

The drones enveloped the group of ARM militia. Ravenous mouth parts stripped their clothing like scythes in a wheat field. The column of insects moved on, pouring from the nearby offices. The drones landed on people, burrowing into their clothes, striking any exposed skin. Hands swatted madly trying to block them. ARM members yanked their shirts over their heads to cover their mouths and eyes. Crushing drones under heel as they fled. A man pounded against a window, soundlessly crying for help. Drone bodies covered the back window and the front. He collapsed under the weight of them. Crawling over hands, buzzing in ears, driving the militia members out of the building.

They cleared the entrance to the roof.

"This was what I had prepared for downtown." Matata peered over the roof's edge.

"This does not reassure me," Ishant said.

"Some friends intercepted me." Matata upticked his chin toward he action on the ground.

Caravans of trucks screeched to a halt, surrounding the ARM vehicles. People hopped out before their trucks slowed. The Deacons arrived. ARM members tumbled onto the ground and concealed themselves, providing cover fire to allow their mob to flee. Standing water turned brown with crushed insect drones. The Deacons marched in relentless assault to set up a new perimeter, further scattering the militia.

"We won't have long until ARM regroups," Matata said.

"Or send word that you're here," Ishant said.

"They don't need evidence that I'm here. That will be the story once the bombs have dropped and no one remains to contradict them." Matata finished his sweep of the landing bay. Punching in a set of codes, he looked to the dark cloud smothering the sky. Lights, bright enough to force them to shield their eyes, cut through the cloud cover; the clouds roiled back to reveal a landing ship.

Extending its wings, it looked like a shadowed ladybug gliding down. It floated several meters over the roof. A column of HOVA gbeto leapt from it. They spread across the roof like honey across a smooth surface. When the ship landed, its bay doors opened. Three people exited the craft. The first two he didn't recognize. Then there was someone who looked like the Deacons' idea of a bargain-basement HOVA. Bayard he knew, despite the casualness of his attire. The last one coming into view made his heart leap.

Jaha.

"Jaha? I . . ." Ishant rushed to her, having not seen her since she ordered him to Oyigiyigi and he joined the Niyabinghi. There was so much to tell her. So much he wanted her to see, how he'd grown. Wanting her to be proud of him.

"Sweetheart, can we do this later," Jaha's voice cut through. "We got drones incoming. The HOVA have evacuated everyone else. It's just us left. Seal the scene!"

Ishant stationed himself next to her for a long time, comforted by her simple presence. Not liking the look of their defensive line, she started shouting new deployment instructions. Jaha barked a few more orders, her eyes blazing trails for them to follow. Determined to remain hard and unflinching in the face of chaos. Glancing at him from the side, she dropped her façade for a moment and rocked into him. Just enough to bump his shoulders.

The remaining column of the HOVA unit skulked into the building, securing the scene. The gbeto looked so young, so battered, so haunted. An expression of loss and anger eclipsed their faces. Caught up in circumstances beyond their control and life-changing. History-altering. And it was only the beginning of their journey. The roof had been secured. Emergency medics tended to Akilah's and Miriam's injuries.

"Things are going to shit fast," Ishant said. "We'll need to do a formal debrief as soon as possible."

"We'll have to split up, regroup later," Jaha concurred. "What about him?"

A contingent of gbeto escorted Matata.

"He's with us. I'll explain later." Ishant pointed to Akilah and Miriam. "We need to get these two to the Dreaming City."

"Take my ship." Matata summoned his Saqqara, a modified glider-type drop ship, except its nose retained its pyramidal shape. "Sorry if this steps on your Muungano sense of agency. . . ."

"The chicken that causes the most trouble gets cooked," Jaha said.

"I want to clear my name. I'm volunteering to stay to continue the organizing work of the Deacons. Here on O.E. On my terms, not Muungano's," Matata said.

"That's why you'll always fall short. It's always about you." Jaha sucked her teeth.

"It's okay. I'll fill you in later," Ishant said.

"You sure?"

Ishant examined his emi. "Yeah."

"Well, I trust you." Jaha clicked, her words untranslatable.

"I'll stay with him." The Energy held his arm out. "Ensuring the job gets done. We don't abandon any of our people."

Matata hesitated, studying The Energy's arm as it hung in the air, before clasping it. "We're all on a journey."

"Everyone needs to head out. The Energy, check in with the Deacons. Ladies, we'll drop you off at the Dreaming City." Jaha turned to Ishant and Bayard. "Let's go get Wachiru."

25

AMACHI ADISA
Mars—The Badlands

Final Lesson

The darkness yawns before you, foreboding yet it claws at you with a sense of desperation. A telltale draft whisks down the corridor of light, catching you in its torrent. Images dance so far away, a distant memory, the stories that form you. They coalesce into a scene that rushes toward you with the urgency of terror. The large window glows ethereal white, catching the escaping moonlight. You freeze at the sight. A man impales Nehanda on the tip of his sword.

The Tigari.

"Nehanda!" you call out. You're not expecting to hear her voice, but you long to hear her voice again.

The Tigari whirls toward you. You catch enough of a glimpse of him to note his surprise at your entrance. He lowers his sword to allow Nehanda to slide free of it. Her limp body puddles at his feet. You focus so intently on her form, you barely notice the furtive movement of his free hand reaching for an object at his waist. The whip issues a deadly whistle, its tip exploding the cave wall above your head, raining down a scree of rock. You snatch your chakram, slicing the air, driving him backward. Your emi searches for a connection. It latches onto the bowl of water behind him. You send a spear of water that pierces his side. His blade clatters to the floor. Pushing against the wall, he scrambles backward, clutching his side. He disappears into the shadows. No longer sensing his presence, you switch your chakram back to your right hand and creep away from the residual glow of the odede in a tactical retreat. Not taking your eyes from the shadows he hid in. Winding around to your left, you keep your back against the wall. Side-stepping along it, you steady yourself. Careful not to make a sound. Checking around you, extending your emi.

Nehanda whimpers and chokes in half breaths. Still alive. Blood pumps from her chest. Its gushes ebb with the slowing of her heartbeat.

"You're hurt." You rush to her side and slap your hands over the wound. The hairs along your arms rise taut, caught in their own electric current.

"Hush, child. There is a natural order to things. This is how things should be. I have spent the last of my energies keeping our enemies at bay." Nehanda coughs.

"You can't go. I . . ." Cradling her in your lap, you wonder if there must be some sort of healing spell.

"What needs to be said is known." Nehanda's voice drifts into something dreamy. Her eyes grow faraway, studying a distant tunnel.

You strain your ears for any sound of pursuit. No footfalls. No scrape of movement, but this isn't an old house with creaking floorboards. Yet something stirs behind you.

Scooping Nehanda into your arms, you make your way to the chute behind the nook carved out as a heart used for venting the cook fire. Slinging her arm behind your neck, you adjust her weight and begin to climb. Were the Tigari to pursue you here, the close quarters would limit his ability to do much more than clamber after you.

Nehanda's breathing slows. Her heartbeats weaken, a waning trickle of the surging river you once knew. You aren't ready for her to leave you. You can't do this on your own.

Sluggish with worry for her, you will your limbs to finish the climb. You emerge into one of the outcrops of stone that ring the Tharsis bulge. You lay Nehanda along the floor of the clearing.

"As I was chosen, now I choose you. You have a natural bent for the old ways. It's in you. Xola had the mind for it. Maulana has the will to use it. But you have the eyes to truly see." Her hand twitches. You wrap yours around it.

Not knowing at all what to say, you stare at your great-aunt. A wave of emotion chokes you. Everything from anger to curiosity, all at the same time. Before you get a chance to utter anything else, Nehanda's head lolls to the side. Your chest hitches, threatening to implode. Your voice filled with fury and sorrow. "Nehanda?"

She doesn't answer. Her chest still, you know her spirit has joined her ancestors.

You are alone. Again.

Everyone who claims to love you leaves you. You begin the familiar script, waiting for the inner chorus of voices to join in. The ones which whisper about how you aren't worth loving. The ones which detail your faults and inadequacies. But they don't arrive. The ache of her death is real. The pain of loss is real, especially piled with so much of late. But you are . . . whole.

You remove Nehanda's necklace and slip it on. It crawls up your neck until its rings encase all of it. You start to fashion a copy of her suit. Your outfit shifts into a black bodysuit, though an open skirt flares from your waist. Your collar forms a design that echoes your chakram along your breastplate. The lightness of a phase suit without the heavy harness. Your boots little more than a thin veneer allowing your feet to feel the contours of the ground beneath you. You place her in repose, a state of waiting because you have unfinished business.

The Tigari cannot hide from you. Not today.

As you march off to cross the desert, your emi screams, a wildfire in search of him. You cannot read the dirt in order to track him. Not that it would matter, if he has found a way to exploit tesseract folds while on the move. Your emi and your entire sabhu work in sync. Out of time. You feel yourself—you will yourself—out of the moment into the future, both present and absent at the same time. Reaching out. Probing. You aren't alone. You touch his mind. At first you don't realize you've made the connection. Somewhere in the black void deep within the cavern, the Tigari lurks. You are in danger. Yet you now know how he thinks. You can visualize how he moves. Making connections, intuitive leaps, anticipating his next attack. Your focus is so intense, you no longer require your eyes to move. He senses you, though not quite the way the rabbit catches the upwind scent of the fox. His mind closes like a well-oiled trap. He casts spells, wards of sealing to shield him from you. To throw you out of his mind. This use of emi is new to you. However, you have his spiritual scent, your emi to his.

Visualizing your surroundings, you see him in your mind's eye, and through your emi. Your heart beats with his, you feel what he feels. The current of wind along his skin. The claustrophobic enclosure he sought shelter in.

He bolts from his hole.

Scrambling up rocky crags, you stalk your prey. You run. Swiftly, you bound across the desert floor. When the Tigari climbs into a rocky alcove, you angle off, driving him back toward the sun. You feel the harsh rays beating down on him. He exists as a herd of one, like a single antelope. Scattering and re-forming, breaking from the pack though swerving. You cannot explain how you perceive him in this moment. Only that it takes all of you. Consumes all of you.

He drops to the ground, attempting to flip the hunt. Crawling along his belly, he hopes to slink into scope weapon range. Perhaps take you out by sniper fire. No, that is not the way of the Tigari, though you don't know how you know that. Their kill must be close. Personal. You have to stand accused of your crime by them, be judged, and then be executed. That is his weakness.

His heavy breathing fills your ears. He gasps. You feel his desperation. He's wounded. His gait favors his right side. Nehanda buried her claws deep within him. He reels from the lingering effects of her water blasts. The bruises from her kicks. He suffers internal injuries from the crush damage of their battle. As he runs, his wounds open, blood seeping through his armor, making him even easier to hunt. Maybe he hopes to make it back to some bolt-hole. Maybe his masters lurk there. But he's not going to make it.

You recall Nehanda's words. *To run an antelope to death, all you have to do is scare it into a gallop on a hot day.*

The pursuit goes on for over an hour.

You move with a languid grace until you catch up to him. The Tigari staggers. His knees buckle and he crashes face-first into the dirt. His strength remains formidable, drawing on eldritch powers outside of him. Recovering enough to straighten, he turns to face you. Gold frames the Tigari's all-black mask. His eyes reminiscent of buttons, triangles alternate in black and white arranged like teeth. Almost two meters tall, over 120 kilograms, his metallic kanzu soaked with blood. Nehanda's blood. His eyes, dark and unblinking, like twin voids. Not realizing that he is already done. When prey is so focused on the chase, they push themselves beyond their limits. They don't even realize they're past exhausted, unaware that they've reached so far beyond the end of their reserves that their body is about to betray them.

"You are the other one. Her agoze." He doesn't turn to face you.

"Her friend," you say.

"You, too, are fated to die. Your entire Egbe circle dies with you." The Tigari tilts his mask at an odd angle, a marionette aware of his strings about to be cut, but with a last burst left in his limbs.

"You're already done. Don't make me do this." You extend your hand. Your heart becomes yours again. One hundred and twenty beats per minute of fury. You inhale.

He draws his hand forward, revealing a coiled mass of shadow. The object relaxes, unwinding to the ground. He shakes the whip to a serpentine semblance of life. The Tigari flicks his wrist.

You hear the whistle of the whip slice through the air before your mind registers what it means. Your head snaps backward, and the whip cracks just above your left eye. Your emi recoiled you an instant before his wrist moved, but your world still explodes in a kaleidoscope of pain. The night dissolves into a spray of fireworks. Molten lightning courses through your body. Your grip on reality slides away. You almost drop your chakram. Wooziness overwhelms you. Staggering backward, you fight against the blackness. If you pass out, the fight, your life, will end. The shock of the sharp pain runs to your core, a searing wave of nausea that nearly topples you. Dimly you're aware of the warmth trickling into your eye.

The Tigari rushes at you with a speed you didn't expect. He gnashes his teeth at you. The action has the weight and force of a curse behind it. His hooked fingers claw your head. The Tigari's mask blurs his face, the fringe about it making him look like melted wax framed by fur. You cross your chakram across his throat, but he bobs backward, just enough. He snatches your wrist and bends it back. The pain shoots along your arm into your brain as if a bullet creases your skull. You are close enough to hear him utter an incantation. The boulder behind you shatters, the exploding rocks hurtling like shrapnel. He plows his elbow into your stomach. You jab the edge of your chakram into his arm.

"You and your kind are an abomination." His voice drifts down to you, an echo along a distant tunnel. You can't tell if he's speaking out loud or directly into your mind. He moves slowly to the right then to the left in pitying appraisal, as if peering at you from deep within an ambush position.

"We just want to exist in peace."

"I offer you eternal peace." Throwing a short punch, he strikes you in the ribs.

You bring your chakram up, but not soon enough to block his leaping kick. The blow drives you back, slamming you into the rocky crag behind you. For a microsecond, you fear defeat, but by the time the thought registers, your body has already shifted. You crouch into your next attack posture in reflex. Tucking into a roll, you spin to your feet. Taking a step toward him, you falter. Your legs buckle, uncertain and awkward. Pinpricks needle down your left arm. You slam your chakram into his temple, the blow glancing from his face shield. He wraps his arms around you. A pivot of your hip sends the two of you rolling across the sand together.

He flings energy projectiles like daggers drawn from the air. Dodging to the left, you spin away in a pirouette, ducking low to slash him along his hamstring.

He jumps over your clumsy swing. All of your movements feel clumsy and slow. You might not have mastered your magics, but you had mastered fashioning. You carve your emi into shards, each slice channeled into a different focus. You sweep your hand across the sand, spreading your nanobots across it with the same movement. When the Tigari lands, you roll and raise your spread fingers as if you are about to give praise. A series of spikes erupt around him.

Ducking under the barrage of his slashing daggers, you drive a stiffened heel of your palm into his chin, driving his head back. He grabs your hair with a flailing hand and yanks you into a rock. The blow jars you, leaving you uncertain as to whether you still have all of the teeth you were born with. He drives the tip of his blade toward your eye, but you roll—finding strength more in panic than technique—and it lands in the sand beneath you. You draw the nanobots deep into the sand, burrowing toward the Tigari. You parry his next blows with your chakram. A feint, as you close your hands into a fist. Your movements swirl the nanobots and they rise up as a spinning buzz saw of metal and whirring sand.

Your hands itch, a near burning, in search of a lost thing nearby.

The Tigari draws his whip and his blade. Nehanda's blood still dries on it. With the last bit of his ebbing strength, he leaps at you. All of your emi reaches out, an act of desperation. Drawing everything to you to stop him. You etch a circle in the air. The glow cracks the air in between you and the Tigari. An electric filament breaching time and space. The world slows down for you. The aching maw widens, moving at your direction. Its edges harden under your control. You open an odede in front of him. He disappears within its luminous embrace.

The portal snaps shut before he clears its borders. The bottom half of a leg rolls to a stop at your feet. Before you can bend over to examine it, a shadow rears over you.

A cyclone of burning sand engulfs you. A desert storm, sudden and unbidden. Perhaps his last gasp. Your arms shield your head as best you can. You hold on and wait. Sand whips your back, your ears. You buckle under its constant lash.

With no strength left to hold you upright, you tumble over the side of the embankment in a graceless dive. Your arms flail about, attempting to protect you. Slow your fall into the waiting gorge. A terrible pain shoots up your left leg. You grab at anything to find purchase. Your scream follows a dull pop. Your hardscrabble descent ends when you hit the ground. All of your training forgotten as you bounce comically into the air. You can only imagine what your rag-doll body looks like. You land on your left leg again. Something wrenches in it. You roll to a stop against an unmoving stone. Shock grips you; your hands claw about, uncertain and unsteady, searching to anchor you in your still-spinning world. You crawl partway up the slope, the pain in your leg making it all but useless.

Sweat drips down your face. You drag yourself along the ground by your hands and your lacerated elbows, and your left leg bumps against a rocky out-cropping. You stifle a cry. As you hover at the brink of unconsciousness, a fig-ure comes into view. You stagger to your feet, not certain how much fight you have left for another Tigari, but certain you will honor your elders with your attempt. Shunting your right leg into an upright position, you turn to better face your attacker. You are a spider scuttling along on six of its limbs; not dead, but far from the feared predator of the webs. Your breath rasps in an uneasy rhythm.

"Who have we here? You look familiar. Maybe we passed each other in the Dreaming City. But your kind wouldn't remember someone like me." He bends low. His emi does not intend violence. He produces a canteen and offers you water. "My name is Hondo."

Your eyes grow blurry, but you don't need them to see. Your sabhu con-nects to your ancestors. Nehanda is here now. The Ban mu Kyidomhene. Astra Black. Even Xola. Your community, within and without. It is understood now, a belonging on a level so deep within us, it has the clarity of life itself. We peer at him, allowing him to fully see us.

"Our name is Amachi Adisa."

26

STACIA CHIKEKE
The *Cypher*—Planet's Orbit

Stacia stood alone, staring down Yahya and Zenith. Stacia's eyes widened for an instant before she hardened her face again. She fought back a wave of nausea. Disgust. Unable to move. She refused to let tears well in her eyes, refused to give into her building scream, refused to have her expression reveal her pain, as to not allow any of them that satisfaction. She closed her eyes. Her face set in a pained expression. The command deck bristled with tension. Kenya crept around the side of the room, waiting on her opportunity to take both men out. Nadina and Anousheh froze, stiff and awkward, as if caught midburglary, not knowing where to stand. Or with whom.

"Zenith." Stacia balled her hands and took a step toward him.

"O Captain, my Captain." Zenith held up his hands in mock surrender. A smile snaked across his face; he was pleased with the no-win scenario he placed her in.

Patting the air, Yahya stepped between him and Kenya. "Hear him out."

"Yahya?" Her gaze accused him of an unforgivable deception. One that neither could see them walking back from. She had never felt so betrayed. So abandoned. She had supported him. Ride or die. But in the end, it hadn't been enough. She hadn't been enough. "You did this?"

"I'm sorry, Stacia. You left me no choice." Yahya's eyes filled with pleading and lament. He wanted the indulgence of relationship—their history—to buy him a moment. The flash of hope faded when he met Stacia's icy glare. Soon, he studied the ground.

Playing back scenes of their life, she imagined the gaps she missed. The distance. Working late, all the time. Her prioritization of duty over their time together. The mission became more important than their relationship. The conversations not had. The missed chances. The tapestry of her world unraveled along invisible seams. She would not let this man, either of them, destroy her. Her emotions roiled in waves. Hurt, confused, shocked, angry. Anger she could work with.

"Let me explain," Yahya said.

"I don't want to hear an explanation. I have all the answers I need." The door of her heart slammed shut, emergency bulkheads sealing off vulnerable parts of her. Stacia sucked her teeth. "Before I have the trash swept from my command deck, tell me what do you want?"

"The same thing your people want: to go home," Zenith said.

"We're all here because of you."

"No, we're here because of your ego. Your narcissism. From the beginning, I've told them the truth. All I needed was to get to the location I gave you and we could find the cure and get home."

"You never gave me the real location."

"I gave it to you." Zenith strode the command deck, assuming full control of his stage. "Your captain likes to believe that she kept me here as a part of her plan. That's the folly of her ego. A person of my rank within LISC does not end up on this level of mission by accident. You just failed to admit to your people that you failed to get us to the right time. We are millions of years off course. Millions. Unless you have a plan involving taking the long way around to get us to the right time and space . . ."

Stacia locked gazes with each member on her command deck, the strength of her will holding them in place. Knowing that she was slowly losing their faith in her, a fistful of hourglass sand slipping through her fingers. "We're working on it."

"We. We who? This is what I mean. You and your secrets. Because most of the crew had no idea of the nature of their dilemma, much less the fact that you were 'working on it.' I ask you, Captain, tell us all—in the Muungano way of having as many witnesses as possible to a conversation—have you been in contact with any representative from the Interstellar Alliance? Have they co-opted you? Are you compromised, Captain?"

"I'm not even going to dignify that. Not from a man who, as a means to an end, dangled the life of my son—our son, Yahya—as both stick and carrot. Is this what things have come to? What you believe about me?"

"I don't know what to believe anymore. I don't know what is true anymore." Yahya backed half a step away from her.

"I never heard a 'no' in there, Captain." Zenith was obviously enjoying himself, practically spraining several muscles to avoid smiling. "Only more of you placing your personal life above the lives of the crew. Tell me, is this the new lesson of what Muungano means when it talks about community?"

Kenya's hand tensed, by her expression, longing to draw a weapon and commence knocking heads into compliance. A to-do list beginning with Zenith and Yahya, but Paki would probably catch hands in a bonus round of ass whuppings.

"We're past that. You can surrender and return to your cell," Stacia said. "Yahya, you can put an end to this charade or I will."

"We . . ." Yahya hesitated before committing to his course. ". . . need a leader who will preserve our way of life. Who prioritizes us, who we are and who we're meant to be."

"That's *him* talking. That's fear talking."

"We *are* afraid, you're just too blind to see it."

"You are not the leader we need right now," Zenith said.

"And who is? You?" Stacia asked.

"I would not presume—especially as an . . . obroni—to attempt to lead. But I'm glad you demonstrated exactly who you are—the Stacia that I've always known—in front of everyone. When you perceive a potential threat to your agenda, you lock them away, or cast them out. Yahya. Me. Tell me you haven't 'lost' Paki again. No, I wouldn't dare. But I would follow Nadina."

Zenith was canny. He stood no shot of leading her crew, and Yahya was too compromised by his relationship with her. Paki would be the logical choice, but by Zenith's calculations, he was too great an uncertainty. Nadina, already blinded by disillusion, wanted to end all of this.

"What?" Stacia didn't bother to disguise her disgust. Nadina sat up straighter.

"Your hesitancy betrays you. Even now, you can't imagine she has what it takes to lead. You never believed in her. Never thought she had what it takes to bring people together."

"Wait, that's not true." Stacia pleaded with her eyes, but it was too late. She'd walked into his trap. This was what he wanted, not just to undermine her but to divide her crew. First Yahya, then Nadina. Exploit the fractures in their relationships to leverage her isolation. Because she couldn't figure out how to heal what they had, she'd lost them. The final wisps of faith the crew had in her snuffed out. She was no longer their voice. Nadina turned away from her.

Smiling, Zenith addressed the rest of the crew. "Many of you don't know me, just the distorted version of me presented by your captain. So I make you this offer: turn from your captain and follow Nadina. I trust her to bring us home. She is our future. We will accomplish all of this, together."

"Stacia, we need you to step aside." Yahya took her by the arm. Too knowing, too intimate a gesture for where they were now. Stacia yanked her arm free. Mabry and Silva flanked her. They moved neither to take her into custody nor to hold the rest of the crew at bay. They waited, drawing all eyes to them, with the crew waiting to see what they decided their next move would be. Silva pivoted. A pehla stick was unholstered along her hip. Whether it was an invitation or opportunity, Stacia grabbed it. Spinning, she ducked, dropping to the ground in a mad scamper to the door. Yahya blocked her way. Springing up, she kneed him in his belly, doubling him over. She rolled across his back to clear space between her and the rest of the crew. Charged pehla stick swinging, she dodged to her left and kicked him in the back of his knee. Kenya rushed toward her. Stacia braced for an attack. Kenya spun, ready to watch her back.

"I'll buy you some time," Kenya said.

"I can't ask that of you."

"I'm not leaving your side any more than you would leave mine." Kenya tapped her helmet with her pehla stick. "You need to regroup."

Stacia ran from the command deck. Running—she knew how to do that well. That and cutting people out of her life. She thought they were a team. They had their problems, but they were fundamentally on the same page. Carving out that piece of herself that contained Yahya, she placed him on the untended shelf in her heart next to Amachi. The people who left her.

Dashing down the hallway, she had to make it to the secondary command deck, the backup CIC space used when the main command deck had been compromised. She skittered past crew members, gauging their response to see if they'd try to apprehend her. She had no idea who was still with her or who had bought into Zenith's lies. They eyed her with a mix of pity and shock, the closest thing to support she had in the moment. If she stayed in the hallways it was only a matter of time before Zenith supporters cut her off and detained her.

She slipped into an isocrawl. Bek loved these things as if they were his own personal hidey-holes. She didn't know how much time he spent in them, not that she ever blamed him. Connecting the entire ship, they also took a person out of view of everyone, rendering them both alone yet still somehow connected. On hands and knees, she crept along the shaft. The walls pressed in on her, the air especially close so far away from the Green Zone. She found it difficult to catch her breath. A hiccupping hitch swelled in her chest. She refused to give in to the panic of tears. She crawled until she reached Maya's central core. The port to the command deck required her personal code.

"Maya are you still with me?"

<Yes. For now.>

"Understood." It wasn't a threat. For her command authority to be overridden, a new captain would not only have to be chosen, but accepted by the leadership council. That would require time. "I need command function routed to my location. On the move. Emergency bypass JywanzaS1W."

<Initiated. Command function rerouted to your location.>

She dropped down into the room. The chamber's shielding was like a hall of mirrors. Her image reflected all about her. Stacia dashed to the nearest console. "I need to lock out systems."

<That cannot be done without secondary authorization.>

Stacia pounded the workstation. She couldn't do this alone. She had to risk trusting someone. "Maya, can you give me a site-to-site channel to Paki?"

<Complete.>

"Paki, how close are you?"

"Problems, Captain?" Sarcasm dripped from his voice. He'd obviously kept up with events.

Stacia couldn't afford to rise to his baiting tone. Though she wasn't about to admit, at least to him, that he might have been right. "Are you still with me?"

"I'm still for the *Cypher*. For getting us home. And finding a cure for your son. I have a theoretical model ready."

"We're on it, Mom," a voice in the background shouted.

"Bek?"

"And me," Marguerite yelled. "Let me know if you need backup."

"I will." Stacia smiled. She still had her family. Most of them. "I need you all to initiate whatever you have to as soon as possible. The *Cypher* can't stay here. I . . . can't hold us together any longer."

"Understood," Paki said.

Stacia monitored the shields and deflection arrays. The invisible protoplanet kept them in its hold much the same way Zenith did. The crew was divided. Some out of loyalty to her. Some simply wanting to go home and calling it loyalty to Muungano. Some had simply been twisted about by Zenith and his promises. Even handing herself over to them would not heal the divide. At least so she told herself. She cursed that Zenith found a way to worm his way even into her head. The reinforced glass ceiling above her shattered.

Nadina lowered her head into the room. "This was the only logical place for you to go."

"We don't have to do this." Stacia crouched to a low attack position, a defensive stance.

"Oh, I need to do this." Nadina leapt. As she fell, she hooked her pehla stick into a conduit and swung. She surprised Stacia with a kick to the face. The captain rolled and sprang up. Stacia wiped the thin trickles of blood from her lip. This was not what she wanted. She did not join the ranks of the scientists at Titan to take up arms against her own people. But this wasn't about that. A wound hid behind Nadina's eyes. A deep-seated anger in need of venting. Even if it was her last act as her friend, Stacia would give her that occasion.

Barely avoiding the thrust of Nadina's stick, Stacia grabbed for the handle. She misjudged it by centimeters. The charge flung her to the wall. Nadina followed up with a loose flurry of punches. Nadina barely passed basic combat Forms. Unfocused and undisciplined, she wasn't built for fighting, not at this level. Sloppy and wide, Stacia parried the initial blows. As captain, her combat training was surpassed only by specialists like Kenya. But this wasn't about winning the fight. It was about her anger.

Stacia allowed Nadina to land a few punches. And a kick. She caught the next punch, however, and flung her hand back at her. "That's enough, Nadina. You've made your point. I don't want to fight you."

"That's too bad. I want to fight you." Nadina charged her.

With a slight sigh, Stacia elbowed her in the neck. Hooking her pehla behind her onetime friend's hand, she tugged Nadina toward the ground as she drove her knee up into her face. Sprawled on the floor, Nadina writhed, barely conscious.

"I. Don't. Have. Time. For. Your. Shit," Stacia said. "Next time, use your words. What we have to work through can wait. For now. Punching it out is so . . ."

"Yo?" Nadina staggered to her feet.

"Exhausting. Is it out of your system, or do we have to go another round?"

A massive gravimetric wave struck the ship with so much force, Stacia tumbled against the wall. The lights blinked out. All the *Cypher*'s systems powered down. A terrible silence filled the ship, as if it held its breath. Power fluttered back in spurts. Stacia accessed vidfeeds throughout the ship. The crew stared up, an existential pause awaiting the inevitable. Making their peace with the Universe. Zenith cowered in a corner.

Anousheh scrambled back to her station. "We can't hold position, our orbit is beginning to decay."

"We can't take another hit like that," Kenya yelled.

Stacia projected her holoimage into the command deck. The deck went quiet and everyone turned to her. She added Paki's workstation holoimage to hers. "Paki, what do you have for us?"

"We need to avoid any more waves like that." He frantically worked at his station. "If we can get up to optimal power levels, we can attempt to jump."

"Jump where?" Yahya demanded.

"Home." Stacia let the word hang in the air between them. "If you'd trusted me, we could've gotten there together. How long do we need to give you, Paki?"

"Ten minutes."

"Let's make that happen." She met the eyes of each member of her command deck. "Can we work together one last time for ten fucking minutes?"

Everyone scrambled to their stations. Stacia took her seat for a command performance. She unlocked her vintage clavioline by setting her command sphere into the keyboards at her station. Closing her eyes, she raised her hands as if in prayer. Whenever she prepared to play, she took a moment to gather herself, to slide fully into the moment. With an improvised performance, she never knew what she might bring forth. Or how. Each new song was a blank page full of infinite possibilities.

"The atoms that make up the human body could be traced back to the stars." Stacia intoned the words with the near reverent whisper of a prayer. Calling on the one thing she truly believed in. Barely aware she spoke the words out loud, much less if she meant them for her or Nadina or both; but she needed to set the intentionality of the music. "Everything is connected. The stars have the ingredients for life itself. The universe is in us and we are in the universe."

One of Stacia's gifts was being able to see music as color. She tapped the first few notes without time to warm up. A nauseous shade of gray filling her mind. That would not be the tenor of this journey. Music was a sound waveform that evolved in time. It had structure. Harmony. And when it resolved, it was transcendent. Stacia began with her motif, the captain's prerogative. She could only trust in the process, her training, her creative instincts, to find her way there. To play her way into the song. To find the familiar, renewing stir of the music.

Progressions of tensions and resolutions, storytelling through wavelength and frequency. She clung to the hope of home. Finding the path of a melody, she allowed it to guide her into verdant shades and tranquil blues, a meadow under a clear sky. The sun setting over a beach view.

Clutching the bamboo frame of her balafon, Nadina joined her.

Her fractal runs formed a smaller piece that mirrored the form of Stacia's larger structure. Expansion was a form of antigravity. Gravity came from bass and drums. Stacia channeled the orbit of Titan in her improvisation. Against her refrain, a balafon solo expanded and spiraled away from their gravity well. With every repetition, the improvisation led to new solos, or permutations of her solo cycle. The melody-of-quantum-field-theory way of connecting the threads of the reality of the song. The subatomic realm knit together by discrete packets, quanta. Slipping quantum symmetries produced forces and particles. Broken symmetry in music structures coming together only as parts resolving into a greater whole.

Sound and music unraveled eternal truths about the universe; improvisation and adaptation with all of its possible uncertainties and outcomes. The energy of the protoplanet, the twin gravities of the black hole and white dwarf. Lights etched the space between them like the outline of a door forming. A tunnel, a golden-hued corridor. When they entered the Orun Gate, they did so by accident. Now they harnessed their energies bound by a driving chorus. Tone and time became hyperspace. Multiphonics become warp drive. The tools to navigate, to unlock, to explore.

"Now!" Stacia commanded Paki.

And the *Cypher* jumped.

27

ANITRA GOUVEI
Nambra—The Abrehot

The armored prefects were walking tanks. A single punch would drop her. The cadre of prefects closed in on her. The nearest one trundled toward her, too confident and too slow in targeting his arm cannon on her.

"Robin, I be in situations." Anitra initiated a site-to-site. "Prepare to drop."

"We'll have pickup in five," Robin said. "Will you be okay for that long?"

"We thank our beloved ancestor, Nathaniel Alexander, for inventing this time-honored weapon in the fight for liberation." Anitra hefted her folding chair.

"Oh no," Robin said.

"The run-up has been initiated, so the done-up must commence. I'll give them a taste of chair jutsu." Any object in Anitra's hands was a perfectly fine weapon choice. The chair was light, constructed with nanobots. "Get you some feel-good even if you don't . . . feel good."

The chair legs caught the prefect in the crease of his chest plate. With the next blow, she hooked the chair around the cannon, wrenching it free. The next prefect parried her lunge. She battered him with the broadside of the chair. Despite the loud whomping echoes, she did little real damage. She swatted them more as a distraction than anything else, drawing their attention away from Chandra.

Ellis dashed straight forward, keeping their body low. They retrieved the dropped arm cannon. The arm cannons were based on previous-generation talons. Designed to be integrated into their mech suits or, if need be, freed for field use outside of the suit. Ellis flipped it over and reprogrammed it for field combat. Their shot caught a guard in the mouth, charring the side of his face.

Bracing against her armor, Anitra brought her knee up to break the prefect's hold before he could fully grab her. Chair in hand, she backflipped, kicking him in the face. She tumbled to her feet. The prefect threw a short chopping punch. She blocked it with the chair. She landed hard, tucking into a roll, bringing the chair up to see who else wanted some. She used the chair as a shield, though it wouldn't survive actual cannon fire. Just trying to buy enough time for her sisters to get into position. Anitra smashed the chair against the closest two soldiers. They staggered back, limbs flailing, their mech suits taking the brunt of the damage. Anitra faced down a cluster of guards preparing to jump up. She ran along the deck and dove behind the lab benches. Anitra let the soldier she'd just punched drop from her grasp. She held up her hand to hold Ellis's fire.

"I know you don't have much field experience with Silent Negro types, but now is an opportunity for field observation. Allow me to explain the nuances of what you are witnessing so you can better appreciate their magnificence." Anitra held her chair at the ready.

A soldier rushed Chandra from the left. A hidden prefect fired from their unseen perch, pinning down Cadgejia and Henam. Ellis fired at the sniper's position, allowing them to scramble for cover. Few had seen Chandra in an actual combat situation. She was a comms prophet, not meant to be in firefights or hand-to-hand combat situations. Though she had the same HOVA genetic modifications as any other gbeto, few understood the ramifications of having a Maya implant, an AI node, grafted into her brain. She was a living transceiver of data, especially combat data.

Without any visible weapon, Chandra marched to meet the armored prefect.

"They are the wrong ones to fuck with." Anitra unfurled the chair and sat down. "Note her approach. It's a 'Who do you think you talking to?' stride. Just so you know, that's not an actual question. Look at her eyes. They say 'I got time today,' which means she's about to clear her schedule for them. They about to catch those hands in Jesus' name."

Chandra moved like a phantom. Spinning, she kicked the soldier charging up on her between the legs. The man paused more in reflexive shock, not remembering his armor. The hesitation was all she needed. Her actions drew the attention of three more prefects, who trundled toward her. With a pivot, she drove him into the center of them. Without looking, she stripped him of his cannon. Reprogramming it with a touch, she targeted the sniper, taking him out with a single shot. She jammed the rifle into the foot of the nearest man and fired three shots.

"See, Ellis, you're learning a valuable lesson. If a Silent Negro type suddenly asks 'What did you just say to me?' the only correct answer is 'Nothing, sorry.'

It's all in the eyes, I'm telling you. Look at them carefully. They say 'You gone learn today,' which means a . . . physical lesson is about to be taught."

Chandra leapt, clearing the two men, but wrapping the last one between her legs. She twisted and flexed midair. His body spasmed and jerked, dead before she landed.

"And that's that on that. If a Silent Negro type says 'Be right back,' you better not be here when she returns."

Chandra dropped and rolled, firing charger blasts into surrounding positions. Soldiers fell from nooks or other sniper nests. Novice Quass gaped in shock, his face spasming so fiercely, he struggled to keep his eyes open. Attempting to unbury himself from the body of one of his fallen comrades that had tumbled onto him. He reached out to grab Chandra by her face. She threw her hand up in a feint that appeared to block his forearm. Instead, she turned in to him, one hand snatching his arm, the other hooking under his shoulder. With him off-balance, she used her weight to drop him to the floor. Kicking her legs out, she allowed her full weight to land on top of him. He grunted, his body reduced to a collapse of limbs, he took the brunt of the fall. She locked his arm and neck in a hold. He spasmed, losing control of his bowels. Plowing his head into the ground, she planted her elbow into his throat. Chandra moved with an unrelenting, brutal efficiency. She drove her stiffened hand under his jaw plate. It jolted his head back. She smashed his visor with the butt of her hand cannon. The sound of his neck bones grinding together sent a sympathetic shiver down her back.

Chandra backed away from the wreckage of bodies. Whatever quip Anitra was about to make dissipated on her lips. Her friend's face was a frieze of sorrow and regret. Leaving carnage and destruction in her wake, she'd become an efficient killing machine. Emphasis on *machine,* judging from the expression on her face. She seemed lost. Partly as if not remembering how she arrived in her location, as if she'd blacked out and woken up after a disastrous party; and partly not knowing who she was anymore. The expression passed in a flash. Back on her business, she led the way.

"Call me Chair Master," Anitra finally said through comms.

<No.>

"Ellis, stay here with our friends. We going to see what he had planned for us."

"But . . . ," Ellis's protest began.

"Robin is on the way to pick us up. We don't want to miss our ride. And we need you to guard our six."

Grabbing the Novice, Anitra ushered him to follow Chandra inside the building most of the prefects had poured out of in case there were any more surprises. The Service of the Order was careful. Setting up their operation in plain sight and yet invisible. A seamless entry into the fabric of Nambra.

At first the entrance looked like a cave wall, with the rough-hewn rock making the building appear carved from a mountain. Succulent weeds grew along its edges. Winding around a bend, the craggy surface gave way to smoother walls. Scarabs etched into corners. The floor a polished stone cool to the touch. The air thickened, still breathable but with greater humidity. The interior walls of the building were covered in intricate carvings made of an amalgamation of metals echoing silver and gold, except much denser. Anitra slowed to take them in, recording the data for later review. Symbols depicted fierce creatures gathered around feasts. Three figures arriving on a barren, gray world. A brocade draped down the wall at the end of the hallway. Its rich woven fabric had designs of a huge tree, its roots stretching deep into the planet, its branches into the heavens. A rumble gurgled within the walls. Chandra tilted her head to the side. She drew the brocade to the side. Extending a finger, she jacked into an unseen port and overrode whatever scanner she encountered. With a smothered hiss of complaint, the wall slid to the side, revealing a mechanical shaft.

Chandra examined the space. A series of bleats and chirps emanated, locks and safeguards disengaged. With a hand flourish, she bade the Novice enter first. Her arm barred Anitra.

<In case I didn't get all of their . . . precautions.>

The Novice glanced about nervously. He punched in additional codes and walked in.

After a few seconds, she allowed the rest of them to enter. When the wall slid back into place, the chamber acted as an air lock. When they stepped out, the hall opened into a large room. Enough comm stations to be a base-camp CIC. Tens of workstations ringed the room. Data streamed continually from holovids, newslinks, and telemetry readings. Security reports, from the vidfeeds of the fallen prefects to satellite defensive grids. Anitra didn't understand much of the equipment, as they were above her pay grade, but from her time stationed on Titan, she recognized a state-of-the-art research facility when she walked into one.

"Sweep the lab," Anitra said.

"We have the right to be out here," Novice Quass protested. "This is our designated mission field."

"I swear, if you say you're on a mission from . . ." Anitra's voice trailed off. Several isolation chambers filled the next corridor. A bank of clean rooms, each with its own isolated air system. Biohazard controls. Gene tanks. A leaden familiarity filled her belly. She remembered the first time she had stepped into a room like this. She had just completed the basic gbeto training, the physical and mental screenings to be accepted into the HOVA. The lab was clean and white, so sterile everyone kept their hands to their sides, afraid to touch anything. The central core reminded her of an altar. The table glowed. "What is this?"

"It's where we receive the Blessed Sacrament." A tenor of pride, bordering on reverence, filled Novice Quass's voice. A supplicant in the throes of ecstasy. "Praise be the blood."

"Chandra?"

<A combination of nanotech mixed with human growth hormone.> Chandra ran her hand along one of the suspension tanks. A body floated in it. A young weusi woman. Tubes inserted into her belly and mouth. Needles periodically jabbed into her for mitochondrial insertion. Other genomic and cellular modifications occurred; for the HOVA this included dual mitochondria to rapidly detoxify reactive oxygen species and other cellular wastes. The procedure that made all HOVA gbeto no longer fully human.

"Through the blood we have life," Novice Quass said. "The Blessed Sacrament allows the body to be repaired and rejuvenated. Never truly aging."

"Only knowing war," Anitra whispered. Whatever this was, it was much farther advanced than the HOVA transition treatments. She tried not to think about how many test subjects the church's science division had expended to perfect their gene therapy. The Service of the Order's personal medical industrial complex. "Why does this feel like . . . Where did you develop this tech?"

"It was stripped from us in the early stages of its development. During the Great Unrest. O.E. declared eminent domain, proprietary state interests. We received word that their scientists advanced it and it was being used in clandestine operations. We were able to reconstruct some of it."

"Clandestine. Joint. Operations?" Anitra steadied herself against the wall. "Shit. Chandra, can you confirm whether this technology was a precursor of or is related to that which was used to create the HOVA."

<Confirmed.> Chandra's voice held a troubled tremor.

"Praise be the blood." Novice Quass beamed at her as if she were a long-lost child.

Anitra blasted him. She'd reduced the cannon's charge down to 1. He'd be all right. The Reapers might not be.

* * *

Three ships locked in formation. The *L.H.S.*, Henam's ship, and now their latest. Epyc Ro's fleet, Chandra-linked, cruising on automatic pilot. Their physical presence would have been too intrusive to the moment, but the Reapers assumed control of the biggest ship. The bridge was a large, circular space with a high, vaulted curved ceiling, with metal ridges along its walls like the exoskeleton of a rib cage. The view ports were vidscreens. In the center of the room was a table made from the same metal ridging the room as well as lining the temple laboratory. The chairs weren't designed for human comfort. Anitra slouched in one, her leg draped over one of the hunches along the seat.

Henam remained on her ship so that the former HOVA could have a measure of privacy to digest what they'd learned. Epyc Ro left a channel open so both she and Cadgejia could hear their deliberations.

They carried their augmentations as badges of service, but the hidden parts of them—from the gbeto to the elders and the architects of Muungano—wrestled with the morality of their decision. Genetic engineering was playing God. Setting them outside the course of natural evolution. No longer on the path of what it meant to be human. Liberation by any means necessary was no excuse. For so long, O.E. framed them as monsters. Abominations. Their transitions portrayed as an act of shame. Looking down on them with tacit hope that their scorn, disdain, and hatred would be soaked up by them and find root in their sabhu. The HOVA still chose to sacrifice themselves for the sake of community. Willing logs placed on the fire of their community's struggle for freedom. To safeguard what Muungano was building.

The HOVA accepted that genetics were not destiny. And their destiny was not in their genetics. They created their own customs and rituals to reclaim the spiritual core of who they were. Though they were still members of the Muungano family, they split off into a separate community. Some might call it a self-imposed exile. They didn't want to be a perpetual reminder of the hard, dark choices required to sustain the dream of Muungano.

"I don't know what to do with this," Anitra said.

"None of us do," Epyc Ro said.

"We had to know this technology didn't occur in a vacuum. Someone had to develop it," Robin said.

"But . . . them? I feel dirty all over." Anitra shifted positions.

"Because the Service of the Order is counter to everything Muungano stands for."

"Do you think the elders know?"

"I . . . don't know. I don't know if I want to know." Robin's voice trailed off. Little more than a whisper by the time she stared out the view port.

Epyc Ro slapped the wall. "Here's what we're not going to do. We're not going to lose track of each other. We're not going to leave the work half-done. We're not going to give even a centimeter of ground. We're not going to give them anything to celebrate. Not today. We have to decide who we are. As long as we are on this side of the Orun Gate, we're Muungano's long-range unit. And we are going to find our way home."

"We sucked at being pirates anyway." Anitra's fingers scrambled across the console. A small red light blinked in warning.

A hole opened up, the kind of energy signature not seen since the Orun Gate. A ship slowly emerged. A giant nose cylinder with two wing units almost like fluttering sails emerged. Several extensions, perhaps eight all told, given how they swirled about as if caught in an ocean current. The appendages unfurled in a halo of eight limbs. The entire structure of the ship undulated like a wave, each limb continued to expand. The alarm blasted. She hoped for a proximity alert, but its blaring insistence meant one thing: battle stations.

"Problem commander: we have a ship entering targeting range," Robin said.

"Where'd they come from?" Epyc Ro asked.

"They just . . . appeared. Emerging from a tesseract fold."

"We've recorded all telemetry scans," Robin said.

<It produced a pulse of Tyson radiation.>

"Tesseract folds. On this scale. We are deep in it," Anitra said. "Maybe they could use that to track them, if we—"

Anitra's words were cut off by the signal broadcasting on all frequencies.

"This is the Templar ship *Piper*. Your vessels are hereby impounded. Prepare to be boarded."

"They aren't big on introductions," Robin said.

"A Templar ship? Those were just rumors. Conspiracy theories about the Service of the Order," Epyc Ro said.

"We have a big-ass ship to port that says otherwise," Anitra said.

"We can't go head-to-head with a battle cruiser," Robin said.

<Hold. Tyson radiation levels are spiking again.>

Another hole began to form. Proximity alarms blared. Gravimetric waves from the wormhole opening buffeted the ship.

"Is it another Templar ship?" Epyc Ro asked.

"One wasn't enough," Anitra said.

"No, whatever it is, its profile is entirely different. A whole new scale," Robin said.

The intricacies of interstellar politics were not Epyc Ro's forte. She already needed a chart in three dimensions to keep track of all of the current players.

<Readings are all over the place. Telemetry is beyond scanning range.>

"The *Piper* is backing off."

"That doesn't make me feel any better. Anyone know what we're dealing with?"

"Ma," Henam said.

"Wait, Henam, did you say something? Your transmission was faint."

No, it wasn't faint. Her voice was reverential. She all but genuflected her words. "Ma is here."

EPILOGUE

MAULANA BUHARI
The Dreaming City

My quarters had become my meditation place. A retreat where I could isolate, as if the purification ritual of Ipebi had been embraced as a rhythm of life. I needed to clear my head, to focus. The Universe, however, conspired to keep me from anything resembling a moment of peace. It was always in conflict, an endless cycle of creating and destroying. Stars exploding and new ones birthed. Nation-states rising and falling, seeking to control resources, life reduced to constant negotiations of enemies and terms. My door signaled.

"We're going to be late." Ezeji's emi tweaked, a mix of enthusiasm and anxiousness. I understood his uneasiness, but I refused to let it drive me. The newslinkage had dubbed First Lady and Secretary of State Teddy Harrison LISC's presumptive VOP. A name both relatable and nonthreatening to the masses, the first salvo in the war of ideas. Reality was whatever we created it to be. They who controlled the minds controlled reality. She had inherited a world awash with a sense of impending doom. With so many unknowns and so much uncertainty about what was next, the present being so taut, she craved a win. Something to launch her administration. She had invited me to a new round of talks. To the public, she painted the picture of wishing to arrange a summit for us to create a path for peace. As if I was to forget her public posturing, the atrocities committed in the name of her restoring security to her streets. Once diplomacy had been exhausted, weapons were deployed, and troops marched to the front lines in the inexorable dance.

"Mzungu will give us fifteen minutes. You have a party that they're at, they're in the driveway waiting fifteen minutes early. At five till, they're walking up to the house." I straightened my vestments. "They operate by a different relationship to time."

"That's why I lie to folks about what time the party starts. Tell them an hour early to get them there on my time." Ezeji plopped into a chair and projected his reports and collated analyses. He scanned linkage reports for the latest news. He was oblivious to how much he'd grown since taking on his new role. Examining reports, cross-referencing the latest updates, forecasting friends. Far from the pyr head he allowed people to believe he was.

"That's one way. For me, the key is to be so good at what you do, to be so essential to the proceedings, that they can't even start the party without you." I stared at my mask of office. "I won't be rushed through our briefing and enter the lion's den unprepared."

Ezeji briefed me on the contingency plans Jaha had drawn up:

-war with O.E. (nearly a hundred possible scenarios)

-war with Mars (tens of scenarios with Mars wanting to expand, colonize the stars)

-the latest technology coming out of Titan

-the possibility of alien incursion (wanting to set up protocols for engagement)

"You know what's happening? Nothing but losses. Got folks running out of LISC so motherfucking fast, they can't stop the bloodletting. All the oldheads."

"Teddy is an electric fence." The final movement of a Collapsing Circle, the secret intelligence code of operating to close off an investigation. LISC's true masters took VOP out using his own security, leaving no leads left to pursue. All that remained was a tidy theory and questions which could never be answered. To my mind, they were regrouping, which meant that something bigger, something likely worse, was coming.

Ezeji leapt to his feet. "We have an override alert coming through."

"What is it?" I waited for Maya to activate an encryption cone, but one never came. Whatever it was, it was broadcasting across all spectrums. Everyone heard it.

"The Oyigiyigi listening station has picked up a . . . beacon." Ezeji's face warped through a gamut of panic. "They're not sure where it's originating from. Deep space. An alien message they're scrambling to translate. A triangulation signal of some sort."

A message had been sent out into the universe, translated throughout in a way everyone intuitively felt down to their core. The kind of summoning signal that attacking forces might use to direct their troops for an assault. Directing them to their target. To Earth.

This changed everything.

✳   ✳

PLANETS OF THE GALACTIC RIM

Darawad—marine civilization

Life-forms resemble octopi with six limbs.

Lei'den—O.E. operatives

Actually the CO/IN claiming to be part of the Interstellar Alliance.

Huzini—designated **Melancholia** by the Lei'den

The moon of CFBDSIR2149 of the AB Doradus Moving Group.

The planet itself is a gas giant, a rogue planet ejected from its system.

Revisio. Floating unicellular things; each strain would be considered an individual.

The Revisio's "resonance" functions as a low-level kind of telepathy.

Derthalen. Long simian arms rippled with burly musculature. Thick brows ridged deep, inset eyes.

When occupied by a Revisio, they become smaller.

Morawi—Amaitjo and the Eciton peoples

Mamerafe, Mother of Nations, the Amaitjo and the Eciton.

"Ma is coming."

Mzisoh—the planet designated Eshu by Muungano

The Mzisoh make no distinction between themselves and their planet.

They appear to be gender fluid, having no sexual identity, per se.

Only once a relationship has been established does sexual maturation occur during the hormone release of being "in love."

Nambra—Ouje people

Ringed by the spaceports of the Angwen.

Nia'quong, a country within the country Angwen.

Horta, the original religion that the Ouje practiced.

GLOSSARY

agoze—initiates to ways of sorcery

Aje—a woman who wields myriad arcane creative, biological, spiritual, and cosmic powers

akata—wild cats

Alkebulan—the Motherland

Amafufunyama—possession by evil spirits, the final step in the journey to become a healer

Asante sana—"Thank you very much"

Asè—the power to make things happen or "So let it be"

Asili—natives of Alkebulan

bagirwa—revered priestess, spiritual head of the Niyabinghi

balafon—a kind of wooden xylophone or percussion idiophone

Basotho blanket—a distinctive form of woolen tribal blanket traditionally worn by Sotho people and unique to the Kingdom of Lesotho

bembe—a drumming party to call down orisha into the body of an initiate

Black Caesar—a device used to pirate link streams

Black Dove—a line of oracles, the Libyan Sibyls

boerewors—a type of sausage

CAP—current aspirational phase

chakram—a gold band that lies in a flat circle about the neck; when activated, it becomes a bladed weapon

djemaas—from North Africa (à la palavers of West Africa)—disputes worked out in public; collective self-criticism

donga—a ravine

Egbe—sect that initiates Iyami

ekpu—ancestor figure

eleye—bird

emi—spirit

fashioning—manipulation of nanobots into objects

funkentelechy—the use of emi to direct nanobots for fashioning

gbedu—big drum

gbeto—soldiers/hunters

Gelede—a society devoted to Iyami

glyph—site-to-site transmitter

gravsuit—combined phase suit and exoskeleton (civilian grade)

Griot Circle—policing force, story investigators

Habari gani—"What's the news?"

Homowo—literally "hooting at hunger," a gratitude ritual

HOVA—military of Muungano; name taken back when O.E. was thrown into religious wars just after the Mars colony was established. O.E. referred to gbeto as "God's army," and Jehovah is another name for God.

Ifa—how the Universe works and what people's relationship to it is. Its tenets balance on three legs: the Universe, its spirits, and the ancestors.

igbodu—the sacred forest

Ijo—governing body of Muungano

ikin—palm nuts

imoles—primordial orisha at the beginning of creation

Ipebi—ritual of isolation

Iwa-pele—one's inner character

Iyami—feminine powers

Iyami Aje—a Yoruba term of respect and endearment used to describe a woman of African ancestry who is considered to be an Aje. No one can choose to initiate as Iyami and only Iyami can choose who they will initiate as Iyami.

jeli—griot officer, court musician

jeliya—griot's ancient art, handlers of the nyama

jijifo—"evasive maneuvers" meant to wrong-foot obroni

kanaga masks—worn primarily at dama, a collective funerary rite for Dogon men whose goal is to ensure the safe passage of the spirits of the deceased to the world of the ancestors

kanzu—shirt

kaross—cloak made of sheepskin, or the hide of other animals, with the hair left on

kheprw crystals—minerals mined from lunar strata as well as the asteroid belt; used to fuel Muungano starships

kikombe cha umoja—unity cup

kizungu—language of the wanderers (English)

kraal—village

kreef—crayfish

Lij—head of a Niyabinghi Order unit; translates as "child"; serves to indicate that a youth is of noble blood

linknet—personal data streams

LISC—Liberation Investment Support Cooperative, the corporate entity running the Original Earth government

lobola—dowry

Maafa—the Holocaust of Enslavement

Maroons—descendants of Africans in the Americas who formed settlements away from slavery

Master Poet—diplomat-level poet, a liaison to other cultures

Muungano—means "Togetherness" in Swahili. Centered on the Terran moon whose capital is called the Dreaming City, Muungano extends to Bronzeville on the Mars colony, to Titan guarding the Orun Gate, and to the distant Oyigiyigi mining outpost.

mzungu—someone with white skin; plural is wazungu

nanomesh—suit like a second-skin interface between wearer and their navsuit/ nanobots for fashioning

navsuit—combined nanomesh and exoskeleton (military grade)

Negus—derived from the Ethiopian meaning "to reign." The title has subsequently been used to translate as "king."

neoniks—the generation fascinated with the late-twenty-first-century era as part of what they called the Remember Revolution

Ngwenya Mine—named for the oldest mine on Earth

Niyabinghi Order—honor guard of the Ijo, taken from the gathering of Rastafari people to celebrate and commemorate key dates significant to Rastafari throughout the year

nyama—the spoken/sung word and the power that storytelling releases

Nyamakalaw—handlers of nyama (civilian head of the Griot Circle)

obroni—outsider

odede—wormholes, the "golden chord"

odu—stories, myths, and history central to Ifa

ogbanje—changeling spirit

ori—the head, the seat of one's intellect, also tied to one's destiny

orisha—deities

Orun Gate—the name of the nearest wormhole

oso—sorcerers

Oyaheya—"Praise the Spirit"

Oyigiyigi—a series of asteroid belts and the mining colony; named for the orisha's eternal rock of creation

panga—daggers

pap—a thick porridge of finely ground corn

PAW—public ass whipping

pehla sticks—charged batons, griots' weapons

phase suits—combined nanomesh and exoskeleton (civilian grade) to control nanobots for fashioning

Ras—civilian head of the Niyabinghi Order; is a rank of nobility equivalent to duke, though it is often rendered in translation as "prince"

Reapers—named for a subset of the Mino, the female fighting units who fought with meter-long straight razors

rondavel—home

sabhu—the language of the soul

Saqqara—ship named for the Saqqara Bird, a bird-shaped artifact made of sycamore wood, discovered during the 1898 excavation of the Pa-di-Imen tomb in Saqqara, Egypt

sebau—"those who give instruction" referring to both teacher and pupil

skia—a home brew of fermented root

sosaties—a traditional dish of meat cooked on skewers

synthed—synthesized

Thmei—the Egyptian goddess of truth and justice

tjwala—a potent home-brewed beer

Toppers—the wealthiest 1 percent of O.E.

Ubuntu—"humanity" or "I am because we are"

Ugenini—children of the diaspora

Uhlanga—according to the Zulu, it is the marsh from which humanity was born; code for Muungano's secret panspermia program

ukuhlanya—the madness that's part of the process in the journey to become a healer

Ukuthwasa—the rite of initiation to become a healer

umbidvo wetint sanga—cooked pumpkin leaves and peanuts

umoja—"unity" in Swahili

upinde mvua—rainbow (Swahili)

Uponyaji—a time of healing

wazungu—the plural of mzungu, people with white skin

weusi—blackness

yankadi—a slow and mellow dance

Yemoja—the leader of Iyami, the owner of Gelede

Yo—the generic term for the O.E. or its mentality or systems

ACKNOWLEDGMENTS

With *Breath of Oblivion,* the middle book in the Astra Black trilogy, it's easiest to think about the theme being about journeys. And who accompanies you on them as you learn (and hopefully grow). And how to hold to your culture, carry it with you, wherever you go. These are lessons brought home by my work alongside the Kheprw Institute: its founding elders (Imhotep Adisa, Pambana Uishi, and Paulette Fair) as well as some of its frontline folks (Diop Adisa, Leah Humphrey, Alvin Sangsuwangal, Aghilah Nadaraj, and Mimi Zakem). A special shout-out to my Café Creative crew.

Also, much love to another group of organized neighbors, The Learning Tree.

Speaking of folks who accompany me on the journey, I'd like to thank my editor, Will Hinton, and new (to me) agent, Bridget Smith. Friends who cheerleaded me along the way, like Hana Soh, Marilyn Chin, Miri Baker, and the B15 crew. Or folks who talked me through the science, like Linda Fowler, Evan Camp, and Andrew D. Gavrin.

Speaking of folks who continue to inspire, push, and challenge me, I can't help but thank many of the local artists around me: Stacia Murphy, Sibeko Jywanza, Ro Townsend, Robin Jackson, Anitra Malone, Chandra Lynch. All the folks who help imagine a better world.

I wouldn't hear the end of it if I didn't thank Bella Faidley, Rianna Butcher, and my other student dreamers from the Oaks Academy Middle School. [I haven't forgotten you, Andre Perez. In our hearts, the name of this book will always be *The Brink of Oblivion.*]

I'd also like to thank the many editors who have published stories of mine that led up to me writing this novel: Jason Sizemore, Bill Campbell, Scott Andrews, Susan Forest, Lucas K. Law, Mur Lafferty (for the story I *did* finish), Lynne and Michael Thomas.

I'd be remiss if I didn't thank the friends who were my cheerleaders along the way. Anthony Cardno. Wayne Brady. And I know I'm forgetting some folks, but luckily there will be Book III . . .

A special thank-you to Rodney Carlstrom.

An even more special thank-you to Chesya Burke.
And the most special thank-yous to my mom
and my sons, Reese and Malcolm
and my wife, Sally.
I couldn't make this journey without you.
[We miss you, Ferb, the most faithful of cats.]

BONUS: Here a list of the books I was reading while writing this:

—*Elite Capture: How the Powerful Took Over Identity Politics (And Everything Else)* by Olúfẹ́mi O. Táíwò
—*Caste: The Origins of Our Discontents* by Isabel Wilkerson
—*Sacred Economics: Money, Gift, and Society in the Age of Transition* by Charles Eisenstein
—*Black Skin, White Masks* by Frantz Fanon

ABOUT THE AUTHOR

A middle school librarian, **MAURICE BROADDUS** is also a fantasy and horror author best known for his short fiction and his Knights of Breton Court novel trilogy. He has published dozens of stories in magazines and book anthologies, including *Asimov's Science Fiction, Black Panther: Tales of Wakanda,* and *Weird Tales.*

Broaddus was born in London, England, but grew up and lives in Indianapolis with his wife and two sons. His mother is from Jamaica, a fact she reminds him of constantly, though she splits her time between there and Indianapolis.

He lives in service to the betterment of his community.